Joseph Mullooly

Saint Clement, Pope and Martyr

And His Basilica in Rome

Joseph Mullooly

Saint Clement, Pope and Martyr
And His Basilica in Rome

ISBN/EAN: 9783744696623

Printed in Europe, USA, Canada, Australia, Japan

Cover: Foto ©Raphael Reischuk / pixelio.de

More available books at **www.hansebooks.com**

SAINT CLEMENT

POPE AND MARTYR

AND

HIS BASILICA IN ROME

BY

JOSEPH MULLOOLY, O. P.

The memory of him shall not depart
away,
And his name shall be in request from
generation to generation ·
(Ecclesiasticus, XXXIX. 13

Second edition enlarged and improved.

ROME.
PRINTED BY G. BARBÈRA
—
1873.

INTRODUCTION.

In a vineyard about a mile from Rome, the foundation walls of a large villa, the chambers of which are filled up with masses of stucco ornaments and coloured plaster, as indeed the whole soil with bits of Pompeian red, fragments of various and rare marbles, mosaics, glass of so many colours that we wonder at the profusion, pottery from the coarsest to the fine thin polished red clay, and, more rarely, seals, and gold ornaments, attest the mansion of a rich Pagan family. In a corner of the inclosure are ruined columbaria, probably for their dependents, with broken cinerary urns still in their niches; and in another place a vast massive round monument of stone for the head of the house, who left to posterity a single sepulchral chamber in the centre. A white marble slab, still preserved, though detached from the building, gives us the title.

A Pagan tomb.

D. M.

M. AVRELIVS SYNTOMVS ET
AVRELIA MARCIANE AEDIFICIVM
CVM CEPOTAFIO, ET MEMORIAM
A SOLO FECERVNT SIBI ET FILIIS
SVIS AVRELIO LEONTIO ET AVRELI
AE FRVCTVOSAE ET LIB. LIBER.
POSTERISQVE EORVM.

D. M.

M. Aurelius Syntomus and
Aurelia Marciana made the building
with garden-tomb and memoria
from the foundation for themselves and
their children Aurelius Leontius and Aurelia
Fructuosa, and their freedmen, freedwomen
and their posterity. »

Its Christian
adaptation.

Here then we have the whole exterior economy
of Roman burial: the *praedium* or farm, and that
disposition of the *monumentum* with its area and
precincts so sacred, and jealously fenced about by
Roman law.[1] With this before our eyes we can

---

[1] According to Roman law, land which had been once used for burial
purposes was protected by special privileges, one of which was that it was
exempted from many of the laws which regulated the tenure and transfer

conceive, were the owner a Christian, how by his
licence, or active zeal, the martyr might be safely
laid at rest upon his estate; and history records
the names of many noble ladies who thus gave
honourable burial to the martyred dead.

The breviary says of S. Andrew that « Maxi-
» milla, dear to Christ, bore the Apostle's body to
» an excellent place, and buried it with spices. » [1]
Not long ago several martyrs were found, with the
sponges which were used to collect their blood, in the
church of S. Pudenziana. In 119, Severina, the wife
of Count Aurelian, buried Pope Alexander, Eventius
and Theodulus, on her farm seven miles on the
Nomentan way, and made a cemetery for them.
When the emperor Adrian, in 120, put to death
Symphorosa and her seven children at Tivoli, their
Acts say: « After this the persecution ceased for a
» year and six months, during which time the holy
» bodies of all the martyrs were honoured, and
» deposited with all care, in tombs constructed for
» them. » [2] Two Lucinas were celebrated for this
pious work. The first, the sorrowful widow Pom-

of property. In the technical language of the time it became *Religiosus*
« Religiosum locum unusquisque sua voluntate facit, dum mortuum infert
in locum suum. » (Marcian Digest. 1, 8, 6, §. 4.) It was inalienable, and
exclusively belonged to the families of those who were buried in it.

[1] Maximilla Christo amabilis tulit corpus Apostoli, optimo loco cum
aromatibus sepelivit. Antiph. IV. ad Laudes.

[2] Ruinart, Acta Sincera, p. 19.

ponia Graecina, who, as De Rossi thinks, buried S. Paul, and, in 251-252, another Lucina, who buried Pope Cornelius at night, with Cereale and Salustia. and twenty one others on her farm in a crypt next the cemetery of Callixtus on the Appian way. And, even under Diocletian, in 301, the martyr Restitutus was thus interred. « Justa, a pious and reli-
» gious matron, with some ecclesiastics, a few Chri-
» stians, and her servants, at night, on account of
» the wickedness of the Pagans, gathered up his
» body, went to her house towards the *meta sudans,*
» and there sprinkled it with aromatics, and placed
» it in a snowy windingsheet. Whilst it was yet
» dark night, she put it in her chariot to take
» it to her grounds on the Nomentan way. And
» whilst she was going there, she dispatched a mes-
» sage to the bishop (Stephen by name) who lived
» on the same road, that he might come to meet
» it with the priests, deacons, and other clerks,
» with the servants of God and the sacred vir-
» gins. Early in the morning they arrived, and
» with hymns and canticles brought the holy body
» to the sixteenth milestone and there worthily
» interred it. »

But here, on the lands of Aurelius Syntomus, there are no vestiges of the Christian dead, no arenaria, no crypts, and above all no loculi, arcosolia and chapels, [1] for the commemoration and *cultus* of the martyr. The first Christian members of the family were obliged to make arrangements for themselves, under the protection of the law, with such decorations as their means and taste afforded. The earlier the conversion of any Roman family the more certainly will their funeral monuments puzzle us by an intermixture of Pagan ornaments. For they had no other at hand, and so long as they were not peculiarly identified with Pagan worship, there was no reason for rejecting them. Whether the convert had **to fear a** family council upon foreign superstition, such as sat upon Pomponia Graecina **the wife of** Aulus Plautius, who conquered Britain

---

[1] The proper term is *cella*, or *cella memoria*, which was a rectangular chamber cut in the rock, with *loculi*, that is single places for bodies, (sarcophagi being usually on the floor, though in Domitilla's cemetery some loculi were closed with imitations of sarcophagi), and an *arcosolium*, that is an arched recess for the altar-slab over the body. Behind a wall built for concealment in the above mentioned cemetery De Rossi found an arcosolium with marble slabs, and a marble table having two large bronze rings to lift it, beneath which were two bodies, one in cloth of gold, the other in purple with a *terra-cotta* vase at its head. Pope Eutychian, A. D. 275-283, who was himself a martyr and interred in the cemetery of Callixtus, buried there a hundred and sixty two martyrs with his own hands, and forbade the faithful to bury a martyr without a dalmatic, or a purple garment called *colobium*. De Rossi says that the Fathers, especially in Africa, and the Pontifical Book, call such cellae « *cellae memoriae* of the martyrs », to distinguish them from the cellae or chambers in the temples and baths. S. Augustine tells the Manichaean Faustus : « The Christian » people celebrate together the memories of the martyrs with religious » solemnity; both to excite imitation, and to be made partakers of their » merits, and be helped by their prayers. So however, that we sacrifice

under Claudius, or notoriety had provoked imperial
edicts, sculpture above ground was not so safe a
work as painting below. Pure symbolism must necessarily be the growth of leisure and instruction;
and the more exclusively Christian its character the
less we should expect to find it among the primitive converts. Hence if we see the vine and vintage (Bacchanalian emblems as classical conceit has
christened them) upon the mosaic vault of S. Co-
stanza, or carved on the sarcophagus of her grand-
mother S. Helen, whilst they may have had an
indirect reference to the mysteries of faith, it does
not follow that they had or were anything more
than customary embellishments.

» to none of the martyrs, but to the very God of the martyrs, although
» we erect altars at the *memorias* of the martyrs. » And again : « To our
» martyrs we build not temples as to gods, but *memorias* as to men whose
» spirits are living with God. » And the fifth Council of Carthage,
Cau. XIV , forbids *aedes* to be built for martyrs except there be on the
spot either the body, or some sure relics, or where the origin of some habitation, or possession, or passion, has been transmitted from a most trust-
worthy source. And in his fifth hymn Prudentius describes the tyrant
threatening to destroy the bones of Vincentius lest the people of the Lord
worship and fix martyrs' titles over them. The whole technical phraseo-
logy is found in the inscription from Caesarea in Mauritania quoted in the
Bollettino of April 1864 :

> « Aream at sepulcra cultor verbi contulit
> Et cellam struxit suis cunctis sumptibus
> Eclesiae sanctae hanc reliquit memoriam
> Salvete fratres puro corde et simplici
> Evelpius vos satos sancto spiritu

ECLESIA FRATRVVM HVNC RESTITVIT TITVLVM M. A. I. SEVERIANI C. V. »
Ex ing. Asteri.

We do not mean that the Christians did not rejoice in images of the vine, but that the earliest converts chose it perhaps as the most easy and least offensive of Pagan ornaments. S. Jerome says « that the Syrian tongue naturally lent itself to » parable. It was one of the mediums which the » wisdom of our Lord adapted for teaching the » people. » The images in the catacombs were scriptural images; and perhaps more familiar to the Christians of Palestine and Africa than to the Romans. S. Asterius of Amasea bitterly inveighs against a singular abuse of them. « Whenever then » they go out dressed, as it were depicted among » themselves and pointing out with their fingers » the picture on their garments, they follow too at » a good distance and keep back not indiscreetly; » for there are lions there, panthers, bears, bulls, » dogs, woods, rocks, and hunters, and everything, » in short, that exercises the industry of painters » expressed in imitation of nature. For as it seems » not only walls and houses must be so adorned, » but their very tunics too and the cloaks thrown » over them. But the men and women of those » rich folks that are more religious give the wea- » vers subjects out of the Gospel history: I mean » Christ himself with all his disciples, and every » one of the miracles in the very way it is told.

» You will see the marriage at Galilee, and the
» waterpots, the paralytic carrying the bed on his
» shoulders, the blind man who is cured with the
» clay, the woman who labours under an issue of
› blood taking hold of the hem, the sinner approach-
» ing to the feet of Jesus, **Lazarus** returning to
« life from the tomb; and whilst they do these
» things, they suppose that they are acting pious-
» ly, and putting on garments pleasing to God. »[1]
It was about the year 400 that the bishop of Pontus complained of these walking catacombs.

Classical
learning
insufficient
to elucidate
Christian
ruins.

Convenience has a large share in funerals as
well as in other human actions, and the antiquary
who desired to make deductions from a series of
coffinplates, would probably arrive at conclusions
very derogatory to the respectable deceased. The
ancient dead did not undertake to teach theology
to remote posterity, and the attempt to reconstruct
their tenets from the slabs of their sepulchres, mutilated and dispersed, seems not of the wisest. It
is imperfect at best, and hopeless without more
enlightened erudition from other sources. If a
candid traveller were to examine the magnificent
ruined abbey churches of Ireland and England, he
might with moderate acumen make out that they

---

[1] Sermo de Divit. et Lazar, p. 6.

were of no sort of use to the practices of the present Establishment; but he could hardly understand the perfection of their purpose without some knowledge of the Catholic Church. He could not mistake that some deplorable flood of ruin had recently swept over the land, and that the variety of sects had not yet repaired its ravages. But he could not learn from the ruins alone that a great living society had never ceased to practise the rites for which those churches were originally designed. But what, if the field of his observations was not for three hundred, but for eighteen hundred years? What, if he would track the footsteps of an Apostle in a country that had literally been ploughed up by waves of ruin again and again for fifteen centuries at least?[1] Our traveller upon the waste of the Roman Campagna, even with Murray in his hand and Horace in his head, would find his chances of discrimination wonderfully small. And if he had been qualified by an University education to

---

[1] The description of S. Gregory the Great, in the year 600, is well known. « The savage Lombard race drawn out of the sheath of its dwell- » ing-place has been fattened on our necks, and has cut down and dried » up the race of men that in the excess of multitude had risen in this land » like a thick cornfield. For the cities are unpeopled, camps overturned : » churches burnt, monasteries of men and women destroyed, farms made • desolate of men and stript of every cultivator, the earth lying waste in » solitude : no owner inhabits it, beasts have occupied the places hitherto » held by a multitude of men. » Dial. b. 3.

identify the *memorabilia* of Roman grandeur, to step out on the road to Brundusium, and exhaust the poetry of his affections upon a race whose perishing had been predicted long before Moses went up to mount Pisgah, [1] he might find it convenient to forget what mould of man founded his « Alma Mater, » and politic to decline the distasteful task of grubbing up the soil for Christian ideas. The value of each spadeful of earth would depend less upon the contents than upon his understanding what he found. He might spell out a name upon a bit of leaden pipe, or be very learned upon the marks of the tilemakers; but « cui bono » if he knew nothing of the first founder's means and motives for choosing the spot, nothing of his family affections, nothing of his progenitors or descendants: nothing but that once he was and now is not? « Ne sutor ultra crepidam. » Classical literature is not sufficient for the purpose of decyphering Christian antiquity; and whatever sermons may be found in stones, the monuments of the Catholic Church have a language of their own. Whether they were hastily constructed, or studiously framed to suit the discipline of the « secret; » whether

---

[1] « They shall come in galleys from Italy. They shall overcome the » Assyrians, and shall waste the Hebrews, and at the last they themselves » also shall perish. » Numbers, ch. 24. v. 24.

stamped on the legend of a royal coin, or printed in the encyclical of the living Pope, **they require** an initiation and instinct to understand them. **And** we say in no spirit of controversy, but simply as a fact, that no man who is not of the Church can appreciate them. **If** men will not hearken to the voice of the living Church, **how can they catch its** echoes in the past?

With the exception of some savages who laid their friends out to dry on little platforms in the open air, or others who ate them at a certain age,[1] mankind in general seem to have put their dead out of sight, if not under ground. Whether they burnt them and put their ashes in urns, embalmed and packed them in a series of painted cases, or **gave** them coffins of lead or stone, the actual place of deposit was not usually on the very level of the high-way. Catholics did not burn their dead; [2] **but** restored them to the earth, whence they **came; and** incremation was not likely to be recommended by the example **of** the persecutors **who** did burn them, and scattered the ashes the Christians venerated to

Christian cemeteries, and why constructed

---

[1] The Recognitions of S. Clement notice, « that of the whole world » only the Medes solemnly cast out people still breathing to be devoured » by dogs; that the Indians burn their dead, and the wives are voluntarily » burnt with their husbands : that very many Germans end their lives » with a noose ». Book 9, chap. 25.

[2] Execrantur rogos, et damnant ignium sepulturas. — Minucius Felix. Oct. c. II. p. 451. « They execrate funeral piles and condemn burial in fire. »

the winds and streams. The learned De Rossi tells us that the Pagans made the same crypts and loculi as those in the Christian cemeteries, but they were only family vaults, not general, ramifying, well-closed places for worship as well as burial : that among them sarcophagi were in vogue in the days of the Antonines, and that in the fifth century Macrobius writes « urendi corpora defuncto- » rum usus nostro seculo nullus est, » « in our age » it is not the custom to burn the bodies of the » dead. » But from the first the Catholic sleeping places «coemeteria» were meant to preserve the bodies whole, and in most instances singly, and securely, apart from Pagans and heretics, conveniently for the rites of the Church whether at the deposition or commemoration. About Rome the Christians dug into the hill-sides as the Etruscans had done before them; but not so much for private sepulture, as to provide one common place of rest laid out in regular tiers and passages, with economy of space, and choice of strata, where the rich and noble felt it a privilege to be found among the poor, and all yearned to lie not far from the martyrs of Christ. They were not thereby precluded from monuments or chapels above ground,[1] and

---

[1] See De Rossi's *Bullettino di Archeologia Cristiana*, on the monument of S. Domitilla. December 1865.

in case of distinguished martyrdom they were sure
to construct such *memories,* which when persecution
had ceased became basilicas. For if the Catholic
Church has one stamp of truth more decisive than
another, it is that she hallows and consecrates every
legitimate human affection. She honours more the
call of God in the vow of the virgin, **and** the ordination of the priest, but she has set the seal of
the sacrament upon the first act of Christian life,
baptism, upon the indissolubility of marriage, and
the last act of passage to the tomb. The spot where
Christian blood was shed for faith, to her was holy
ground. She never forgot it; for it was registered
by the Church in heaven, and as far as the vicissitudes of time and the malice of the world allowed, she sought to protect, to cherish and make
it a monument for ever. Literally « aromatibus
sepelivit, » [1] she buried with perfumes. She embalmed the memories of those holy dead with the prayers and incense of her daily sacrifice, stupendous

---

[1] « Aromatibus sepelivit. » This expression seems to have a technical
force equivalent to saying, buried as a saint. De Rossi quotes Prudentius:
« We will sprinkle, both the inscription and the cold stones, with liquid
» perfume, » as applicable to the tazze, marble vases, placed upon a short-
pillar near the tombs of the saints. Roma subterranea, pag. 282. Perhaps
in the East such pillars, besides holding the balsamic vessel, were inscribed. At least S. Asterius says: « We, disciples of the martyrs, learn to
» preserve the true religion even in the extremest dangers by merely look-
» ing upon their sacred *thecae* as pillars inscribed with letters, and accu-
• rately manifesting the agony of their martyrdom. »

monument of love not bound by time or space. Poor
Horace had done his best : « Exegi monumentum
« aere perennius. »[1] In the Church the names of
the early martyrs will cease to be repeated only
with the Eucharistic sacrifice itself, ending with the
world and passing triumphantly to the knowledge
of the new names in heaven.[2] Nor did she neglect
the meaner memorials of time. Died they in their
house? She set up an altar on the very spot. Witness S. Caecilia, SS. John and Paul, S. Pudentiana,
and many more. Was it afar off? Her fondness
grew excessive. She begged, she bought, she risked
life and limb to get their dear remains, and their
possession was made the choice of conquerors and
articles of peace.[3] She made much of giving a cloth
that had touched them, wool soaked with the oil
of the lamps that burned before them, mere dust
that gathered over them. She rejoiced in distributing their relics to the churches throughout the

Relics.

---

[1] Ode XXIV, lib. III.

[2] See Apocalypse, ch. 3. v. 12; ch. 2, v. 17; ch. 22, v. 4. And Isaias
ch. 65. v. 15. « And you shall leave your name for an execration to my
» elect. and the Lord God shall slay you, and call his servants by another
» name, in which he that is blessed upon the earth shall be blessed in
» God. Amen. »

[3] The holy Cross was recovered from Chosroes in this way. The
crown of thorns was chosen by S. Louis, who paid the loan to the Vene-
tians for it. Childebert, A. D. 542, raised the siege of Saragossa for the
stole of S. Vincent, and built the church of S. Ge main les Prés at Paris
to receive it.

world, and never did she erect an altar anywhere, that was not enriched with some portion of their blessed remains. Enjoying the sunshine of the Real Presence, she desired that these memorials of His friends should be found there too. Nay, she became in love with death and treasured up the instruments of agony, and set them, too, like jewels at her shrines. People call it superstition. The Church upon earth, who knows her own mind and her Master's, never grows weary of canonizing the sanctity which He has been pleased to perfect. She loves the saints and martyrs, because they mirrored Him. If she dwells with greater fondness upon the blessed wounds of our Lord, she contemplates with love the sufferings of those who died for Him. She does not forget them, because she knows that He has not forgotten them, and is pleased that they remember her.

The leading idea then in any Catholic church, but more evident in the older historical basilicas, is that we are dead to the world and buried with Christ. On Holy Thursday we literally do bury our Lord in the sepulchre and visit the spot where He is laid. In the Mass we repeat the sacrifice, and represent the circumstances of His cruel death. And if He has deigned to be with us all days, even to the consummation of the world, His

To bury the dead, a sacred duty.

presence may be said to be, in regard to the manifestation of His glorified existence and our inability to bear it and live, even yet swathed and
shrouded in the tomb. Man again is a most glorious work of His, and our confraternities by keeping up that charity of burying the dead which the
angel commended in Tobit, honour the Creator in
that slime of the earth which He means to raise
again from the tomb. Even the natural instincts
of the Pagan Romans granted great legal privileges
to burial-clubs. These privileges were confirmed by
an edict of Septimius Severus A. D. 200. The burial
of those bodies that had been once the temples of
the Holy Ghost is for Christians so sacred a duty
that in the nervous language of S. Ambrose, « hu-
» mandis fidelium reliquiis vasa Ecclesiae, etiam
» initiata, confringere, conflare, vendere, licet. » It

The Church obliged to pray for the dead.

is a duty of religion, and not of simple convenience,
just as prayers for the dead is a duty for the
whole Church, as well as for the survivers. « Lay
» this body anywhere, » said S. Monica to her son
Augustine ; « let not the care of it anyway disturb
» you: this only I request of you that you re-
» member me at the altar of the Lord wherever
» you be. »[1] Intercessory prayer was all the dying

---

[1] « She (S. Monica), the day of her dissolution being at hand, be-
» stowed not a single thought upon having her body sumptuously swath-

mother asked, not some peculiar place of sepulture. And it was to give opportunity for the kind
of prayer for the dead which she requested that Catholics desired to be buried together, and marked
the loculus with a hurried sign or more deliberate inscription.

Now it is not easy, but very difficult, to make
those, who think that the reading of the will after
the funeral is the chief duty to the deceased, really
appreciate the necessities of the Catholic dead. For
them to be buried away from the rest was to
separate from communion, and withdraw from that
jurisdiction which the Pope and bishops exercised
over the cemeteries. With the single exception of
some Mithraic tombs, De Rossi has found in the catacombs no Pagans, or heretics, who intruded themselves among the faithful dead. The notion, after
robbing the Catholic dead, of dressing up in his
clothes, stickling for his name, and insisting upon
being buried with him, seems to be almost an idle
modern invention. And if that request, which is
usually felt to be so urgent, because it comes from
dying lips, is to be disregarded as for superstitious

» ed .... but only desired a commemoration to be made of her at the
» altar, at which she had, without the intermission of a day, rendered her
» service, whence she knew was dispensed the holy Victim, by which the
» handwriting that was against us is blotted out. » See S. Augustine,
t. I, l. IX. *Confess.* n. 36, col. 389.

uses, because it asks for prayer, how can we understand the language of S. Cyprian? « To the bodies
» also of those who, although they were not put
» to torture in prison, nevertheless depart by the
» outlet of a glorious death, let a more zealous
» watchfulness be given; for neither their resolution
» nor their honour is the less, so as to prevent them
» too from being classed among the blessed mar-
» tyrs. Finally note also the days on which they
» depart that we may celebrate commemorations of
» them also among the memories of the martyrs. » [1]
When the cross was a reality, and the roaring lion
physically ready to devour, the heretic was not so
eager to assume the Catholic name. What Maxi-
minus said to S. Tarachus had few attractions to
those without. « I will not merely slay thee, that,
» as I have already said, they may wrap thy relics
» in linen cloths, and anoint them, and worship
» them. » Or again: « Dost thou think, most
» wicked man, that thy body after death will be
» venerated and anointed by silly women? But
» this also shall be my care that thy remains be
» utterly destroyed. » [2] Nor was the boast of S. Hilary of Poitiers more inviting. « We owe more to
» your cruelty Nero, Decius, Maximinian, than to

---

[1] Ep. XXXVII ad Clerum.
[2] Passio S. Tarachi et Soc. Ruinart, p. 475, 476.

» Constantius; for through you we have conquered
» Satan: everywhere was the holy blood of the
» martyrs received, and their venerable bones are
» a daily testimony, while evil spirits howl at them;
» while maladies are expelled, while wonderful works
» are seen. » [1]   The chief use of the churches then
was not to shelter the congregation from the weather,
but to provide for the relics, and the commemorations of the dead.   The Christians met to pray for
the living and the dead; and with greater fervour,
because the mortal remains of saints were before
their eyes, whose intercessory prayers they knew
to be most acceptable to God.

The reason again for the greater honour to the
martyrs was not alone for the illustration of the
Church, nor for the romantic circumstances of their
deaths. Our Lord himself has pronounced it.   « No
» man hath greater love than this that he lay down
» his life for his friends. » [2]   They were not merely
witnesses of the truth, but of the Author of truth,
and especially of His resurrection; that He whom
the Jews and Gentiles had conspired together to
blot out from the land of the living was nevertheless a living man, powerful to protect the Church

*Greater ho-
nour due to
the Martyrs,
and why.*

---

[1] S. Hil. lib. II, de Trinit. n. 3, lib. III , adv. Constant. n. 8, p. 1243.
Ed. Ben.
[2] John, XV, v. 13.

that had loved Him; and the first martyr looking
up steadfastly to heaven deserved to see the glory of
God, and to bear witness: « Behold! I see the hea-
» vens opened and the Son of man standing at the
» right hand of God. » If love for God was to be the
measure of the admiration of the Church, it was
found most conspicuously in the martyrs. The charity which worketh love and unites the soul with
God, was to be found among all classes, the beggar and the king, the founders of religious Orders
and the hermits, the suffering nun and the active
apostle; and if it were approved by miracles the
Church set it before her children as an inheritance
and example, (for it is not the Church, but writers
in evil days who have said, that the actions of the
saints are rather to be admired than imitated);
but she gave the first place to that faithful love
which was sealed with blood. For that blood was
her cement and seed; and that sanctity contained
the special token that the world had striven to destroy it, and striven in vain. She has hardly watched
with the shepherds through the night of the Nativity before she celebrates the stoning of Stephen.
The cry of the little babe of Bethlehem is upon her
ear, and she listens to « Rachael weeping for her
children, because they are not. » The mystic gifts
are offered by the kings, and she sings:

« Crudelis Herodes, Deum regem venire quid times?
» Non eripit mortalia, qui regna dat coelestia. »

« **Our God**, the coming King, why dost thou,
» cruel Herod, dread?

» He snatches **not at mortal things** who heavenly
» gives instead. »

She feels that the persecuting malice of the
world is an additional wreath for the champions
of Christ, whose kingship was mocked and set at
nought by the great ones of the earth; a sign of
the world's fear, and a prize for those it hates.
That little phial of witnessing blood in the silent
passages of the earth was her ruby jewel. The
lips of the martyrs, opened by the Holy Ghost, spoke
the truth. Hence the Popes were so solicitous to
preserve their Acts that they appointed notaries and
deacons for that purpose in the several districts,
or regions, of the city, and built so much in the
cemeteries, and set ecclesiastics over them. [1] Hence

Diocletian's persecution.

---

[1] Pope Zephyrinus, A. D. 202-218, set Callixtus over the cemetery.
Of Pope Fabian, 236-250, the breviary says : « Septem diaconis regiones
» divisit, qui pauperum curam haberent. Totidem subdiaconos creavit, qui
» res gestas martyrum a septem notariis scriptas colligerent. » « He al-
» lotted the regions to seven deacons to have charge of the poor; and
» created as many subdeacons to collect the Acts of the martyrs written
» by the seven notaries. »

Pope Cornelius, A. D. 251, 252, testifies that there were forty six
priests in Rome, that is with parishes and cemeteries; but there were in

when, owing to the desolating persecution of Diocletian, the churches and sacred books had been
burnt, and the lands and cemeteries confiscated, we
find Marcellus, A. D. 308-310, set twenty five titles,
or titular churches, like dioceses within the city
for the many Pagan converts, and for the burial
of the martyrs, and invited Priscilla to make another cemetery on the Salarian way. When the suburban cemeteries were ruined by the barbarians, the
Popes brought the martyrs' bodies into the city.
When they had repaired the damages in vain, and
the cemeteries were no longer safe, they brought
them in greater numbers into the basilicas. Even
as late as 560-573, John III restored the cemeteries of the holy martyrs, and had Masses and lights

---

the city only twenty five basilicas. In the time of Pope Damasus, A. D.
366-384, every title had two priests, and a recently discovered inscription
in S. Clement's shows that their colleagues were called « *Socii*. » In the
following inscription from the cemetery of Domitilla we read the jurisdiction of those priests :

ALEXIVS ET CAPRIOLA FECERVNT SE VIVI

IVSSV ARCHELAI ET DVLCITI PRESB.

And in this other from S. Callixtus we find the jurisdiction which the
Popes themselves peculiarly exercised over that cemetery. Marcellinus governed the Church from 296 to 304.

CVBICVLVM DVPLEX CVM ARCISOLIIS ET LVMINARE

IVSSV PP SVI MARCELLINI DIACONVS ISTE

SEVERVS FECIT MANSIONEM IN PACE

SIBI SVISQVE.

☞ We may observe here, once for all, that our notices of the catacombs are chiefly taken from De Rossi's *Roma subterranea* vol. I, and his
Bollettino di Archeologia Sacra.

supplied every Sunday from S. John Lateran's. It
is recorded of Sergius I, who lived in the seventh
century, that, when he was a priest, he was un-
wearied in celebrating Mass in the different cemeteries. Gregory III, 731-741, provided a priest to
celebrate in the catacombs on the principal martyrs' feasts. It was not only that the martyrs were
the earliest saints, but their blood was the seed of
the Church, the pledge of fidelity to the last. If she
did not honour those chosen instruments of faith,
whom should she honour? If she prized chastity,
they had died to keep it. If she reverenced old age,
her venerable bishops and priests while tortured were
admired even by the Pagans. If she needed miracles, the martyrs were miracles. If the Holy Ghost
inspired her, the Spirit spoke also by their lips.
If generous devotedness could move her, these had
indeed given up all. If gratitude became her, she
must raise her eyes to heaven and to them. Hence
the feeling which moved the learned Benedictine
Abbot, Gueranger, to ask leave of Pius IX to renew
the celebrations in the catacombs at the grave of
S. Caecilia. Hence the joy of the Church at the
canonization of the victims of the Calvinists of Gor-
cum, and the beatification of the martyrs of Japan.

About the year 405, the noble Spanish poet
Prudentius came to Rome to satisfy his devotion,

and has left graphic passages relating to the catacombs. Two lines of his describe their locality better than a volume.

« Haud procul extremo culta ad pomeria vallo
Mersa latebrosis crypta patet foveis. »

« Not far from the last rampart, at the cultiva-
» ted boulevards, a crypt lies open plunged in lurk-
» ing pits. »

And he enables us to judge of the decorations of
the crypt, and its purpose; for he tells us that in
the cemetery of S. Cyriaca he saw the body of
S. Hippolytus, with an altar by it, at which priests
celebrated and distributed the divine mysteries; and
that on the walls was a picture of his martyrdom,
the faithful gathering his scattered relics, and with
cloths and sponges sucking up his blood on the
briars and ground. To the confusion of those whose
tender piety is scandalized by the sign of the Cross,
and much more by the image of the Crucified, who
date their new birth from the Holy Ghost, but abhor
the emblem of the dove, whose whitewashed walls
receive no light from the illumination of the Church,
whose dreary devotion denies to Mary the prophetic
title « Blessed; » and who, dating their conversion
from the Apostles, neither know nor care to know
what became of them when they dispersed to teach

the Gentiles, and fear their pictures more than sin, the profusion of paintings with which the early Christians decorated their cemeteries must appear a singular impiety and revolting mistake. After so much devastation enough still remains below ground (without reckoning the peculiar symbols of private graves, doves, anchors, palms, and monograms of Christ) to furnish us with painted ceilings, and pilasters, and altar-tombs, with multiplied effigies of our Lord, the Mother of God, and the saints, the miracles of either Testament, types of the Sacraments and especially of the Eucharist. S. Jerome who died soon after Prudentius visited Rome, speaks of the inlaid glasses, now preserved in our museums: « *in cucurbitis vasculorum, quas vulgo Sancomarias vo-* » *cant solent apostolorum imagines adumbrari.* » « In the » bowls of the little vessels commonly called San- » comarias the images of the apostles are wont to » be shadowed. » [1] And wall painting would not be wanting where painted vases were esteemed. But the *cella* above ground, all that art had done in

Pictures destroyed by Diocletian.

---

[1] Tertullian, A. D. 195-218, had asked: « Where is the lost sheep » sought for by the Lord, and carried back upon His shoulders? Let the » very pictures of your chalices come forth, if even in them the interpreta- » tion of that animal will clearly shine forth, whether it pourtray the » restoration of a sinner that was a Christian or a Gentile. »

It is only recently, and by fragments, that we have recovered the Christian inlaying of glass with gold images of our Lord, our Lady, and the Apostles. But it was so common and popular that S. Ephrem, *Sermo I de*

oratories, perished in Diocletian's persecution, and it may be questioned whether Christian decorative art ever recovered that loss. We know that the fine arts had so declined in the age of Constantine that the triumphal arch erected by him owes whatever sculptured beauty it possesses to the skill of those who had lived at an earlier age than his own. In the third century there were forty six churches, in Rome. What was the style of their decoration? In the cemeteries, De Rossi thinks that « towards » the end of that century, the arts, which flou- » rished in the times of Trajan, Adrian and the Anto- » nines, visibly declined. »[1] If this is to be understood of the representation of mere outward natural form, it is probable enough; but it may be ques-

---

Poenitentia XV, uses it as an illustration of the sacrament of penance. « Penance is a great furnace: it receives glass and changes it into gold. It » takes lead and makes it silver .... Have you seen glass how it is made » of the colour of beryll, emerald, and sapphire ? You cannot doubt too » that penance makes silver of lead, and gold of glass. Besides if human » art knows how to mix nature with nature and change what was before, » how much more will the grace of God be able to effect still more ? » Man has added gold leaf to glass, and in appearance that seems made » gold which before was glass. So grace to him who yesterday was unjust » and a transgressor of the law makes to-day a servant of God, not only » superficially, but also as to the conscience according to God. For if man » had chosen to mix in gold the glass would have been made golden ; but » avoiding the loss he invented the fitting together and insertion of the » thinnest leaf. » The vaunters of progress might describe inventions more grandiloquently, but the elegant simplicity of the deacon of Edessa is nearer the truth.

[1] Roma sott. I, 196, 197.

tioned whether the decline affected symbolism, and
the power of representing Catholic religious feeling;
just as while the more celebrated painters of religious
subjects, since Perugino, have given the natural with
greater truth, they have not always depicted the
supernatural, and religious affections, with as much
force as other hands inferior to them in the mecha-
nism of art. If Greek art surpassed Roman, and
Pagan art rapidly declined, neither in fancy nor design did Christian art ever come near it. It is not
possible that the obscure sect described by Tacitus
could ever get artists of any reputation to paint
in the dark; on which account catacombic art, taken
by itself, is a fallacious standard. Not possess-
ing the early Church pictures, we can only judge
by the mosaics, restored and altered, but not changed in character, that Christian Catholic art by no
means declined in elaborate ingenious symbolic ornamentation, and ability to represent what it wanted to inculcate. The drinking fountains of Paris
or London, expensive as many of them have been,
would not give a fair idea of the appreciation of
art either in France or England. Eusebius, A. D.
325-328, says: « You might see at the fountains,
» in the middle of the market-places representa-
» tions of the good Shepherd well known to those
« acquainted with the divine word, and Daniel with

Christian
drinking-
fountains.

the lions, fashioned in brass. » [1] And speaking of a tablet which the emperor Constantine placed before the vestibule of his palace to be seen by all, the same historian says: « The saving sign of the Cross is represented as it were resting on his head ; but that enemy and adverse wild beast, which, by means of the tyranny of the ungodly, had vexed the Church, he represented under the shape of a dragon rushing headlong down. » [2] And he adds: « I am filled with wonder at the powerful understanding of the emperor, who, as it were, by a divine inspiration, symbolized those things which the words of the Prophet had long before proclaimed. » He also says that « the house of the woman healed of the issue of blood was shown at Caesarea Philippi, and that he had himself seen the circumstance represented in brass before the door of it. And that it is no wonder, for the images of Peter and Paul, and even of Christ himself are preserved in paintings. » [3]

In the fourth century, S. Asterius bishop of Amasea gives a minute account of a picture of the martyrdom of S. Euphemia. This celebrated virgin martyr

---

[1] De Vita Constant. l. 3, c. 40.
[2] Lib. 3, c. 3.
[3] Hist. of Euseb. b. 7, c. 18,

of Chalcedon is represented with her contemporary S. Catharine of Alexandria, in the niche of the Madonna in our subterranean basilica. S. Asterius says: « Her fellow-citizens and associates in the religion » for which she died, admiring her as a resolute » and holy virgin, reverencing her sepulchre, and » also placing her bier near the temple, pay her » honour, celebrating her anniversary as a common » and crowded festival. » He saw this picture accidently and was affected to tears; and it appears from his description of it, that it must have been an admirable composition. He particularly notices her after sentence of death was pronounced against her. « After this there is a prison, and again the » venerable virgin in her dark robes is seated alone, » stretching out both her hands to heaven, and call - » ing upon God, the helper in trouble : and there » appears to her whilst in prayer, above her head, » the sign which it is the custom of Christians both » to adore and represent in colours, a symbol, I » think, of the passion which awaited her. The » painter then, a little further on, has lit up, in » another compartment, [1] a blazing fire..... and has » placed her in the midst of it, with her hands » stretched out towards heaven; her countenance

---

[1] This seems like the exemples in our subterranean basilica of several episodes in our composition.

» bears on it no sign of sadness; but, on the con-
» trary, is lit up with joy, for that she is depart-
» ing unto a blessed and incorporeal life. » [1]

Pope Adrian I, in his letter to Charlemagne concerning holy images, quotes Gregory the Great's letter to the hermit of Ravenna. « We have sent » you two cloths containing the picture of God » our Saviour, and of Mary the holy Mother of » God, and of the blessed apostles Peter and Paul; » and one Cross: also for a benediction, a key which » has been applied to the most holy body of S. Pe- » ter the prince of the apostles, that you may re- » main defended from the enemy. » De Rossi shows distinctly, from the type of the two apostles on the sarcophagi, and from the ancient representation of them, that there was a traditional set of portraits with features peculiar to each. Pruden-

Other church pictures.

tius, A. D. 405, narrates an incident in his journey to Rome. « I was lying prostrate on a tomb, which » a sacred martyr, Cassian, with his body dedi- » cated to God, made beautiful. Whilst with tears » I was considering within myself my wounds, and » all the labours and bitter pains of life, I turned » my face upwards; there was before me, painted » in dark colours, the image of the martyr co-

---

[1] Combefis, t. I, Enar. in Martyr. S. Euphem. p. 207-210.

» vered with countless wounds, lacerated in eve-
» ry limb, and with the skin minutely punctured.
» Around him, oh sad sight! there was a countless
» crowd of boys who with their pens pierced the
» wounded limbs... The keeper of the building said
» 'in answer to my inquiries,' that which thou
» seeest, stranger, is no empty or idle fable. The
» picture tells a history. These are the circumstan-
» ces which, expressed in colours, have excited thy
» wonder. This is Cassian's glory. If thou hast
» any just or praise-worthy desire, if there be any
» thing that thou hopest for; if thou be inwardly
» troubled, but whisper it. The most glorious mar-
» tyr, believe me, hears every prayer; and those
» which he sees deserving of approval he renders
» effectual. I then ran through the list of my se-
» cret difficulties; I then murmured forth my de-
» sires, and my fears, my household left behind
» in hopes of future good. I am heard. I visit
» Rome; I am successful; I return to my home, and
» I loudly praise Cassian. »[1] S. Paulinus of Nola,
who died a year after S. Augustine, in 431, describes a basilica apparently covered with paintings.
He says, expostulating with Severus for placing his
portrait in the baptistery of his basilica beside

---

[1] Galland. Vol. 8, Hymn 9, p. 452-3.

S. Martin of Tours: « You did right to have a paint-
» ing of S. Martin in the place where man is formed
» anew: he by a perfect imitation of Christ pour-
» trayed the image of a heavenly being. » S. Ni-
lus, 448-451, advises his friend, Olympius, who was
going to build a church in honour of the martyrs,
« to represent in the sanctuary, towards the East,
» one only cross, and cover the building on every
» side with the histories contained in the Old and
» New Testament, done by the hands of the most skil-
» ful painters, in order that they, who are not ac-
» quainted with letters, and are unable to read the
» divine Scriptures, may have a remembrancer of
» the worthy actions of those who have nobly served
» the true God. » S. Asterius says boldly: « Were
» there no martyrs, gloomy and gladless would
» our life be; for what is worthy to be compared
» with those solemn assemblies! What so venerable
» and everyway beautiful, as to behold a whole city
» pouring forth all its citizens, and repairing to
» the sacred place to celebrate the pure mysteries
» of the most true religion! But true religion is
» both to worship and honour those who have so
» resolutely endured torments for Him. » This
bishop of Pontus says: « The Gentiles and Euno-
» mian heretics (new Jews, as he calls them) de-
» tested the honours paid to martyrs and their

» relics. » He describes in his own country, pre-
cisely what Prudentius saw in Italy, « that on the
» solemnities of particular martyrs, which were kept
» by the people, all Rome and the neighbouring
» provinces went to adore God at their tombs, kiss-
» ing their relics. » And if we would know how
such festivals were kept, in the fourth century,
in the East, we have it in S. Gregory of Nyssa.
« Let us view the present state of the saints, how
» very excellent it is, and how magnificent! For
» the soul indeed having attained unto its proper
» inheritance rests gladly, and, freed from the body,
» dwells together with its compeers. Whilst the
» body, its venerable and spotless instrument, which
» injured not by its peculiar passions the incorrup-
» tibility of the indwelling spirit, deposited with
» great honour and attention, lies venerably in a
» sacred place; reserved as some much honoured
» valuable possession unto the time of the regene-
» ration, and far removed from any comparison
» with the bodies which have died by a usual and
» common death, and this though they are natu-
» rally of the same substance. For other relics
» are to most men even an abomination. Whereas
» whoso cometh unto some spot like this, where
» we are this day assembled, where there is a mo-
» nument of the just and a holy relic, his soul is

S. Gregory of
Nyssa's descrip-
tion of the
Christian
shrine.

3

» in the first place gladdened by the magnificence
» of what he beholds, seeing a house, as God's tem-
» ple, elaborated most gloriously both in the mag-
» nitude of the structure and the beauty of the
» surrounding ornaments. There the artificer has
» fashioned wood into the shape of animals; and
» the stonecutter has polished the slabs to the
» smoothness of silver; and the painter has in-
» troduced the flowers of his art, depicting and
» imaging the constancy of the martyrs, their resis-
» tance, their torments, the savage forms of the
» tyrants, their outrages, the blazing furnace, and
» the most blessed end of the champion: the repre-
» sentation of Christ, in human form, presiding over
» the contest; [1] all these things, as it were in a
» book gifted with speech, shaping for us by means
» of colours, has he cunningly discoursed to us of
» the martyr's struggles, has made this temple glo-

---

[1] S. Basil also, A. D. 379, alludes to this same introduction of Christ
into the canvass. « Rise up now, I pray you, ye celebrated painters of the
» good deeds of these wrestlers. Make glorious by your art the mutilated
» image of their leader. With colours laid on by your cunning make il-
» lustrious the crowned martyr by me too feebly pictured. I retire van-
» quished before you in your painting of the excellencies of the martyr. I
» rejoice at being this day overcome by such a victory of your bravery. I
» shall behold the struggle between the fire and the martyrs depicted more
» accurately by you. I shall see the wrestler depicted made glorious by
» your representation. Let demons weep at being now also smitten in you
» by the brave deeds of the martyr. Again let the burning hand be shown
» them. Let Christ also, who presides over the struggle, be depicted on
» your canvass. »

» rious as some brilliant fertile mead. For the
» silent tracery on the walls has the art to dis-
» course, and to aid most powerfully. And he who
» has arranged the mosaics has made this pavement
» on which we tread equal to a history. And hav-
» ing gratified his sight with these sensible works
» of art, he then desires to approach the very shrine
» itself, believing that the touching it is a hallow-
» ing and benediction. And should some one allow
» him to carry away the dust which lies on the
» surface of that resting place, the dust is received
» as a gift, and the earth is treasured up as a va-
» luable possession. For to touch the relic itself,
» if ever by so great a good fortune one could ob-
» tain leave, how very much this is to be desired,
» and what a concession to the most earnest sup-
» plication, they know who have had experience,
» and have accomplished this desire. For the be-
» holders, with joy, embrace it as if a living and
» unfading body, applying it to eyes, and mouth,
» and ears, and to all the senses; and shedding
» then a tear of veneration and sympathy for the
» martyr, as though he were entire and visible before
» them, they supplicate him to intercede, beseeching
» him as an attendant upon God, calling upon him
» as receiving gifts whenever he pleases. »   This
beautiful passage was written before the year 395.

Although veneration of the martyrs is based upon spiritual relationship and supernatural motives, even in the natural order a rude inhumanity would appear in not treasuring their remains. « We » are moved, » says Atticus to Cicero, « by the » very places, where the footprints of men we ad- » mire, or love, are present. That very Athens of » ours does not delight me so much by the magni- » ficent works and exquisite arts of the ancients, » as by the remembrance of the chiefest men, where » one was wont to dwell, where to sit, where to » argue: I studiously contemplate their tombs. »

But our purpose is more with the external mode of honouring than with the sentiment. Granting that Christian art, contrasted with the classical, was never of the highest order, and that (especially in Africa where the cemeteries above ground were more exposed to Diocletian's persecution) it was mercilessly swept away, there is ample evidence that, within fifty years after Constantine gave peace to the Church, able artists had done much to repair the damage. It is very true that religious feeling is often awakened by inferior external forms but the productions described in such noble language by S. Gregory of Nyssa and S. Asterius could not have been mere daubs. We shall see that the latter speaks of a picture as resembling the style of an artist whose name he gives, and compares it with the old masters. The Vatican bronze medallion of S. Peter and S. Paul, found in S. Domitilla's cemetery, the earliest known representation of these apostles, shows a good style of execution; and if we consider the rank and riches of the noble converts in Rome, it is unlikely that the first Pope, who lived in the palace of a Senator whose daughters were his zealous pupils, or the other apostle who lived in his own hired house, should have failed of competent artists if their portraits were wished for at all. And in the same way, directly the Church had breathing time, whatever the style of the pictures may have been, it is evident that the bodies of the martyrs and their pictures were honoured together, and that in the fourth century pictorial art in the churches was public and profuse. Naked form and classical outlines were not to be got, nor probably desired; but it is difficult to believe that the decorations of the Church were deficient in poetry, execution, and effective art.

Earliest medallion of SS. Peter and Paul.

Profusion of art in the 4th century.

If the chief motive for Church decorative art was to embellish the places of sepulture and chapels connected with them, and if the embellishments themselves, under the pressure of necessity, were confined to symbols, or very simple adaptations of Christian facts, we should expect to find with

Disuse of the subterranean cemeteries, and their destruction by the Barbarians.

greater liberty, greater freedom of composition.
When the empire became Christian, the sufferings
of the martyrs would naturally be chosen for historical religious pictures, and the Roman artist
would be no longer doomed to the obscurity of the
catacombs, but would enjoy the more favourable
light and grander dimensions of the basilicas. The
Popes themselves were no longer buried in the subterranean crypts. Melchiades, A. D. 311-314, the first
to sit in the Lateran, was the last to be buried
under ground: « in coemeterio Callixti in crypta. »
Sylvester, A. D. 314-336, was buried in the cemetery
of Priscilla in an open-air basilica. Mark, A. D. 336,
similarly in the cemetery of Balbina outside the Ar-
deatine gate, not far from the cemetery of Callixtus on the Appian way. The Constantinian basilicas, S. Lorenzo, S. Agnese, and S. Alexander, even
cut away many loculi and crypts to make a level.
After the death of Julian the Apostate, in 363, De
Rossi says, « that the use of subterranean cemete-
• ries visibly declined. » In the public distress they
were neglected and fell into the hands of private
fossors, and, after the year 454, he finds no interment
in them at all. The liturgies of the second half of
the fifth century constantly refer to burials in the
basilicas; and in the sixth century burial was common within the walls of Rome. As for the Pagan

emperors, the first direct public attack upon the
cemeteries was that by Valerian, in 257, and it
only lasted three years; for his son Gallienus, whose
mother, Solinina, was a Christian, recalled it, and
ordered the religious places to be restored to the
bishops, on which account Dionysius, bishop of Alexandria, calls him, « more friendly to God. » [1] It
is recorded of his contemporary, Pope Dionysius,
that he allotted the churches and cemeteries to
priests, and constituted parishes and dioceses. In
303, Diocletian burnt and ravaged every thing. De
Rossi thinks that from 370 to 373 there was again
a fashion to be buried near the martyrs. Perhaps
the zeal of Damasus for restorations, and his own
recorded wish to be laid by the martyrs, had something to do with it. But the invasions of the
barbarians were the real cause of the destruction
of the cemeteries. Alaric marched three times
against Rome. The first time he arrived within a
few miles of the city, and, deterred by a mysterious
power, suddenly retreated. But he appeared a second time, in 408, when he besieged the city, and
after reducing it to extremities by famine and pes-
tilence, accepted a ransom of 5000 pounds of gold,
30000 of silver, 4000 vestments of silk, and 3000

---

[1] See De Rossi's *Bollettino di Archeologia Sacra*, for January 1866,
page 6.

dyed furs. On the 24th of August 410 he returned
a third time, entered the city through treason at
the dead of the night, and the blast of the Gothic
trumpet announced to the inhabitants that the barbarian invaders had passed through the Salarian
gate. Genseric the Vandal, about the year 460,
destroyed all Rome and its suburbs, with the exception of the three principal basilicas. Before the
end of the fifth century Ricimer the Suevian Goth
besieged and destroyed the doomed city, but was
obliged to evacuate it by Belisarius. In the absence of Belisarius, Totila, after taking Fiesole, commenced another siege of Rome in 545. The citizens
made a heroic resistance, but suffered cruelly from
famine and disease. The Isaurian soldiers, who
guarded the Porta Asinaria, no longer able to support the fatigues and privations of a protracted
siege, consented to admit the invader by treason,
and Totila entered the city in triumph, April 546.
He spared the inhabitants for a time, but having
learned that the Greeks had defeated the Goths in
Lucania, he compelled the entire population to emi-
grate into the province of Campagna; and thus, as
Procopius narrates, « Rome was left absolutely a
» wilderness of ruin, and desolated mansions; a city
» without sound or tread; abandoned to the fox
» and wolf. » Belisarius retook the city and rebuilt

its walls. Totila subsequently returned, but was forced to retire with much slaughter. He besieged the city again in 549, and, as before, entered by the Porta Asinaria. He remained in peaceful possession until 552, when Justinian sent Narses to renew the war in Italy with greater energy. Narses completely defeated the Goths in a general engagement in the passes of the Apennines, and among the slain was Totila himself. Narses then marched to Rome, and the Goths, on his approach to its defenceless walls, retired to the Castle of S. Angelo, which they defended for a short time, but were obliged to capitulate on condition that their lives should be spared by the conqueror. The resting places of the dead were not, of course, spared during those terrible ravages. In 648, 682, the bodies of the martyrs were brought in from the suburban towns, such as Porto and Nomentum. Astolphus and the Lombards ruined the cemeteries in 760. Paul I, who was elected Pope in 757, brought the bodies of the martyrs into the city, because the cemeteries were in decay. Adrian I and Leo III tried to restore them. Paschal I, in 817, removed the body of S. Cecily with many others. Sergius II and Leo IV brought in some that were still left. Nicholas I attempted, in 867, some catacombic restorations, and they were the last.

— 42 —

From these brief notices we may arrive at several general conclusions. 1ˢᵗ That any attempt to construct a religious system from the presence or absence of catacombic data alone, is quite fallacious, owing to the original character and extremely mutilated state of the monuments. 2ᵈ That in so far as art attended upon burial, and that peculiar kind of burial had almost ceased within thirty or forty years after the peace of the Church, we must look elsewhere for it. 3ʳᵈ We shall find pictorial art still busy about the dead, and the relics of the martyrs removed into the city between 600 and 800, that is in the great basilicas. 4ᵗʰ Whether we look to Christian art for a peculiar class of artistic ideas, or for religious instruction, it is singularly absurd to restrict our inquiries to the more meagre instances of it in the catacombs, and overlook the profusion of it in the basilicas; because if the Christians were fond of painting under all the disadvantages of the catacombs, they would certainly develop their taste upon a grander scale in the basilicas; and if their thoughts are interesting to us when depicted in the obscurity of difficult times or persecution, we should expect a fuller utterance when they were at peace and free. Hence, on the religious side, the proper test is not whether what we find in the basilicas is different

A religious system cannot be constructed from the catacombs alone.

After the peace of the Church, art followed the bodies of the Martyrs transferred into the basilicas.

from the little we may know of the catacombs, but
whether the basilicas contradict the catacombs.
And in this view *even the latest frescoes* in S. Clement have a peculiar interest; because if they were
painted when Leo IV was alive, or those relating
to S. Nicholas, S. Clement, and S. Cyril, soon after
the events they represent, they are a link in religious art, especially as being votive pictures, by
which we can trace the ideas which prevailed when
the catacombs had fallen into desuetude. Without
a single symbol of the catacombs, or a single figure imitated from them,[1] they contain a distinct,
formed, and characteristic school of painting. The
ideas elicited from them do not contradict the catacombs. And on the side of art, as compositions,
they are superior to any we possess in the catacombs. With all the defects of drawing and perspective, the colouring is pleasing, they tell their
story well, and they exhibit a grouping and movement for which we seek in vain through the catacombs, or indeed in most of the Pagan frescoes
which have come down to us.

S. John, in the Apocalypse, saw under the altar
the souls of them that were slain for the word of

Votive pictures
discovered in
S. Clement's,
bolder in com-
position than
catacombic
pictures, and
linking Chris-
tian art with
the early Ita-
lian school.

---

[1] On the pier that contains the fresco of the miracle of Sisinius at
S. Clement's mass, there is a painting of Daniel in the lions' den, but
its treatment is quite different from that of the same subject frequently
found in the Catacombs.

— 44 —

God, and for the testimony they held. The basilicas continued the *cultus* of the dead. The Church brought their bodies in from the Campagna, and placed them more conspicuously beneath her altars. When S. Peter's was ringing with the voices of the tens of thousands giving glory to God for the dogma of the Immaculate Conception, the « Veni Creator Spiritus » intoned by Pius IX, was answered from the Nomentan way. There the ancient Christian basilica was again given to view, the oratory at the cemetery. There appeared the altar-tomb of the martyr Pope Alexander. But if we would venerate his relics, we shall find them with an inscription in the more sumptuous crypt of S. Sabina on the Aventine. The little loculus in the catacombs, with its phial of precious blood and tiny lamp, gave occasion for the oratory, the oratory for the country church; the danger of the sacred deposit of the Church for the securer and grander basilica within the walls of Rome. There is no lapse or hiatus, any more than there is in the succession and teaching of the Popes. Bosius reckons six cemeteries of the Apostolic age. The first, on the via Cornelia, that of S. Peter's in the Vatican. The Pontifical Book says: « Anacletus memoriam » beati Petri construxit, et loca ubi episcopi con- » derentur. » If those bishops of Rome did not

Discovery of S. Alexander's basilica in 1854.

date from S. Peter, they had no date at all. The ancient Acts of SS. Peter and Paul state that their bodies remained a year and seven months in the catacombs, « quousque fabricarentur loca, ubi po- » sita sunt in Vaticano et in via Ostiensi. » The catacombs were crypts at S. Sebastian's to which alone the name of catacomb, for some time, exclusely applied. [1] Pope Damasus, in 384, gives us verses upon the spot.

> « *Hic habitasse prius sanctos cognoscere debes*
> *Nomina quisque Petri pariter Paulique requiris.* » [2]

> « Thou ought'st know that here the saints did dwell the first of all,
> Whoe'r thou art that seek'st the name of Peter and of Paul. »

And of the Vatican cemetery again he writes:

> « *Cingebant latices montem, teneroque meatu*
> *Corpora multorum cineres atque ossa rigabant.*
> *Non tulit hoc Damasus, communi lege sepultos*
> *Post requiem tristes iterum persolvere pœnas.*
> *Protinus aggressus magnum superare laborem,*
> *Aggeris immensi dejecit culmina montis.*
> *Intima sollicitè scrutatus viscera terræ*
> *Siccavit totum quidquid madefecerat humor :*
> *Invenit fontem, præbet qui dona salutis.*
> *Hæc curavit Mercurius levita fidelis.* » [3]

> « The streams the mountain girt, and with their tender rill
> Of many, bodies, ashes, bones, with moisture fill;
> Nor bore this Damasus, by common law who lay
> When once at rest again sad penalties should pay;
> He set to work at once the labour vast surmount,
> Of bulk immense threw down the summit of the mount;

---

[1] The names of all the other catacombs, occurring so frequently in the Martyrologies and Lives of the Popes, appear to have been confused with this particular spot; because it always retained its place in the *Libri Indulgentiarum.*

[2] Carmen IX.   [3] Carmen XXXVI, de fontibus Vaticanis.

The inmost bowels of the earth explored with care
And dried the whole whate'r the moisture wetted there:
He found the fountain that the gifts of safety lends,
All this Mercurius the faithful levite tends. »

In this particular instance we have the Pope himself describing his care for the cemeteries. At that date (366-384) it was as easy to ascertain a circumstance relating to the coming to Rome and death of S. Peter, as any now relating to the religious revolution by Henry the eighth. The substructions of S. Peter's conceal the Vatican cemetery. The new basilica of S. Paul shows that the Popes have not yet forgotten the graves of either apostle.

But the Basilican churches of Rome were sometimes built upon the martyr's own house, whether interred there as in the case of SS. John and Paul, officers in the army under the Apostate Julian, or not, as in the instance of S. Clement who was mar-
tyred in the Crimea. Tradition has always maintained that the church of S. Clement is upon the actual site of his house. When we visit it, we cannot be blind to the inveterate faith with which Catholics venerate the relics of the dead, and the magnificence with which holy Church surrounds the bodies of the saints. For reduced, as this Constantinian basilica may be said to be in its present state, to mere brick and mortar, whilst we admire the beauty of the precious marble pillars, we must re-

Basilica of S. Clement built upon his own house.

Style of its decorations.

place in imagination what was removed to construct the church above; the noble marble panels
of the choir, and especially the two of basket-work
-*transennæ*- once probably protecting the relics of the
saint; the various intricate patterns of the rich opus
Alexandrinum of the pavement. If we add frescoes
from top to bottom, and from end to end, elegant
in their ornamentation, and harmonious in colouring, deficient indeed in perspective and void of class-
ic type, but noble and expressive in telling their
story; if we introduce the lights and crowd, and
priests at the high altar, we shall conceive no small
idea of the Catholic basilica. Nor will it be a hin-
derance that the frescoes were not all painted at the
same time. Their presence, and the votive character of the most striking, show that the religious
spirit which painted the catacombs was not lost with
them, and in this respect the pictures in S. Clement's are unique. If we were in possession of those
with which S. Damasus adorned his church of Saint
Lorenzo in Damaso, and which were extant four
hundred years afterwards, that is about the year 800,
we should have an ascertained series of pictures to
supply the link which seems wanting in Catholic decorative art between the catacombs and those compositions in mosaic, which, though some may be
of the sixth and seventh, are more generally of the

Its frescoes the earliest Christian compositions now left to us — a peculiarity in their arrangement. ninth and later centuries. Independently however of any other interest, the frescoes in our basilica of S. Clement go far to fill up the gap; for in them we have the earliest large wall-paintings of church compositions now left to us, certainly in Rome at least: ingenious in their arrangement and replete with piety. They were designed by worshippers who understood that passage of the psalm: « I have » loved, o Lord, the beauty of thy house; and the « place where thy glory dwelleth. » If we agree, from the square nimbus about his head, that Leo IV, introduced in the picture of the Assumption of our Lady, was painted before his death, in 855, we can judge in some degree (even without the pictures lost in the interval, and taking no account of the Crucifixion and other earlier frescoes in S.Clement's) by comparison with Catholic art of the fourth century, such as the glasses inlaid with gold, and the latest representations in the catacombs, how much has been lost in the lines of drawing, and what progress made in more crowded compositions. Again if we refer the great picture representing the translation of S. Clement's relics, from the Vatican to his own basilica, to the time of S. Nicholas I, who died in 866, we shall not think, even by comparison with the catacombs, that Catholic art had miserably perished. We may find a certain analogy,

though a less delicate execution, between them and
the frescoes by Masaccio in the upper church. But
our point of comparison is itself inaccurate, that is
between simple symbols and historical pictures. It
is observable that the bishop of Amasea, S. Asterius, compares the picture of the martyrdom which
he saw at Chalcedon between the period of Euphe-
mias' death in 307, and his own about 400, with
older productions. « You would have said it was
» one of Euphranor's skilful pieces, or of one of
» those old painters who raised their art to so great
» an eminence, making their canvas (tables) well nigh
» breathe into life. » Again the composition itself
was large, truthful, and forcible; and, as far as mere
description goes, not unlike more modern arrangements. « The judge is seated aloft on his throne,
» looking at the virgin intensely and fiercely. There
» are the magistrate's attendants, and numerous sol-
» diers, and men with their writing tablets for their
» notes, and styles in their hands; one of whom
» has raised his hand from the wax and looks ear-
» nestly at the virgin who is being questioned, with
» his whole countenance bent towards her as though
» bidding her to speak louder. The virgin stands
» there in a dark robe, indicating her wisdom by
» her dress, and is of a beautiful countenance as the
» painter has fancied her, but, in my judgement,

*Excellent com-
position of a
church-picture
in the 4th cen-
tury.*

4

» beautified in mind by her virtues. Two soldiers
» force her towards the president, one dragging her
» forward, and the other urging her from behind.
» One of the soldiers has seized the virgin's head
» and bent it back; and presents her face to the
» other soldier in a favourable posture for punish-
» ment, and he standing by her has dashed out her
» teeth. The instruments of punishment are seen
» to be a mallet and auger. At this I burst into
» tears, and my feelings intercept my words. For
» the painter has so plainly depicted the drops of
» blood that you would say they were really flow-
» ing from her lips, and you would go your way
» sorrowing. » This picture seems, like several in
S. Clement's, to have contained three subjects in one.
The Saint then describes the trial and torture, the
virgin martyr in prison, and lastly her passion. « A
» little farther on the painter has lit up, in another
» compartment, a blazing fire, and placed her in
» the midst of it with her hands stretched out to
» heaven; her countenance bears on it no sign of
» sadness, but, on the contrary, is lit up with joy
» that she is departing to a blessed and incorpo-
» real life. » It may be doubted whether the notices of our imperial or royal academies supply more
critical description, and whether the religious pieces of modern painters present more able arrange-

ment and matter for thought. We derive this consolation, at least, from what we can no longer see
and admire, this point of comparison from the early
churches of Asia and Rome, that upon the largest
scale, and with all the available resources of art the
memories of the sainted dead were perpetuated for
public reverence. The peace of the Church brought
with it the fruits of peace, public joy, and hope,
and regard for those who fought the good fight.
That puritanical iconoclastic mania, which, like every dereliction from truth, dries up the heart and
impoverishes the understanding, never had any place
in the bosom of the Catholic Church. When the
iconoclastic emperor Leo, in 813, threatened the
bishops in his palace, the bishop of Sardes replied :
« For these eight hundred years past since the com-
» ing of Christ there have always been pictures
» of Him, and He has been honoured in them. Who
» shall now have the boldness to abolish so ancient
» a tradition? » It is not without reason that the
Acts tell us, when the great persecution at Jerusalem dispersed all, except the Apostles, that devout
men took care of Stephen and made great mourning over him. The same affection for the saints
distinguished the noble Roman matrons in the first
three centuries. The very same urged S. Cyril to
bring S. Clement's relics to Rome, and Methodius

The iconoclas-
tic mania.

Christian affec-
tion for Mar-
tyrs, from
S. Stephen
downwards, il-
lustrated by
the pictures
found in S. Cle-
ment's.

to desire that his brother should repose beside them. The very same sent no less a Pope than Gregory the Great to preach in S. Clement's over the corpse of the poor cripple Servulus, who used to lie in its porch. The same affection had carried thither also what remained of the bones of S. Ignatius ground by the teeth of lions in the Coliseum to become the pure bread of Christ. The same laid under the high altar the body of the martyr-consul Clement. The same depicted on the walls the crucifixion of S. Peter, the death of S. Alexius, and the tomb of S. Clement. And what men learned to love and praise, what eloquence extolled and piety revered, the spirit of martyrdom, the actions of the martyrs and their remains, were felt to be no disgrace to the hand of the artist, and no unseemly memorial in the house of God.

If it had not been for the malice and ignorance of the enemies of the Church, we should never have heard of anything so absurd as that Christians should not paint the exploits of the heroes of Christ. Saint Ephrem gives the common sense practice of the fourth century in his letter to John the Monk. « But those » who are yet weakminded need some examples » to excite them to imitate and cultivate the same » virtue. Take this example. Those who according » ing to the world show themseleves strenuous in

» war make images describing the history of the war
» on walls and in pictures; as how these strike with
» arrows, others inflict wounds, some fly, others make
» incursions, others using their swords beat their
» adversaries down like ears of corn. And this they
» do for the emulation of posterity, and commemo-
» ration of those who bore themselves bravely in war
» against opposing enemies. But others paint in
» domestic oratories the contest of the saints for
» the imitation of cowardly hearts, and delight of
» the spectators. »

LIFE OF S. CLEMENT

POPE AND MARTYR.

CHAPTER I.

S. Peter in Rome — His preaching in that city — Lineage of S.Clement — His birth-place — His conversion by S. Peter.

« T<small>HE</small> providence of the universal Ruler, » says Eusebius, « led, as it were, by the hand to Rome, » that most powerful and great one of the Apostles, » and, on account of his virtue, the mouthpiece or » leader of all the rest, Peter, against that pest of » the human race *(Simon Magus).* He, like a noble » commander of God, fortified with divine armour, » brought the precious merchandise of the revealed » light from the East to the dwellers in the West, » announcing the light itself, and the salutary doc- » trine of the soul, the proclamation of the king- » dom of God. » [1] In Rome itself the home of Pagan superstition, and mistress of error, (for she

---

[1] H. E. B. II, c. 14, p. 63-4.

welcomed to her hearths and temples the gods and creeds of every race) and central seat of military power, the Prince of the Apostles determined to fix his See.[1]   In that great metropolis of the world he decided on founding the fortress of faith, to attack Satan in the stronghold of his tyranny, to light up the dark valley of the shadow of death, and, thence by diffusing the gospel, facilitate the conquest of the rest of the world to the kingdom of Jesus Christ. Rome was to the Gentiles what it has been to the Catholic world, no insulated or merely national capital city, but the focus of thought, of civilization, and the most authoritative power. With no theories

---

[1] In the whole range of ecclesiastical history there is not a statement better authenticated, or more satisfactorily proved than S. Peter's visit to Rome, his preaching there, his founding the Roman Church, and his martyrdom in that city. Nevertheless such critics as Marsilius of Padua, John of Janduno, Oldaricus Velenus, Bower, and a few others have denied or thrown doubt upon his having been ever there at all : and a modern philologist, Dressel, has carried his prejudices so far as to confound the death of Peter the Apostle with that of Peter the martyr, bishop of Alexandria. But the evidence of writers, Protestant as well as Catholic, is against them. Among the former, Cave, Hammond, Pearson, Grotius, Joseph Scaliger, Blondel, Young, Buddeus, Le Clerc, Kipping, Basnage, Newton, Leibnitz. etc. Among the latter, S. Clement, S. Ignatius, Papias, Cajus, Origen, S. Irenaeus, Eusebius, S. Leo, S. Jerome, S. Augustine, the Author of the Carmen against Marcion, S. Hippolytus martyr, S. Epiphanius, S. John Chrysostom, S. Gregory the Great, Anastasius the Librarian, S. Thomas Aquinas, S. Bonaventure, Baronius, Orsi, etc. etc.   And yet, within the last year, a few apostate Friars, calling themselves evangelicals, had the effrontery to deny a fact so well attested, and provoke a public discussion on the subject, in the very City of Rome, the result of which has proved how ignorant of church history are those soi-disant evangelicals.   See also *La Venuta di S. Pietro in Roma*, by D. Cataldo Caprara, Rome, 1872.

to suit the imperial mind, with no schemes drawn from family ambition and masked by an hypocritical life, S. Peter, directed by the spirit of God, left Antioch, and, single-handed, entered the Babylon of human power to preach Christ crucified to its licentious, proud, and fanatically idol-worshipping inhabitants. From the Jewish quarter to that inhabited by the Gentiles the mystery of the Cross spread through the city. [1] The burning zeal and inspired eloquence of the Galilean fisherman were so irresistibly impressive that all regarded him as a man mighty in word and work. He was only fulfilling the promise of his Lord : « I will give you a mouth » and wisdom, which all your adversaries will not » be able to resist and contradict. » [2]

Much as has been written about the conversion of Rome a great deal more requires to be added to

---

[1] The learned Dominican Ciaconius, author of the lives of the Popes, says in his biography of S. Peter that « he sojourned for some time among » the Jews, who, as Philo and Martial narrate, lived in the Trastevere, be- » fore he began to preach to the Gentiles : but, when the fame of his preach- » ing became known, Pudens, believing in Christ, received and treated » him hospitably in his own palace.
» For breast-plate take faith, like a grain of mustard believing in » the consubstantial and indivisible Trinity. For the mustard seed is » altogether round, having no cleft, no angle ; but is entirely round and » has a remarkable heat. Relying on that Peter the prince of the apo- » stolic order when he had confessed Christ to be the Son of the living » God received the keys of the kingdom of heaven, and obtained the » power of things heavenly and terrestrial. » S. Ephrem de panoplia ad Monachos.
[2] Luke XXI. 15.

it. We read indeed in the Acts of the martyrs how
the rich and noble were victims of their faith: most
touching the simple innocence with which youthful
and delicate virgins, whose names and memories are
yet household words among their fellow citizens,
gave up all that the world prizes: most admirable the
courage (is it for ever gone!) with which illustrious
men and noble matrons devoted life and fortune to
the assertion of truth, and the burial of the martyred
dead. But the rapidity with which the leaven hid in
the three bushels of meal, the secret strength of the
gospel in the three centuries Christianity groaned
under imperial infidels, leavened the whole mass of
their autocracy and prepared the civilized world for
the freedom and sovereignty of the Church in Rome,
the jealousy of their political power which animated
the emperors of those days and whetted the rancour
of their prefects, and the divine power by which
tender souls were changed at once and strengthened
to bear the worst persecutions of the state, can only
be understood from an intimate acquaintance with
the genealogy and connexions of the Patrician families. « Men cry out, » says Tertullian A. D.
195 - 218, « that the state is beset, that the Chris-
» tians are in their fields, in their forts, in their
» islands: they mourn as for a loss that every sex,
» age, condition, and now even rank, is going over

» to this sect. » [1] We cannot open the Acts of the early martyrs without perceiving that their rank and estates were aimed at as in much more modern religious proscriptions.

Crowds then from every quarter rushed to listen to S. Peter. If miracles also bespoke the presence of an Apostle, we must not forget that the sudden conversion of multitudes upon hearing of his words was one of the greatest. The infidels who try to account for the reception of Christianity by natural causes alone, and believers who ascribe it to the miracles of healing which strike the sense of sight, seem to have overlooked that grace given to speech, which penetrates and makes the soul captive to faith, without striking eloquence, without learned disquisition, without merely human motives and passion, with a simplicity apparently inadequate to its marvellous effects — a phenomenon in the lives of many of the saints. Among those who had ears to hear was the noble youth Clement. Zazera thinks that he belonged to the Octavian family. [2] To the Claudian as Hesychius Salonitanus asserts. [3] To the Senatorial and Caesarean family, as Ciaconius, Si-

---

[1] Apol. n. 1, p. 2.
[2] See notes of Oldoinus in Vita S. Clementis.
[3] Paternum illi genus ex antiquissima Claudiae gentis Neronum familia.

anda, Burius, Boscus, Audisius and many others
maintain on the authority of the celebrated letter
of S. Eucherius bishop of Lyons to his kinsman Valerian A. D. 427. [1] Also the Recognitions (falsely
attributed to S. Clement) published in Greek in the
beginning of the second century and translated into
Latin by Rufinus priest of Aquileia towards the end
of the fourth, represent Clement as related to the
Caesars. « Peter says, no one in truth is superior
» to thee in race. I replied there are indeed many
• powerful men come of Caesar's stock (prosapia).
» For to my father, as to his relation and brought
» up with him, he gave a wife of an equally noble
» family by whom he had twin sons before my-

[1] Ciaconius, Vitae et res gestae Pontificum Romarorum, in vita
S. Clementis. Sianda, Breviar. Hist. Burius, Rom. Pont. Brevis not. pag. 7.
Bosco, Vita dei Sommi Pontefici, in S. Clemente. Audisius, Storia dei
Papi, in S. Clemente.

2

Genealogical tree

As given in De Rossi's *Bullettino*

TITVS F
u.

• TITVS FLAVI
u.ror VESPAS

TITVS FLAVIVS SABINVS
u.ror (*Plautia.* . . . ?)

(Flavius . . . ?)   († PLAVTILLA)   † TITVS FLAVIVS CLEMENS   TITVS FLAVI'
(u.ror . . .)   conjux . . . .   u.ror † FLAVIA DOMITILLA   SABINVS
                                                           u.ror IVLIA A

(† *Clemens pp.* ?)   † FL. DOMITILLA VESPASIANVS IVN. DOMITIANVS IVN.

» self. »[1] In this no doubt tradition was followed. De Rossi remarks that if we were to read in the lives of the saints that christianity, almost at the death of S. Peter and S. Paul, was so nigh to the imperial throne that the cousin and niece of Domitian were not only Christians, but suffered exile and death for the faith, the incredulous would laugh, and yet he proves it from profane authors alone. He distinguishes Marcus Arecinus Clemens twice consul, first A. D. 73, and next under Domitian who had him put to death, from the martyr consul Titus Flavius Clemens son of Vespasian's eldest brother Titus Flavius Sabinus many years prefect of Rome; and he conjectures that pope Clement was the child of an elder son of Sabinus and consequently nephew to the martyr.[2] Others, from a phrase in S. Clement's epistle to the

---

[1] Recogn. lib. VII.

Flavian family.

·cheol. *Crist.* Roma Marzo 1865

:TRO
:RTVLLA

BINVS
)LLA

| TITVS FLAVIVS VESPASIANVS AVG. | | FLAVIA (*Polla* vel *Petronilla*) | |
| *uxor* FLAVIA DOMITILLA AVG. | | | |

TVS FLAVIVS VESP. AVG.	TITVS FLAVIVS DOMITIANVS AVG.	FLAVIA DOMITILLA	
ores ARRECINA TERTVLLA	*uxor* DOMITIA LONGINA AVG.	*conjux*	
MARCIA FVRNILLA			

| IVLIA AVG. | . . . . . . | † FLAVIA DOMITILLA | |
| *uxor* *T. Fl. Sabini* | | *conjux* *T. Fl. Clementis* | |

Corinthians, set aside unvarying tradition, and will
have him to be a Jew. The arguments adduced by
Tillemont, Ceillier, Baillet, Gallicciolli, and others to
make him out a Jew or a Greek are so feeble as
to excite surprise. They say he calls Jacob « our
father » [1] and therefore he must have been a Jew.
But these critics should have reflected that when
Abraham was constituted « a father of many nations, » [2] all those who were converted to the faith
had a right to call Abraham and Isaac their fathers,
and to consider themselves fellow-citizens with Ju-
dith, the Machabees, and other confessors of the old
law. Nor because the priest is of the order of
Melchisedech, who was not a Jew, is he therefore
according to the flesh of the stock of that royal
priest. The alliance between God and Abraham
was spiritual: « Know ye therefore, » says S. Paul,
« that they who are of the faith the same are the
» children of Abraham. » [3] With the same acumen
by which Tillemont makes him a Jew, Hefele maintains that he was a Greek and Philippian, because
he assisted S. Paul in his evangelical labours among
that people. If he travelled with that Apostle in
Greece, S. Luke of Antioch did the same, and was

---

[1] « Through envy our father Jacob fled from the face of Esau his
» brother. »

[2] Gen. XVII. 4. [3] Gal. III. 7.

martyred in Achaia. The faith could not be pent up within the narrow limits of Judea, and independently of the facilities for travelling in the more settled parts of the empire, many Scripture personages fled from the persecutions of the Jews to Rome and Gaul without having been born there. We believe that S. Clement was a Roman, and a noble Roman citizen.

Passing from the question of S. Clement's country to that of his parentage, we find it generally admitted that his father's name was Faustinus, or Faustinianus, or Faustus, [1] and his mother's Matidia, or Macidiana, of the most noble family of the Anicii: [2] and that he was born on the first of July, in the consulship of Sextus Ælius, and Cajus Sentius Saturninus, the very day on which Tiberius was adopted by Augustus. [3] We read that he had two brothers Faustinus and Faustus. S. Zosimus, one of the most illustrious occupants of the pontifical throne, informs us that the noble youth Clement was so affected by the words which fell from the lips of S. Peter that, without any deliberation, he submitted to the sweet yoke of the gospel, and was regene-

---

[1] See Rondinini, de S. Clemente ejusque Basilica, lib. 1, cap. 1, § 4.

[2] « Maternum illi genus e gente Anicia. » Hesych. Salonitanus.

[3] « Clemens natus Romae Kalendis Julii, ipso die quo Tiberium Augustus adoptavit, Sexto Aelio et Sentio Saturnino Coss. »

[4] Epist. ad Aurelium et episcopos Africanos.

rated in the waters of baptism. Considering his noble ancestry and accomplished education, « a man re- » plete with all knowledge and most skilful in the » liberal arts, » [1] we are not surprised that he was very dear to S. Peter, and also to S. Paul who calls him one of his fellow-labourers in the mystic vineyard of the Lord, « whose names are in the » book of life. » [2] Eusebius, Origen, S. Jerome, S. Epiphanius, Rufinus, and many other ancient and modern historians do not hesitate to affirm that the Clement mentioned here by the Apostle was the suc- cessor of S. Peter in the apostolic chair: [3] and also the Church, as Martini, the learned archbishop of Florence, observes, seems to favour this opinion by ordering a part of that epistle to be read at the al- tar on the festival of S. Clement. [4] Therefore, con- cludes Rondinini, [5] little or no attention ought to be paid to Oldoinus and a few others who endeavour to controvert and contradict it.

But although we willingly adhere to the opinions of the abovenamed holy Fathers and celebrated wri-

---

[1] « Omni scientia refertus, omniumque liberalium artium peritis- » simus. » S. Hieron. Comment. ep. ad Philip. IV, 3.

[2] S. Paul to the Philippians, IV, 3.

[3] See Calmet's Commentaries on S. Paul to the Philippians, IV, 3. Also Cave, Baillet, Ladvocat, Cesarotti; Rohrbacher's universal history, vol. IV, book 26. Audisius, etc. etc.

[4] See notes by Martini on S. Paul to the Philippians.

[5] Rondinini, de S. Clemente, lib. 1, cap. 1, §. 4.

ters, who make S. Clement the companion and fel-
low-labourer of S. Paul in his apostolic missions,
we cannot admit that he was a Canon Regular or a
Carmelite, or that he was the first bishop of Velletri, or of Cagliari in Sardinia, or of Sardis in Lydia.
As for the abovementioned religious Orders which
are anxious to add this rare and precious gem to
their treasures, it is certain that they have not authentic titles for doing so, and that the former, as
Rondinini observes, has attempted it « *inani prorsus
conatu,* » and the latter « *levi pariter traditione.* » [1]
With regard to those who assert that S. Clement
was the first bishop of Velletri the capital of the
Volsci, Oldoinus, quoted by Rondinini, says: « Those
» writers who enumerate S. Clement among the bish-
» ops of Velletri must have been deceived either
» by a similitude of name, or by a love of country,
» for I cannot, as well as I recollect, find that state-
» ment affirmed by any ancient historian. » [2] And
to this similitude of name may also be ascribed the
mistake of those who, with Phara in the first book
of his history of Sardinia, assert that S. Clement
was sent by the Apostles, a short time before he was
elevated to the Popedom, to govern the church of

---

[1] Oldoinus' annotations on Ciaconius, and his book on the Clements.
[2] Rondinini, de S. Clemente, lib. 1. cap. 1, § 18.

5

Cagliari. Or perhaps the mistake arose from the passage which Godfrey Henschenius quotes from Cardinal Sirletti, « *Clemens qui ex gentibus conversus factus* » *est Episcopus Sardorum,* » and of which he says in his Acts of Apelles, Lucius, and Clement, « here men-» tion is made of the Sardi the inhabitants of Sardis » the metropolis of Lydia under Croesus, according » to the Poet: « *Quid Croesi regia Sardis.* » [1] And the same learned critic in his remarks on these words which he quotes from another very ancient calendar, « *Clemens primus ex gentibus credens episcopus Sar-* » *dicae,* » says « that some writers have erroneously » asserted that Clement here mentioned was after-» wards raised to the pontifical chair.» [2] But we have dwelt long enough on this subject, and our limits do not permit us to proceed with the investigation of assertions which require much stronger evidence before the inference drawn from them can be applied to the subject of our inquiries. For the same reason we omit the extracts given by Ughelli, in the sixth book of his « Italia Sacra, » from a Greek menology of the tenth century preserved in the Vatican library, in which he con-

---

[1] Horace, book, 1, ep. 11.

[2] One of the writers here alluded to is evidently Raphael of Volterra who in the 19th book of his Commentaries says « Clemens Praesul Sardicensis, postea Pontifex, primus ex gentibus Christianus. »

founds the person and martyrdom of Clement of Ancyra with the person and martyrdom of Clement of Rome.

———

CHAPTER II.

S. Clement consecrated bishop by S. Peter, and appointed his coadjutor in the apostolic ministry — Chronological order of succession of the three first Popes who governed the Church after Peter — Opinions of ancient writers on this subject — Opinions of modern writers — The Ebionite and Marcotian heresies condemned by S. Clement.

We now come to facts connected with the life of our Saint, which can be more satisfactorily proved, and are more interesting to the reader. Ciacónius, on the authority of the epistle of the martyr Ignatius to the Trallians, tells us that S. Clement was baptized by S. Peter, and afterwards on account of his rare merits ordained deacon for the purpose of assisting him in his sacred ministrations. [1] He made great and rapid progress in the path of virtue, and converted many souls to Christ by the persuasive

———

[1] « A Beato Petro baptizatus Clemens, et diaconus sibi assistens ut » Ignatius tradit.... ordinatus. » Ciaconius in Vita S. Clementis. De Rossi asserts that out of the seven Roman deacons each Pope chose an archdeacon whose office was very much such as that of the cardinal Vicar now.

powers of his preaching, and the silent eloquence
of his example. The Prince of the **Apostles** observing **the** excellent qualities of his deacon Clement,
ordained him priest, and shortly after raised him
to **the dignity of the** episcopacy and made him his
own coadjutor in the apostolic ministry. So earnestly and zealously did Clement labour in his vocation that **Rufinus** calls him an **apostolic man,** nay
almost **an Apostle.** [1] Clement Alexandrinus styles
him an Apostle, [2] a distinction accorded to him by
all antiquity, as Isaac Vossius, Godfrey Vendolinus,
and many other renowned writers most satisfactorily prove. [3]

It has not escaped our attention that some historians assert that Clement preached the gospel to the
inhabitants of Metz, and afterwards became the **first**
bishop **of that city,** then one of the most important and populous in France. Even Audisius, frequently quoted by us, refers in his life of our Saint
to the origin of this tradition, and says « that Cle-
» ment preached the gospel in France is evident
» from the acts of Metz, which formed the subject
» of a work by Paul the deacon a distinguished writer
» of the middle ages. » Oldoinus also adverts to

---

[1] Rufinus, de adulteratione librorum Originis.
[2] Clemens Alexandrinus Stromat. lib. IV.
[3] Vossius, Judicium de Barnaba.

this in his commentary on the 14th of October of
the Gallican Martyrology. But he says that the
Clement here mentioned is not our Saint, but his
uncle of the same name and the companion of the
Prince of the Apostles during his travels. [1]

Writers of the most remote antiquity are loud
in their praise of our holy Pontiff, in whatever sphere
of action they regard him. But of all the virtuous
qualities with which he was adorned we may say :
velut inter ignes Luna minores, [2] that virginal purity
shone the brightest. If the « book of Recognitions »
be styled apocryphal, that only means that the
name of its compiler is uncertain, and that those
who ascribe it to Clement do so without sufficient proof. It is however generally admitted that
it is a production of the second century, [3] when there
still were living eye and ear witnesses of the words
and writings of our venerable Pontiff. In the first
page of that work we read: « I Clement born in the
» city of Rome, from my earliest age cultivated chas-
» tity, whilst the natural inclination of mind kept

---

[1] «Tres invenio Clementes Apostolorum temporibus apud probatae fidei
auctores. Tertius hujus Romani Pontificis patruus ab ipsomet Apostolorum Principe, cujus fuerat in itineribus comes, Metensis episcopus ordinatus, et ad Gallos missus ».

[2] Horace, lib. 1, Od. 11.

[3] «Eosdem libros saeculo secundo in lucem prodiis o ferunt». Rondinini,
de S. Clemente lib. 1, cap. 11, § 6. Origen also mentions them.

» me bound as it were with certain chains of anxiety
and grief. » [1] Words which are almost literally
repeated in the Clementine homilies. « Be it known
» to you, my Lord, that I Clement who am a Roman
» citizen and have wished to pass the first age of
» life with modesty and moderation, when I had
» taken to heart a thought which had crept in upon
» me I know not whence, and begat for me frequent
» musings upon death, I was living with labour and
» anxiety. » [2] And in that part of the letter to the
Philadelphians attributed to S. Ignatius martyr, but
interpolated by some very early unknown hand, in
which mention is made of those who were extolled
for having preserved intact the flower of their virginity, we read: « Would that I might enjoy your
» sanctity, like that of Elias, of Josue, of Melchise-
» dec, of Elisaeus, of Jeremias, of John the Baptist,
» of the beloved disciple, of Timothy, of Titus, of
» Evodius, of Clement who went out of life chaste. »[3]

---

[1] « Ego Clemens in Urbe Roma natus ex prima aetate pudicitiae stu-
» dium gessi, dum me animi intentio velut vinculis quibusdam solicitudinis
» et moeroris innexum teneret. »

[2] « Notum sit tibi, Domine mi, quod ego Clemens, qui Civis Romanus
» sum, et primam vitae aetatem pudice ac moderate transigere volui, quum
» animo percepissem cogitationem, quae nescio unde irrepserat, crebrasque
» mihi de morte meditationes pariebat, cum laboribus et anxietatibus vi-
» vebam. »

[3] «Utinam fruar vestra sanctimonia ut Eliae, ut Josue filii Nave, ut
Melchisedeci, ut Elisaei, ut Hieremiae, ut Baptistae Joannis, ut Dilecti Di-
scipuli, ut Timothei, ut Titi, ut Evodii, ut Clementis, qui in castitate e vita
excesserunt».

And since, as Adelmus, a writer of the middle ages, remarks: « S. Clement, even before his conver- » sion, led a pure and chaste life, how much more, » and to what a greater extent, must those virtues » have become the cherished objects of his life » after he was regenerated with the waters of bap- » tism, and began to practice evangelical perfection, » by imitating the example set him by the Apostles, » and recommended by our Divine Saviour himself. »[1]

This seems a proper place to ask, - who was the immediate successor of S. Peter ? which has occu- pied the attention of some of the most eminent ec- clesiastical historians. Peter, Linus, Cletus, Clement: such is the order of the succession of the Popes, as asserted by the tradition and offices of the Church. Linus of Volterra, Cletus and Clement of Rome, and all three consecrated bishops by Peter. It is said that Clement was instituted by Peter to be his immediate successor.[2] If we could admit that S. Peter had no inspiration of the Holy Spirit, and that so vital a matter as the form of the succession of the Vicars of Christ was left to chance, that the Papacy instead of becoming an elective (and elective with the special assistance of the Holy Ghost) was on the point of being a delegated power, we might admit

[1] See Adelmus.
[2] See Clement's letter to S. James bishop of Jerusalem.

that S. Peter did ordain Clement to be the second
Pope; and that his prudence and modesty declined
the honour, upon the death of his patron, until after
the martyrdom of the two other bishops.   We believe, however, that S. Peter did no such thing. If
he expressed a hope, a preference, a conviction of
his disciple's future elevation to the Pontificate, that
has not been a rare foresight or inspiration. If he
ordained him bishop, many Popes have done the like.
But what is perplexing is that scarcely two authors
agree about the precise chronological order of the
four first Popes. There are many Sees which can
trace their bishops with more or less precision from
the first induction by an Apostle. At Smyrna, for
instance, S. Polycarp ordained by S. John. S. Ignatius of Antioch, who succeeded Peter there after the
death of Evodius, was a disciple of S. John. S. Irenaeus of Lyons says of Polycarp: « that he not only
» had been instructed by Apostles, and had con-
» versed with many who had seen the Lord, but was
» also appointed by the Apostles bishop of Smyrna
» in Asia; that he had seen him, [1] and that he

---

[1] « I can tell you the very place where the bishop Polycarp sat as he
» discoursed: and his goings out and his comings in, and the character of
» his life and his bodily appearance, and the discourses which he addressed
» to the multitude, and how he narrated his daily intercourse with John
» and with others who had seen the Lord; and how he commemorated
» their discourses, and what were the things which he had heard from

» came to Rome under Pope Anicetus. » The visit would have been about a hundred years after the martyrdom of S. Peter. S. Irenaeus was made bishop a very few years later, viz, A. D. 177. He was a man remarkably zealous for apostolical tradition, active in the affairs of the Church at Lyons, to which Rome and Roman information were easily accessible, very near to the facts themselves; one would suppose that of all men he should know the list of the Popes. « The blessed Apostles, » says he, « having founded and built up that Church, conferred the public office of the episcopacy upon Linus, of whom Paul makes mention in his epistle to Timothy. To whom succeeded Anacletus, and after him the third from the Apostles who obtained that episcopacy was Clement, who had seen and conferred with the blessed Apostles, and who still had before his eyes the familiar teaching and tradition of the Apostles; and not he only, for many were then still alive who had been instructed by the Apostles. But to this Clement succeeded Evaristus, and to Evaristus Alexander. Next to him,

---

» them concerning the Lord, and concerning his miracles and his doctrine;
» how Polycarp having received them from those who had seen the Word
» of Life narrated the whole in consonance with the Scriptures. These
» things did I, at that time, hearken to eagerly, through the mercy of God
» then shown me, making remembrance of them, not on paper, but in my
» breast, and by the grace of God I ever revolve them in my mind. »

» thus the sixth from the Apostles, Sixtus was ap-
» pointed, and after him Telesphorus who suffered a
» glorious martyrdom; next Hyginus, then Pius, after
» whom was Anicetus. To Anicetus succeeded Soter,
» and to him, the twelfth in succession from the
» Apostles, succeeded Eleutherius who now holds the
» episcopate. By this same order and succession
» both that tradition which is in the Church from
» the Apostles, and the preaching of the truth have
» come down to us. » The singularity is that Cletus
is suppressed altogether, and Anacletus, whom the
breviary places after Clement, comes next after Linus. Tertullian, who was of the same age as Irenaeus, seems to introduce another confusion and to
insinuate, though he does not expressly say, that Clement was next to Peter. « Let them make known
» the origin of their churches, let them unroll the
» line of their bishops, so coming down by succes-
» sion from the beginning that their first bishop had
» for his author and predecessor some of the Apostles,
» or of apostolic men, so he were one that conti-
» nued steadfast with the Apostles. For in this man-
» ner do the apostolic churches bring down their
» rolls; as the church of the Smyrnians recounts
» that Polycarp was placed there by John, as that
» of the Romans does that Clement was in like man-
» ner ordained by Peter, just as also the rest show

» those whom being appointed by the Apostles to
» the episcopate they have as transmitters of apo-
» stolic seed. » **Another** source of confusion (and
worse, because it palms off an account of Clement's
appointment to succeed S. Peter as if given by Clement himself) occurs directly after the time of Irenaeus and Tertullian in the pretended epistle of Saint
Clement to S. James. The very language is sufficient
to convict it of forgery. It is contained in the Clementines, which, according to Gallandius, were written A. D. 230, whereas Irenaeus died A. D. 202, and
Tertullian twenty years after him. The Clementine
Recognitions again were written in the second century, and the Apostolic Constitutions may be set
down as of the middle of the third century. Eusebius, who was made bishop of Caesarea, in 314, says:
« Linus was the first after Peter to obtain the epis-
» copate of Rome..... but in the progress of this work,
» in its proper place according to the order of time,
» the succession from the Apostles to us will be no-
» ticed. » And accordingly in book III, c. XI, he
says: « Anacletus after having occupied the See of
» Rome for twelve years consigned it to S. Cle-
» ment. »[1]

---

[1] « In Urbe vero Roma duodecim Anacletus annis in episcopatu exac-
» tis, Sacerdotii eolem Clementi tradidit. » Butler says in his life of Cletus, April 26, « that Eusebius a Greek easily made mistakes in similar

So far the oldest authorities, giving the order
of succession of the Popes professedly, set S. Clement in the third place after S. Peter.   S. Irenaeus'
work has come down to us in a very fragmentary
state: whether a copyist conceived Cletus and Anacletus to be one and the same person, and so wrote
Anacletus instead of Cletus, or Anacletus, by an
error of transcription, was left out after Clement,
we are unable to determine.   As far as the place
occupied by S. Clement in the series is concerned,
S. Irenaeus supports tradition and the breviary.
With regard to Tertullian the difficulty is less; because he was not treating of the collocation of the
Popes, but of the apostolicity of churches.   He was
saying what S. Clement himself says in his first
epistle to the Corinthians , « preaching through
» countries and cities, they appointed their first
» fruits, having proved them by the spirit, bishops
» and deacons of those who were about to believe. »
Or as the Presbyter of Africa who lived in the
middle of the fifth century says more in detail: «For

» Latin names, and confounded Cletus with Anacletus, Novatus with No-
» vatian, Pope Marcellus with Marcellinus.   But the Latins who had au-
» thentic records by them, especially the author of the first part of the Li-
» berian Calendar, which appears in most particulars to be copied from the
» registers of the Roman Church, could not be mistaken: which authori-
» ties make it appear that Cletus sat the third and Anacletus the fifth
» bishop of Rome. »

» it is iniquity to rend unity, tearing, as it were,
» the garment of Christ, and the nets, as it were,
» of the fishermen the Apostles: from whose fel-
» lowship all heretics are strangers; who, having
» abandoned the peace of communion and of the
» one bread of God and the Apostles, preach in
» their not churches but squares; and do not com-
» municate in their memories, or, in places de-
» dicated to their memories: separated from the
» whole, assume for themselves the name of catho-
» lic. Whereas in Jerusalem, James, and Stephen
» the first martyr; at Ephesus, John; Andrew and
» others, in various parts of Asia; in the city of
» Rome, the Apostles Peter and Paul, delivering to
» their posterity the church of the Gentiles (in
» which they taught the doctrine of Christ our
» Lord), at peace, and one — hallowed it with their
» blood. »[1]   For Tertullian's argument was, that
on points of doctrine only apostolic churches deserve to be heard.   « On this principle therefore we
» shape our rule of prescription, that if the Lord
» Jesus Christ sent the Apostles to preach, no others
» are to be received as preachers but those whom

---

[1] Iniquitas est scindere unitatem . . . . . . relictâ pace communionis, et
panis unius Dei et Apostolorum, in suis non ecclesiis, sed plateis praedi-
cant, et eorum memoriis non communicant, separati a toto Catholicum
sibi nomen adsciscunt . . . . . pacatam unamque suis posteris tradentes.

» Christ appointed; 'for no man knoweth the Fa-
» ther save the Son and he to whom the Son hath
» revealed Him.' [1]   Neither does the Son seem to
» have revealed Him to any other than to the Apos-
» tles, whom he sent to preach, to wit, that which
» he revealed unto them.   Now what they did
» preach, that is what Christ revealed unto them,
» I will here also rule, must be proved in no other
» way than by those same churches which the
» Apostles themselves founded, by preaching to
» them as well *viva voce*, as men say, as afterwards
» by epistles. » Again he says : « But if any here-
» sies dare to place themselves in the midst of the
» apostolic age, (that they may therefore seem to
» have been handed down from the Apostles because
» they existed under the Apostles) we may say: Let
» them make known the origin of their churches,
» let them unroll the line of their bishops etc. »[2]
It is simply by implication, caused by his mentioning the notorious fact that Polycarp ordained by
John was the first bishop of Smyrna, and that *in
like manner* Clement was ordained by S. Peter, that
Tertullian appears to place Clement next to Peter,
whereas dealing not with the regular order of
succession, but with the ordination, it would have

---

[1] Mathew, XI.
[2] Tertullian, de Praescript. advers. haeret. No. 21, 32.

served equally to say that Linus or Cletus was so
ordained: but the argument is carried incidentally
over a longer space of time by mentioning the ordination of Clement who was the most distinguished
of the three. And that such was the scope, and
not the order of succession of the Popes, appears
from what he says afterwards. « Come now, thou
» that wilt exercise thy curiosity to better purpose
» in the business of thy salvation, run over the
» apostolic churches in which the very chairs of the
» Apostles to this very day preside over their own
» places, in which their own authentic writings are
» read echoing the voice and making the face of
» each present. Is Achaja near to thee, thou hast
» Corinth. If thou art not far from Macedonia, thou
» hast Philippi, thou hast the Thessalonians. If thou
» canst travel into Asia, thou hast Ephesus. But if
» thou art near Italy, thou hast Rome, whence we
» also have an authority at hand. That church, how
» happy! on which the Apostles poured out all their
» doctrine and their blood; where Peter had a like
» passion with the Lord; where Paul was crowned
» with an end like the Baptist's; where the Apostle
» John was plunged into boiling oil and suffered no-
» thing, and was afterwards banished to an island;
» let us see what she hath learned, what she hath
» taught, what fellowship she hath had with the

» African churches likewise. » In short Tertullian was speaking of the uninterrupted episcopal succession in all the apostolic churches, [1] and not of the primacy or the succession of Popes. He was not saying that Linus did not succeed S. Peter, but that the succession in Clement was unbroken.

The apocryphal Clementine writings were sure to create fresh difficulties. Eusebius of Caesarea in Palestine must first have felt their influence. A. D. 384, died Optatus, bishop of Milevis in Numidia, who agrees with Irenaeus and Eusebius in making Linus the first; but where Irenaeus has set Anacletus he puts Clement. « Peter therefore first » filled that individual chair which is the first of the » gifts of the Church; to him succeeded Linus, to » Linus Clement, to Clement Anacletus. » Here Cletus again is doomed to disappear from the roll of the early Popes. A. D. 403, S. Epiphanius bishop of Salamis died in the island of Cyprus. He, like Irenaeus, places Clement in the third place. « In Rome » Peter and Paul were the first both Apostles and » bishops; then came Linus, then Cletus, then Clement the contemporary of Peter and Paul, of » whom Paul makes mention in his epistle to the

[1] « Clear it is that no one has founded churches throughout the whole » of Italy, the Gauls, Spain, Africa and Sicily, and the interjacent islands, » except those whom the venerable Apostle Peter or his successors appoint- » ed priests. » Pope S. Innocent I, epist. 25 ad Decentium, A. D. 416.

» Philippians. And let no one wonder that, though
» he was the contemporary of Peter and Paul, for
» he lived at the same time with them, others re-
» ceived that epicopate from the Apostles. Whether
» it was that while the Apostles were still living he
» received the imposition of hands of the episcopate
» from Peter, and having declined that office he re-
» mained unemployed..... or whether after the death
» of the Apostles he was appointed bishop by Cletus,
» we do not clearly know..... However the succes-
» sion of the bishops of Rome was in the following
» order: Peter and Paul, and Cletus, Clement, Eva-
» ristus, Alexander, Sixtus, Telesphorus, Hyginus,
» Pius, Anicetus. » Here two points are to be noticed, that treating expressly, like Irenaeus, of the
order of S. Peter's successors, he gives Clement the
third place as Irenaeus did. He leaves out Anacletus, and refers cursorily to Clement's episcopal consecration by S. Peter, but without any nomination
as successor. Through the mistake of a transcriber
Linus has been left out in the order of the succession, although Epiphanius had named him before as
next to the Apostles.

The next author, Rufinus, priest of Aquilaeia, died
in Sicily about A. D. 410. He published and relied
upon the Clementines *in extenso*. S. Augustine died
A. D. 430. To prove that no Donatist bishop ap-

G

pears in the Roman succession he begins it: « To
» Peter succeeded Linus, to Linus Clement. » Here
again Cletus disappears. It is worth noticing that
both African bishops Optatus and **Augustine** agree
with Irenaeus, Eusebius, and Epiphanius in making **Linus** the immediate successor of S. Peter; and
it is a fair inference that either they did not take
their countryman Tertullian to mean that Clement
was that successor, or that they rejected his opinion.
So far we have given almost all the ancient authorities we know of. But as we are more concerned
to fix some place in the series of Popes for Clement,
than to distinguish between Cletus and Anacletus,
and as S. Irenaeus and S. Epiphanius were both
writing upon the actual Roman succession, and their
Sees were nearer to Rome, we prefer their argument
which makes S. Clement the third in succession from
S. Peter. Peter, Linus, Cletus (or Anacletus),[1] Cle-

---

[1] There exists an historical doubt, which has been fruitful of controversy, whether Cletus is different from Anacletus, or not, Critics are divided on the question; but the learned researches of Papenbrock, Laz-
zari and other Bollandists, seem to have settled the question by adopting
the identity of the two names in the person of the same Pontiff. According to their opinion, Cletus, elected the successor of Linus A. D. 78, was
included in an order of exile against the Christians, enacted, under Vespasian, by the governor of Rome. During the reign of Titus, Cletus, returning to his See, took the name of Anacletus, or *iterum* Cletus, Cletus *again*:
and thus is reconciled the authority of the ancient Fathers and Calendars,
who name this Pope sometimes Cletus, sometimes Anacletus, and sometimes, as by Eusebius, Anencletus.

ment. The same opinion is adopted by S. Jerome. [1]
We shall now say something of modern authors,
and their dealings with Linus and Cletus as sitting
before Clement. If the Apostolic Constitutions, and
Clement's letter to S. James of Jerusalem were not
apocryphal, those who give the second place after
Peter to Clement would have more weight; but the
older authority of S. Irenaeus would still be against
them, and the two oldest authorities after those apocryphal writings, viz: Eusebius and Optatus, whilst
they agree with the Apostolic Constitutions and Irenaeus by giving Linus the first place, flatly contradict the letter to S. James, which pretends that
Peter gave the keys to Clement. The Apostolic Constitutions, A. D. 270, say that « Linus the son of
» Claudia was ordained, by Paul, first bishop of
» the church of the Romans, but, after the death of
» Linus, Clement was ordained second bishop by Pe-
» ter. »[2] Rufinus' version of the letter to James says:
« I make known to you, my Lord, that Simon Peter,
» who by the merit of true faith, and spreading of
» entire preaching was designed to be the founda-
» tion of the Church, on which account also by the

---

[1] Lib. de Script. Eccl. cap. XV.
[2] « Linum Claudiae filium Ecclesiae Romanorum Episcopum primum
a Paulo ordinatum, post mortem vero Lini Clementem, quem ego Petrus
secundum ordinavi. » Lib. VIII, c. 47.

» Lord's mouth he was surnamed **Peter; who was**
» the first fruits of the election of the Lord, first
» of the Apostles, to whom **first God** the Father
» revealed the Son, on whom too he suitably con-
» ferred blessedness...... But in those days in which
» he felt the end of life at hand, set in the assembly
» of the brethern, taking **hold of** my hand and
» rising suddenly, he uttered these words in the ears
» of the whole Church..... this Clement I ordain your
» bishop to whom alone I deliver the Chair of my
» preaching and doctrine..... on which account I de-
» liver to him the power of binding and loosing
» delivered to me by the Lord, that of all things
» whatsoever he shall have decreed on earth this be
» decreed also in heaven. For he will bind what
» ought to be bound and loose what it is expedient
» to loose, as one who has clearly known the rule
» of the Church. Him then do ye hear, knowing
» that whosoever **has grieved the** teacher of truth
» sins against Christ and exasperates God the Fa-
» ther of all, on which account he shall also be de-
» prived of life. »[1]

---

[1] « Notum tibi facio, Domine, quia Simon Petrus, qui verae fidei me-
» rito et integrae praedicationis obtentu, fundamentum esse Ecclesiae defi-
» nitus est, qua de causa etiam Domini ore cognominatus est Petrus, qui
» fuit primitiae electionis Domini, Apostolorum primus, cui et primo Deus
» Pater Filium revelavit, cui et competenter beatitudinem contulit . . . In
» ipsis autem diebus (quibus vitae finem sibi imminere praesensit) in con-

It is amusing after the recent definition of Papal Infallibility to read these early assertions of teaching authority.

Butler learnedly demonstrates that the Apostolic Constitutions cannot be ascribed to Clement, nor to any Apostle, and Rondinini quotes Epiphanius to prove that the heretics misinterpreted them, as is also declared by the third oecumenical council of Constantinople. [1] For the letter to S. James some quote the epistle of S. Ignatius to the Trallians; but no stress can be laid upon it, because the best critics prove that it also has been interpolated. We have explained before that Tertullian in his book of Prescription (c. 32) was speaking of the certainty of Clement's consecration by S. Peter, and not of his place in the list of Popes. And that if Rufinus in his preface to the apocryphal book of the Recognitions, which he dedicated to Gaudentius bishop of

---

» ventu fratrum positus, apprehensa manu mea repente consurgens, in au-
» ribus totius Ecclesiae haec protulit verba . . . . . Clementem hunc Epis-
» copum vobis ordino, cui soli meae praedicationis et doctrinae cathedram
» trado . . . . . Propter quod ipsi trado a Domino mihi traditam potestatem
» ligandi et solvendi, ut de omnibus quibuscumque decreverit in terris, hoc
» decretum sit et in coelis. Ligabit enim quod oportet ligari, et solvet quod
» expedit solvi, tanquam qui ad liquidum Ecclesiae regulam noverit. Ipsum
» ergo audite, scientes, quia quicumque contristaverit doctorem veritatis,
» peccat in Christum, et Patrem omnium exacerbat Deum, propter quod
» et vita carebit.» Epist. I Clementis ad Jacobum fratrem Domini, p. 133.

[1] « Aliqua in eis haeretici nequiter interpretati sunt. Ab eisdem multa
» fuere corrupta. »

Brescia, does certainly place Clement before Linus, just as certainly did he rely upon the forgery he was editing. That able schismatic Photius ᴀ. ᴅ. 878, who, if we are to believe Nicetas of Paphlagonia, was a good hand at forgeries himself, says: « Some suppose
» that Clement was the second bishop of the city of
» Rome after Peter ; but others the fourth, for that
» Linus and Anacletus intervened as Pontiffs between
» them. » [1] Archbishop Rabanus Maurus of Metz, a learned monk who lived in the middle of the ninth century, adopted the opinion of Rufinus, but with some modifications, as we read in his treatise on choral bishops, which Labbè inserts in his collection of the councils. « In the epistle to James you will
» find in what way the Church was committed to
» Clement by blessed Peter, therefore Linus and Cle-
» tus will not be enrolled before him, because they
» were ordained by the Prince of the Apostles him-
» self to show forth the sacerdotal ministry. » [2]
» He concludes again that Linus and Cletus per-
» formed the ordinations of priests » (which is now the office of the cardinal Vicar and the bishop Vice-gerent of Rome) « and that after the martyrdom

---

[1] « Clementem secundum post Petrum Urbis Romae episcopum fuisse
» quidam autumant, alii vero quartum; Linum enim et Anacletum inter
» utrumque Pontifices intercessisse. » Codex CXII.

[2] Vol. VIII, p. 1853.

» of Peter not they but Clement succeeded to the
» honour of the chair. » [1]   The whole if this seems
to be mere guesswork mixed up with heretical opinion. Isidore Mercator, who lived towards the end
of the ninth century, agrees in some respects with
Rufinus and Rabanus Maurus. In the first letter of
his Collections he adheres to the apocryphal letter
to S. James. In the letter he is said to have addressed to Pope John III, [2] he says: « But if Pe-
» ter the Prince of the Apostles adopted Linus and
» Cletus his assistants, nevertheless he did not for-
» mally deliver to them the pontifical power either
» of binding or loosing, but to his successor S. Cle-
» ment, who deserved to hold the apostolic See and
» pontifical power after him by delivery of blessed
» Peter. Linus and Cletus indeed administered outer
» matters, but, the Prince of the Apostles, Peter was
» earnest in word and prayer. For nowhere do we
» read that Linus and Cletus ever discharged any
» function of the pontifical ministry as Ordinaries,
» but only used to do as much as was enjoined upon
» them by blessed Peter. » This again is obviously
special pleading borrowed from the account in the
Acts of the first institution of deacons: neither they

---

[1] Vol. VIII, p. 1853.
[2] N. 559-72.

nor Clement could exercise any pontifical powers in Peter's lifetime except by direct delegation. Rabanus and Mercator rest evidently upon the apocryphal letter to S. James. Nor are solid reasons wanting to refute their assertions that Linus and Cletus were choral bishops; on which subject we refer the reader to the learned work of Peter Coustant in his preface to the epistles of the Roman Pontiffs.[1] At the close of the tenth century, Aymon, a monk of Fleury, says in his third book « *de Christianorum moribus*: » « Some, who have investigated the Chair
» of the Roman Church say that Linus and Cletus
» did not sit as Pontiffs but as coadjutors of the sove-
» reign Pontiff to whom in his lifetime blessed Peter
» intrusted a dispensation of things ecclesiastical,
» but himself spent the time only in prayer and
» preaching. Whence as ordained by him with so
» great authority they deserved to be placed in the
» catalogue of sovereign Pontiffs. But blessed Peter
» himself constituted Clement as his own successor,
» as seems besides to agree with the Canons and
» the epistle of Clement to James. But Clement,
» who was flourishing in becoming manners so as
» to be agreeable to Jews and Gentiles, and all the
» Christian people, had the poor of each of the re-

---

[1] N. 7.

» gions written down by name, and those whom he
» had cleansed by the sanctification of baptism he
» did not allow to become subject to public men-
» dicity. » As our answer to this is already given,
we need not here repeat it.

Taking S. Peter as the root, it is certain that
Linus came next to him and then Cletus; for in
fixing this order of succession all the Calendars of
the Roman and Italian churches agree, as well as
the pictures in S. Paul's on the Ostian way: the Calendars preserved in other churches, the testimony
of ancient writers, the Canon of the mass, uninterrupted universal tradition, and the dearth of facts
and arguments, or even probable conjecture to the
contrary. In like manner the authorities which
assign the third place to Clement are so grave and
satisfactory that little or no doubt can remain regarding it. If Pagi, [1] Vendelinus, [2] Henschenius, [3]
Bianchini, [4] Orsi, [5] Muratori, [6] and others of less ce-
lebrity, rely upon the Liberian Calendar, and the
opinions of S. Optatus Milevitanus and S. Augustine
to give the second place to Clement instead of Cle-

[1] Franc. Pagi ad an. Christi.
[2] Vendelinus, Comment. in epistolam Clementis.
[3] Henschenius, Apparat. ad Chronol. Pontif. exercit. 5.
[4] Bianchini, Not. Chronolog. in Pontificat. S. Clementis et S. Cleti.
[4] Orsi, Stor. Ecclesiast.
[6] Muratori, Annal. d'Italia, an. 66-67.

tus, weighty and respectable writers though they
be, they cannot counterbalance a host of others.
The Liberian Calendar is the only one which puts
Clement in the second, Cletus in the third, and
Anacletus in the fourth place. « *Clemens annis IX,*
» *mensibus XI, diebus XII. Cletus annis VI, mensi-*
» *bus XI, diebus X. Anacletus annis XII, mensibus X,*
» *diebus III.* » Ancient and valuable as this Calendar is, it need not be preferred to the agreement
of almost all the early writers who have learnedly
discussed this subject. Coustant remarks in his life
of Cletus : « the mere antiquity of the Liberian Ca-
» lendar should affect no one, since it contains many
» patent errors regarding facts in the early ages. »

We have already remarked upon S. Optatus and
S. Augustine, and preferred to them S. Irenaeus and
S. Epiphanius, and we may add S. Jerome.[1] Rondinini
asserts that « the old authors of ecclesiastical matters
» bear witness unanimously that Clement succeeded
» Cletus. »[2] Burius however says: « *Disputat hic mundus
sit quartus, sitne secundus:* » [3] or taking Peter as the
root, whether he was the third or first. In our opinion the whole may be traced to the apocryphal letter

[1] Irenaeus, adversus haeres. lib. III, c. 3. — Epiphanius, Tom. I, adv.
haeres. (27) p. 107. — Eusebius, Hist. Eccl. lib. III, c. 13. — Hieronymus,
de Script. Eccl. c. XV.

[2] Rondinini, lib. 1, c. 1, §. 2.

[3] Burius, Elench. not. Roman. Pontif. See c. XXX.

to S. James: the eagerness and veneration with which
such documents were received, and the impression,
in the absence of decisive authority, which they naturally produced upon the later writers that there
must be some ground of truth in them. « *Nihil
est tam incredibile, quod non dicendo fiat probabile.* » [1]
It may have been through this veneration with which
S. Clement's writings were received next after the
scriptures that S. Jerome, without stopping to distinguish the spurious from the true, remarks: « most
» of the Latins suppose Clement to have been the
» second after the apostle Peter, »[2] that is before
Cletus. There are many who although convinced
by tradition that Clement held the third place and
not the second, did not like to contradict S. Jerome.
We do not allude to Henry Hammond who thought
that Linus, Cletus, and Clement governed the Church
together: the two first the Gentile converts, and the
latter the Jews, and, after the death of his colleagues, both together, an hypothesis by which he
tried to defend the Episcopalians against the Pres-
byterians, but which by no means pleased his own
colleague John Pearson, who repudiates it in his
posthumous works, [3] as contrary to the discipline by

---

[1] Cicero.
[2] Hieronymus, de viris illustribus, c. XXV. We adhere to the opinion
expressed by S. Jerome in his work on Ecclesiastical writers. Ch. 15.
[3] Pages 180-181.

which only one bishop should preside over the same diocese. [1] But we allude to the **opinion of Baronius**, [2] which others maintain, and among them Coteler, [3] and the Bollandists, [4] who affirm that Peter consecrated Clement bishop of Rome , and nominated Linus his successor. Clement, however, for reasons not assigned, (perhaps **because** they never existed, though merely alluded to by S. Epiphanius), [5] resigned the pontifical chair to Linus, who was succeeded by Cletus, after whose death he assumed the government of the universal Church.

Linus suffered maytrdom on the 23rd of September A. D. 82, and Cletus glorified God with his blood in the year 92 or 93, and was buried in the Vatican near **S. Linus**, where his relics are still preserved. [6] After his death Clement had no excuse for **not** accepting the government of the Church. The Latin **and** Greek fathers unanimously attest with what zeal and assiduity he laboured for the salva-

---

[1] Tillemont, note sur S. Clément.
[2] An. 60, n. 43.
[3] Const. Apost. p. 31.
[4] Propyl. ad Act. Sanctor. p. 15.
[5] Adversus haeres. XXVII, n. 6.
[6] **The** beginning of S. Clement's pontificate dates, according to **different** writers, from 90 to 93. Butler says that Cletus governed the Church from 76 to 89. Ciaconius, in his life of Cletus, relates that he **was crowned** with martyrdom on the 26th of April 92. Natalis Alexander **ad soec. pr.** records the same. Baronius, ad an. 1, says in 93.

tion of souls. He was adorned with every public
and private virtue, and all antiquity is loud in his
praise. It is not our scope to describe in what heroic degree he practiced each virtue, but we cannot
refrain from some notice of those writings which
constitute his peculiar characteristic. He laboured
strenuously to preserve intact and inviolate the sacred
deposit of faith, to condemn heresy, and root out
vice. S. Epiphanius, writing against the Ebionites,
says: « There are other books too which they use,
» as the Itinerary of Peter compiled by Clement, in
» which book, with the exception of a few words,
» they have made the rest supposititious: as Cle-
» ment himself rebukes them in those circular epis-
» tles which, written by him, are read in the very
» holy churches; from which it is certain that his
» faith and speech are very far abhorrent from the
» things which in those Itineraries under his name
» have an adulterated existence. »[1] He also points
out two of these discrepancies. « Clement teaches
» the observance of virginity, they reject it. He

---

[1] « Sunt et alii libri, quibus utuntur, velut Petri circuitus a Clemente conscripti, quo in libro paucis verbis relictis cætera supposuerunt,
quemadmodum Clemens ipse omnibus illos modis redarguit iis epistolis
circulatoribus, quæ ab eo scriptæ in Sacrosanctis Ecclesiis leguntur. Ex
quibus constat longe ab iis, quæ in circuitibus illis sub eius nomine adulte-
rina existant, illius fidem ac sermonem abhorruisse. » S. Epiphanius, adv.
hæres. XXX, p. 15.

» recommends Elias , David , Samuel , and all the
» prophets, they detest them. » [1] Nor were Clement's learning and authority confined to the vindication of the orthodox doctrine of virginity against
the Ebionites,[2] and the harmony which results from
the legal, prophetic and christian economy as in
contradiction to the dreams of the Cerinthians.[3] He
likewise condemned the Marcotian heresies. Praedestinatus, who lived in the fifth century, tells us
in his first book on heresy, part 14th: « The four-

---

[1] « Etenim virginitatem Clemens edocet, isti repudiant: ille Eliam,
Davidem, et Samuelem, omnesque Prophetas commendat, Ebionitæ de-
testantur. » S. Epiphanius, adv. hæres. XXX, p. 15.

[2] Epiphanius says that S. John went into Asia by the special direction of the Holy Ghost to oppose the heresies of Ebion and Cerinthus.
Ebion seems to have been the father of the Unitarians. After the destruction of Jerusalem he taught the Christian refugees at Pella that
Christ was the greatest of the Prophets, but a mere man, the natural
son of Joseph and Mary; an error which he borrowed from the sect of the
Nazarenes. He mutilated S. Matthew's gospel , pretended that the legal
ceremonies were indispensable, and permitted divorces. The word Ebion,
in Hebrew, signifies poor, and seems to allude either to the low and mean
opinions they formed of Christ, or to the poverty of this sect.

[3] Cerinthus added his share to Ebion's impieties. He defended the
obligation of circumcision, and of rejecting the use of unclean meats.
He extolled the angels as the authors of nature, pretending that the
world was not created by God, but without his knowledge by some distinct virtue; that the God of the Jews was a mere man preeminent
for his virtue and wisdom, pointed out by the dove at baptism , and
proceeding to manifest his father hitherto unknown to the world. He
seems to have invented the myth that Christ fled away at his passion,
and Jesus alone suffered and arose again. The Mahometans have an idea
that when Judas betrayed our Lord, as a punishment for his treachery
his face was changed, and he was crucified instead of Jesus Christ.
Probably this notion was somehow borrowed from the Cerinthians

» teenth heresy was invented by one Mark, who,
» denying the resurrection of the flesh, endeavoured
» to build up that Christ did not suffer truly, but
» by supposition. Him S. Clement bishop of Rome
» and most worthy of Christ, confuting by irrefrag-
» able assertions, and convicting in the Church be-
» fore all the people, punished with eternal damna-
» tion; teaching that our Lord Jesus Christ was
» truly born and suffered, summing up that by Him
» nothing was done under a phantastic form, and
» evidently showing that truth, the enemy of false-
» hood, could have nothing whatever in itself that
» was false, just as neither could light have dark-
» ness in itself, nor blessing malediction, nor sweet-
» ness bitterness: and if those might be mingled to-
» gether, yet did he teach that it is impossible for
» God to be mixed up with a lie. »

As Tertullian says in defending S. Luke's gospel
and the Apocalypse against Marcion : « Wasps build
» nests: Marcionites too build churches. » To trace
the architects of these churches, or builders of
those nests, is not always easy. But we do not know
upon what principle Peter Coustant attempted [1] to
deprive Clement of the merit of having anathematized the idealism of the Gnostics, and vindicated

---

[1] Epist. Romanor. Po..t. pag. 6.

the scandal of the Cross, and the resurrection of the flesh. S. Irenaeus says : « Before Valentinus there » were no Valentinians, nor Marcionites before Mar- » cion ; nor in fact any of the other malignant senti- » ments enumerated above, before there arose in- » ventors and beginners of each perverse opinion. « But the sect called Gnostics, who derive their » origin, as we have shown, from Menander, Si- » mon's disciple, each of them of that opinion » which he adopted, of it he was seen to be the » parent and high-priest. » [1]   He says, however, that before Marcion, Cerdon taught similar errors under Pope Hyginus, A. D. 139-42. Valentinian at the same date revived those of Simon Magus. Me- nander had done it before him. It does not follow that any of these men were the disciples of Simon directly, but only his followers, and imitators. And as Simon practised magic, so Irenaeus mentions that even in Lyons Mark and his followers used love philters, permitted women to consecrate, and made the chalice seem filled with a red liquor which he called blood. Evidently this Mark was later than Clement ; but it does not follow that a previous Mark and Gnostic principles were not condemned by him. The same remark applies to

[1] S. Irenaeus, adv. haeres, lib. III, c. 4.

Eusebius, who says that Mark was living when Valentinian came to Rome under Hyginus, and remained there under Anicetus. [1] S. Paul and S. John, S. Ignatius and S. Polycarp encountered similar heresiarchs long before Hyginus. Even without the authority of Praedestinatus it would be very odd if they had given Clement a truce. In his preface that writer says : « In the detection therefore of » falsehood, and in the defence of truth, we have » followed the footsteps of Catholics, and we have » done it that in the first book the ancient su- » perstition of heresy may be thoroughly laid open. » Clement then the Roman bishop, S. Peter's di- » sciple, most worthy martyr of Christ, fully ex- » plained the heresy of Simon vanquished with » Simon himself by the apostle S. Peter. Him fol- » lowed five holy orthodox men, and each of them » in his own time wrote down the rise and con- » flict and issue of each several heresy in many » books and many thousands of lines, which we, » by God's assistance, have epitomized in this little » book. » [2] As the deposit of faith contains within itself every dogma before it becomes necessary to ascertain it by precise definition, so every heresy like some fungus contains within itself the

---

[1] Eusebius, Hist. Eccl. lib. IV, c. XI.
[2] Apologet. 5.

seed which it scatters to generate its kind. S. Clement was not likely to forget the warning of S. Paul. « Men shall be lovers of themselves, co-
» vetous, haughty, proud, blasphemers, disobedient
» to parents, ungrateful, wicked. Traitors, stub-
» born, puffed up, and lovers of pleasures more
» than of God; having an appearance of godli-
» ness but denying the power thereof. Now these
» avoid. For of these sort are they who creep
» into houses, and lead captive silly women laden
» with sins, who are led away with divers de-
» sires: ever learning, and never attaining to the
» knowledge of truth. » [1] Nor was the apostolic
man who wrote to the Corinthians: « Do ye, there-
» fore, who laid the foundation of this sedition sub-
» mit yourselves to the priests, and be instructed
» into repentance, bending the knees of your hearts,
» learn to be subject, laying aside all proud and ar-
» rogant boastings of your tongues; for it is better
» for you to be found in the sheepfold of Christ lit-
» tle and approved than thinking yourselves above
» others to be cast out of His hope. » He I say was
not likely, when sitting in the chair of Peter to refrain from anathematizing a rebel, whether his name
was Mark, Marcion or Legion. Seeing the licentious

---

[1] II Epist. to Timothy, chapter III, v. 2, 4, 5, 6,.7.

impieties of one Mark at Lyons no long time after
Clement's death, and of that other Manichaean Mark
who afterwards went into Spain and seems, by in-
stituting the Priscillianists, to have anticipated the
Mormons and Agapemone, it is not unlikely that
there may have been Marks enough before them,
who preferred the flesh to the spirit, and deserved
the excommunication of the Church.

CHAPTER III.

S. Clement's solicitude to hand down to posterity the Acts of the Martyrs — He divides the fourteen regions of the city into seven districts, and appoints seven notaries over them, whence he is said
to be the founder of the Prothonotaries called *Participantes* — Roman Martyrology — Its author — Liturgy of the Mass.

To the indefatigable solicitude with which Clement fed the flock and extirpated heresy, we must
add his anxiety to preserve and hand down to posterity the exploits of the champions of Christ. He governed the Church under the reign of Domitian,
who was for cruelty, as Tertullian says, « a piece
of Nero. » [1] « Domitian, » says Orosius, « grew
» through all the grades of crime to dare by edicts

[1] « Portio Neronis de crudelitate. » (Apologet. 5).

» of a most cruel persecution, published every-
» where, to pluck up Christ's Church that was
» greatly strengthened in the whole world. » [1]   In
his persecution, the second against the Church, it
was that S. John, after having come miraculously
out of the caldron of boiling oil at the Latin gate,
was exiled to Patmos, where he had those visions
which he recorded in the Apocalypse. « Like Herod
» the emperor feared the advent of the Messiah,
» and had the descendants of the house of David
» searched out and put to death. » [2]   But what
most exasperated him was to see the number of
the Christians, in spite of his sanguinary edicts,
daily increasing in Rome, nay in his own family
and palace. He had no respect for dignity of position or nobility of birth : not even for those of
his own kindred. And here we may quote from
the Prophet: [3]   « For there is no truth, and there
» is no mercy, and there is no knowledge of God
» in the land, cursing, and lying, and killing, and
» theft, and adultery have overflowed, and blood
» hath touched blood. » Domitian beheaded his
cousin german the consul Flavius Clement, and ba-

---

[1] « Per omnes scelerum gradus crevit, ut confirmatissimam toto orbe
» Christi Ecclesiam, datis ubique crudelissimae persecutionis edictis,
» convellere auderet. » (Oros. VII, 10).

[2] Eusebius, Hist. Eccl. III, 19.

[3] Osee, chapter IV, v. 1, 2.

nished, to Pandatereia, [1] his wife Flavia Domitilla [2] whose sons [3] he had adopted and destined for his successors; and his niece Flavia Domitilla, for having embraced the christian faith, he transported to the island of Ponza. The persecution spread like a fire throughout the empire, and torrents of noble and innocent blood were poured out to slake the insatiable thirst of that imperial monster. Examples of the most heroic fortitude daily presented themselves to the Christians who were to be immolated, and to the Pagans who ridiculed and scoffed at their madness, and in their scoffing were sometimes converted to the faith by the patience of the martyrs, and condemned to perish by their side. No age, sex, or condition could escape the sword of the ruthless tyrant. Imagine what sweet incense of confession rose up to the throne of God from the lips of those devoted victims, questioned about their faith, tempted by the most deceitful promises, racked by demoniacal tortures. But the most cruel punishments seemed light to them, believing as they did in the promise of their Divine Saviour: « Fear not them that kill the body,

---

[1] Pandatereia is an island opposite the gulph of Gaeta half-way between Ponza and Ischia, now known by the name of Sᵃ Maria.

[2] This Flavia Domitilla was Domitian's sister.

[3] Vespasian junior, and Domitian junior who had for their tutor the famous Quintilian.

» and are not able to kill the soul.... every one
» therefore that shall confess me before men, I
» will also confess him before my Father, who is
» in heaven. » [1]   That these confessions of the
faith, so consolatory to the christian heart, so
dear to God, might not be lost, Clement divided
the fourteen regions of the city into seven districts
over which he appointed as many ecclesiastics distinguished for learning and piety. Their duty,
as Baronius tells us, [2] was not alone to collect the
Acts of the Martyrs and the records of their sufferings, but also to register the answers they made
to their persecutors, when arrested or put on trial,
or condemned to death. In them we possess the
most luminous practical proof of Catholic truth,
for in them the gospel was put in practice before
a raging world. « Why have the Gentiles raged,
» and the people devised vain things? The kings
» of the earth stood up, and the princes met to-
» gether against the Lord and against his Christ. » [3]
In venerating them we bow our heads to the God
of the martyrs, humbled, but consoled to see how
frail nature was elevated by grace, how the prophetic words of Christ were fulfilled, how his chil-

---

[1] Matthew, X chap. v. 28-32
[2] An. 238.
[3] Psalm. II, verse 1, 2.

dren, of whom the world is not worthy, preserved
to the last the priceless treasure of their faith, how
their triumphs eclipsed and have survived the triumphs of the Capitol by how much the nearer they
were made like to Calvary. O how true is the ex-
clamation of S. Eucherius bishop of Lyons! « The
» minds of the children are set in arms whilst
» the triumphs of their fathers are rehearsed; for
» from them we understand how much that life
» eternal should be longed for, which we see sought
» for through torments, through wounds, through
» insupportable toils; which we know to have been
» purchased with the price of blood. » [1] Rondinini says of these seven Clementine notaries that
« their name, and office partly, passed formerly,
» to the seven Prothonotaries whom they call
» *Participantes;* » and they, increased by Sixtus V,
to the number of twelve, were enriched with very
notable privileges, especially with the power of
conferring, like the most illustrious Universities of
the world, the degree of Doctor. These Prothonotaries, in the pendent seal which they annex to
the doctoral diploma, are wont to print an image
of S. Clement with the epigraph *S. Clemens Collegii
Prot. Part. Fundator.*

---

[1] Homily of S. Eucherius on S. Peter and S. Paul.

Whereas the principal origin of the most ancient Martyrologies is only an epitome of the acts of the martyrs collected by those clerical notaries, S. Clement is called by many writers the author of the Roman Martyrology. Bencini in his notes to the life of S. Clement, published by Anastasius, says: « Out of » these Acts related in the churches the oldest mar- » tyrologies and lessons are made up. » [1] And to them may be traced the origin of other martyrologies which even yet deserve to be studied by the learned. Hence Boldetti says: « Those notaries dili- » gently registered in the ecclesiastical Tables the days » that were called Fasti, from which were compiled » the Martyrologies, out of which were read, on the » day before, the names of the martyrs whose festivals » occurred the next day, in order that the memory » of their triumph might be celebrated with greater » spiritual solemnity on the anniversary of their mar- » tyrdom which was called their birth day. » [2] In the choirs of monastic Orders the same is done to this day. The Acts were not collected for entertaining historical reading, but that, as far as possible, the Church upon earth might join on the very day with the Church triumphant in heaven, where are the souls

---

[1] Acta Martyrum, pag. 541.
[2] Boldetti, Osservazioni sui Cimiterii de' Martiri, lib. I, c. XI.

of them that were slain for the word of God, and
for the testimony which they held. [1]

In addition to the other works which distinguished our Saint, we must not omit the liturgy of
the Mass, of which, according to Baronius, Proclus,
Usher and others, he was the author. Baronius
writes: « Moreover there is a tradition that Clement
» left in writing the rite of offering the sacrifice which
» he had received from S. Peter, to wit the Mass it-
» self of the Roman church. » To which tradition
Proclus adheres in these words: « Many other di-
» vine pastors too who succeeded to the Apostles, and
» ancient churches, explaining the reason of the sa-
» cred mysteries of that heavenly Mass, have deli-
» vered the order of the Church in writing: amongst
» whom first and foremost blessed Clement, disciple
» and successor of that sovereign Prince of the Apo-
» stles, who published those most holy mysteries re-
» vealed to him by the sainted Apostles. » So says
» Proclus, bishop of Constantinople (in 447), of Cle-
» ment, with whom others of the Greeks who have
» written commentaries upon the sacred rites equal-
» ly agree; though some have supposed that by the
» liturgy of Clement we must understand what are
» held as written by him of the same most holy sa-

___
[1] S. Cyprianus, Epist. ad Clerum. XXXVII, pag. 114.

» crifice in the seventh book of the Constitutions, [1]
» and in the eighth. [2]   But the form of holy Mass
» which is prescribed to the Latins and the whole
» Western Church, some things excepted which
» were added or changed not only by Clement but
» by the prince of the apostles Peter himself, ancient
» tradition vindicates to itself, since there is nothing
» else to point out its beginning and origin. » [3]

The consent of authors is sufficient to show that
Clement had a true zeal to provide for the worship
and religious decorum of the Catholic Church, whether he actually committed anything regarding the
sacred liturgy to writing or not; nor does it seem
more inconvenient that the chief part should be preserved as a standard in some authentic roll than that
the epistles and gospels should be copied.   On which
account it is not worth while to examine the opinion
of Peter Le Brun who maintains « that no liturgy
» was published either in Greek or Latin before the
» sixth century. » [4]   If this means publication for
general circulation it may be likely enough; for the
Christians had seen so many of their volumes committed to the flames, so many scattered to the winds,

[1] C. XXV, XXVI, XXVII.
[2] C. XV, et seq.
[3] Baronius, An. CII, 23.
[4] Disputatio liturgica, vol. III.

and had smarted so severely for bringing out the
treasures of the Church, that common prudence
would warn them, even after the peace of the Church,
to be chary of diffusing the mysteries. And again if
it means that nothing was written down, it would
be contrary to human nature among so many literary
bishops and priests, even with the utmost religious
veneration for secrecy, that no notes or manuscripts
should ever be made, and contrary, we may say to the
very necessity of the case, so prolonged was the initiation of the Church in comparison with modern times.
Usher says: « In the Arabic catalogue of Chaldaean
» and Syrian liturgies, which belonged to Ignatius
» the late Patriarch of Antioch, is reckoned [1] one of
» Pope S. Clement composed in Greek, which one
» Thomas Harchalanus translated into Chaldaic 407
» years after the Nativity of our Lord; and another
» of S. Ignatius composed in Greek at Antioch twen-
» ty seven years after our Lord's Ascension, which
» James, bishop of Rehanus did into Chaldaic. And
» Clement is reckoned by the Patriarch Proclus among
» the first who delivered a written exposition of the
» liturgy to the Church. Bessarion in his book of
» the Sacrament of the Eucharist thus replies to the
» Greeks urging his (Clement's) authority: ' Though

[1] See Cornelius Schulting, Biblioth. Theolog. tom. III, p. 1.

» these words of Clement be usually enumerated
» among apocryphal writings, yet we are willing
» to assent to them as true in present circumstances;
» but that liturgy is a certain part of the eighth
» book of those which in some *Codices* bear the title
» Διδασκαλιας of doctrine, in others of Διαταγῶν, or of
» Apostolic Constitutions written by Clement. » [1]
It is obvious however in reference to Proclus who
did not write before the middle of the sixth century, that he has given a merely imaginary account
of the long chanted prayers with which the Apostles
celebrated the mystic sacrifice, and probably he had
no authority for saying that the Apostles themselves
dictated the Roman liturgy to S. Clement; though
he may have been correct in saying that S. Basil
and S. Chrysostom, to meet the degeneracy of the
times, abridged the one they used. Pope S. Innocent I, who held the See at the beginning of
that (5th) century, declared that the Roman liturgy is of apostolic origin, which, it may well be,
whether oral or written. Waterworth says in his

---

[1] Usserius, de Ignatii Martyr, epist. Consult also, Liturgia Orientalis
by Eusebius Renaudat, book 3, page 186. Les anciens liturg. by John
Grancolas, page 96. Bibliotheca Orientalis by Simon Assemanni, tom. 1,
ex codice Vitriensi III. Liturgical codex of the whole Church by Lewis
Assemanni, book 4, p. 2. In the 4 vol. part. 1, p. 137, he (Assemanni) and
Muratori in his dissertation *de rebus liturgicis*, completely demolish the
assertion of Le Brun.

extracts from the fathers of the first five centuries, that from the testimony of several of the fathers there is reason to believe that no public liturgy of any church was written earlier than the middle of the fourth century, and that the Clementine is no exception; for as compiled in the Constitutions it is not known to have been used in any church service whatever. [1] But Oldoinus in his notes to Ciacconius' life of S. Clement enumerates a number of liturgical observances as enforced by S. Clement, and Moroni repeats the same in his erudite ecclesiastical dictionary. It is also said that he was the first to introduce into the liturgy of the Mass the salutation *Dominus vobiscum*, and the *Orate Fratres*. [2] *Non nobis tantas componere lites.* All we wish to show from their disputes is that Pope Clement has a traditional claim to zeal for liturgical observance.

---

[1] See the specimens he gives of all the liturgies, referring them to three sources, to wit, that of S. James, S. Mark and S. Peter, besides the Gothic fragments of Spain and Gallia Narbonensis published by Mabillon in 1685.

[2] See Gem. lib. I, cap. 87.

CHAPTER IV.

Zeal of S. Clement to diffuse the Gospel of Christ — Missionaries sent
by him to France, Spain, and elsewhere — His letters to the Corinthians, and to Virgins — The Book of Recognitions — The
Clementine Homilies, and Epistle to S. James — The Apostolic
Canons.

Not alone did S. Clement provide with unwea-
ried vigilance for the unity of the faith and the
decorum of public worship, but like one who heard
his Master's words ringing in his ear: « And other
» sheep I have that are not of this fold, them also
» must I bring, and they shall hear my voice, and
» there shall be one fold and one shepherd. »[1] He
spared no pains to maintain uninterrupted the succession of the hierarchy, and propagate the Kingdom of
Christ. We read in the pontifical book that he held
two consecrations in the month of December in which
he ordained ten priests, two deacons, and fifteen bishops. He baptized the son of Tarquinius a Roman,[2]
initiated him in holy orders, and sent him to France
with S. Denys, S. Ursenius, S. Gratianus, S. Saturninus, and S. Nicotius. Some modern writers have
disputed the authenticity of these facts, but, as Rondinini observes,[3] they cannot succeed in subvert-

[1] John, c. 10, v. 16.
[2] See Roman Martyrology, 11 of August.
[3] Book 1, ch. 1, §. 5.

ing the more ancient authorities. We read in the
chronological manuscript of S. Ivo, quoted by Patrick Young, that Clement sent Pothinus to Lyons,
Paul to Narbonne, Gratian to Tours, and Julian to
Mans. Bernard Guidoni cited by cardinal Mai in
his Specilegium attests the same. « He also sent
» many bishops to different regions: Pothinus to
» Lyons, Paul to Narbonne, Gratian to Tours, Denys
» the Areopagite to Paris where he suffered mar-
» tyrdom by decapitation, together with his com-
» panions on the ninth of October in the ninetieth
» year of his age. » [1] The Maurist Fathers follow
the same opinion. « No matter what modern wri-
» ters may say it is very probable that the mission
» of the first bishops into Gaul, such as S. Tro-
» phinus of Arles, S. Gratian of Tours, S. Denys
» of Paris, S. Paul of Narbonne, S. Austromonius
» of Clermont, and S. Martial of Limoges, is due to
» Clement and not to S. Fabian. » Nor is it likely that these were all he sent, or to Gaul only.
Oldoinus and other writers say that « he consecrat-
» ed Eugenius first bishop of Toledo, and that in
» the second year of his Pontificate, when blessed
» Mark of Atina had borne the palm of martyr-
» dom by orders of the president Maximus, he made

---

[1] See Cardinal Mai's Spicilegium, vol. 6, p. 13.

» Fulgentius bishop of the same city who presided » over the church of Atina thirty one years, seven » months and twenty eight days. »[1] Atina was then a flourishing city near the Pontine Marshes.

If S. Clement earnestly laboured to diffuse gospel truth, he knew that it was essential to preserve it pure and undefiled, and that that could only be done by submission to a divinely constituted authority. A scandalous schism broke out among the Christians at Corinth, in which some of the laity rebelled against the priests, and carried their secrilegious violence to the point of preventing them from exercising the functions of their ministry. Fortunatus, who is mentioned by S. Paul,[2] was sent to Rome to lay the whole matter before the Pope. Clement bitterly deplored the ruin impending over that portion of his flock, and addressed to them, in the name of the Roman Church, a very pathetic and instructive epistle. Writing with the effusion of the paternal heart he does not forget the firmness without which dignity becomes a bauble and the authority, which is meant to check, a provocation to fresh aggressions. Eusebius styled it « an admirable work, »[3] and all the Fathers of

---

[1] See Oldoinus, ad vitam S. Clementis per Ciacconium.
[2] Corinth, XVI, v. 17.
[3] Hist. Ecclesiast. lib. 3, c. 16.

the first four centuries spoke of it with admiration.
It may give an idea of the difficulty of ecclesiastical researches, since the vast destruction of original
documents, that this epistle, which was read in the
churches next to the Scriptures, was entirely lost.
For several centuries not a trace of it could be found.
Baronius deeply deplored its loss, and collected all
the extracts he could find of it from the works of
Irenaeus, Dionysius bishop of Corinth, and Eusebius of Caesarea. Fortunately, however, to the
great delight of the learned, it was discovered at
the end of a very ancient Alexandrian manuscript of
the Bible written about the time of the first council of Nice, by an Egyptian woman named Thecla.
Cyril Lucarius the schismatical patriarch of Constantinople brought it from Alexandria and presented it
to James I of England. The royal librarian Patrick
Young published a copy of it at Oxford in 1633.
Pages 58, 59, 60 are still wanting. It begins:
« The Church of God which is at Rome to that of
» Corinth, to those who have been called and sancti-
» fied by the will of God in our Lord Jesus Christ,
» may the grace and peace of Almighty God be
» increased by Christ Jesus in every one of you. »
He reminds them of their former peace. « At that
» time your virtues, piety and zeal, your inviola-
» ble attachment to the law of God, were the ad-

» miration of all who knew you. You were then
» submissive to your Pastors, you respected your
» superiors: you set an exemple of sobriety and
» modesty to your children, you established and
» maintained good order within your own families.
» More ready to obey than command, more eager
» to give than to receive, you cherished the senti-
» ments of moderation and humility in your hearts.
» Content with the common gifts of Providence for
» your support in life, you turned your thoughts
» to God and studied the observance of His holy
» law. Thus you enjoyed the sweetest tranquilli-
» ty and peace of mind. Being animated with the
» purest charity you felt a warm desire and seized
» every opportunity of doing good. Full of confi-
» dence and zeal you never ceased lifting up your
» hands to the throne of mercy, humbly begging
» forgiveness for the sins of frail mortality. Day
» and night you poured forth your prayers for the
» salvation and happiness of your brethren in Jesus
» Christ that the number of the elect might be
» speedily filled up. You were then void of ma-
» lice, your conduct was sincere and blameless.
» You held in abhorrence the very name of con-
» tention and discord. You pitied your deluded
» neighbour, and bewailed his faulty oversights
» as your own. But how sadly has this prospect

» changed since then! How clouded and how dis-
» mal the view which was once so bright and de-
» lightful! In place of content and harmony, jea-
» lousy and disunion prevail among you. » He
puts his hand at once upon the root of the evil,
speaks with just indignation of their disgrace, and
exhorts the refractory to more generous and cha-
ritable sentiments. « Wherefore are these conten-
» tions and swellings and dissensions, and wars a-
» mongst you? Have we not one God and one
» Christ, and one Spirit of Grace poured out upon
» us, and one calling in Christ? Wherefore do we
» rend and tear in pieces the members of Christ,
» and raise a sedition against our own body, and
» come to such a height of folly as to forget that
» we are members one of another? Remember the
» words of our Lord Jesus, how he said: ' Woe
• to that man by whom scandal cometh: it were
» better for him that he had never been born than
» to scandalize one of my elect: it were better for
» him that a millstone should be hanged about his
» neck, and that he should be cast into the sea, than
» that he should scandalize one of my little ones. '
» Your schism hath perverted many, hath cast ma-
. » ny into dejection, many into doubt, and all of us
» into grief; and yet your sedition continues ....
• Take up the epistle of the blessed **Paul the**

» Apostle. What did he first write to you at the
» beginning of the gospel? Verily he did by the
» spirit admonish you both concerning himself and
» Cephas and Apollo; because that even then you had
» formed particularities amongst yourselves, though
» that your particularity had led you into less sin,
» for you were partial to tried apostles and to ano-
» ther who had been approved by them. But now
» consider who they are who have led you astray,
» and have lessened the majesty of your much spo-
» ken brotherly love. It is shameful, my beloved, it
» is most shameful and unworthy your Christian
» profession that it should be heard that the most
» firm and most ancient church of the Corinthians,
» on account of one or two persons, is in a sedi-
» tion against the priests.... « Who then amongst
» you is generous, who that is compassionate, who
» that is filled with charity? Let him say: ' If
» sedition and strife and schism be through me,
» I will go and depart whithersoever you please, and
» do whatever is appointed by the multitude, only
» let the flock of Christ be at peace with the consti-
» tuted priests. ' » He exhorts them by the example
of God himself to be patient and long suffering and
to acknowledge his benefits to all: each in his degree. « Behold the Creator of the world, and think
» how patient and gentle he is towards his whole

» creation. The heavens, the earth, the oceans and » worlds beyond them, are governed by the com- » mand of this great Master. Let every one be » subject to another according to the order in which » he is placed by God. Let not the strong man » neglect the care of the weak, let the weak see that » he reverence the strong, let the rich man con- » tribute to the necessities of the poor, and let » the poor bless God who hath given him one to » supply his wants. Let the wise man show forth » his wisdom not in words but in good works. Let » him that is humble never speak of himself, nor » make show of his actions. Let him that is pure » in flesh not grow proud of it, knowing that he re- » ceived the gift of continence from another. In » our body the head without the feet is nothing, » nor the feet without the head, and the smallest » members of our body are yet useful and neces- » sary for the whole. » Not content to appeal to the necessary harmony of parts, he warns the ring- leaders to make a voluntary submission and not to incur excommunication. « Do you therefore who laid » the foundation of this sedition submit yourselves » to the priests, and be instructed unto repentance. » Bending the knees of your hearts learn to be sub- » ject laying aside all proud and arrogant boast- » ing of your tongues: for it is better for you to

» be found in the sheepfold of Christ little and ap-
» proved, than thinking yourselves above others to
» be cast out of His hope. »

He points out to them the source of Catholic
and Episcopal power, and that disputes for prelacy
and precedence were foreseen and provided against;
and he insists upon the strictness of ritual observance. The Apostles have preached to us from the
Lord Jesus Christ, Jesus Christ from God. Christ
then was sent by God, and the Apostles by Christ....
Preaching therefore through countries and cities
they appointed their first fruits (having proved them
by the spirit), bishops and deacons of those who were
about to believe. « And what wonder if they to
» whom in Christ such a work was committed by God,
» appointed such as we have mentioned when even
» that blessed and faithful servant in all his house,
» Moses, notified in the sacred books all things that
» had been commanded him..... Our Apostles knew
» through our Lord Jesus Christ that contentions
» would arise upon the name of the episcopacy, and
» for this cause, having a perfect foreknowledge,
» they appointed the aforesaid and then gave di-
» rections in what manner, when they should die,
» others should succeed them in their public mi-
» nistry. Wherefore we account that they who
» have been appointed by them or afterwards by

» other eminent men, the whole Church consenting,
» and who have ministered blamelessly to the flock
» of Christ with humility, peacefully, and not illi-
» berally, and who also for a long time have been
» approved by all; that such are not to be without
» injustice thrown out of the ministry. For it would
» be no small sin in us, if we should cast off from
» the episcopacy those who offer up the gifts blame-
» lessly and holily. » Refusing to sacrifice any
bishop to popular clamour or secret prejudice, he
speaks of the due order of Church functions. « As
» these things are manifest to us, it behoves us
» looking into the depths of the divine knowledge
» to do all things in order whatsoever the Lord
» hath commanded to be done; at stated times to
» perform both the oblations and the liturgies; and
» not at random and disorderly hath He commanded
» this to be done, but at determined times and
» hours. And He himself hath ordained by His su-
» preme will both where and by what persons He
» wills them to be performed; that all things being
» holily done, unto all well pleasing, they may be
» acceptable unto His will. They therefore that
» make their oblations at the appointed times, are
» at once accepted and blessed, because that fol-
» lowing the institutes of the Lord, they sin not.
» For there are proper liturgies delivered to the

» chief priest, and a proper place assigned to the
» priests ; and there are proper ministrations in-
» cumbent on Levites, and the layman is adjudged
» to the appointment of laymen. Let every one of
» you, brethren, give thanks to God, in his proper
» station with a good conscience, with gravity, not
» going beyond the prescribed canon of his liturgy. »
He desires them to send back his legates to acquaint
him of the restoration of peace. « Those that have
» been sent to you by us, Claudius, Ephetus, Va-
» lerius, Vito together with Fortunatus also, send
» back to us again with all speed, in peace and in
» joy; that they may the sooner acquaint us of
» your peace and unanimity so much prayed for and
» desired by us. So that we may speedily rejoice
» at your good order. »

The authenticity of this epistle is generally acknowledged ; but assuming for a moment that it is
a forgery, it is, by its adaptation to circumstances,
by the moderation and elevation of its language,
one of the most skilful literary forgeries ever penned. It is filled with the spirit of papal authority.
And viewing it from the ground of Catholic principles, it would be no small compliment to Clement that so weighty, reasonable, and eloquent a
document could be attributed to no less a man. The
soul of the priest responsible for the souls of others,

the heart of the Christian man, the mind of the Vicar of Christ laying his obligations at the foot of the altar of his Lord ; the spirit of the prelate commanding in the place of the Apostles, the peaceful order of the ecclesiastic consecrated for his office, are conspicuous in every line of it. It is a pleasure to believe it produced the desired effect. The holy Pontiff's prayers were heard, all dissensions ceased, the laity became submissive to their pastors, and peace and concord reigned again in the church of Corinth.

A very considerable fragment of a second letter to the Corinthians was found in the same Alexandrian manuscript. S. Dionysius of Corinth tells us [1] that it was read in that church, but was not so celebrated among the ancients as the first. It recommends the faithful to despise the world and its allurements, to subdue their passions, and to keep their minds always fixed on heaven.

In addition to those two letters to the Corinthians our Saint addressed two others to Virgins. Westein, a Lutheran, found them in a Syrian manuscript of the new Testament, in 1752, and published them the same year at Amsterdam with a Latin translation, and again in 1757. The authen-

---

[1] L, 1, c. Jovinian. ch. 7.

ticity of these letters was impugned by Henry Ve-
nema, a German Lutheran, but his objections, as
we read in the Acts of Leipsic, for January 1756,
were refuted by Westein, who also acknowledges
that Clement differed much in his opinion of celi-
bacy from Martin Luther. « But it has not been
» proved, » says the Protestant writer, « that his
» opinion has been wrong. »   « For, if any one de-
» nies himself what it is allowed him to enjoy, that
» he may the better, and the more freely apply
» himself to the care of the Church, why ought he
» not hope to receive a great recompense in the
» life to come? »   S. Jerome alludes to these letters
in his book against Jovinian:[1] « In these epistles
» which S. Clement, the successor of the apostle
» Peter, wrote to them, that is to certain eunuchs,
» almost his whole discourse turns upon the excel-
» lency of virginity. »   Butler remarks that they
are not unworthy of the great disciple of S. Peter.
They expound the counsels of S. Paul regarding ce-
libacy and virginity, the practice of which they
recommend without diminishing the respect due to
the holy state of matrimony.

Many other works have been attributed to, and
circulated under, the name of Clement, but the uni-

---

[1] C. 7, p. 527.

versal consent of almost all writers regards them
as either apocryphal, or supposititious. These, as well
as the genuine works of our Saint, were collected
and published by Coteler at Paris in 1672. We
have alluded already to the Book of Recognitions,
as a production of the second century. The Clementine Homilies and the Epistle to S. James were
got up about the year 230 by some learned and
clever unknown writers. Gallandius thinks that the
Apostolical Constitutions should be referred to the
year 230. They are quoted by S. Epiphanius,[1] and
are a compilation of ancient pastoral regulations.
Bzovius translated them from Greek into Latin in
1603. Turrianus illustrated them, and Servius and
Burius inserted them in their collection of the Councils. They have been erroneously ascribed to Clement, as Pagi, Baronius, Natalis Alexander, Coteler,
and almost all modern writers, except Whiston, satisfactorily prove. They comprise eight books, and
contain much valuable information, regarding the
liturgy, discipline, and practices of the primitive
Church, although neither the precise time when they
were written, nor by whom, can be ascertained.

The Apostolical Canons were thought by some
really to have been written by the Apostles. Others

---

[1] Hom. 45, 35.

referred them to the close of the fifth century. They
are a compilation from various synods, and are now
generally supposed to be not later than the beginning of the third century. They were 85 in all, and
were all received by the Greeks in the sixth century.
The Latins received only the first 50, and even
these with some reserve, particularly Canons, 7, 46,
47, rejecting altogether the last 35. Turrianus, a
writer of the 16th century, strains every nerve in defence of the whole. Bellarmine,[1] Baronius[2] and
Bassenius in his « Apparatus sacer » think the first
fifty to be authentic. Burius[3] admits all but 65 and
84. Natalis Alexander[4] explodes them all together.
It is certain that not a single Father, except S. John
Damascene, has placed them among the canonical
writings. They are not quoted by Eusebius, Jerome,
Athanasius, Epiphanius, or any of the early Fathers
in their vindication of the discipline of the primitive
Church. Of some of them, however, the antiquity
cannot be denied, for they were quoted at the Council of Nice; but it is admitted that they were adulterated at a very early period, and that their number
was increased to 85 in the ninth century. Whether

[1] De script. eccl. in Clemente.
[2] Ann. in an. 102.
[3] Vol. I. Concil.
[4] Hist. eccl sæcu'i primi

any of the Canons drawn up by Clement is comprised or not in these compilations, no one can say. We are content to rest his reputation, as an author, upon his Epistle to the Corinthians, and his character as a prelate, upon the general approbation of antiquity : an apostolic man, a martyr Pope, whose name is registered in the Book of life. The petty disputes of critics about uncertain writings may obscure but not elucidate his career.

CHAPTER V.

Morality of Roman emperors in the days of S. Clement — S. Ignatius of Antioch condemned to death by Trajan — His journey to Rome, and martyrdom in the Coliseum — S. Clement exiled to the Chersonesus by orders of Trajan — Condition of the Christians in that penal settlement — Fruits of his Apostolic labours among its inhabitants — His martyrdom — Miraculous recovery of his body by S. Cyril who brought it to Rome, and deposited it in the Basilica dedicated to him at the foot of the Coelian Hill.

It is the fashion of writers, led away by classical enthusiasm, or rather by their indifference to true religion, to speak, sometimes with apology, sometimes with praise, of the pagan despots, who one after the other possessed the imperial throne of Rome. The epithets, *just, humane, and virtuous*, are bestowed upon men who, in the recesses of their dwellings, probably led no more decent lives than the rest of the idolatrous aristocracy, who have left after them obscene pictures, indelicate statues, and a foul mythology, to justify the reproaches which the martyrs cast upon the infamous vices of the heroes and gods they cherished and adored.

True, that the Roman eagle hovered over that cunning, lust, and cruelty, from which at various periods even Christian emperors have not been free, as well as over the reigns of princes less base; and that, as in more modern times, in the courts of emperors and kings, flatterers could be found, by winking at their vices, by dissembling their hypocrisy, by shutting their eyes to everything but the external glitter of their rule, to prate of justice, benevolence and freedom. But glory based upon a lie cannot endure. [1] Men who are liable at any moment to be seized and transported to unhealthy exile, by imperial order, to have their homes suddenly invaded, their means of subsistence confiscated at the pleasure of the Prince, nay even to be burnt alive in villages by the commander of his troops, to be flayed before the tribunal of the judge, to be hooted and

---

[1] We have seen this in the fate of the Imperial adventurer of France. In a night the fungus springs up, is filled with insects and rots. History will record the fate of foreign potentates in Mexico, Spain and Italy.

hunted, and branded as useless members of society, execrated as adverse to civil government, reviled as superstitious wretches, who deserve no mercy but to be driven forth to beg — such men, indeed, have learned that, between Pilate and Herod, between Octavius, who seated himself upon the ruins of the Republic and thought to number the whole world, and Nero who drove his vile mistresses in the imperial chariot, reviling the Christians the while, between Domitian who debauched his own niece, and, as Suetonius and Eusebius say, took the titles of Lord and God, who varied his amusement of impaling flies by the delight with which he beheld the most barbarous executions, and Nerva, whose philosophic indolence gave the Christians a respite of fifteen months, there were, as in modern crowned tyrants, gradations of vice and brutal power without, scarcely, a single redeeming quality. Nero was a man of taste, loved music and songs, and theatres and their accompaniments, did not disdain races, nor to dress and drive like a charioteer; if he did not write pamphlets and memoirs, he composed poetry; he had an extravagant passion to make a new Rome which should be built in a more sumptuous manner; he wanted room in particular to enlarge his own palace, which after the destruction of the quarters of the city adjacent to it, he immediately rebuilt

of an immense extent and adorned with whatever
the world afforded that was rich and curious, and
no doubt with sumptuous quarters for his imperial
guard. Of course he had no love for Christians. He
permitted his satellites to defame them as much as
they pleased, though his hypocrisy could not escape
the satire of the public; and the legal officers he let
loose upon them rather excited compassion for their
sufferings, than respect for themselves or their chief.
He was the first that made a general indiscriminate
persecution of religion, and thought perhaps that by
cutting off the Pope and his fellow-martyr S. Paul
to put an end to what he considered a farce and an
obstacle to his own arbitrary power. He miserably
ended his days by committing suicide.[1] How S. Clement escaped him, how he got through the first ten
years of Domitian's reign, and especially the next
five years after he sat in the Apostolic chair, history
does not record. A prince was coming who had
some literary pretensions and more ambition: before
printing was invented he had his own way of inscrib-
ing his name and actions, and got the nickname of

---

[1] Tertullian says, that it was the glory of the Christian religion
that the first emperor that drew his sword against it was Nero, the
sworn enemy of all virtue. This tyrant, four years after he had begun
to persecute the Christians, in his extreme distress attempted to kill
himself; but wanting resolution, he prevailed upon another to help him
to take away his life, and perished under the public resentment of the
whole empire, and the universal detestation of all mankind.

« wall-dauber » for his advertisements: he had his eye upon the East, and promoted foreign expeditions. He lived in incest with his sister. Like Vespasian and Domitian he ordered all who were of the race of David to be put to death; and, accused of this as well as of being a Christian, the bishop of Jerusalem, S. Simon, who was over his hundredth year, was tortured for several days and then crucified. He originated the third, as Domitian did the second general persecution. As usual, there have not been wanting men to style him « a just and virtuous prince, » and he affected moderation. From the beginning of his reign he prohibited the assemblies of Christians; but he directed his Prefects to punish those only who were legally convicted, and not to go out of their way to arraign them for supposed criminality. He punished informers as well as the accused. Thus he seems not to have adopted espionage, and he rejected anonymous charges as repugnant to the equity of his government, and required for the conviction of those to whom the guilt of criminality was imputed the positive evidence of an open accuser. Trajan especially after he had marched towards the Danube and achieved victories over the Dacii and Scythians, who may be taken as the ancestors of the Russians, shewed his native superstition and policy, out of gratitude to his imaginary deities. The next year, A.D. 106,

9

the ninth of his reign, he set out for the East on an expedition against the Parthians and entered Antioch with the pomp of a triumph. What compliments he paid and received from the chiefs and tribes, what respect the Caesar showed for their polygamy and polytheism, we know not. His first concern was about the affair of religion, and the worship of the gods. And for this purpose he resolved to compel the Christians either to own their divinity and to sacrifice, or to suffer death. Of the way in which this « *excellent and equitable Prince* » presided at trials, we have a specimen in the Acts of S. Ignatius the Martyr bishop of Antioch.

« Who art thou, wicked demon, that dare trans-
» gress our commands and persuade others to pe-
» rish? »

Ignatius mildly answered: « No one calls Theo-
» phorus a wicked demon. »

Trajan said: « Who is Theophorus? »

Ignatius: « He who carrieth Christ in his breast. »

Trajan: « And do we not seem to bear the gods
» in our breast whom we have assisting us against
» our enemies? »

Ignatius: « You err in calling them gods who
» are no better than devils, for there is only one God
» who made heaven and earth and all things that
» are in them, and one Jesus Christ his only Son

» into whose kingdom I earnestly desire to be ad-
» mitted. »

Trajan asked: « Do you not mean him who was
» crucified under Pontius Pilate? »

Ignatius: « The very same: who by his death
» has crucified sin with its author, overcame the ma-
» lice of the devils, and has enabled those who have
» Him in their breasts to trample on them. »

« Do you then carry within you this crucified
» Jesus? » Asked the Emperor, with a sarcastic
smile.

Ignatius: « Yes, for it is written: ' I will dwell
» in them and walk among them.' »[1]

Trajan then dictated the sentence. « It is our will
» that Ignatius who saith that he carrieth the cru-
» cified man within himself be bound and conducted
» to Rome, to be devoured by wild beasts for the
» entertainment of the people. »

The holy martyr, having heard the sentence
pronounced against him, cried out with a heart
full of joy: « I thank Thee, oh Lord! for having
» vouchsafed to honour me with this pledge of per-
» fect love for Thee, and to be bound with chains of
» iron, in imitation of the apostle Paul, for Thy
» sake. » He was then put in chains and consigned

---

[1] Corinth. VI, 1C.

to a troop of savage soldiers to be conducted to
Rome. On arriving at Smyrna he had an interview
with S. Polycarp, the disciple of S. John the Evangelist, and addressed most affecting and instructive
letters to the churches of Ephesus, of Magnesia, of
the Trallians, and to the Christians of Rome. He
then implored S. Polycarp and others to unite their
prayers with his, that the ferocity of the lions might
soon present him to Christ; and with this view he
also wrote to the faithful at Rome, beseeching them
not to deprive him of his crown by praying to God
that the beasts might spare him, as they did other
martyrs. « I fear your charity, » he says, « lest it
» prejudice me. For it is easy for you to do what
» you please, but it will be difficult for me to obtain
» God if you spare me. I shall never have such
» an opportunity of enjoying God, nor can you, if
» ye shall now be silent, ever be entitled to the
» honour of a better work. For if ye be silent in
» my behalf, I shall be made partaker of God, but if
» ye love my body, I shall have my course to run
» out. Therefore a greater kindness you cannot do
» me, than to suffer me to be sacrificed unto God;
» whilst the altar is now ready, that, so becoming a
» choir in love, in your hymns ye may give thanks
» to the Father, by Jesus Christ, that God has
» vouchsafed to bring me the bishop of Syria, from

» the East into the West to pass out of the world
» unto God, that I may rise again unto Him. Ye
» have never envied any one. Ye have taught others.
» I desire, therefore, that you will firmly observe,
» that which in your instructions you have prescribed
» to others. Only pray for me that God may deign
» to give me both inward and outward strength
» that I may not only say, but do, that I may be
» not only called a Christian, but be found one; for
» if I shall be found a Christian, I may then de-
» servedly be called one, and be thought faithful
» when I shall no longer appear to the world. No-
» thing is good that is seen. A Christian is not
» a work of opinion, but of greatness, when he is
» hated by the world. I write to the churches and
» signify to them all that I am ready to die for
» God, unless you hinder me. I beseech you that
» you show not an unreasonable good will towards
» me. Suffer me to be the food of wild beasts, that
» I may be found the pure bread of Christ, whereby
» I may attain unto God. Rather entice the beasts
» to my sepulchre that they may leave nothing of
» my body, that being dead I may not be troublesome
» to any one. Then shall I be a true disciple of
» Jesus Christ when the world shall not see so much
» as my body. Pray to Christ for me that in this I
» may become a sacrifice to God. I do not, as Peter

» and Paul, command you; they were Apostles, I
» am an inconsiderable person; they were free, I
» am even yet a slave; but if I suffer, I shall then
» become the freeman of Jesus Christ, and shall
» arise a freeman in Him. Now I am in bonds for
» Him, I learn to have no worldly or vain desires.
» From Syria, even unto Rome, I fight wild beasts
» both by sea and by land, both night and day,
» bound to ten leopards, that is to say a band of
» soldiers, who are the worse for kind treatment.
» But I am the more instructed by their injuries,
» yet I am not therefore justified. I earnestly wish
» for the wild beasts that are prepared for me, which
» I heartily desire may soon dispatch me, and whom
» I will entice to devour me entirely and suddenly,
» and not serve me as they have done some whom
» they have been afraid to touch; but if they are
» unwilling to meddle, I will even compel them to it.
» Pardon me this matter, I know what is good for
» me. Now I begin to be a disciple, so that I have
» no desire after anything visible or invisible, that I
» may attain to Jesus Christ. Let fire or the cross,
» or the concourse of wild beasts, let cutting or
» tearing of the flesh, let breaking of bones or cutting
» off limbs, let the shattering in pieces of my whole
» body, and the wicked torments of the devil come
» upon me, so I may but attain to Jesus Christ.

» All the compass of the earth, and the kingdoms
» of this world will profit me nothing. It is better
» for me to die for the sake of Jesus Christ than
» to rule unto the ends of the earth. Him I seek
» who died for us. Him I desire who arose again
» for us. Pardon me, brethren, be not my hin-
» drance in attaining to life, for Jesus Christ is the
» life of the faithful; whilst I desire to belong to
» God, do not ye yield me back to the world.
» Suffer me to partake of the true light. When
» I shall be there, I shall be a man of God. Permit
» me to imitate the passion of Christ my Lord.
» If any one has Him within himself, let him consider
» what I desire, and let him have compassion on
» me, as knowing how I am straitened. The prince
» of the world endeavours to snatch me away, and to
» change the desire with which I desire, with which
» I burn, of being united to God. Let none of you
» who are present, attempt to succour me. Be ra-
» ther on my side, that is on God's. Entertain no
» desire of the world, having Jesus Christ in your
» mouths. Let no envy find place in your hearts.
» Even were I myself to entreat you when present,
» do not obey me, but rather believe what I now
» signify to you by letter. Though I am alive while
» writing this, yet my desire is to die. My love
» is crucified, the fire that is within me does not

» crave any water, but being alive and springing
» within says: Come to the Father. I take no plea-
» sure in the food of corruption, nor in the enjoyment
» of this life. I desire the bread of God which is the
» flesh of Jesus Christ, and for drink His blood which
» is incorruptible charity. I desire to live no longer
» according to men, and this shall be if you are
» willing. Be then willing, that you may be ac-
» cepted by God. Pray for me, that I may pos-
» sess God. If I shall suffer, ye have loved me. If
» I shall be rejected, ye have hated me. Remember
» in your prayers the church of Syria, which now
» enjoys God for its shepherd instead of me. I am
» ashamed to be called of their number, for I am
» not worthy, being the last of them, and an abor-
» tive, but through mercy I have obtained that I
» shall be something, if I enjoy God. » The holy
martyr arrived in Rome on the 20th of December,
and was immediately sent to the amphitheatre where
he was devoured by lions « *for the entertainment of
the people.* » Thus it is ever. Whether a S. Ignatius
of Antioch, a S. John Chrysostom, a S. Thomas of
Canterbury, a Gregory VII, or any exiled bishop
of the nineteenth century, is to be persecuted, and
if possible, doomed to suffer death, the pretext of
crowned tyrants is ever, the well-being, and « *the
entertainment of the people.* » The Christians, to the

lions! was the shout of the popular diversion then
— then as now war upon Catholic priests and prelates was the maxim of men whom God, who waiteth
patiently to repay, permits for his own wise purposes to disgrace for a while the thrones of the
earth. — S. Ignatius, as we have said, was instantly
devoured by the lions that were let loose upon him,
and nothing of his body remained but the larger
bones, which, as S. John Chrysostom relates, were
religiously taken up and « carried in triumph on
» the shoulders of all the cities between Rome and
» Antioch » where they were laid in a marble urn
as an inestimable treasure. Evaristus writes [1] that
« at first they were deposited outside the Daphnitic
» gate, but in the reign of Theodosius the Younger
» were translated with extraordinary pomp to a
» church in the city, which had been a temple of
» Fortune, and which has ever since borne his name. »
They are now in our church of S. Clement in Rome,
whither they were translated when, in 637, Antioch
fell into the power of the Saracens.

To the bishop of Rome the head of the state
adopted that policy of grinding exile which more
petty kings, since then, have used, lacking the
courage to consummate a greater crime, whilst

---

[1] Hist. eccl. lib. 1, cap. 16.

their works point out the bent of their will. The enemy of the Church could not bear the Sovereign Pontiff even a prisoner in his own palace : he could not suffer him in Bologna, Ancona, Naples, or in any of the great Italian towns. The decay of nature and the expectation of an old man's death under oppression was not enough for his hatred of the head of **Christians**. That he had succeeded in planting military colonies in various places, won some victories over men brave, but not numerous enough to defend themselves effectually, and gained fresh cities, was not enough so long as there was a bishop with the soul of a freeman, and whom the consciences of men voluntarily o-beyed. The greater the virtues, talent and holiness of such a man the more obnoxious to the prince by reason of the contrast of his character with his own : the warmer the affection in which he was held by the moderate and good, the more jealous the suspicion with which he was watched by the magistrates and their master. Clement was accused of being the leader of what then was called a new sect, and the organizer of their meetings. Accordingly he was cited before Mamertinus the Prefect of the city. As was not unusual with persons of noble birth, he was treated with a certain degree of urbanity. He had only to do what many

persons nobly born have found it convenient to do,
to betray his Sovereign, to renounce his faith, to
prostrate body and soul before the ideas and will
of the Caesar. He had only not to know Christ
the King, to give up what he was assured was
superstitious excess, and offer incense to the gods,
the protectors of the empire. His common sense
ought to show him that the stronger were the
best judges, and that his private opinions, even if
he were consecrated to herald them to the world,
ought not to be pushed too far in opposition to
the material interests and wishes of so well-judging
a prince.[1] But Clement was the Bishop of bishops,
and he assented not to such suggestions. A report
of the trial was submitted to the emperor, who ordered him to be banished to Cherson beyond the
Euxine sea. Under an escort of soldiers he set
out on his long and dreary journey. If we would

---

[1] We have in the martyrdom of S. Chrysogonus which the Church
celebrates on the day after the feast of S. Clement, an example of this
method of persuasion. He was shut up in Rome for two years, and his
wants supplied by Anastasia. Diocletian ordered all the Christian prisoners to be put to death, but Chrysogonus to be sent to him to Aquileia.
« I sent for you » said the emperor « to increase you with honours, if
» you will bring your mind to worship the gods. » « I do venerate »
was the answer « with mind and prayer Him who is truly God: but the
» gods who are nothing else but images of devils I detest and execrate. »
The emperor had him beheaded. It has been well said that there are more
ways than one of sacrificing to the infernal deities; and modern iniquity
has not been at a loss for victims to the prejudice, passion and injustice,
of which those deities are the authors.

know how such prisoners were treated, history furnishes us with many examples, and among them that of S. Ignatius already referred to, that of S. John Chrysostom exiled from Constantinople to Comana Pontica in Cappadocia, that of Pius VI from Rome to Valence. If we would know how an imperial jailor can treat his victims, we can read it in Napoleon the First bullying Pius VII at Fontainebleau. And if we would estimate the only value such men set upon moral and religious authority, we find it where that emperor tells his agent to treat the Pope as a power of a hundred thousand bayonets. S. Helena was the only fit comment, or Sedan. Wicked men grasp power, kings usurp; but God does not always wait for their death to hurl them from unjustly acquired eminence. The Pagan emperors resembled modern kings in their reliance upon brute force, but they were not paracides and did not style him they stript, imprisoned, mocked and murdered, their Holy Father. They despised or hated the Pope as their religious rival. They did not send for his blessing when they wreaked their malice on him. We may doubt whether their injustice was greater than that of royalty in the progress of the nineteenth century: but if they seemed more ferocious, they were certainly less hypocritical and mean.

The power and the stones of ancient Rome were literally cemented with blood. When the sentimental traveller visits the Coliseum by moonlight, or deplores the wreck of marble columns, he seldom thinks with what agonies and deaths of slaves those masses were quarried and set up. At that great day when the just will stand with confidence against their oppressors, to Caesar will be given the things that are Caesar's, the dross of the metals he coveted for his filthy pleasures, the armour of his legions, the stones ransacked from every quarter of the world for his buildings and his statues. Perhaps the last of those fallen columns which has been set up again in Papal Rome to bear aloft the image of the Mother of Christ, that pure and immaculate creation who never knew a stain of sin, was hewn and polished and consecrated by the toil and misery of Christian men. Clement found two thousand Christians doomed to hopeless slavery in the marble quarries of the Chersonese. What a consolation commingled with feelings of the deepest grief, must it not have been to those martyrs of Christ to see the Supreme Pastor descend into those gloomy prisons! He taught them to bear with fortitude the trials they were subjected to, reminding them that they were not better than their Master, who suffered the direst persecutions, and shed His blood for their redemption; and that if they would imitate His example, they should share His glory. His admonitions produced the desired effect. They submitted to the tyranny of their masters, to the severity of their labours, and to the gloom of their prisons, with Christian meekness and fortitude. They were obliged to carry water from a long distance under a parching sun; like another Moses, Clement caused a limpid stream to gush from a rock that was miraculously pointed out to him. This fact is best explained by the Antiphons of Lauds, which are read in the Office for his feast, on the 23^d of November.

1st « Whilst Clement was in prayer, there appeared to him the Lamb of God. »

2nd « Not by my merits; the Lord has sent me to you to be a partaker of your crowns. »

3rd « I saw upon the mountain the Lamb standing, from underneath whose feet is welling out a living fountain, »

4th « From underneath whose feet flows forth the living fountain; the gushing of the stream makes glad the city of God. »

5th « All the people around believed in Christ the Lord. »

The fame of this supernatural event spread

throughout that entire region, and the result was that most of its pagan inhabitants embraced the Christian faith, broke their idols, razed, to the ground, the temples in which they were enshrined, and upon their ruins built no less than seventy five churches. When Trajan was informed of the miracles wrought by S. Clement, and the innumerable conversions made by his preaching, he became so incensed that he despatched his prefect Auphidianus armed with full powers to take proceedings against the Christians, and punish their temerity for violating the laws of the empire and insulting the gods, its protectors. Auphidianus on arriving at Cherson caused numbers of its inhabitants to be put to death by various kinds of torture. But seeing that, owing to the persuasive and inspired eloquence of Clement, they met their fate with cheerful resignation, he ordered the Pontiff to be thrown into the sea with an anchor fastened to his neck. The sentence was executed in the presence of an immense crowd. The Christians being grieved that they could not recover his relics, were advised by his disciples, Cornelius and Phoebus, to have recourse to God by prayer, and humbly implore of Him to indicate to them the spot where the holy martyr's body lay. As their prayers ascended to heaven, the sea miraculously retired from

the shore : they followed the receding waters, and
having gone to the distance of about three miles,
they found, to their astonishment, and inexpressible
consolation, a marble temple, and within it an urn
containing the holy Pontiff's body, while near it
lay the anchor, the instrument of his martyrdom.
Falling on their knees they returned thanks to God
for having recovered so priceless a treasure. For
more than two hundred years the sea used to retire on the anniversary of S. Clement's martyrdom,
leaving a dry path to the faithful for visiting his
tomb, which remained accessible for the seven following days, when it was again covered by the waters, as is recorded by S. Ephraim, the martyr
bishop of Cherson, by S. Gregory of Tours, Peter
de Natalibus, and many other trust-worthy authors.
Trajan thought to disperse the sheep by striking
the Shepherd, but he little knew that « the blood
» of martyrs is the seed of the Church. » The
miracles wrought by S. Clement during his exile,
and after his martyrdom, had such an effect on
the inhabitants of Cherson that they all embraced
the Christian faith, so that, as Bosco informs us,
neither Jew, nor Pagan, nor heretic, nor schismatic, was to be found in any part of that country;
and the penal settlement of the Christians became
a nursery of Saints. As we stated above, the mi-

raculous reflux of the sea continued for more than two hundred years; but owing to the frequent incursions of the barbarians, the primitive inhabitants were gradually eradicated, so that, before the ninth century, the whole of that region was repeopled by a new race of men, and even the very spot, where once stood the celebrated temple of S. Clement, was forgotten, and of the sacred treasures it contained nothing was known until they were miraculously discovered by S. Cyril.

Not as Pope wrote, in his « Moral Essay, »

« Where London's column pointing at the skies
« Like a tall bully, lifts the head and lies; »

do the two great sculptured columns of pagan Rome reflect upon the victims of persecution. The Antonine column records the rain, in answer to the prayers of the Christian soldiers, who saved the army of Marcus Aurelius from perishing by thirst. Where tier upon tier the sculptured marble gives the exploits of Trajan in minute detail, we see nought to remind us of his vindictive cruelty against the Christian martyrs, but we miss the anchor there. Generally speaking, when the pagan Romans had slain men, they let them be buried : they did not root out their ashes; they did not destroy their

10

sepulchres: to purify, they did not burn down their
temples : they did not take much pains to blacken
their reputation after death. It was done sometimes, but not for long. Neither Nero nor the se-
nate built a column to record that the Christians
set fire to Rome. Perhaps though they tortured
men, they did not wish to boast of it. They did
not think their power was built on that. We
gaze indeed upon that proud monument of Trajan's
triumphs, but the figure which crowns it is that
of an Apostle. We look upon the shattered granite pillars of his forum, where Constantine proclaimed the empire Christian. We smile at the
impotent conventions of emperors and kings, and
bless the providence of God. In the midst of persecution the Catholic in Rome has only to look upon
her monuments to read the persecutor's fall.

We have seen something of one of the first of
S. Peter's disciples, a Roman, a Pope, and a Martyr. That first Christian century began with the
stoning of Stephen, it ended with S. Clement's exile,
and the second commenced with his having been
hurled into the sea. We must pass over seven centuries to find him again. The ninth century was
one of great men, and of great events. It began
with a great Catholic emperor, Charlemagne, it
ended with a greater Catholic king, Alfred the

Great. Both were self-taught men, and both were full of Catholic instincts. Sir **Henry Spelman**[1] thus panegyrizes the character of the Monarch of **England**: « O, Alfred, the wonder and astonishment » of all ages! If we reflect on his piety and re-» ligion, it would seem that he had always lived » in a cloister; if on his warlike exploits, that he » had never been out of camps; if on his learning » and writing, that he had spent his whole life in » a college; if on his wholesome laws and wise ad-» ministration, that these had been his whole study » and employment. »

The monarch of France was active in war and in peace, constant at Mass, a linguist and a legislator, who began too old ever to write well, yet the friend of Alcuin. He retored the States of the Church, and, in 800, was crowned at Rome, by Leo III, emperor of the West. It is possible that Alfred stood before the fresco of our Lady's Assumption in S. Clement's; at least if Leo IV, whose figure forms part of the subject, was, as is supposed with the greatest probability, living, when the painting was executed; for twice Alfred was brought, by his pious father Ethelwulph, to Rome, and Leo adopted him for his son, and anointed him for future

[1] Con. Brit.

king. This is no place to dwell on the glories of
his reign, but no greater king ever graced the English throne. If he appears less conspicuously on
behalf of the Popes, it was for no want of will. He
thought Peter's pence no detriment to the realm,
and we have recorded the names of the noblemen
who carried his presents to Rome. [1] Nor was the
ninth century without its missionary Saints. Charlemagne had subdued the Sclavonians by his arms,
S. Cyril won them to Christ in the warfare of the
faith. It is not uncommon in the lives of the Saints
that the child is marked, as it were, by the finger
of God, and pointed out for future sanctity; perhaps
that when death crowns the work, men may remember that it was one of patience and love and not
of man's doing. Thus Peregrina, the pious mother of
the great bishop of Fiesole, S. Andrew Corsini, dreamt
that she gave birth to a wolf which ran into a church
and was turned into a lamb; and the young rake
actually did retire to the Carmelite church which
he did not leave until he had put on the habit of that
Order. Thus the Blessed Jane of Aza, the mother of
S. Dominic, dreamt that she brought forth a whelp
with a lighted torch in his mouth, which set the
whole world on fire; and that is the arms of the Order

---

[1] See Asserius, William of Malmsbury, and Matthew of West
minster.

to this day. From his early youth Constantine Cyril of Thessalonica, the son of a senatorial Roman family, was called the Philosopher from his rare talents and aptitude for learning. Happier than others who had the same title, he dedicated the education he received at Constantinople to God's service in the priesthood. It was not a mean one. He knew Greek, Latin, and the Sclavonian languages, and he learned the Turcic spoken by the Huns, Chazari, and Tartars, that he might become the Apostle of their country. In 848, the Chazari, the descendants of the Huns of European Scythia, then settled on the Danube, sent to the emperor Michael III. and his pious mother Theodora, an embassy unlike modern embassies, for it was for priests to teach them the faith of Christ.[1] The empress sent for the patriarch S. Ignatius, and, by his advice, Cyril was charged with this important mission. Recommending his undertaking to God, he set out, and in a short time after entering the field of his missionary labours, he instructed and baptized the Cham together with his whole nation. He then committed his church to the care of pious and zealous pastors, and returned to Constantinople, absolutely refusing to accept the

[1] In the reign of D. Sebastian of Portugal Alvaro I. king of Congo sent an embassy for a similar purpose to the Portuguese.

rich presents which the new convert and his people wished to bestow on him; while he assured them that he valued, more than all the gifts they could give him, a promise that they would emancipate their Christian slaves, which they accordingly did. [1]

Cyril's second mission was to the Bulgarians, in which he was assisted by his brother Methodius. [2] Perhaps the circumstance which led to the conversion of Boigoris their king, had something to do with the previous embassy; for his sister had long been a hostage in the court of the empress Theodora, and became a Christian there. Her prayers, doubtless, ascended night and day to the throne of God for the conversion of her brother, which is said to have been effected, like many others in our own day, by a picture. Methodius was an artist monk; and when Boigoris asked the emperor for a painter to adorn his new palace, Methodius was selected. The king ordered him to execute a subject which would strike terror into all who saw it, and the

---

[1] « Illi (Chazari) plurimi exhilarati, et in fide catholicâ roborati gratias referebant, offerentes philosopho maxima munera, qui illa omnia respuens rogavit eos, quatenus pro muneribus quotquot captivos haberent Christianos servituti deditos, dimitterent liberos; quod protinus est adimpletum. Quo facto philosophus reversus est Constantinopolim. » MS. Blauber.

[2] « Egressus igitur (cum Methodio germano suo) prius venit ad Bulgaros, quos gratia cooperante sua predicatione convertit ad fidem. » MS. Blauber.

good monk thinking nothing more awful than the *last judgement*, executed it in the most lively colours. The terrors of the scene and the explanation of it had so powerful an effect on Boigoris that he instantly desired to be baptized, and took the name of Michael. His subjects hearing of his conversion rose in arms against him and marched to attack his palace; but he put himself at the head of his army and defeated them. The rebels thus checked returned to their allegiance, and shortly afterwards followed the example of their sovereign by embracing the Christian faith. A thorough convert, this prince sent letters and ambassadors to Nicolas I. begging his Holiness to let him know what more he should do.[1] The Pope gave him the instructions he desired, and sent Legates, in 867, to congratulate him on his conversion to the faith. He also answered many difficulties that were proposed to him, and declared baptism administered, in case of necessity, by laymen, and even by infidels, to be good and valid.[2] Boigoris Michael renounced his crown in 880, and, putting on a monastic habit, led an evangelical life on earth. The year of his death is unknown. From Bulgaria Cyril and Methodius passed into Moravia, by invitation of

[1] Anastas. Bibl. in Nicolao I, et ipse Nicolaus ep. 70. Hincmar etc.
[2] See his response ad consulta Bulgarorum. Conc. t. 7. p. 1542.

king Rastices, whom they baptized with most of his
people. Augustine, in his catalogue of the bishops
of Ulmutz, [1] and Dubravius [2] assert that S. Cyril was
the first bishop of the Moravians. Also, the Bohe-
mians, under God, owe their faith to our Apostolic
monks. Dubravius writes that Borivorius, or Bori·
way, duke of Bohemia, was converted to the faith
by hearing the holy missionaries preach, and being
baptized by Methodius he invited him to Prague
where he instructed his wife Ludmilla, their children,
and many of his subjects, and regenerated them with
the waters of baptism. Methodius also built at Prague
the church of our Lady and several others. Stre-
dowski, in his « *Sacra Moraviae historia* », styles SS. Cyril and Methodius the apostles of Moravia, upper
Bohemia, Silesia, Cazaria, Croatia, Circassia, Bulgaria, Bohemia, Russia, Poland, Dalmatia, Pannonia,
Dacia, Carinthia, Carniola, and of almost all the kingdoms in which the Sclavonian language is spoken.
Pope John VIII, in 879, in his letters to count Spen-
dopulk, writes that the Sclavonian alphabet was invented by S. Cyril. « The Sclavonian letters or alphabet invented by Constantine the philosopher that the
praises of God may be sung, we justly commend. » [3]

---

[1] Inter rerum Bohemiae scriptores. Hannoviae 1632.
[2] Hist. Bohemiae, lib. 4.
[3] Ep. 247 ad Spendopulchrum comitem.

The brothers also translated the liturgy and Mass into that tongue. In 1631, the Sclavonian missal was revised by Urban VIII, and his approbation of it was confirmed by Benedict XIV. It was not until after S. Cyril's death that Methodius, who was made archbishop of Moravia, obtained from John VIII. permission to use the Sclavonian language in the Mass. Both brothers came to Rome by invitation of Pope Nicolas I. Cyril died there and was buried in the church of S. Clement.

It is necessary to know what we may style the family affections of the Church in Rome even in unhappy times, what brotherly rejoicing in the canonization of a saint, what devotion in united prayers, what interest the good take even in the trifles of their father, to appreciate the eagerness with which the Roman people received the news of the arrival of the missionary saint, bringing with him the relics of S. Clement. The contemporary bishop of Velletri, Gaudentius, has given us an account of the translation of the relics of S. Clement which he witnessed; and Rondinini thinks that he may have had the account of their discovery from S. Cyril himself. When Constantine Cyril went to Pontus, the present Crimea, to study the language of the Turci for his mission to the Chazari,[1] he tried in vain to learn

---

[1] The Chazari were a tribe of Turci, the most numerous and power-

something about S. Clement's relics. The people,
who were not the tribes of Clement's day, but others
who had come in since then, could give no
information about them; and, for more than five
centuries, the miraculous receding of the sea had
ceased. He applied to George, the bishop of the
diocese, and they agreed to search what they supposed to be the original spot. « Taking ship on
» a calm day, under the guidance of Christ, they
» took their way, to wit, the aforesaid Philosopher,
» with the bishop, George by name, and the re-
» verend clergy, and some of the people as well.
» Sailing then with great devotion and confidence,
» hymning and praying, they reached the island in

---

ful nation of the Huns in European Scythia. In the sixth century
they were divided into seven, sometimes into ten tribes, governed by
so many independent chagans, that is chams or kings. They drove the
Avares, and other nations of the Huns, from the banks of the Ethel,
now called Volga, towards the Danube, in the reigns of the emperors
Mauritius and Tiberius, who both honoured them with their alliance,
and two pompous embassies, minutely described by the emperor Constantine Porphyrogenetta in his « Pandextae Hist. de Legationibus p.161. »
From these ancient Turci some think the Turks among the Ogisoian
Tartars to be descended, as well as the Tartars of the Crimea. Cos-
tantine Porphyrogenetta (l. de regendo imperio ad Romanum filium)
and other Byzantine writers, call also the Huns and other northern nations, whether of Europe or Asia, by the same name, Turci. The Chazari
took possession of the territory bordering on Germany, upon the banks
of the Danube, which Porphyrogenetta describes in his time to have had
the Bulgarians on the east, the Patzinaciticae (who came also from the
Volga) on the north, Moravia on the west, and on the south the Serobati,
a tribe of Bulgarians who lived in the mountains.

» which they supposed the holy martyr's body to
» be. Getting round about it then, and searching,
» with great brilliancy of lights, they began, more
» and more earnest in their holy prayers, very
» anxiously, and without intermission, to dig in
» that mound where so great a treasure was sus-
» pected to rest. After working there for some
» time, and with much holy desire, on a sudden,
» as if God grave some brilliant star, one of the
» precious martyr's ribs shone forth. At which
» spectacle all filled with immense exultation, and,
» not now without some excitement, vying with
» each other to dig out the earth more and more,
» his holy head also in due course appeared. And
» then behold after a little while again, as it were
» out of some parcels of holy relics, by degrees,
» and at moderate intervals, the whole was found.
» And last of all there appeared the anchor with
» which he had been cast into the deep. After the
» celebration, by the bishop, of the sacred myste-
» ries upon the spot, the holy man lifting the chest
» of the sacred relics upon his own head, bore
» them to the ship; *then transported the glory* [1] *to the*

---

[1] « Deinde *Gloriam* metropolim transportavit. » Rondinini thinks it
should be *Georgiam*. See Rondinini, lib. I, § II. Or *Gloriam* may be a
misprint for *Georgiam*, and if so, the meaning would be - he transported
the relics to Georgia the Metropolis.

» *metropolis.* On the following morning the entire
» population of the city getting together, and tak-
» ing up the chest of sacred relics, went round
» the town with much thanksgiving, and coming
» to the greater basilica honorably placed them in
» it. » If any one should suppose that this account is fabulous and incredible, he would betray
his ignorance of Church history. When S. Helen
recovered the true Cross, it was distinguished, from
the other two which lay beside it, by a miracle
of healing. S. Ambrose relates how he himself recovered the relics of SS. Gervasius and Protasius.
« Whilst I was dedicating the basilica, many began,
» as with one voice, to call upon me saying: ' Let
» this be dedicated as was the Roman basilica. S.Am-
» brose: I will do so, if I can find martyr's relics" and
» instantly there came upon me an ardour which
» presaged something. What need of many words?
» The Lord granted the favour. And though even
» the clerics were alarmed, I ordered the ground
» to be dug up before the gates of SS. Felix and
» Nabor. I met with suitable indications. We
» found two men of wonderful stature. All the
» bones entire and much blood. The crowd was
» great throughout the whole of the two days. In
» a word, we translated them when the evening
» was near at hand to the basilica of Faustus, and

» on the following day to the basilica which they
» call the Ambrosian. Whilst we were translat-
» ing them, a blind man was restored to sight. »
In the three instances here mentioned, search was
made at a particular spot, where the relics were
suspected to be. The reclics of S. Cecily were
found, by Pope Paschal I. in the catacombs,
through a dream in which the saint appeared to
him after he had actually abandoned the search
as useless. The recovery of the relics of the protomartyr, the deacon S. Stephen, was still more
extraordinary. In the year 415, while Lucian, a
venerable priest who was attached to a church in
the small town of Caphargamala, about twenty
miles from Jerusalem, whilst sleeping in a room
near the sacristy where he lived in order to guard
the sacred vessels, he dreamt that a tall comely
old man appeared to him clad in a white garment
edged with small plates of gold and decorated with
crosses, and holding a golden wand in his hand.
Approaching Lucian, and calling him three times
by name, he ordered him to go to Jerusalem and
tell bishop John to come and open the tombs in
which his remains and those of other servants of
Christ lay; Lucian asked his name, and he replied:
« I am Gamaliel [1] who instructed Paul in the law,

---

1 Gamaliel was of the sect of the Pharisees, and a legal doctor of

» and on the east side lieth Stephen who was stoned
» **to death by the Jews** outside the **north gate.**
» His body was left there exposed one day and one
» night, but was not touched **by** birds or beasts.
» I exhorted the faithful to carry it away during
» **the** night, and had **it** secretly brought to my
» **house** in the country, **where I** celebrated his ob-
» sequies **for** forty days, and then buried him in
» my own tomb. Nicodemus who came to Jesus
» by night, lies in another sarcophagus. He was
» expelled the synagogue for following Christ, and
» **then** banished from Jerusalem, whereupon he came
» to my house, where I kept him till his death
» and buried him near S. Stephen. I also buried
» there my son Abibas: his body is **in a** coffin
» higher up in which I myself was also interred. »
Lucian, unable to understand the vision, begged of
God that if it came **from** Him, he might be fa-
voured with it a second and a third time. And

---

high reputation in his day at Jerusalem. We read in the acts of the
Apostles, ch. 22, n. 3, that S. Paul recommended himself to the Jews **by**
saying that he had been his scholar. When the Jews were **contriving to**
put the Apostle to death, Gamaliel dissuaded them by **proving that the**
christian religion was the work of God. And this he did with such prudence that he did not incur the least suspicion of favouring the Nazarenes, **as the Christians were then called. He was not then** a Christian,
but **S.** John Chrysostom assures us **that he embraced** the faith before
S Paul. See Acts of the Apostles, ch. **V, v. 34. Hom. 20.** S.Joannis Chrys.
in Joan. Hom. **14, in Act.**

so it was, Gamaliel appeared to him in a dream a
second and a third time, in the same dress as before, and commanded him to obey. Lucian communicated his vision to the bishop of Jerusalem. The
search was made, the coffins were found, one of
which was higher than the others, and in it lay
the bodies of an old and a young man, and one
in each of the other sarcophagi. On the lid of the
highest coffin, or sarcophagus, were engraved in
large letters *Gamaliel, Abibas*. On the second *Cheliel*,
the Syriac name of *Stephen*, or *crowned;* and on
the third *Nasuam*, which in Syriac means Nicodemus, or *victory of the people*. Lucian immediately
sent messengers to communicate the discovery to
bishop John, who was at the time assisting at the
council of Diospolis. The good tidings filled the
heart of the holy old man with joy; and forthwith
he set out accompanied by Eutonius, bishop of Sebaste, and Eleutherius, bishop of Jericho, to visit
the place where the relics were found. On opening the coffin of S. Stephen, the earth shook, a
balmy perfume was diffused, such as no one there
present ever smelt before, and no less than seventy
three persons afflicted with various maladies were
cured on the spot. The history of this miraculous
discovery written by Lucian, and translated into
Latin by Aritus, a Spanish priest and an intimate

friend of S. Jerome, is published by the Benedictine monks in the appendix to the seventh volume of the works of S. Augustine. The same is attested by Chrysippus, a learned and holy priest of Jerusalem, as well as by Idatius, Marcellinus, Basil bishop of Seleucia, by S. Augustine, Bede, and several other Fathers and historians of the early Church. S. Augustine says that the place where the martyrs of Milan lay hid, was made known to S. Ambrose by a vision. « I was there, I was at Milan. I know » the miracles wrought. A blind man,[1] very well » known to the whole city, recovered his sight. » He ran. (He caused himself to be led to touch » the bier with his handkerchief). He came back » without a guide. We have not yet heard that » he is dead: perhaps he is still living. He dedi- » cated himself to serve during his whole life in » that basilica of theirs, where their bodies are. »

---

[1] The name of this blind man is Severus. He had been a butcher, but was obliged, by the loss of his sight, to give up his profession. S Ambrose, in his letter to Marcellina his sister, relates that many lame and sick persons were cured of divers maladies by touching the shrouds which covered the relics, and that devils, in possessed persons, confessed the glory of the martyrs, by declaring that they were not able to bear the torments which they suffered in their presence. He also observes, that the Arians at Milan, by denying the miracles of these martyrs, showed that they had a different faith from that of the martyrs; otherwise they would not have been jealous of their miracles; but this faith, says he, is confirmed by the tradition of our ancestors, which the devils are forced to confess, but the heretics deny.

Paulinus says, in his life of S. Ambrose: « To this
» very day, he (the blind man) lives as a religious
» in the same basilica which is called the Ambro-
» sian, whither the bodies of the martyrs were re-
» moved. » The very energy of Augustine's language shows his belief in what he says. But
the festival which the Church keeps on the 3rd of
August for the finding, in 415, of S. Stephen's relics is still more remarkable — they were discovered entirely by a dream several times repeated,
and more than ordinary miracles confirmed its
truth in divers places. Augustine's friend Evodius,
bishop of Uzalis, published two books recording the
miracles. [1] In his own church were perserved two
phials of the martyr's blood, and some fragments
of his bones, by which several miracles were performed, a list of which he had publicly read, and
as the name of the person cured was called out, he
was desired to go up to the apse that he might
be seen by the people. So that here is a case notorious enough, in which the Church, not satisfied
with solemnizing the martyrdom on the 26th of December, has appointed a special festival to celebrate a
dream and its results. If, as S. Gregory Nazianzen
energetically says, « such is the veneration of truth,

---

[1] See S. Alfric's Homilies, Vol. I. In festo Sti Stephani Proto-
martyris.

11

» that a little dust, or some small relic of old
» bones, or portions of hair, or shreds of a rag, or
» a stain of blood, are enough to have the same
» honour as the whole body, » the Church does
not shirk the marvellous in the discovery of relics; but celebrates together the dream vouchsafed
from God to do honour to His saint, and to bring
blessings on His people in the gifts of healing which
followed upon the finding of the relics. « *Magna et
in exiguâ sanctorum pulvere virtus.* »

Cyril, after having deposited the chest containing S. Clement's relics in the metropolitan church of
Pontus, set out for his mission to the Chazari, and,
after having converted that people, he returned to
Constantinople. On his way he passed again through
Pontus, and obtained from the bishop S. Clement's
relics, which he always carried about on his missions, and finally brought them to Rome when called thither together with his brother Methodius by
Nicholas I. Nicholas died before they arrived, and
was succeeded by Adrian II. who being informed
that they were not far distant from the city, and
had brought with them the relics of S. Clement,
went out to meet them together with the Roman
clergy and people.[1] Gaudentius, who assisted at

---

[1] « Papa Hadrianus exhilaratus valde cum clero et populo procedens
illis obviam honorifice eos cum sacris suscepit reliquiis. » Ms. Blaub

their deposition by the Pope's orders in S. Clement's church, [1] says that they were the instruments of many miracles. [2] In a short time after, Cyril died in Rome, and the Pope had him interred in the Vatican, with pontifical honours, in the marble sarcophagus he had prepared for himself, and sealed it with his own ring. The two brothers before setting out on their mission to the Bulgarians, had promised their pious mother that if either should die, the survivor would bring his remains to the monastery and there bury them with suitable honours. [3] Methodius, mindful of this promise, begged of Adrian to allow him to take back his brother's remains to his native country. The sequel we give from the Duchesne manuscript: « Although

---

[1] « Sepelierunt autem corpus sanctum in ecclesia quæ in nomine eius diu antea fuit constructa. » Ms. Blaub.

[2] « Cœperunt itaque ad præsentiam sanctarum reliquiarum per virtutem omnipotentis Dei sanitates mirabiles fieri, ita ut quovis languore quivis oppressus fuisset, adoratis pretiosis martyris reliquiis sacrosanctis, protinus salvaretur. Quapropter tam venerabilis apostolicus, quam et totius Romani populi universitas, gratias et laudes Deo maximas referentes, gaudebant et iucundabantur in ipso qui iis post tam prolixi temporis spatia concesserit in diebus illis sanctum et apostolicum virum, et ipsius Apostolorum principis Petri successorem in sede sua recipere, et non solum urbem totam, sed et orbem quoque totum Romani imperii signis eius ac virtutibus illustrari. » See Gaudentius in Rondinini, pag. 40.

[3] « Mater cum multis lacrymis obtestata est, ut si aliquem ex nobis antequam reverteremur obiisse contigerit, defunctum fratrem frater vivus ad monasterium eum reduceret, et ibidem illum digno et competenti honore sepeliret. » Ms. Blaub.

» it seemed somewhat grievous to himself, the Pope
» did not see fit to refuse a petition and desire of
» that kind, but having closed the body carefully
» in a marble chest which he sealed with his own
» ring, after seven days gave him leave to re-
» turn.   The Roman clergy taking counsel with
» the bishops and cardinals and nobles of the city,
» came together to the Pope and said: ' Venerable
» Father and Lord, it seems to us very unworthy
» that so great and magnificent a man, through
» whom our city and church has had the fortune
» to recover so precious a treasure, and whom God
» has designed of his gratuitous compassion to bring
» to us out of 'such distant foreign regions, and
» even to take to His kingdom from this place,
» should be allowed by us to be translated to other
» parts; but here rather would we have him hono-
» rably interred...   Then Methodius prayed that he
» might be laid in the church of blessed Clement,
» whose body found again by his great labour and
» zeal he had brought thither. The most holy
» Pontiff, assented to this petition, and, with a
» great concourse of the clergy and people, with
» great gladness and much reverence, they laid him,
» together with the marble chest in which the
» Pope had placed him before, in a monument,
» purposely prepared in the basilica of S. Clement,

» on the right side of the altar. »[1] That pious office having been performed, Methodius, with a heart laden with grief, set out alone from Rome and returned to Moravia to attend to the duties of his ministry. Having incurred the displeasure of the archbishops of Saltzburg and Metz, by celebrating Mass in the Sclavonian tongue, they, conjointly with their suffragans, addressed two letters to Pope John VIII, which are still extant, complaining of the novelty introduced by Methodius. The Pope, in 878, called Methodius, whom he styles archbishop, to Rome. He obeyed and gave ample satisfaction to his Holiness, who confirmed him in

1 « Tunc supradictus frater eius Methodius accedens ad Sanctum Pontificem (scilicet Hadrianum II), et procidens ad vestigia eius petiit sacrum corpus..... Non est visum apostolico, quamvis grave sibi aliquantulum videretur, petitioni et voluntati huiusmodi refragari; sed clausum diligenter defuncti corpus in locello marmoreo et proprio insuper sigillo signatum, post septem dies dat ei licentiam redeundi. Tunc Romanus clerus simul cum episcopis, cardinalibus et nobilibus urbis, consilio habito, convenientes ad Apostolicum cœperunt dicere: Indignum nobis valde videtur, Venerabilis Pater et Domine, ut tantum tamque magnificum virum per quem tam pretiosum thesaurum urbs et ecclesia nostra recuperare promeruit, et quem Deus ex tam longinquis regionibus et exteris ad nos ex sua gratuita pietate perducere, et adhuc etiam ex hoc loco ad sua regna est dignatus assumere, qualibet interveniente occasione, in alias patiamini partes transferri, sed hic potius placet honorifice tumuletur..... Tunc Methodius oravit ut in ecclesia Beati Clementis cuius corpus multo suo labore ac studio repertum huc detulit recondetur. Annuit huiusmodi petitioni Præsul sanctissimus, et concurrente cleri et populi maximâ frequentiâ cum ingenti lætitiâ et reverentiâ multâ, simul cum locello marmoreo, in quo pridem prædictus Papa condiderat, posuerunt in monumento ad id præparato in basilicâ Beati Clementis ad dexteram partem altaris ipsius. » Mr. Duches.

all the privileges of the archiepiscopal See of Moravia, exempted him from the jurisdiction of Saltzburg, and approved of the Sclavonian language in the liturgy and office of the Church, as it continues to be to this day. He lived to an advanced age, but the year of his death is uncertain. Dubravius affirms that he died in Rome and was buried with his brother in the church of S. Clement, where his relics wrought many miracles. The same is mentioned by Baronius in his notes on the Roman Martyrology; by Panciroli in his « *thesauris absconditis Almæ Urbis,* » and by Heinschenius, who, morever, adds, that some portion of his relics were sent to Moravia and enshrined in the collegiate church of Brunne.

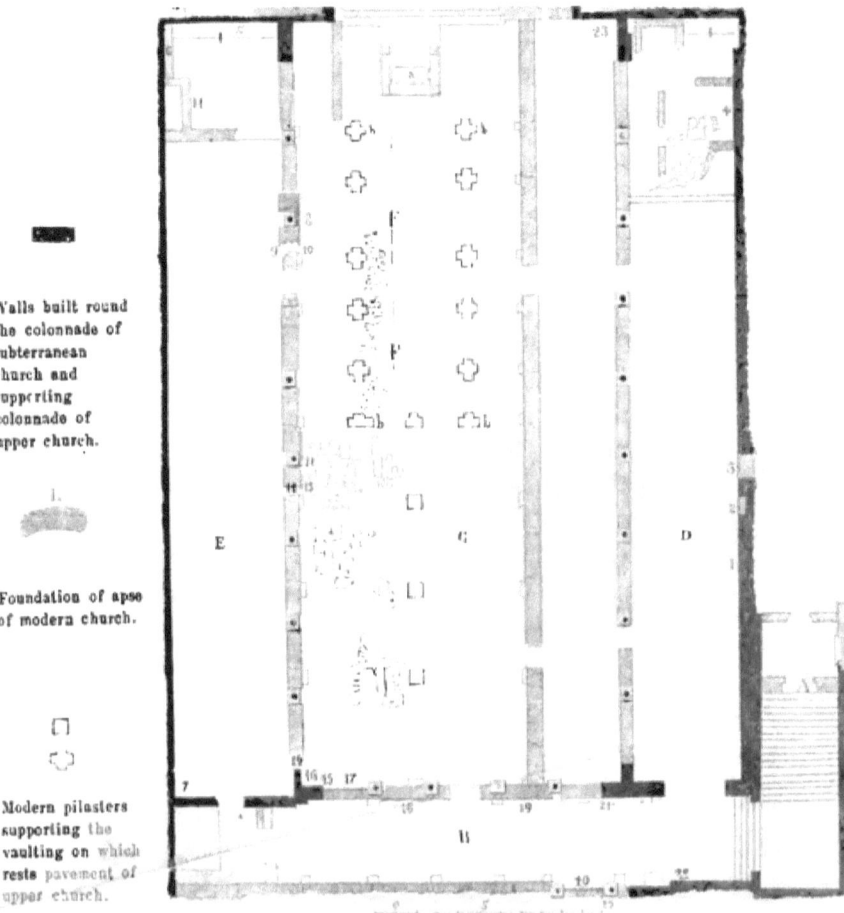

Walls built round the colonnade of subterranean church and supporting colonnade of upper church.

Foundation of apse of modern church.

Modern pilasters supporting the vaulting on which rests pavement of upper church.

GROUND PLAN OF SUBTERRANEAN BASILICA.

A. Entrance to the subterranean basilica. B. Narthex. C. Nave. D. North aisle. E. South aisle. FF. Site of ambones and marble enclosure of choir. GGG. Apse of subterranean basilica. H. Supposed tomb of S. Cyril. I I. Passage leading to the walls of the imperial, republican, and kingly periods. a. Altar. bbbb. Modern pilasters from which spring vaults supporting the pavement of modern church. 1. Fresco of the martyrdom of S. Catharine of Alexandria. 2. Niche of the Madonna. 3 Council-painting. 4. Mutilated figure of our Saviour. 5. Martyrdom of S. Peter. 6. Baptism by S. Cyril. 7. Miracle of Libertinus. 8. Installation of Clement by S. Peter. S. Clement celebrating mass, and Miracle of Sisinius. 9. 10. S. Antoninus. Daniel in the lions' den. 11. Life, death, and recognition of S. Alexius. 12. 13 S. Giles. S. Blaze. 14. S. Prosper. 15. Crucifixion. 16. The Marys at the Sepulchre, descent into Limbo, and marriage feast at Cana. 17. Assumption of the B. Virgin. 18. Translation of S. Clement's relics from the Vatican to his own church. 19. Miracle at the tomb of S. Clement. 20. Our Saviour blessing according to the Greek rite. 21. 22. Heads of unknown personages. 23. Our Saviour delivering Adam from Limbo.

SUBTERRANEAN BASILICA
OF S. CLEMENT.

CHAPTER I.

Basilica — Its meaning and purpose — Christian churches called basilicas, and why? — Pagan basilicas converted into churches — Basilican-design carried out in S. Clement's — Oratory of S. Clement replaced by a basilica in the 4th century — Diocletian's doings in Nicomedia — Churches restored to the Christians by Licinius and Constantine — *Memoria*, technical meaning of — *Memoria* of S. Clement.

THE Greek word Βασιλική — Basilica — means a royal hall, and in this sense it is used at the end of the Recognitions of S. Clement, where it is stated that Theophilus, the first citizen of Antioch, « domus suae ingentem basilicam ecclesiae nomine » consecravit, » for the reception of S. Peter's chair. It was a covered building, not like the forum, an open place surrounded by covered porticoes. The first great basilica in Rome was built, A. U. C. 568, by Cato the elder (Marcus Portius), whence it was called Portia; the second was called Opimia; the third, that of Paulus, built at so great expense,

and with such magnificence, that it was called Regia Pauli. Julius Caesar built, under the direction
of Vitruvius, the basilica Julia, which served not
only for the hearing of causes, but also for the
audience and reception of foreign ambassadors. It
was supported by one hundred marble columns in
four rows, and enriched with decorations of gold
and precious stones. Pagan Rome contained many
other basilicas also, such as the Emilian, the Ul-
pian, the Constantinian, etc. Ecclesiastical writers
generally use the word to signify a church of great
magnificence, and in that sense it is frequently employed by S. Ambrose, S. Augustine, S. Jerome, Si-
donius Apollinaris, and several other writers of
the fourth and fifth centuries. Some, with the
learned Jesuit Alexander Donati, and Rondinini,
assert that the ancient churches were called basilicas from their having been built in the style of
the Roman halls, while others maintain that those
halls were given to the Church for the celebration
of Christian rites, as may be collected from that
passage in Ausonius, where he tells the emperor
Gratian : « The basilicas, which heretofore were
» wont to be filled with men of business, are now
» thronged with votaries praying for your safety. »
These words clearly indicate that at least some of
the Roman basilicas were converted into Christian

churches. The design of the basilica was simple
and grand : oblong in form, with a nave and two
aisles, separated by lines of columns from which,
in many instances, sprung arches to support the
walls that sustained the roof. At the extreme end
opposite the door was a raised platform for the
tribune, and the apse in which it stood was often
ornamented with mosaics. The main entrance to
the building was through a portico supported by
five or seven columns according to the size of the
structure. All these arrangements are still preserved in the modern basilica of S. Clement, the
style of which, we presume, was borrowed from the
ancient one. Bottari,[1] Agincourt,[2] Raoul Rochette[3]
and Father Marchi[4] have maintained that the style
of the Christian basilica was borrowed from the
chapels in the catacombs. But these chapels were
rather modelled after the plan of the ancient Roman basilica, as it was natural for the Christians to
adopt the designs to which they were accustomed.

History,[5] as well as tradition, informs us that

---

[1] In his Roma Sotterranea, 6, 3, pag 75.
[2] Histoire de l'art par les monuments, liv. I, pag. 25.
[3] Tableau des catacombes.
[4] Monum. delle arti primitive, architettura.
[5] See Ciacconius, in Vita S. Clementis. Pompeo Ugoni, Sacre Sta-
zioni, Chiesa di S. Clemente. Rondinini, lib. II, c. 1. Panciroli, Tesori
nascosti dell'alma città di Roma. Baronius, etc.

Clement, shortly after his conversion, erected an
oratory in his own palace at the foot of the Coelian Hill, to which the catechumens and Christian
neophytes used to repair for instruction in the mysteries of the faith, to assist at the celebration of
the sacred rites, and eat of the bread of life. How
long this oratory existed after the exile and martyrdom of its founder there is no historical proof;
but judging from the veneration in which the primitive Christians held the abodes of the martyrs,
there is every reason to believe that it witnessed
and withstood all the persecutions which assailed
the Church from Nero to Diocletian, and that it
was replaced by a basilica of great size and magnificence in the beginning of the fourth century.
The first act of Diocletian's sweeping persecution,
in 302, was to level to the ground the lofty Christian church of Nicomedia, whilst he and Galerius
looked on from a balcony of the palace. The pre-
tence was that certain just men hindered the ora-
cles of Apollo; and the emperor Constantine records
this in an edict issued by him which is preserved
by Eusebius. « Thee I call to witness, most high
» God. Thou knowest how I being then very young,
» heard the emperor Diocletian inquiring of his
» officers who these just men were, when one of
» his priests made answer that they were the Chri-

» stians ; which answer moved Diocletian to draw
» his bloody sword, not to punish the guilty, but
» to exterminate the righteous whose innocence
» stood confessed by the divinities he adored. »
Lactantius says : « When they are sacrificing to
» their gods, if there stand by one who has his
» forehead *signed* (that is with the sign of the Cross),
» they cannot proceed with their sacrifices. *Nec*
» *responsa potest consultus reddere vates.* And this
» has been often the chief cause why wicked kings
» have persecuted righteousness. For certain of
» ours, who were in attendance on their masters
» as they were sacrificing, by making the sign upon
» their foreheads put to flight their gods, so that
» they could not descry in the bowels of their
» victims what was to happen. » He evidently
alludes to what actually happened in 302, when
Diocletian was sacrificing at Antioch ; who there-
upon compelled the whole court to come and sacrifice or be scourged, and all the soldiers to sacrifice or be disbanded. The palace of Nicomedia
was twice set on fire, and, like the burning of Rome
under Nero, it was attributed to Christian incen-
diaries. Eusebius says of the imperial edicts: « We
» have seen with our eyes the sacred temples le-
» velled to the ground and overturned from the
» foundations, the sacred books of divine scriptures

» burnt in the midst of the forum. » But all the churches were not destroyed, for he says that, under Licinius, many were levelled to the ground, and others were closed by the provincial Presidents; and he gives the decree of Licinius and Constantine ordering the churches to be restored to the Christian corporations. « And since the » same Christians themselves are known to have » had not only the places in which they used to » meet, but others too which did not belong to » each of them individually, but to the body, all » these according to the law commemorated by us » you will, without any doubt, order to be restored » to the same Christians, that is to each body and » assembly of them. » [1] It was, therefore, a necessity, at the peace of the Church, to repair the old and build new ones. « But now, » says the same Eusebius, « who can fully describe the num- » berless crowds of men daily taking refuge in the » faith of Christ ? Who the number of churches » in each city ; who the illustrious concourse of » people in the sacred *aedes ?* whence it happens » that now, not satisfied with the old buildings, » they erect spacious churches from their founda- » tions in every city. » And it would have been

---

[1] Book 10, c. 5.

strange if Constantine, who owed his empire to the miraculous sign of the Cross, and set it upon his statue in the imperial city, remained indifferent to these buildings. Again Eusebius says: « He sup- » plied God's churches with many benefits out of » his treasury, partly enlarging and raising aloft » the sacred buildings, partly adorning the august » oratories of the churches with very many votive » offerings. »

The preamble of the decree preserved by the same historian shews that it contemplated a general and public restoration. « Since up to this day im- » pious presumption and tyrannical violence have » persecuted the ministers of our Saviour, I hold » it certain and am evidently persuaded, that the » buildings of all the churches, either spoilt through » carelessness, or through fear of the assailing ini- » quity of the times, are less honourably cared for. » It is reasonable to suppose that the oratory of S. Clement was not forgotten in these Constantinian restorations. S. Jerome, in his catalogue of ecclesiastical writers, informs us that the church built in Rome keeps the memory of « his name to this day. » [1] We do not read of any other church having been ever

---

[1] « Nominis ejus memoriam, usque hodie Romae extructa ecclesia custodit. » S. Hieron. Cat. de script. ecclesiast.

dedicated to S. Clement in Rome except this one. Besides this, the word *memoria* has a technical meaning; it does not mean simply the remembrance of his name. S. Augustine writing against Faustus, the Manichean, says: « The Christian people frequent » the *memorials* of the martyrs, with religious so- » lemnity, both to excite imitation and that they » may share in their merits, and by their prayers » be helped; so however that we sacrifice to none of » the martyrs but to the very God of the martyrs, » although we set up altars in the *memorials* of the » martyrs. » [1] Again he says: « We build to our » martyrs not temples as to gods, but *memorials* as » to dead men whose spirits are living with God; » nor do we erect these altars on which to sacrifice » to martyrs, but to the one God, both of the mar- » tyrs and our own, we immolate the sacrifice. » [2] So the Pontifical Book records that Felix I. appointed Masses to be celebrated over the tombs and memorials of the martyrs; and that «Anacletus built » and put together the *memoria* of blessed Peter, » seeing that he had been ordained priest by blessed » Peter; and also other places, in which the bishops » might be buried: but where he himself also was

---

[1] Lib. 20, cap. 21.
[2] De Civitate Dei, lib. 22, c. 10.

» buried near the body of blessed Peter. »[1] A Pagan inscription records that « Servilius Troilus, » whilst living, provided the *memoria* for himself and » his, and for his wife Ulpia Successa etc. » And in another to the Diis Manibus and eternal memory of Q. Vereius Laurentinus, an incomparable man of Lyons, their son records that he laid the said Laurentinus and his wife in the *memoria* which Laurentinus had made for his very dear wife. The inscription at the beginning of this volume records the pagan *memoria* of Aurelius Syntomus. In the case of the martyr Pope S. Clement there was a special reason why the *memoria* should be styled the memorial of his name. The religious inclination of the Christians naturally led them to build the *memoria*, or *memorial* over the martyr's body.

When the body of S. Boniface was brought from the East in Diocletian's time, « Aglae, straightway » rising up, took, with her, clerics and religious men, » and thus with hymns, and spiritual canticles, and » all veneration went to meet the body and laid it » five stadia from the city of Rome till she could » build him a house worthy of his passion. »[2] About

---

[1] « Hic (Anacletus) memoriam Beati Petri construxit, et composuit, dum presbyter factus fuisset a Beato Petro, seu alia loca, ubi episcopi reconderentur sepulturae. Ubi autem et ipse sepultus est juxta corpus Beati Petri. »

[2] Ruinart, Acta Mart., p. 290.

the same time Primus and Felicianus were beheaded
at Nomentum (modern **Mentana**), **and thrown** into the
fields, but the Christians carried them into an arena-
rium and afterwards buried them near it. Miraculous
cures ensued; and when the persecution of the Pagans
had ceased the Christians built a basilica in their honour at the fourteenth milestone from Rome. The
martyrs Chrysanthus and Daria were buried on the
Salarian way. Many years after, A. D. 284, a multitude of Christians were keeping their birth day,
that is the anniversary of their martyrdom, when
Numerian walled them in, and threw down a mass
of gravel on them. « Among them were Diodorus
» the priest, Marianus the deacon, and very many
» clerics; but of the people neither the number nor
» names were collected. » Ciampini says that small
buildings were constructed over the cemeteries or
their boundaries, called confessions, *memorias*, and
martyria, (which has been illustrated by De Rossi's
recent discovery of the entrance to the cemetery of
S. Domitilla) and that the Acts of Chrysanthus and
Daria, quoted by Arringhi, show it. There Hilaria,
the relict of the martyr Claudius, is described as
placing the bodies of her sons in separate sarcophagi;
she is taken at prayer at the most holy confession,
and in the hands of her captors utters this beautiful
prayer: « Lord Jesus Christ, whom I confess with

» my whole heart, unite me to my children, whom
» from my womb thou didst call to martyrdom, »
and so expired. Her two maids buried her with the
most loving diligence, and built a little church over
her, for the place in which she died was her own
garden, and, from the time the saints had suffered
there, she made it her dwelling place. **But in**
the case of S. Clement, his relics remained at the
scene of his martyrdom until S. Cyril brought them
to Rome in the ninth century. His *memoria*, then,
was not of the body, but of some other title. The
fifth council of Carthage [1] forbids *aedes* to be built
for martyrs except there be on the spot either the
body, or some certain relics, or where the origin of
some habitation, or possession, or passion of the martyr, has been transmitted from a most trustworthy
source « fidelissimâ origine. » The memory of Clement's name, preserved in the church mentioned by
S. Jerome, was that of his traditional dwelling place.
This saint and doctor (Jerome), to whom the Church
owes the Latin version of the Scriptures, died in 420,
only a hundred years after the Christian religion was
made free throughout the empire, and we **may well**
suppose that the basilica, which had been raised over
S. Clement's paternal house at the base of the hill

---

[1] Can. 14.

to which the Etruscan leader Coelius Vibenna had given his name,[1] would not have escaped that indefatigable restorer of shrines, S. Damasus, if it had need of repairs. De Rossi argues, from the collar [2] of a fugitive slave, that S. Clement's had its « proprio clero, » that is its own clergy, or regularly constituted body of clergy, in the middle of the fourth century. The brand of slavery was abolished by Constantine, and such collars as that above mentioned substituted instead. Upon this thin bronze-plate, referred to by De Rossi, is engraved, on one side: « Hold me for I have fled, and recal (return) » me to Victor the acolyte of the *dominicum* of Cle-» ment, »[3] together with the Constantinian mono-

---

[1] The Coelian hill lies to the east of the Palatine, and, according to Tacitus (*Annal.*, liv. IV, cap. 65) its ancient name had been Querquetulanus, from the oaks that covered it ; and that subsequently it was called Coelian from Coelius Vibenna a leader of the Etruscans who came to the assistance of Rome, and was settled on that hill by Tarquin: or who, according to Varro (*De Ling. Lat.*, lib. IV), came to assist the Romans against the Sabines, and was located there by Romulus. The ancients distinguish the *Mons Coelius* from the *Coeliolus*, (Varro, *De Ling. Lat.*, lib. IV), and antiquarians do not agree as to the precise place of the latter. It is certain that the Coeliolus was in the second Region of the City, and Nardini and Nibby assign it to the eminence on which the church of S.Gregory now stands. Under the church of SS.John and Paul are ancient quarries of tufo lithoide, which supplied building material for the walls of Servius Tullius.

[2] In the museum of Lelio Pasqualini, a contemporary of Baronius. De Rossi, in the Bollettino di Archeologia Cristiana N. 4, proves that the above mentioned collar is of the time of Constantine.

[3] Fabbretti, Inscr., p. 522, n. 365.

gram of Christ. On the obverse side the inscription
is « I have fled from Euplogius ex-prefect of the
city.» This inscription is rudely scratched, as if with
the point of a knife, and below it is the monogram
of Christ encircled by a laurel crown having ᵖₑ on
one side, and a pal.n branch on the other.

TENE ME Q

VIA FVG . ET REB

OCA ME VICTOR

·I ACOLIT

O A DOMIN

ICV CLEM

ENTIS

☧

FVGI EVP

LOGIO EX .

PRF . VRB .

For our part, we will hope that, if Victor of S. Clement's kept a serf at all, he had him, as S. Paul says
of Onesimus : « Not now as a slave, but instead of
» a slave, a most dear brother , especially to me
» but how much more to thee » (Philemon) « both in
« flesh and in the Lord. » [1]

---

[1] S. Paul to Philem., v. 16.

CHAPTER II.

We will not infer the primitive respectability of our Clementine clergy from the circumstance mentioned at the end of the preceding chapter, but rather from the fact that Renatus, the priest deputed by Leo the Great, and who fled from the Eutychian *latrocinale* of Ephesus, twenty years after S. Jerome's death, was titular of S. Clement's. Or from the fact that Pope Zozimus chose this church in 417 for his sentence of condemnation of the Pelagian Celestius : « We sat, » says the Pope, « in
» the basilica of S. Clement, who imbued with the
» discipline of blessed Peter, with such a teach-
» er amended ancient errors, and had such sure
» confirmation as even to consecrate by martyr-
» dom the faith he had learned and taught ; viz,
» that for the salutary castigation the authority
» of so great a priest might be an example in

» present knowledge. » [r] Or because the beggar, S. Servulus, lived and died in the porch of this church, and no less a man than Gregory the Great found time, amidst the incursions of the Lombards, the storms and earthquakes on all sides, and his missionary engagements for the conversion of the Angli, to come to this basilica and preach his panegyric. We should conclude that both Church and clergy were flourishing in 600. Two hundred years after, whatever may have been the cause, the basilica was falling into ruin. Anastasius the librarian tells us that Adrian I, who died in 795, restored the roof. Stephen III, who died in 757, restored the basilica of blessed Laurence *super Sanctum Clementem*, which seems to have been the chapel *Sancta Sanctorum*, at the Lateran palace, which Anastasius, in his lives of the Pontiffs, frequently calls the basilica of S. Laurence and S. Theodore. Of Adrian he says : « The title of blessed » Clement, which was even about to fall and be » laid in ruins , of the third region, he made

---

[r] « Resedimus *in Sancti Clementis basilicâ*, qui imbutus Beati Petri » apostoli disciplinis tali magistro veteres emendasset errores, ratosque » profecto habuisset, ut fidem, quam didicerat et docuerat, etiam mar- » tyrio consecraret, scilicet ut salutiferam castigationem tanti sacerdotis » auctoritas praesenti cognitione esset exemplo. » Epist. S. Zosimi ad Africanos.

» anew. » One of the columns of the original basilica is broken, and perhaps the brick pier in which it and several other pillars of the old church are imbedded, are Adrian's work. Certainly that Pope, who sent his legates to the council against the Iconoclasts, which in its seventh session defined that not crosses only (which Iconoclasts admitted as do the Lutherans) should be set up in churches, and on the walls and ceilings of houses, but holy images and pictures be honoured with incense and candles, like the gospels and other holy things, would have been pleased to see depicted, on one of these piers, S. Clement saying mass and the miracle of Sisinius. His successor Leo III is said to have given several splendid vestments to S. Clement's. Perhaps they were antependiums, or frontals, such as that which Anastasius says was given by Leo IV to another church, « and upon the altar » itself he made a vestment shining throughout » with white pearls, and, on the right and left, » gemmed tablets having, with disks of gold round » about, the distinguished name of the bishop » written in full. » S. Leo IV deserved to have his portrait painted in the fresco of our Lady's Assumption in our basilica. He shewed that he knew how to use the sign of the Cross; for by it he extinguished the great fire that broke out in the Vatican quarter of the Borgo. He might well have said, with David : « Blessed is the Lord » my God, who teacheth my hands for the battle » and my fingers for war. » [1] He gave no countenance to the paradox that the Church is not to make use of the secular arm against Church robbers ; for after the Saracens had carried off the silver with which Honorius I, in 626, had covered the confession of S. Peter and the doors of the basilica, he fortified that quarter of the city ; and hearing that they were on their march to plunder Porto, he went down himself to Ostia to meet the Neapolitan troops. He gave them his blessing and the holy communion, and they totally routed the infidels. He restored the doors of S. Peter's and enriched them with many silver bas-reliefs. To our church of S. Clement he gave six silver salvers, cornucopia-lamps, a silver basin and the *regnum* of gold which used to hang over the high altar. When Leo died, in 855, the basilica, restored but six years before, must have been in good order. Then came that memorable event, in 867, when the apostle of the Sclavonians, S. Cyril, arrived in Rome with the relics of S. Clement, beside which his own body was one day to be laid. The mi-

---

[1] Ps. 143.

racles which followed on the translation of the relics of these saints, and the devotion they excited among the Romans, would naturally lead one to suppose that the pictures relating to them were painted soon after this event, rather than that the piety of individuals was rekindled at a later period. Whether they were painted upon the brick pier, which may be attributed to Adrian I, or on piers constructed at a later period, can only be conjecture. It is a matter of great regret that these paintings of an age from which modern European history may be said to date, the age of Charlemagne of France, and Alfred of England, should be now so damaged, and the history of some of them so obscure. The freshness of their colours when first discovered, shews that the basilica was, for some reason or other, abandoned and purposely filled up, and the modern church built upon it whilst its walls were yet in a highly decorated state. We can suggest but two reasons for this. The great earthquake of 896 which shook the old pillars of S. John Lateran's, and may have reached this church; or the destruction of this quarter of the city from the Lateran to the Capitol by Robert Guiscard, who came to Rome, in 1084, to rescue the great monk of Cluni, Gregory VII, who died the following year at Salerno, saying: « I have loved justice and hated

» iniquity; therefore I die in a strange land. » A thorough Italian, Tuscan by birth, educated at Rome in the monastery of our Lady on the Aventine, consecrated Pope on S. Peter's day, wounded and imprisoned on Christmas night by a Roman baron, deposed by a mock council, confronted by an excommunicated antipope, besieged by foreigners in S. Angelo, at last he was driven into exile to end his days in that city where lies the body of the Evangelist whose Gospel ends with our Lord's words: « All power is given to me in heaven and on earth. » Going therefore teach ye all nations, baptizing » them in the name of the Father, and of the Son, » and of the Holy Ghost, teaching them to observe » all things whatsoever I have commanded you: » and behold I am with you all days, even to the » consummation of the world. »[1] S. Gregory was a true type of the contest between Christ's Vicar and the ambition of temporal princes. Probably it was in his age that our venerable basilica disappeared, and as, though the stones of old Rome would speak again, it appears, once more, in the pontificate of Pius IX.

The basilica disappeared and was forgotten, so that, notwithstanding the industry of Roman archaeo-

---

[1] Matt. c. XXVIII, v. 18, 19, 20.

logists, every record and tradition relating to it was
referred to the comparatively modern church built
upon its ruins. However the basilican style was followed in all its details in the latter, which caused
it to be regarded by all archaeologists as the most
perfect example existing of the early Christian basilica. In fact any one who visits the subterranean
basilica, will see that the upper church is simply a
reproduction of it, though on a somewhat smaller
scale. But a particular study of the topography of
this part of the city, as well as a minute inspection
of the marbles in the choir, induced the writer of
these pages to suspect, so far back as 1848, that the
church spoken of by S. Jerome, Pope Leo the Great,
Symmachus, and Gregory the Great, could not be
that described by Ugoni, Panciroli, Rondinini, Nibby
and others : and, therefore, that the former must be
either beneath, or somewhere near the latter. Just
as these conjectures were about to be tested, Rome
became the theatre of an unprovoked and sacrilegious revolution, which caused unheard of abominations within, and the most shocking desolation without, its walls. The contemplated researches were,
therefore, deferred, but not abandoned. In progress
of time, what had been but conjectures ripened into
convictions, and, in 1857, the researches were commenced by opening a passage through a chamber

containing some remains of ancient walls, and thence through another, quadrangular and vaulted. Here, having made an aperture in the wall, and removed a quantity of rubbish to the depth of fourteen feet, we discovered three columns standing erect, *in situ*, and some fragments of frescoes representing the martyrdom of S. Catharine of Alexandria, and a group of nineteen heads with an equally poised balance and the inscription, written vertically: « Stateram auget modium justum. » These discoveries removed all doubt, as to the site and existence of the primitive basilica.

It would be tedious to give a detailed account of the progress of the excavations year by year, and the difficulty of removing the immense mass of compacted rubbish with which the abandoned basilica had been purposely filled up to make a foundation for the church above, without damaging the walls and whole structure of that church. In fact some parts of the upper church had no foundation but that rubbish, more than one hundred and fifty thousand cart-loads of which had to be carried up the same way that Maximin made the martyrs Thraso and Saturninus carry gravel from the arenaria to build Diocletian's baths, that is in baskets on the shoulders. Suffice it to say that the architect Cavaliere Fontana succeeded admirably, and without

a single accident, in supporting the upper church on
brick vaults and arches; and that the lower basilica
is made easy of access in its whole extent. From
what was hitherto the sacristy of the modern church,
a wide and admirably constructed staircase, of
twenty three steps of Alban peperino, made in 1866,
descends at once to the floor of the subterranean basilica. Here the first object that attracts the attention of the visitor is the inscription engraved on a
marble slab, which we give in the next page.

PATERNAS . AEDES

A . D . CLEMENTE . APOSTOLORVM . PRINCIPIS . DISCIPVLO . ET . SVCCESSORE

SACRO . RELIGIONIS . CVLTVI . DEVOTAS

PETRI . PAVLI . BARNABAE . APOSTOLORVM . PRECIBVS

BINIS . GREGORII . MAGNI . CONCIONIBVS

ET . DEBELLANDAE . PELAGIANAE . HAERESI

S . ZOSIMI . PONT . CONCILIO . CELEBRES

VENERANDIS . LYPSANIS . SANCTORVM

CLEMENTIS . PONT . FLAVII . CLEMENTIS . VIRI . CONS . IGNATII . ANTIOCHENI . MM .

SERVVLI . C . NECNON . CYRILLI . ET . METHODII . SLAVORVM . APOST . DITATAS

TEMPORVM . INCVRIA . LONGO . SAECVLORVM . **TRACTV** . IGNOTAS

FR . JOSEPH . MVLLOOLY . ORD . PRAED . **PROVINCIAE** . HIBERNIAE

HVIVS . COENOBII . PRAESES

FELICITER . DETEXIT . **MENSE . SEPT** . MDCCCLVII

AGGESTAS . MACERIES . REMOVERE . INSTITVIT

SACRAE . ARCHAEOLOGIAE . COETVS . REM   ALIQVAMDIV . CONTINVAVIT

RELICTAM . PRAESES . RESVMPSIT . PERFECIT

SCALAS . AD . HYPOGEVM . CONDIDIT

ARCVS . ET . FORNICES . SVSTINENDAE . SVPERIORI . **BASILICAE . EREXIT**

PECVNIA . AD . TANTVM . OPVS . CONLATA

A . PIO . IX . PONT . OPT . MAX .

ET . MVNIFICIS . VNIVERSI . ORBIS . LARGITORIBVS

PIVS . IX . PONTIFEX . OPTIMVS . MAXIMVS

HANC . DIVI . CLEMENTIS . MEMORIAM

NON . SINE . DEI . NVMINE . INVENTAM

QVATER . INVISIT

AN . DOM . MDCCCLXVIII .

On the walls to the right and left are inscriptions by S. Damasus, and of the time of his successor Pope S. Siricius. Of the Damasine inscription only a few letters remain, so few that their meaning cannot be even guessed at, owing to the difficulty, or rather the impossibility of supplying those that are wanting. They belong to three different metrical lines, and De Rossi thinks that, at least, one of them forms a part of some hexameter verses composed by that Pope in honour of S. Clement. The genius of that most eminent of living archaeologists has supplied in italics the letters that are wanting in the other inscription, which is as follows:

Salvo SIR*icio ep*ISC*opo* ECCL*esiae s.* GA . . . . [1]
PRESBYTER *s.* MARTYR*i Clementi h*OC
VOLVIT dedicatum (?)

The pieces of marble containing the letters in Damasine character were found in different parts of the upper and lower churches, and the inscription in a single line shows that they must have originally stood side by side, probably forming a screen similar to that in the *Chorus cantorum.* Thus we have a record of some restoration made in our basilica

---

[1] Gabinus, or Gallus, or Gaudentius.

by Pope S. Siricius who governed the Church from 384 to 398.

On a marble bracket near the foot of the stairs is a mutilated statue of S. Peter as the « Good Shepherd. » It was found in the old Oratory of S. Clement, and so far as we know it is unique in Rome. Bas-reliefs representing S. Peter in that quality have been found in the Catacombs and on sarcophagi, but no statue. It is well finished, and of a very good style of art. The drapery is also very fine. The crisped beard and hair, and furrowed cheeks, so well known to Archaeologists as characteristic of S. Peter, leave no doubt as to whom it represents. He is carrying the lost sheep on his shoulders. A little farther on are plaster casts of two columns which formerly stood at the high altar in this subterranean church. The foliage, flowers, and birds with which they are decorated are admirably chiseled. The capitals are very handsome, and on the rim of one of them is the following inscription: † Serbus † Dni † Mercurius PB † Sce Ecclesiae Catholicae off. The originals are in the upper church. We shall refer to them hereafter.

The basilica consists of a nave, two aisles, and a narthex. Its entire length is 146 feet. The nave is 52 feet 3 $\frac{1}{2}$ inches wide; the width of the northern aisle is 18 feet 6 inches, and that of the

southern 13 feet 10 inches; the narthex, which
runs the whole width of the church is 91 feet 8
inches. From the narthex we enter the north
aisle which is divided from the nave by a line of
seven columns of various marbles imbedded in a
wall, built, for the most part, of the *debris* of
ruined temples and broken statues. These columns
are twelve feet high, and eighteen inches in diameter; and all stand in their original positions.
The first, of *verde antique*, is of marvellous beauty
and very remarkable for its vermillion spots vary-
ing its surface of vivid green and pure white: it is
considered an unique specimen of its kind in Italy.
The second is Parian; the third and fourth are
of Numidian marble; two others of Oriental granite, and the seventh of *settebasi* of the rarest quality. Some of these pillars have been stript of
their capitals, others retain them, and, although
all are valuable and beautiful, they lack unifor-
mity both in height and diameter, which shows
that they must have been taken from still older edi-
fices, perhaps porticoes or Pagan temples. Springing from these columns are arches of early construction supporting the northern wall of the upper
church. The columns seem to stand on a uniform
plinth, running along the aisle, but, in fact, it is
a brick wall of the imperial period. The wall

opposite this line of pillars was once entirely covered with paintings of which only some fragments
remain. We admit that we do not possess the
necessary technical skill to give an artistic description of them as they stand, nor have we much
confidence in assigning the age or date of such
pictures by mere comparison of hands and styles,
seeing the very scanty materials even the learned in art possess for that purpose, and the egre-
gious mistakes which have been made in classifying
pictures so modern as those of the Italian schools.
We will rather suggest thoughts naturally arising
from the subjects themselves, and where we fail,
those more skilful than we can easily correct us.

These fragments have more of what is called
the Byzantine style than the other pictures of the
church. The subjects also are more ancient than
the rest, with the exception of the group of scriptural subjects at the west end of the south aisle
and the heads in the narthex. Hence if we knew
that the wall was repaired by Pope Adrian, we might
suppose that they were painted by pupils of artists who had fled, some seventy years before, from
the image-breaking persecution of Leo the Isaurian
at Constantinople. But the niche of the Madonna,
the most Byzantine of all, was evidently broken
through these pictures after they were painted.

S. Gregory the Great had been at Constantinople, before 590, and it is not probable that the religious pictures which he sent to various missionary countries were all imported from the East, or that the city of the Popes was devoid of native artists. Whenever they were painted the modern plan of dividing the episodes of one subject into divers panels by gilt rectangular frames was not adopted. One large decorated border incloses a group separated only by the discrimination of the spectator's eye. In that of S. Catharine there were six. The eye soon becomes accustomed to this arrangement; and the perpendicular lettered inscriptions introduced in some places interfere much less with the general effect than the horizontal scrolls or tablets held by angels, in productions of a later age. The anxiety of these church artists was to tell the story well, because it had a religious interest, and they chose rather to write the saint's name beside him than that the beholder should make a mistake, or be forced to get by heart some conventional system of emblems that he might make out, among the well-draped muscular figures before him, which was which.

Alexandria was as dear to Pagans as Mecca is to Mahommedans; for there was the great temple and monstrous idol of Serapis. In the reign of Julian the Apostate the Pagans again used Pagan standards in the army, and boasted that they would exterminate the Christians. Thirty years after, in May 392, the emperor of the West, Valentinian II, was strangled, in his palace-gardens on the banks of the Rhone, by his Pagan general, Arbogastes, who set up Eugenius as emperor. That same year the Patriarch of Alexandria, clearing out a deserted temple of Bacchus, by a rescript from Theodosius to convert it into a Christian church, found infamous figures in the *adyta*, which he caused to be exposed for public reprobation. The Pagans rose and martyred many Christians. In 394, Theodosius, with difficulty, defeated Eugenius. He ordered the idol of Serapis at Alexandria to be burnt, and two churches were built on the site of his temple. All over Egypt the temples were demolished. In those of Alexandria the cruel mysteries of Mithras were discovered, and, in the secret *adyta*, the heads of many children which had been cut off, mangled, and superstitiously painted. For the Church, Alexandria had another interest. It was a great school of Chistian philosophy. The method of the blind reading by touch was taught there; for Dydimus, born in 308, and deprived of sight in childhood, got his letters cut in wood, and became so great a scholar, especially of the

scriptures, that he was set over the school, and
S. Jerome profited by his teaching. The cemeteries that contained the memories of the martyrs
to which, on the abatement of Diocletian's persecution, the faithful of Alexandria crowded, are now
known. The most frequented was that of S. Peter
their archbishop, situated in a suburb, where, on
account of the martyrs buried there, he had built
a church to the Mother of God, Mary ever Virgin.
One of these cemeteries contains a painting, perhaps
a restoration of the seventh century, of the miraculous feeding with loaves and fishes, in which
S. Andrew has his square nimbus and our Lady
is indicated by name. The words « eating of the
» eulogia of Christ, » found in this painting, refer
to the well known passage of S. Paul: « The cha-
» lice of the *eulogia*, which we bless is it not the
» communion of the blood of Christ ? And the
» bread, which we break, is it not the partaking
» of the body of the Lord ? » [1] S. Peter excommunicated Arius whom he had ordained deacon :
and the patriarch S. Cyril, who died in 412, the
great opponent of Nestorius, who denied the Incarnation, constantly uses the word *eulogia* for
the sacramental species. S. Peter, whom Eusebius

---

1 Corinth., chap. 10, v. 16.

styles « a doctor of religion, and a divine ornament of bishops, » was beheaded with three of
his priests, when Maximin Daza, who had been
named Caesar by his uncle Maximin Galerius, came
to Alexandria, and renewed the persecution in 331.
The visitor who has admired in the chapel of S. Catharine of Alexandria, in the upper church of S. Clement, Masaccio's paintings of her life and sufferings,
has there a proof of the tenacity of Catholic traditional devotion ; for it is only a repetition of the
same subject in the old basilica ; and the rude
picture of her martyrdom in the subterranean
church is perhaps the oldest representation of it in
existence. The great emperor Basil says she
was of royal blood, so true a scholar that she
confuted and converted the philosophers sent by
Maximin to argue with her; they were cast into
a fire and then beheaded. Some think that she
was the Christian lady mentioned by Eusebius, illustrious for birth, wealth and singular learning,
who resisted the brutal debauchery of the Caesar.
Maximin seeing her ready to die would not behead
her, but seized her estates and banished her. Tradition says that our Saint was placed bound, between
four wheels set with sharp spikes, to be torn asun-
der, but was freed by an angel loosening the cords;
that while in prison she converted the persecutor's

wife and his general Porphirius, both of whom were
martyred. She was always honoured by the Greek
Church. When the Saracens oppressed the Christians of Egypt, in the eighth century, her body
was translated to the monastery on mount Sinai
in Arabia, first built by the empress S. Helen, and
beautified afterwards by the emperor Justinian, as
several old inscriptions and mosaics testify. There
is an admirable composition, by Masaccio, in the
upper church of S. Clement, of her entombment
by angels. [1]   S. Paul the hermit of mount Latra
in Bythinia, who died in 956, had great devotion
to her.   In the eleventh century a monk of Sinai,
coming for the yearly alms of Robert duke of Normandy, left some of her relics at Rouen.

---

[1] Monks were called « angels » and their life the « angelic » life.
May not some of these legends of angels refer to the early coenobites
and hermits? Not that I mean to deny in any way that angels have
been employed for such purposes, — witness what S. Paul says about
the body of Moses, and S. Michael contending for it with Satan.

CHAPTER III.

NORTH AISLE.

MARTYRDOM OF S. CATHARINE OF ALEXANDRIA.

On the wall to the right, a little beyond the
second arch, as we enter this aisle, is a painting,
representing the martyrdom of the illustrious virgin S. Catharine of Alexandria, the colours of which
are nearly obliterated. In the wide border, on the
left, at the top, is an angel. The first subject
is a private audience before Maximin, who is seated between two guards; a philosopher occupies
a lower seat. Maximin and the philosopher are
gesticulating with much animation; the Saint,
richly robed, stands intrepidly addressing them.
The middle compartment is destroyed; the stoles
of one or two figures remaining on the left of
it indicate ecclesiastics. On the right the let-
ters $_\Lambda^K$ identify the Saint, who is tied, almost naked,
to the wheel, which a man is turning, while two

others seem to hold her against it. The judge is seated in advance of the crowd, and a person, perhaps one of the discomfited philosophers, turns away. Three angels, over the judge's head, are flying towards her. Perhaps their number, besides the picturesque effect, is intended to refer to the blessed Trinity, as her contemporary Arius denied the divinity of Christ, whose angel delivered her. The three lower subjects are scarcely visible. On the left she seems haranguing, perhaps, while in prison. In the centre is her beheading, before the judge. On the right a crowd of persons appears advancing, past two columns of a temple in the back ground, towards an elevated figure, but the subject cannot be made out. While standing before these old walls pictured with the cruel sufferings of the martyrs, with the Councils of the Church, the lives of her Saints, and viewing a Christian oratory changed into a pagan den of Mithras, our thoughts revert to the last throes of the declining empire. Nothing can be more dramatic than the closing scene of the Pagan Caesars. Diocletian was forced by Galerius to abdicate, and he died in 314, hearing that Constantine had thrown down his statues with those of Maximin and Maxentius. His own slaves could not bear the stench from the corpulent Galerius swarming with vermin, and he died wretchedly, after publishing an edict

in favour of the Christians, whom, during his reign,
he so barbarously persecuted. We have seen the
boy Constantine present at Diocletian's sacrifices,
and Galerius kept him a hostage for his father Constantius, ruling in Gaul, Spain and Britain. The
young prince ran away, avoided pursuit by starting
at night, and, travelling with all speed, he reached
his dying father at York in 306. Licinius, whom
Galerius had made his imperial colleague, extirpated
the whole of Diocletian's family, beheading his mother and widow, and casting their bodies into the
sea. Then came that famous march of Constantine
on Rome: the Cross in the sky: « In this shalt thou
» conquer; » Maxentius in his flight perishing in
the Tiber, and Maximin Daza, compelled by Licinius to repeal his edicts against the Christians, flying
to Tarsus in 313, and dying a withered and dried
up skeleton in acute torment, deprived of sight, his
eyes starting from their sockets.

COUNCIL-PICTURE.

Passing the niche of the Madonna for a moment,
we find the Greek cross in the medallion at the
top of the border of the next picture; and at the
foot a hart springing. « Flee away, o my beloved;
» and be like to the roe, and to the young hart

« upon the mountain of aromatical spices. » [1] The subject in the centre of the picture below the window is well nigh totally destroyed. Judging from the crowd arranged in rows, it represented some public spectacle or assembly. On the left are many female heads: some seem religious, and others have their hair gathered in decoraded nets. There are also tonsured men of the Latin rite. On the right the figures appear to be Eastern, and one more prominent than the rest, is not unlike a Greek emperor in one of the diptychs. Over what seems the entrance there is the balance with the words « stateram auget; » and over the large font below it « modium justum. » A female figure is next to the font, and a lighted taper appears behind it. The words so often quoted by Saint Clement recur to the mind: « The city set upon the mount cannot » be hid; nor do they light a candle and put it » under the modium, but upon a candelabrum that » it may shine to all who are in the house, that » those who are entering in may see the light. » Or those assigned to him in his first epistle to S. James, where he directs the priests, instead of secular judges, to hear the business of the brethern, and adds: « Weights, measures, steelyards, keep

[1] Canticles, chap. VIII, v. 14.

» most accurate for every place: deposits faithfully
» restore. » Possibly the subject may have been
the condemnation of the Pelagians by S. Zosimus.
Perhaps the very circumstance that the niche containing the Immaculate Mother of God full of grace,
and Abraham's sacrifice, the type of the necessity
of atonement for original sin, was broken into the
border of the picture, may favour this idea. Such
heresies usually came from the East. The Pelagians
held Unitarian errors, denying original sin, and the
necessity of divine grace against which they extolled
the philosophical virtues of the Pagans; hence the
most direct answer was the divine provision by
which the Virgin was filled with grace that she
might never be subject, in birth or life, to the least
contagion of sin. After the destruction of Jerusalem, Ebion and Cerinthus taught that Christ was
only a greater angel, born of Joseph and Mary like
other men, but surpassing them in virtue and wisdom.
What the Apostle who received our Lord's Mother
from the Cross thought of this doctrine is appa-
rent from the anecdote which Irenaeus heard from
the lips of S. John's disciple Polycarp. That S. John
going to bathe at Ephesus hurried forth from the
bath without bathing, exclaiming: « Let us fly for
» fear the bath fall, as Cerinthus the enemy of truth
» is within. » And that Polycarp, when Marcion

once met him and said: « Dost thou know us? » replied: « I know thee as the firstborn son of Satan. » To Judaizing Christians the errors spoken of above were readily suggested by isolated texts. For instance « the Jews murmured at him, because he » said: ' I am the living bread which came down » from heaven; , and they said: ' Is not this Jesus » the son of Joseph, whose father and mother we » know? How then said he: ' I came down from » heaven? ' » [1] which evidently raises a difficulty, continuing to this day, in the consecration of the blessed Eucharist, for all who deny the teaching authority of the Church. Pope, S Victor, A. D. 192, 202, excommunicated the Ebionites, Theodosius the banker, who pretended that Melchisedec was greater than Christ, and another Theodosius, the apostate tanner of Byzantium, who asserted that he was nothing more than a mere man who called himself the Son of God. About the year 400 the Syrian Rufinus at Rome taught his errors to Pelagius. They were of the same bitter root; for evidently if Adam's sin did not prejudice posterity, and children are now born in the same state in which they would have been if Adam had never sinned, and if they, dying

---

[1] S. John, VI, 41, 42.

THE BLESSED VIRGIN AND CHILD

without baptism, inherit eternal life, there was
no occasion for the atonement of a divine mediator. The African S. Augustine, who had expe-
rienced the call of divine grace, and personally felt
that without it he could not rise from the degrada-
tion of carnal sin, wrote vigorously against Pelagius. S. Germanus of Auxerre, whose life was a
perpetual miracle of grace, who on his way to Britain, as Legate of Pope Celestine, blessed S. Genevieve then a child of seven years, and foretold the
sanctity which made her the patron saint of Paris,
silenced the British Pelagians at Verulan by word
and miracle in 429. When Celestine's successor Zosimus sent his excommunication of Pelagius and Celestius to Africa and the East, the emperors Honorius and Theodosius published an edict throughout
the empire banishing those heresiarchs, and condemning to perpetual banishment and confiscation
of their properties, all who maintained their doc-
trines.

NICHE OF THE MADONNA.

We approach the little niche, between the two
pictures we have just noticed, with feelings of reverence, for that little recess (six feet by three,
sunk eighteen inches into the wall) contains the
representatives of the Christian world : Christ in

his incarnate nature and in his glory, his Immaculate Mother, angels, virgins, martyrs, saints, men
instruments of his providence and heirs of his promise. These paintings were at first concealed by
others, much ruder, painted upon a coat of plaster
which fell away. The Byzantine school is here
strongly marked, particularly in the overloaded
jewelled head-dress of our Lady, and the decorations
of her throne. The artist knew very well that
this exuberance of ornament, and the elongated arm
supporting the divine child on her lap were not
natural. Let us try to see the spirit of his composition in that mystic art of which Angelico of
Fiesole was the best exponent. In the crown of
the niche a medallion shows our Lord ever youthful
and radiant with glory. On the sides are heads
of the virgin-martyrs S. Catharine of Alexandria
and S. Euphemia of Chalcedon ; and beneath them
respectively Abraham brandishing a sword to strike
and an angel shielding Isaac. The very difference
between the heads of S. Catharine and S. Euphemia
with hair flowing down from their jewelled crowns,
figuring human nature decked with the jewels of virginity and martyrdom, and the countenance of our
Lady enshrined in the mass of ornaments without a
single lock appearing, typical of human nature totally
transformed by grace, indicates the limner's scope.

Our Lady is the chief figure immediately opposite the eye, and occupying the whole front of the niche. Abraham's sacrifice is painted on the side of the niche. The painter does not give a naked Isaac tied up like a bundle and cast upon a heap of sticks. There seems a mystic meaning in the figure of Abraham, which when first discovered had a chalice of blood, in its left hand, since fallen away, and a shower of blood seems falling from a circle above his head. Whether it was an allusion to the passion, or a type of the avenging and destroying angel, whilst the opposite angel of healing, taking Isaac by the hands, points to the true child of sacrifice upon his Mother's lap, we do not say. We are so accustomed to the mere natural outward form, from the days of Raphael downwards, that we are apt to miss the interior life. Not so the Fathers of the Church. They speak of the Mother of God with a tenderness which could not, and ought not to be found in earthly love. They regard her in a triple sense, as the human creature prepared by the perfect union of her will with God's to receive His gifts: as the divine seat richly prepared by grace: and as the Mother, sustaining the human nature she had communicated to her Son. It would also be true to say that they look upon her, after her Assumption into heaven, as crowned with glory to be our

advocate ; because the interests of the Son are dear
to the Mother, dearer as she is placed above the
obscurity of earth in the full fruition of divine
love, and nothing is so dear to the Son as the
salvation of our souls. We see her in the cemetery of S. Agnes veiled, with a single necklace on
her neck, and her hands outstretched in prayer,
an unusual attitude when the Child is seated on
her knees. That face, as compared with others of
hers in the catacombs, partakes of that peculiar
set expression which is characteristic here of the
calm, almost stern face, encircled with the halo of
glory. « The queen hath stood at thy right hand,
» girt about with variety : all the glory of her,
» the daughter of the king, in golden fringes girt
» about with varieties, is from within: virgins after
» her shall be brought to the king, her neighbours
» shall be brought to thee. » [1] We see them next
to her. The head of our incarnate Lord with its
parted hair is marked but by the glory of the
Cross ; but theirs are decorated with the triple row
of gems, viz grace, virginity and martyrdom, which
He bestowed upon them, surmounted by the cross
wherein they found their great reward. But all
the gifts of grace are signified by the necklace,

---

[1] Ps. 44.

breastplate, and the immense jewelled headdress with its triple crown borne by our Lady. It has no cross; for that is beaming about the Saviour's head, sitting on her lap and sustained by her hand beneath his foot. On earth his sufferings were her cross; but now in the peace of glory, totally resplendent from his beauty, as he is blessing, the Gospel in his hand, so she who gave the Author of the Gospel to the world has her hand also raised to bless. From that hand nothing but blessing could flow; and in their own private need or in public distress the saints have held but one language, that she, his Mother, continually intercedes with her divine Son, imploring his compassion for that human nature which through her he was pleased to take. S. Ephrem calls Mary « My Lady » and he spoke the familiar language of the Church; just as says S. Peter of Alexandria sixty years before him: « Our » Lord and God Jesus Christ having been born according to the flesh of the holy, glorious, Mother » of God, Mary our Lady. » Many prayers to the martyrs, and for the dead, are scratched in the catacombs; and it is supposed that, at some spots, where the names of priests are very numerous, they had descended to say mass. On the painting we are now speaking of, the names of two priests are scratched beside the throne, John and Salbius;

14

and between them « Rosa, Bituli. » Who they were
we don't know. S. Euphemia suffered in the same
persecution as S. Catharine. She was a chief martyr
amongst the Greeks, and her festival is kept generally in the East. The Council of Chalcedon often
mentions her *martyrium* in that city, and it held
its sessions in her church under S. Leo the Great,
in 451, to condemn the Eutychian heresy which
denied two distinct natures in our incarnate Lord.
There was a church of hers in Rome in the days
of S. Gregory the Great. We should almost suspect from the eastern figures in the Council picture
here, and the heads of S. Catharine and S. Euphemia on either side of our Lady, that that picture
represented the Council of Chalcedon rather than
the condemnation of Celestius. S. Cyril, indeed, at
Ephesus in our Lady's great church, had condemned,
in the name of Pope Celestine, successor of Pope
S. Zosimus, the opposite error of Nestorius who
maintained a divine and a human person in Christ,
and eastern figures would be expected to appear
in a picture of the Council of Ephesus. But seeing
the inscription lately found among the relics under
the high altar which refers to Leo I, the Council
is more likely that of Chalcedon. That Council
was, as it were, the summing up and anathema of
three heresies: the Pelagian which left human na-

ture as it was by itself without grace; the Nestorian which, indeed, admitted original sin, but denied the necessity of grace and that God was made man; and the Eutychian which out of horror to the Nestorians admitted only one nature in Christ, and the author of which wrote to Pope Leo I to complain of his having been condemned and anathematized in the Council held by S. Flavian.

MUTILATED FIGURE OF OUR SAVIOUR.

We pass on to the end of this aisle, and mount three steps leading to the ancient tribune. There, on the right, is a colossal figure of our Lord, the head and shoulders of which were destroyed in building the upper church. He stands with sandaled feet upon a jewelled footstool. Two books are in his left hand, one resting upon the other. They probably represent the Old and New Testament.

A little more to the left is a fragment of an inscription of which only the following can be deciphered: « Quisquis has mei nominis literas lege- » ris lector dic indigno Joanni miserere Deus. » « Whoever reads these letters of my name, let him » say God have mercy on unworthy John. » Who this John was who is begging the prayers of the passing reader, we do not know. Under this, as

well as under the southern aisle, several chambers
have been discovered, and are supposed to be some
of the original chambers of Clement's house.   Only
three of them have been, as yet, partially explored.

When the excavations reached the west end of
the north aisle, it was found that this ancient basilica stands on the ruins of much earlier struc-
tures.   Observing that the lower part of the west
wall was built of a quality of brick far superior
to that above it, the ground was dug to the depth
of fourteen feet, and three walls of three different
constructions, as well as of three different periods,
were discovered.   One is of the finest brickwork
of the imperial times, and probably belonged to
Clement's palace.   It forms, as it were, the chord of
the apse.   Parallel with it, leaving a space of only
twenty five inches, is another wall of *tufo lithoide*,
which if it be not anterior to what is called with
little truth, in our opinion, the era of the foundation of Rome by Romulus, is, very probably, part
of the walls of Servius Tullius the sixth king of
Rome.   Upon this wall is built another of the Republican period of colossal blocks of travertine, va-
rying in length from eight to ten feet.   These walls
have been traced 98 feet from north to south ;
from east to west the travertine wall was traced 410
feet, and the *tufo* wall upwards of 500 feet, without

finding its termination either way. A depth of about 20 feet is still buried in the earth, which shows how low the level of Rome of the kings must have been.[1] A thorough exploration of the length and depth of these walls could not fail to throw great light on the topography of this quarter of Rome.

ANCIENT ORATORY OF S. CLEMENT.

Ascending from the intramural passage, just described, to the west end of the south aisle, and turning to the right, we find a spacious staircase of twenty steps, constructed for easy access to the rooms of a fine Roman dwelling-house. Its walls are of imperial brickwork, and the style of the stucco decorations on the vault of the largest chamber induces us to assign them to the age of S. Clement. This chamber is precisely under the tribune of the basilica. In fact it occupies almost the same position under the high altar as the Confession of S. Peter does in the Vatican basilica, so

---

[1] Some Archaeologists are of opinion that this portion of the valley, between the Coelian and Esquiline hills, was not included within the circuit of the Servian walls, and consequently the *tufo* wall found here must have belonged to some important building within the city, perhaps the palace of Tarquin, or the Mint in the early days of the Republic.

that there can be no doubt that it is the *memoria*
mentioned by S. Jerome in his notice of S. Clement written towards the end of the fourth century. It was startling to find in this Christian
crypt an altar of Mithras; but the subsequent
discovery of the Mithraeum itself shows that, with
the exception of this chamber, it had been deli-
berately transformed into a cave for the celebration of the Mithraic mysteries. The chamber forms
a part of the oratory and there is no proof that
the Christians ever lost possession of it.

It was not twenty years after the convert Praefect of the City had broken and burnt a cave of
Mithras and his images, that S. Jerome speaks
of the church in Rome still preserving the *memoria* of S. Clement: and although we might desire
to think that the zeal of Gracchus was exercised
upon our Mithraeum, it seems natural to suppose
in that case that S. Jerome would mention it in
connection with the church. Victor also, the acolyte of the *dominicum* of S. Clement, (see page 179)
is a witness that it existed in his time. S. Cyprian
says [1] that in the days of persecution the place
where Christians assembled for divine worship was

---

[1] Liber de opere et eleemosina, pag. 482, lit. A. — Note 30 ad
librum de op. et el., pag. 489.

called *dominicum*. After the fourth century it is
not found in Roman inscriptions. The Emperor Constantine would not permit the slave's forehead to
be branded, on account of the divine image, and
substituted instead a *bronze plate*, on one of which
Victor's name appears. It is reasonable then to
say that, before Constantine's death, in May 337,
the clergy of S. Clement's were known to be in
possession of his *dominicum*. Again, S. Jerome wrote
about the *memoriam Clementis* after Gratian had
ordered the idolatrous temples to be demolished in
382, after Gracchus had destroyed the Mithraeum in
377 [1] and two years only before they were totally
extirpated in 394. If the crypt got into Christian hands, and was merely added to the church
after the destruction of the Mithraeum at a period when Christianity was freed from all fear,
it seems likely that the Christians would have purified it, and have re-stuccoed the vault, or even
included the whole Mithraeum. But nothing is
more natural than that, if this chamber was always under the apse, and did not, like the rest
of the Mithraeum, fall into Pagan hands, they

---

[1] « Ante paucos annos propinquus vester Gracchus, nobilitatem pa-
» triciam sonans nomine, cum Praefecturam gereret urbanam, nonne spe-
» laeum Mithrae, et omnia portentosa simulacra, quibus Corax, Gryphus,
» Miles, Leo, Perses, Helios, Bromius, Pater initiantur, subvertit, fregit,
» excussit ? » S. Hieronymi Epist. VII, ad Laetam.

should preserve it as it was. Some of the stuccoes
are in a pretty good state of preservation, and
not offensive in character, and it was the practice of the Christians, in those days, not to obli-
terate imagery without necessity. It is also very probable that the classical decorations of this
vault would have been altered by the constructors
of the Mithraeum, had it been in their power.
The Eastern rites superseded classical mythology:
their struggle in Rome with legalized Christianity,
a struggle mostly at private expense, would have
been signalized by the destruction of so important
an historical site as this *memoria*.

TEMPLE OF MITHRAS.

Just beyond the apse of the basilica, the side-
wall of the *memoria* showed three arches filled up
with excellent brickwork, and imbedded in it
two square pilasters of Parian marble. These pilasters have debased Corinthian capitals contrast-
ing strongly with the classical style of the stucco
vault. The roughly chiseled foliage reminds one
of the arch of Gallienus: it shows declining art, and
was not executed until about the middle of the
third century. Breaking through the brickwork
a long narrow passage was found, twenty eight

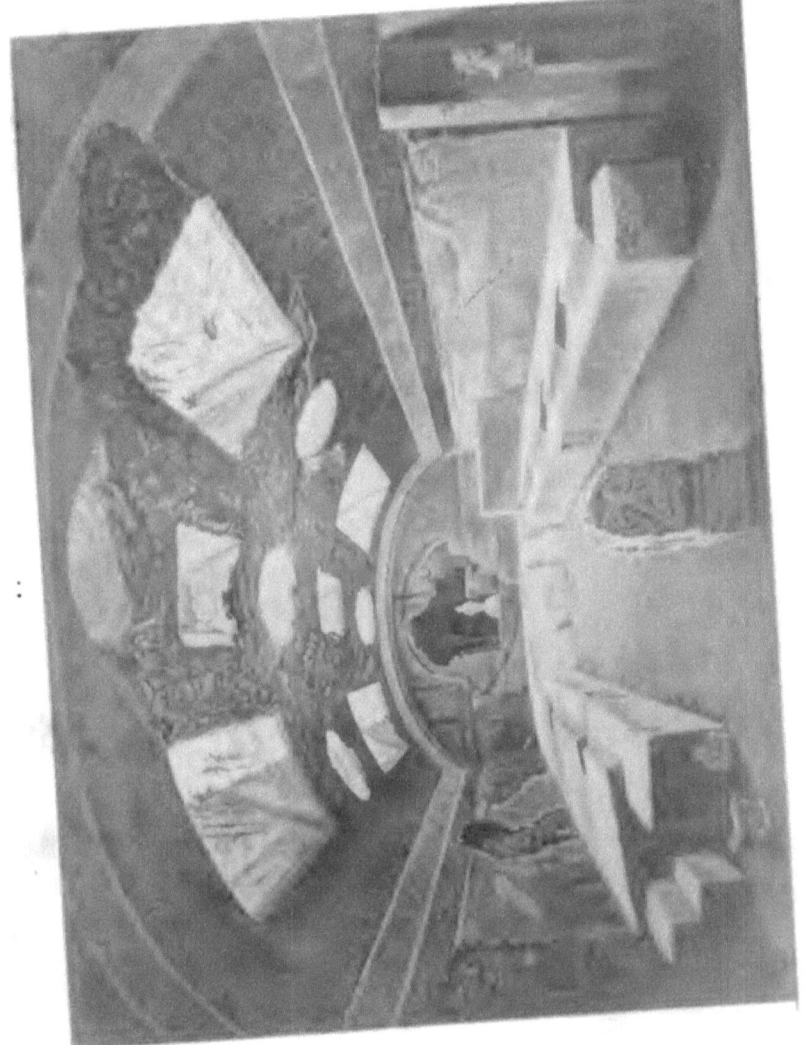

feet by six feet ten. A few inches beyond the pi
lasters is a fragment of a large column of Numidian
marble sunk into the pavement. Opposite to this
was a doorway, also bricked up. On breaking
through it a large hall was discovered thirty feet
long, twenty wide, and almost entirely filled with
earth. The first impression was that this was the
real oratory, the vestibule answering to the ambu-
lacrum intersecting the well known basilica in the
Catacombs of S. Agnese, and, as in that basilica, the
smaller chamber under the apse constituting the part
reserved for the altar. The circumstance also that
there had been a door, at the extreme end, strengthened the idea. The vault was pierced by eleven
luminaria, or skylights, some round, some square,
and all decorated with mosaics. Mosaic bands also
run around the sides and at the ends. The simplicity of the decorations and the absence of Pagan
forms, gave strength to the conviction that it was
the first Christian oratory. Much of the ceiling
however was made of small mineral stones artifi-
cially imitating a grotto; and when the whole was
cleared out, as we see it, there remained no doubt
that it was one of those caverns in which Mithras,
whose altar had been already found, was habitually
worshipped. It was evident that it was not originally
a Mithraic cave, but a large room changed and adapt-

ed to the Mithraic mysteries. At Ostia, the emperor
Commodus gave up the palace crypt to the priests of
Mithras. The like had been done here. Along the
walls are raised platforms ascended by three steps.
They have been found in other Mithraeums, but here
there is a peculiarity : they are not level, but form
an inclined plane towards the walls. They are six
feet wide and three feet three inches from the
ground. It is difficult to say for what purpose they
served. They may have been occupied by the initiated in the mysteries; or, as De Rossi thinks, they
were *triclinia* on which the guests reclined while
participating in some sacred feast held in this cave,
which is by no means improbable; for in the Mithraic mysteries there was a profane imitation of
the Sacrament of the blessed Eucharist. And, according to the usage and ideas of the ancients, in
every feast, even of the mystic kind, the guests used
to put themselves in reclining positions. Along
the outward extremities of these benches there is
a depressed edge on which are five semicircular
niches, two on the right hand and three on the
left. They were formerly covered with marble, fragments of which still remain. In the Mithraeum
discovered a few years ago at Ostia, there is a
similar edge on which were placed lamps, fire - vases,
and small altars of *terra cotta*. The five semicir-

cular niches probably contained the figures or statues called *Signa Sacrorum*, symbolizing the five grades of initiation in the Mithraic mysteries, to which we shall hereafter refer. High up in the wall, at the end of this temple, is a niche, which formerly must have contained a statue of Mithras: and lower down is a small square cavity built of brick. It might have contained water for religious purification, or perhaps served as a receptacle for the blood of victims. Near it, on the floor, there still remains a portion of an altar, and, a few inches in front, a small round piece of marble upon which, it is supposed, burned the sacred fire that was kindled and preserved in the two small square furnaces, facing each other in the sides of the benches. The learned Cavaliere Visconti thinks that the round piece of marble we are just after noticing, served as a pedestal for the conical shaped stone that was found here representing the birth of Mithras. The deity is seen issuing from the top of the stone, which is a well known symbol of Mithras; « for, » as Lajard and others write, « owing to the comparison between him and his symbol, fire, it was said that he had been generated from a stone, from the fact that a spark is produced by striking two flint stones together, which was the way fire was first discovered. » Mithras therefore was called

Θεὸς ἐκ πέτρας, and hence the stone itself was called his mother. This statue is twenty five inches high: the deity from the knees upwards has emerged from the stone; he stands erect and wears the Phrygian cap. The arms from the elbow are wanting. It was broken into three pieces which were found at various periods during the progress of the excavations, and is the only one of the kind in Italy. There was in the beginning of this century a Θεὸς ἐκ πέτρας in the Justinian Museum, but we have not been able to learn what has become of it. *Caulus* was one of the appellations of Mithras, and a *cippus* was also found here, with the words *Caute sacr.* or sacred to Mithras.

Near the square pilasters, already alluded to, was discovered the ara or altar, now placed on the floor in the centre of the Mithraeum. The upper part of it, on which probably were represented the chariots of the rising and setting sun, and the symbols of the seven constellations, is quite gone. It is of Parian marble, and, in its mutilated state , is four feet high, two feet five inches across the front and back, and twenty inches along the side. On the front of it is the background of . a grotto, in the centre of which is the Taurobolium or sacrifice of the bull. Mithras is clad in a short tunic with his clamys or cloak fluttering over his left shoulder·

He wears the Phrygian cap, and is looking earnestly towards the heavens. He has his left knee on the bull stretched on the ground before him, and while he holds him by the nostrils with his left hand, he plunges a dagger into his shoulder with his right. A dog and a serpent lick the blood that flows trickling from the wound, and a scorpion or cancer knaws the scrotum. The tail of the bull ends with ears of corn. Two genii cloathed like Mithras stand as his assistants, one with his torch erect to indicate the rising sun, and the other with his torch depressed to indicate his setting. On the edges of the upper part of the grotto, to the right and left, are fragmentary figures of the sun and moon, and within it is a raven. Low down, on the right of the spectator, is the head of a lion, which, so far as we know, has not been, as yet, found on any other monument representing the *taurobolium*. [1]

Several altars representing the Mithraic sacrifice, and in some respects similar to the one we are after describing, were found in Rome, Ostia , Heddernheim in Germany, near Wiesbaden,[2] Bourg-Saint-Adeol in France , near Schewarzenden in Rhenish

---

[1] See Monum. vet. Ant. by Monsignor della Turre, Cap. IV.
See Habel, Die Mithras-tempel in den römischen Ruinen bei Edderuheim.

Prussia, [1] in Hungary , [2] and elsewhere. Flaminius Vacca, who lived in the sixteenth century , gives the following description of one that was discovered, in his own time, under the Capitoline hill. « I remember, when a little boy, to » have seen an opening leading into a cave under » the *piazza* of the Capitol, and some people return- » ing from it said that they had seen in it a wo- » man riding on a bull. A short time afterwards, » my master Vincenzo De Rossi, told me that he » had gone down into the same cave, and seen a » bas-relief in marble representing the fable of Ju- • piter and Europa sitting on a bull. » The bas-relief here mentioned is now in the Louvre at Paris, and is called the « Borghese Taurobolium. »

Another bas-relief was found near the church of S. Vitale between the Quirinal and Viminal hills, and is thus described by the aforesaid Flaminius Vacca: « I remember the discovery made in a vine- » yard, belonging to signor Orazio Muti, opposite » the church of S. Vitale , of a marble idol four » palms high, standing on a pedestal in an empty » chamber the door of which had been walled up. • Around it on all sides there were many lamps

---

[1] See Lajard, l. c. pl. LXXXVI ; Rouchier, Histoire du Vivarais, T I, pag. 158 - 172, 204 - 206, and Renier, pag. 584 - 588.

[2] See Mittheilungen der K. K. Central - Commissio zur Erforschung Baudenk - malei, Vienna 1867, p. 119-132.

» with three becks for lights, and all turned
» towards the idol who had a lion's head and a
» human body. Under its feet there was a ball or
» globe out of which grew a serpent encircling the
» idol, and entering headforemost into its mouth.
» Its hands were placed upon its breast, in each
» of which there was a key, and it had four wings
» on its shoulders, two pointing towards heaven
» and two inclined towards the earth. I do not
» consider it very ancient; for it is not the work
» of a good artist: or if it is ancient, it must have
» been executed before the era of good art began.
» Signor Orazio told me that a friend of his had ex-
» plained to him the meaning of these things. ' The
» idol, he said, signified the devil, who in Pagan
» times held the earth under his feet: the serpent
» that entwined it and entered into his mouth meant
» the power of prophecying by giving ambiguous
» answers : the keys in its hand symbolized do-
» minion over the world: and the wings ubiquity
» of presence.' I did my best to see this idol, but
» signor Orazio having died, his heirs knew not what
» had become of it. It would not surprise me if
» signor Orazio, acting on the advice of his friend,
» sent it to the furnace to have the moisture taken
» out of it; for many and many a year it must have
» been under ground. »

A somewhat similar Mithraic leontocephalus was discovered, at Ostia, by M.ʳ Fagan in the begining of the present century, and is thus described by Montfaucon : « The god is represented as the solar
» deity, and keeper of the two portals, of which
» he holds the keys, called respectively those of
» heaven and earth, or of mortals and immortals.
» The lion is his symbol; because the sun attains
» its greatest altitude in Leo, and the serpent that
» entwines Mithras symbolizes the tortuous and
» spiral path which the ancients assigned to the
» sun when above the eclyptic : and the serpent,
» from the peculiarity of its casting off its slough
» annually, is symbolic of the ever renewed youth
» of the sun. The bowl between his feet repre-
» sents the water which is necessary for the pro-
» duction of every species of living being, and the
» serpent putting his head into that vessel reaches
» the humid element. Thus is indicated that mix-
» ture of heat and moisture on which the growth of
» every thing depends. The four wings of Mithras
» are also solar symbols, and, in general, signify the
» elevated regions which constitute his domain, while
» more particularly the two upper pinions refer to
» the ascending movement of the luminary when he
» culminates above our hemisphere , and the two
» lower ones point to the opposite declension. »

During the reigns of Pius VII and Pius IX, several caves or temples dedicated to Mithras were brought to light at Ostia, besides a great many inscriptions referring to that Persian deity, which is a proof that his worship must have prevailed to a very considerable extent in that once flourishing and populous city. Indeed it is generally admitted that it was in Ostia this Asiatic worship first found a home in Europe : that from Ostia it made its way to Rome, and thence was propagated throughout the Empire.

According to Plutarch, in his life of Pompey the Great, Mithraism was not known in Europe until the time of the piratic war, that is about seventy years before the birth of Christ. The pirates of Cilicia who swept the Adriatic and Mediterranean seas with their galleys and attacked the Roman fleet at Ostia, were finally defeated by Pompey in the year of Rome 687. After that successful expedition the fleet returned to Ostia to undergo some repairs, and it is generally believed that it was then the seeds of the Mithraic worship were first sown in that soil.

The German and French schools of archaeology, respectively headed by Von Hammer and Lajard , do not agree about the origin of the worship of Mithras. The German school derives it from the

15

mythology of India, and the French finds its traces
in the doctrine of Zoroaster which is contained
in the Zendavesta, [1] the Bun Dehesch , and other
old ceremonial books of the Persians. This latter
opinion is more generally received, and followed.
The Persians, like other Oriental nations, admitted a duality of godhead : the god of good was
their Oromazdes, or Urmazd, or Hormizdas: the

---

[1] Zendavesta, by contraction Zend, or, as it is vulgarly pronounced,
Zundawestou, or Zund, denotes the book ascribed to Zoroaster , and
containing his pretended revelations; and which the ancient *Magians* and
modern *Persees*, called also *Gaurs*, observe and reverence in the same
manner, as the Christians do the Bible, and the Mahomitans the Koran.

The word, it is said, originally signified any instrument for kindling
fire, and is applied to this book to denote its aptitude for kindling the
flame of religion in the hearts of those who read it.

It has been much disputed, among learned writers, who Zoroaster
was, and in what age he lived. Dr. Prideaux, and several others, are of opinion that Zoroaster was the same with the Zerdusht of the Persians, who
was a great patriarch of the Magians, and that he lived between the beginning of the reign of Cyrus, and the latter end of Darius Hystaspis. Dr. Nar-
burtan censures Hyde and Prideaux for making an early Bactrian lawgiver
to be a late Persian false prophet. Baumgarten, likewise, represents it as
doubtful whether the Persian Zoroaster ever existed. The learned M. Bryant
(Anal. Anc. Mithol. vol. III, p. 107) observes that there are more persons than
one, spoken of under the character of Zoroaster ; though there was one
principal to whom it more truly related. Of men, styled Zoroaster, he
says, the first was a deified personage, reverenced by some of his posterity,
whose worship was called Magia, and the professors of it Magi. This
worship was transmitted from the ancient Babylonians and Chaldeans to
the Persians, who succeeding to the sovereignty of Asia, renewed under their
princes, and particularly under Darius the son of Hystaspes, those rites
which had been in a great degree effaced and forgotten. The Persians,
says this learned writer, originally derived their name from the deity
Perez, or Parez, the Sun, whom they also worshipped under the title of
Zor-Aster.

god of evil was Arimanes or Hariman, or Aberman : the former the creator, the latter the destroyer, and each of them assisted by genii of the same nature. According to Celsus they believed in the transmigration of souls, and supposed that the souls issuing from the fixed firmament of heaven, the residence,. of Hormizdas, and passing across the moveable firmament through the seven planets and the constellations of the Zodaic, descended to the earth, and, after remaining for some time there, they reascended to the empyrian of heaven by the same path, and assuming different forms during their journey through the planets and constellations, purified themselves from the stains of gilt they had contracted here below. Arimanes, the malignant genius, set his snares for them on their journey, and endeavoured to bring them into the kingdom of darkness over which he presides : but to defend them from his assaults there was another divinity called Mithras who was a kind of mediator between man and Hormizdas, and whose principal employment was to offer to the supreme being an expiatory sacrifice for the human race.

Though the worship of Mithras had been brought to Rome in the time of Pompey, yet the mysteries of that god were not well known until about the second century. As the Persians had no temples, but celebrated the mysteries of Mithras in caves, as they had learned from their legislator Zoroaster, who first, according to the testimony of Porphyrius,[1] chose for that purpose a den watered with springs and covered with turfs, so the Romans, after their example, celebrated the same mysteries in dens and caves as is affirmed by Tertullian, S. Justin, Julius Firmicus, S. Jerome, S. Augustine, and other early writers. Moreover we still possess the names of many persons who consecrated caves to that god, as for instance :

« Deo soli invicto Mithrae Sosimus spelaeum constituit. »
« Spelaeum Tib. Claudius voti compos dedit. »

In those caves various objects symbolizing the universe were displayed, especially the moveable

---

[1] De Antro Nymph. Statius addresses the following invocation to the sun.

« Adsis, o memor officii, Junoniaque arva
Dexter ames; seu te roseum Titana vocari,
Gentis Achemeniae ritu, seu praestat Osirim
Frugiferum; seu Persei *sub rupibus antri*,
Indignata sequi torquentem Cornua Mithram. »

Lactantius (in lib. I Th.), explaining this passage, says, « the Persians were the first who worshipped the sun in dens and caves, and that they did so to denote his eclipses. Some of the ancients were of opinion that the bull signified the earth, and that the dagger, which Mithras plunges into his shoulder, indicated that the sun by his rays penetrated the surface of the earth, and rendered it fruitful. »

planets in which Mithras was supreme. And as fire was considered by the Persians to be the most pure symbol of Mithras, the rites and religious offerings made to him should necessarily be celebrated in the presence of that element. But although such were the essential constituents of the ancient Mithraic worship, in the course of time it underwent different changes in the various nations through which it had been diffused. The Romans confounded Mithras with the Sun, as we learn from the inscriptions on the altars and marbles dedicated to him in which he is invariably called :

« Deus sol invictus Mithra. — Soli invicto Mithrae: »

In the reign of Adrian the worship of the Sun was substituted for that of all the gods, as is manifest from the inscriptions on the coins of the third century. They exhibit on one side the figure of the Sun and on the other side the epigraph *Sol dominus imperii Romani,* which proves that Mithraism must have been greatly developed throughout the empire at that time. But it was from the end of the third century to the middle of the fourth that it obtained its greatest number of adherents. During that period Christianity was embraced by persons of all ranks, and threatened the overthrow of polytheism. The religion of the empire was in danger, and the

Pagans and Neoplatonists in order to resist the faith of Christ especially employed the mysterious rites of Mithras, and endeavoured to demonstrate that the worship of the Sun had been the primitive and true religion of mankind. Mithraism was better suited to obtain that end than any of the other religions then practiced in Rome; for in addition to its teaching the existence of a god acting as a mediator and atoning for the sins of men, it imitated some of the sacred rites of the Christian Religion, especially the Sacraments of baptism and the eucharist. They sprinkled the initiated with water and presented them with bread and wine, in order, as they said, to regenerate them, and give them a new life. « Per lavacrum, si adhuc me-» mini, » says Tertullian, « Mithra signat illic in fron-» tibus milites suos, celebrat panis oblationem, et » imaginem resurrectionis induit et sub gladio re-» dimit coronam. » [1]

The priests who were initiated in the mysteries of Mithras assumed various names, or titles taken from the animals, which, in their solar system of worship, had a symbolical signification. Thus we find in the writings of the ancients [2] that they were called Coraces, ravens; Hieroco-

---

[1] Lib. de baptismo, c. 5.
[2] Porphyrius, de abstinentia, c. 6. 18. S. Jeronym. Ep. ad Laetam, c. 51.

races, sacred ravens; Leones, or Leontini, lions; Persia, Heliaca, and the priestesses **Leaenae**, Lionesses for Mithras had his priestesses too, as appears from a passage in the second book of Justin, where it is said that Artarxarses consecrated Aspasia to the worship of that god. All these priests wore the figures of the animals whose names they bore. The Leontini alone, as Porphyrius seems to insinuate, had a right to assume the figures of any animal they pleased. Hence the mysteries were called Coracia, Hierocoracia, Leontica, Griphia, Persia, Heliaca.

There were stated days for the celebration of those mysteries as we learn from the following inscriptions found, in the sixteenth century, in a Mithraic cave near the church of S. Silvester in Capite.

In the consulship of Datianus and Ceralis, (A. D. 358) **Victor** Olympius of Senatorial rank, Pater Patrum, and Aurelius Victor Augustus, Senator, Pater, auspiciously conferred the **Persian Orders**, the day before the nones of April.

Under the aforesaid consuls, they conferred the Leontic Orders auspiciously, on the 17 of April. On the 24 of April they displayed the Gryphian mysteries.

In the consulship of Eusebius and Hypatius, Nonnus Victor Olympius, and A.Victor Augentius, both

Senators, conferred the Leontic Order auspiciously ou the seventh of March.

Under the consulship of Datianus and Cerealis, Nonnus Victor Olympius, Senator, Pater Patrum, in the thirteenth year of his consecration, conferred the Cornacean Order, and on the same day displayed the mysteries auspiciously. [1]

From the foregoing we must conclude that not only had those Festivals their fixed days, but also that their ceremonies were different; otherwise they would not have borne different names on the different days on which they were celebrated. And moreover the priests named Coraces presided over the Coracia, the Leontini over the Leontica , etc.

The priests celebrated their respective mysteries in the habits which distinguished their Order, that is whereon were painted or embroidered the animals whose names they assumed, or were made of their skins, which must have made them very ridiculous, as we are given to understand by Archelaus, bishop of Mesopotamia, who reproached Manes with his having played the part of a buffoon in his celebration of the mysteries of Mithras.

The austerities, pains, hardships and tortures to which those persons, who aspired to be initiated in

---

[1] For these particulars, see M. Della Torre, pag. 204-221 ; and Chifflet, De Gemm. Abra.

the mysteries of Mithras, were subjected, are almost
incredible. Nonnus writes that they were obliged to
pass through eighty different grades of trials. [1] They
began with the easiest probations: first of all the aspi-
rant took a bath for several days, then he was
obliged to throw himself into a fire: next he was
confined to a solitary place, where he was obliged
to fast, and thus go on through other severer
trials or probations until he passed through eighty.
And if he survived he was initiated in the sacred
mysteries of Mithras. Nicetas writes that [2] « in the
» very beginning of their probation they were obli-
» ged to fast for fifty days: then they were whip-
» ped for two whole days, and for twenty put into
» the snow. » [2]

Nicetas confirms the statement of Nonnus about
the eighty probations, as we learn from a very old
Greek manuscript preserved in the Laurentiana library at Florence, which Montfaucon translated into
Latin. The Scholiast says « that those persons who

---

[1] « Hi vero serie quadam suscipiebantur, primum quidem levioribus
» suppliciis, deinde atrocioribus inflictis. Nam primum ei diebus multis
» aperienda est aqua. Deinde necessario ipsi faciendum est, ut se in ignem
» coniiciat: postea in solitudine versari, sibique ipsi inediam imperare ne-
» cesse habet; atque ita ad alia pergere quousque LXXX suppliciorum ge-
» nera defunctus fuerit. Quibus si supervixerit, tunc demum sacris Mi-
» thriacis initiatur. » Nonnus in collectione historiarum, No. 5-45.

[2] « In ipso probationis ingressu, per quinquaginta totos dies eos fame
» cruciant, deinde duos dies flagris cædunt, tum in nivem viginti dies
» immittunt. » Episcopus Nicetas ad Nazianzenum.

» were to be initiated in the mysteries of Mithras
» were subjected to certain grades of probations.
» They began with the lightest trials and were by
» degrees subsequently subjected to the more se-
» vere. For example they were obliged to fast for
» fifty days: which if they constantly supported they
» were whipped for two days, and then were to
» practice the same kind of trials for twenty two
» days more: the tortures being increased on the
» condition that if they bore them patiently, they
» were finally taught the more perfect mysteries. » [1]

These mysteries were not less impious than abo-
minable; for human victims were therein offered up,
as Porphyrius insinuates. [2] It is true that the emperor Adrian abolished the custom of offering human
sacrifices, [3] but the emperor Commodus restored it,
since, according to Lampridius, he polluted the mysteries of that god by homicide. [4] We cannot of course

---

[1] « Qui Mithræ mysteriis initiabantur, quibusdam ceu gradibus cru-
» ciatus probari solebant: ita ut primum leviore pœnarum genere adfi-
» cerentur, ac deinceps vehementiore. Exempli causa, primo initiandos
» fame adfligebant quinquaginta diebus, ac si hæc constanter tolerarent,
» illos biduo cædi curabant, ac deinceps eodem pœnæ genere singulos
» exercebant viginti octo diebus: eoque pacto auctis cruciatibus, si qui
» initiabantur hæc patienter ferrent, tunc demum perfectiora mysteria
» edocebantur. »   Nicetas, Episcopus Pamph.

[2] Lib. 4, cap. 56, De abstinentia.

[3] « Hadrianum imperatorem prope omnes humanæ hostiæ mactatio-
nes sustulisse. » Porphyrius ibidem.

[4] « Sacra Mithriaca homicidio vero polluit. » Lampridius in vita
Commodi.

conclude from this that the homicide was a real
sacrifice: but the fact which Socrates relates in his
ecclesiastical history (Book 3, c. 2) leaves no doubt
that human victims were offered to Mithras ; for he
tells us that « there was a place in that city (Alex-
» andria) which had long been abandoned to ne-
» glect and filth, wherein the Pagans had formerly
» celebrated their mysteries, and sacrificed human
» beings to Mithras. This being empty and other-
» wise useless, Constantius had granted it to the
» Church of the Alexandrians: and George, wishing
» to erect a church on its site, gave directions that
» the place should be cleansed. In the process of
» clearing it, an *adytum* of vast depth was disco-
» vered which unveiled the nature of their heathen-
» ish rites: for there were found therein the skulls
» of many persons of all ages, who were said to
» have been immolated for the purpose of divination
» by the inspection of their entrails, when the Pa-
» gans were allowed to perform these and such-like
» magic arts in order to enchant the souls of men.
» The Christians on discovering these abominations
» in the *adytum* of the temple of Mithras, thought
» it their duty to expose them to the view and
» execration of all; and therefore they carried the
» skulls throughout the city, in a kind of trium-
» phal procession, for the inspection of the people. »

The principal festival of Mithras was that of
his nativity, which a Roman Calendar, of the age
of Constantine, placed on the eigth of the kalends
of January, that is on the 25th of December. It is
true that the Calendar does not name this god it
only says « VIII. kal. Jan. n. Invicti. CM. XXIV. [1] The
eighth of the kalends of January the birth-day of
the invincible, twenty four chariots drawn by horses
entered the Circus. » But the learned have judged
from the epithet « Invincible, » so often applied
to Mithras [2] as we learn from the inscriptions « Deo
Soli invicto Mithrae — Soli invicto Mithrae » relating to him, that he is here indicated. And the
games in his honour must have been very splendid,
whereas so many chariots entered the Circus. We
must not however infer from this that the Pagans
meant to celebrate that festival on the same day
that the Church celebrates the Nativity of our Divine Lord. They intended thereby to signify that
the sun, after having been at a distance from our
hemisphere since the autumnal equinox, approaches
it and comes after the winter solstice, which falls
on that day, to warm and fructify this other half

---

[1] Octavo Kalendas Januarii, Natalis Invicti, Circenses, Missus XXIV.
See M. Della Torre, pag. 219.

[2] See Monsignor De la Turre, De Mithra, c. 11, p. 179; and Gruter,
pag. 33, 34.

of the globe: on which account they regarded the 25th of December as his birth day, and celebrated it as such. Nor must we, with Father Harduin,[1] say that the western Christians, on account of that feast, transferred their Christmas from September to the same day; for S. Augustine,[2] S. Ambrose,[3] the author of the Apostolic Constitutions,[4] S. John Chrysostom,[5] and all the early Fathers prove that the festival of the Nativity of our Divine Lord had been, from the days of the Apostles, always celebrated in the Roman Church, on the 25th of December.

Of all the temples dedicated to Mithras in Rome our Clementine one alone remains. It is in a very good state of preservation, considering the vicissitudes through which it has passed, and the number of centuries it has been buried in the earth. Its interest is enhanced by its being, in all probability, a part of the *memoria* of the martyr Pontiff S. Clement, which was hallowed by the footprints of S. Peter, S. Paul, S. Barnabas, and many other illustrious heroes of the primitive Church. When we visit it, our thoughts revert to the struggle between Paga-

---

[1] In Antirrhetico de nummis antiquis, pag. 65.
[2] In Psalm. 132, et De Trinit., lib. 4, c. 5.
[3] Sermo, § 10, 12.
[4] Lib. 5, c. 13.
[5] Homilia 31, Tom. 5, pag. 417, de Natali Christi.

nism and Christianity, and the basilica raised above it proclaims the victory of the Cross of Christ over the polytheism of the Roman empire.

Let us now take leave of these relics of Pagan and Christian antiquity, and retrace our steps to the basilica built on their ruins.

SOUTH AISLE.

CRUCIFIXION OF S. PETER. — BAPTISM BY S. CYRIL. AND OTHER FRAGMENTS OF FRESCOES.

Greatly do we deplore the ruin of the pictures which once covered the whole wall at the west end of this aisle; for the fragments that remain display a beauty and purity of style much beyond the other paintings in this basilica. The subjects appear to have been arranged in two horizontal lines, one above the other; and the figures in panels, singly, or in pairs. The ornamental border, a little above the floor, is a pattern divided into compartments, and in the centre of each compartment is a large globe and four small ones, and birds, like storks, on either side, pecking at what seems to be an undulating stream of light descending from the large globe.

On the top line, at the right, two feet tied to a cross indicate S. Peter's crucifixion with his head downwards: beside it is the head of an aged saint tonsured and with the nimbus. On the extreme left are two very beautiful heads of angels. The centre of the lower line shows , in a circle , the feet of an animal, which, no doubt, was the mystic lamb; for a figure next it, on the right, of which the lower half only remains, extends the hands towards it in the manner of supplication, or adoration, so usual in Christian monuments. There seems to have been a kneeling figure behind this one: then two beautiful angels, and then two saints, standing in order; and what remains of the countenances exhibits great devotion. The subject on the left is quite gone. It had been replaced by a panel of very inferior execution. We say replaced, because it seems scarcely possible that this painting, almost grotesque in character, could be the original one just placed side by side with the other well executed figures. The subject is a crowned emperor seated on a throne under a canopy. S. Cyril, with a nimbus, kneels before the emperor. His name *Cirillus*, is written vertically behind him. The monarch seems, by the action of his left hand, to be addressing two persons who are standing behind the saint. Most probably it represents S. Cyril's parting audience of Michael III, to whom, in 848, the Chazari of the Danube had sent an embassy for priests, and he is directing

the ambassadors to take care of the chosen missionary. Were this picture part of the original series,
we should suppose that the figure on the right of
the lamb with the one on its knees represented a
subject we shall find on a larger scale in the narthex; for the spiral columns and their capitals
behind the emperor are precisely the same as those
on either side of the narthex picture. The subject
at right angles to this, on the southern wall, represents an archbishop, with the Greek pallium,
baptizing, by immersion, a young man of barbaric
type. From its position, next to that representing
the beginning of S. Cyril's first mission, it probably
may be the baptism of the Cham of the Chazari:
if not, that of Rastices duke of Moravia, or Boigoris
Michael duke of Bohemia: for all these were converted by S. Cyril and his brother Methodius. A
few steps further on along this wall is a projecting
inclosure of brick, which may have been an altar,
and which De Rossi supposes to have been the original monument prepared to receive the marble
chest in which S. Cyril's body was removed from
the Vatican where it had been buried at first.

LIBERTINUS.

No pictures remain along the rest of this wall.
At the east end of the aisle, immediately under

S. Catharine's chapel, there are rude remains of a group of Benedictine subjects. S. Gregory the Great, who out of his own estates built six monasteries in Sicily, and took the habit himself in that of S. Andrew which he founded on his father's house at Rome, had true Catholic love for the supernatural manifestations of God's providence, and has preserved many anecdotes in his Book of dialogues. He particularly mentions S. Benedict's prophecy of the plunder of Monte Cassino, and its accomplishment, by the Lombards a hundred years after, before his own eyes; and from his marked love for that saint and familiarity with his order, Mabillon maintains against Baronius that he chose S. Benedict's rule for his own monastery. The subjects here were taken from his dialogues, and were therefore probably painted shortly after his death in 604. Honoratus, an emancipated serf of the Patrician Venantius, built a Benedictine monastery at Fondi, in Campania, for two hundred monks, of whom he was the superior. He was a holy man, and among the miracles wrought by him was his stopping, by invoking the name of Jesus, a descending mass of rock which threatened destruction to the house. At the upper monastery in Subiaco, even to this day, there is a rock in a similar threatening position, apparently detatched and ready to fall and

16

crush the monastery. S. Benedict appears to have
had skill in detecting shams, whether they were
dressed to imitate his own monks, or in the more
gorgeous habits of secular ambition. As Totila,
the Arian king of the Goths, marched through Campania in 542, he sent word to the saint that he
would visit him, but played a trick to test his
powers. « Put off, my son, these robes you wear,
« and which do not belong to you, » said Benedict to Riggo who presented himself in the royal
purple, attended by three noblemen and a train of
pages. He afterwards saw Totila, rebuked him, and
foretold his death. Libertinus, whose story is the
subject of two of the paintings just referred to, ap-
rears to have lived in the time of Totila. We have
in the one with the inscription « ubi Abbas Liber-
» tinus veniam petit » « where the Abbot begs
» pardon of Libertinus, » an example of how human passions may break out in the peace of the
cloister, and how meekness and humility may overcome them. The Abbot who succeeded Honoratus
was not favourable to Libertinus. One day, in a
rage, the Abbot, for want of a stick, took up his
footstool and beat Libertinus severely with it about
the head. He went quietly to bed, and early the
next morning presented himself at the bedside of
the Abbot, who thought that he was leaving the

monastery, and that the abrupt departure of so holy a man would not serve his own reputation. Stung with remorse when he saw that Libertinus had come, as usual, to ask for his blessing, before setting out on the business of the monastery, he rose, and we see him prostrate on the floor of his cell, while Libertinus gives him the benediction of forgiveness he had asked for.

Libertinus had such veneration for the deceased Honoratus that he used to carry one of his clogs or sandals in his bosom. On his journey to Ravenna, a woman with her dead child in her arms seized his mule by the bridle, and insisted that he should restore the child to life. The traveller could not escape, and so strange a demand alarmed his humility. Moved with compassion, he said: « Do not weep. » At length he alighted, placed the clog upon the child's breast, and whilst he prayed life returned. Laurence, who survived him, told these two anecdotes to S. Gregory, as well as the following. The monk, who acted as gardener, was annoyed by some one stealing the vegetables. He found out the place where the thief used to get in, and seeing a snake by it told him to keep guard. While the monks were at their *siesta*, the thief returned, as usual, and seeing the snake, he took fright, and fell, so that his leg became entangled in the hedge. The monk on

returning released him, and quietly conducting him
to the door of the monastery, gave him some vegetables, saying: « My son, why will you steal? If
» you want any vegetables, come to me and I will
» give them to you. » If any of our readers are
scandalized at this simple conventual gossip with
which so great a Pope employed his leisure, and
others did not disdain to paint, we recommend to
them the more serious remarks of Leibnitz. « It is
» not one of the least prerogatives of that Church
» which alone has retained the name and character
» of Catholic, that she alone offers and propagates
» eminent examples of all the excellent virtues of
» the ascetic life. In truth, I own that I have al-
» ways singularly approved the Religious Orders ;
» the pious associations, and all the praiseworthy
» institutions of their kind, which are a sort of
» heavenly militia upon earth, provided that, apart
» from abuse and corruption, they are directed ac-
» cording to the rules of their founder, and that
» the Sovereign Pontiff applies them to the wants
» of the universal Church. What can there be in
» fact more excellent than to carry the light of
» truth to distant nations across the seas, and
» through fire and sword ? To be occupied with
» nothing but the salvation of souls ; to interdict
» oneself every pleasure, and even the sweetness of

» conversation and society, in order to be at lei-
» sure for the contemplation of supernatural truths
» and divine meditations; to be devoted to the edu-
» cation of youth, to give it a taste for knowledge
» and virtue; to go and carry help to the unhappy,
» to men lost in despair, to prisoners, to those who
» are condemned, to all those who are stript of
» every thing, or in fetters, or in distant regions,
» and in those services of the most expansive cha-
» rity not even to be frightened by the terror of
» the plague. Whoever does not know, or despises,
» these things, has only a cramped and vulgar idea
» of virtue; and foolishly thinks to have fulfilled
» his obligations to God when he has discharged
» outwardly some worn-out practices with that
» cold custom which is generally accompanied by
» no zeal or sentiment. » Evidently the learned
German philosopher who dwells upon these works
of the active and retired religious life would not
have stript Communities of their houses, churches,
and lands, and would have subscribed to the condemnation contained in these words of Pope Pius IX :
« With consummate impudence they do not hesi-
» tate to assert that divine revelation not only is
» of no use, but even injurious to human perfec-
» tion : and that divine revelation itself is imper-
» fect, and therefore subject to a continual and

» indefinite progress corresponding to the progres-
» sion of human reason. Nor thence are they
» ashamed to boast that the prophecies and mira-
» cles set forth and told in Holy Writ are the fan-
» cies of poets ; and the most holy mysteries of our
» divine faith the sum of philosophic investigations ;
» and that, in the divine books of either Testament,
» mythic inventions are contained, and that our
» very Lord Jesus Christ, horrible to tell ! is him-
» self a mythic fiction. »[1]

N A V E.

The nave is separated from the south aisle by a line of eight columns, of which only five remain. One is broken and imbedded in a brick pier for support. The front and sides of these piers are co-vered with frescoes, which for perfection of preser-vation, beauty of execution, and their ecclesiastical subjects, are the most interesting Christian compo-sitions ever discovered in Rome, or perhaps else-were. The pictures in the catacombs give us in-deed a class of parabolic and scriptural subjects familiar throughout the early Christian world, and some few figures of saints and Popes. But these,

---

[1] Encyclical of June 1862.

S. CLEMENT CELEBRATING MASS
SISINIUS MIRACULOUSLY STRUCK BLIND

besides such figures, give us also well contrived compositions of Roman devotion, and spirited records of historical events in the Church, after the catacombs were disused, and long before modern pictorial art was developed. They appear to have been part of a series painted about the same time, and, when the colours were fresh, the basilica must have presented a brilliant appearance very different from that puritanical baldness, which some suppose, but very falsely, as we have proved in the Introduction to these pages, to have been the undefiled condition of church walls in the early ages.

INSTALLATION OF CLEMENT BY S. PETER.
S. CLEMENT SAYING MASS.
MIRACLE OF SISINIUS.

Near the high altar, on a pier which is fourteen feet high, nine feet six inches in width, and three feet in thickness, we have a large, and admirably well preserved, series of paintings divided into three horizontal compartments. On the highest are nine figures the heads of which were destroyed during the building of the upper church, but the names, inscribed beneath the feet of four of them - LINVS, S. PETRVS, S. CLEMENS PAPA, CLETVS - enable us to understand that the subject represents the installation of Clement by S. Peter. S. Clement is standing on a highly ornamented throne. S. Peter, having one foot on the step of the throne, is leaning over Clement in the attitude of investing him with the *pallium*, symbol of universal jurisdiction. Linus is standing behind Peter; on the other side Cletus is next Clement; and both are in their sacerdotal vestments, but without the *pallium* moreover they occupy lower positions than those occupied by Peter and Clement who are on the same level, so that it would appear that the painter embraced the opinion of Tertullian and others, and intended to represent S. Clement as the immediate successor of S. Peter. But, as we have already observed, that opinion is contradicted by several Fathers of the early Church, as well as by the Canon of the Mass. Ciacconius, Oldoinus and others say that Peter nominated Clement for his immediate successor, but that, either through humility, or divine inspiration, he did not accept of that dignity until after the martyrdom of Cletus. Behind Linus and Cletus are two other priests in the vestments of their order, and behind them again two soldiers in Roman military costume.

The central compartment represents the interior of a church, from the arches of which are suspended seven lamps, symbolizing the seven gifts of the Holy Ghost. That over the altar is circular in form, much larger than the other six, and contains seven

lights, probably typical of the seven gifts of the same
Holy Spirit. Anastasius the librarian, who lived in
the ninth century, makes mention of this form of
lamp, and calls it « *Pharum cum corona*, » « a pharos
with a crown: » a crown from its form, and a pharos,
or lighthouse, from the brilliancy of the light it emit-
ted. [1] He also says that it was in common use in
all the Christian Churches. S. Clement in his pontifical robes is officiating at the altar, over which his
name - *S.Clemens Papa*, - Pope S. Clement, is written
in the form of a cross. He has the maniple between
the thumb and forefinger of the left hand. The altar
is covered with a plain white cloth, and on it are the
missal, the chalice, and paten. The missal is open,
and on one page of it are the words » *Dominus vo-*
biscum, » which the saint is pronouncing, his arms
extended, as Catholic priests do, even to this day,
when celebrating mass. On the other page « *Pax*
Domini sit semper vobiscum, » « the peace of the Lord
be ever with you. » These two phrases were introduced into the liturgy of the Church by Clement
himself and are still retained. On the right of the
saint are his ministers, namely two bishops with crosiers in their left hands, a deacon, and subdeacon.
They all have the circular tonsure, and the Pope in

---

[1] Commendatore De Rossi has published a bronze lamp of this
kind of the fifth century.

addition to the tonsure has the *nimbus*, or halo, the symbol of sanctity. On the left of the saint, but separated from him by the altar, is a group of fourteen persons probably representing the congregation. They are all admirably designed and carefully executed. Two of them have their names - Theodora, Sisinius - written beneath their feet. Theodora wears a rich and gracefully folded dress, and behind her stands a female of noble mien with jewelled headdress. Mombritius, James of Voragine, Panvinius and other early writers inform us that Theodora was the wife of Sisinius, that both were attached to the court of the emperor Nerva, that they were converted to the faith by S. Clement, and afterwards suffered martyrdom. [1] Sisinius, having intruded upon the mysteries, is struck blind, and his helplessness is admirably espressed. He grasps the shoulder of a youth who leads him towards the open door, and turns to gaze upon his eyes, whilst another assisting him behind seems to be telling, what had occurred, to Theodora who is looking at him with amazement and commiseration. It appears that Theodora, who was converted to the faith before Sisinius, had been in the habit of frequenting, without her husband's know-

---

[1] « Has inter Sisinius, necnon uxor ejus Theodora, atque alii Ner- » vae imperatoris familiares Christo nomen dederunt. » See Rondinini, page 8, §. 9.

ledge, the oratory in which S. Clement used to give instructions to the faithful and celebrate the eucharistic rites. Sisinius, on a certain day, followed her to the chapel, to discover what she was doing there. On entering it, he began, as Pagans in those days were wont to do, as well as many nominal Christians in our own, to ridicule the sacred mysteries, and was struck blind by the Almighty in punishment of his sin. But afterwards, repenting of what he had done, through the prayers of S. Clement, and of his pious wife Theodora, he recovered his sight, embraced the Christian faith, and sealed it with his blood. The following fourth stanza, or verse, of the very ancient hymn formerly sung at the first Vespers of S. Clement refers to this fact.

« Tunc convertuntur Christo sacrae virgines,
Magnatum sponsae Deo peramabiles;
Sed Theodorae sponsus zelotypio
Caecus et surdus factus est continuo;
Sed per Clementem credens sanus redditur. »

In the foreground, on the right of S. Clement, and in front of his attendants, are the figures of a man and woman holding in their hands lighted twisted tapers, called by Anastasius *kerostota*. They are of diminutive size, to indicate their humility, as may be seen in many more modern pictures painted three or four hundred years ago. The man has his name - Beno -

written near him, and the woman's name is Mary,
as we learn from the following inscription which separates this compartment from a beautiful border
below it: « Ego Beno Derapiza cum Maria uxore mea
» pro amore Domini et beati Clementis P. G. R. F. C. »
« I Beno Derapiza with Mary my wife for the love of
» God and blessed Clement had it painted for a fa-
» vour received. »

It is evidently mere pedantry to look for accurate
representations of ecclesiastical costumes in these
pictures. The artist has taken the liberty, as all artists do, to suit his compositions: thus the two assistants wear the maniple on the right wrist, which
is always worn on the left, and S. Clement holds his
maniple across the two fore fingers of the left hand.

In the lowest compartment there are four figures,
one of which is in the attitude of giving instructions
to the others who are engaged in dragging a column,
and each has his name written near him: Carvoncelle,
Albertel, Cosmaris, and Sisinius.   The three first are
clad in the short tunic, which is a badge of servi-
tude. Sisinius wears the toga and paludamentum of
a Roman tribune, and is addressing the men in the
following terms: « Falite de reto colo palo Carvon-
» celle, » « get behind the column, Carvoncelle, with
» a lever. » « Albertel, Cosmaris trai, » « Albertel,
» Cosmaris draw it up. »   « Fili dele pute traite, »

« Sons of — draw it up. » Interpolated under the arches « saxa traere meruistis : duritiam cordis » vestris (sic). » « For the hardness of your hearts » you have deserved to draw stones. » This compartment may, perhaps, have some allusion to the building of the church of S. Clement.

The above phrases may also be referred to the following fact which is recorded by several early writers in their lives of our Saint. On a certain day Sisinius, a noble Roman citizen, went to a church which his wife Theodora was in the habit of frequenting, in order that he might discover her motives for going there. He found S. Clement celebrating mass, and the saint, knowing why he intruded on the sacred mysteries, like another Eliseus, prayed the Lord to strike him with blindness. Sisinius finding himself deprived of his sight as well as of his speech, intimated to his servants to conduct him out of the church, but they could not find the door until Theodora begged of S. Clement to allow them to go away, which he accordingly did. Some time afterwards S. Clement visited Sisinius and restored his sight ; but the ungrateful man took the saint for a magician, and ascribing the loss and recovery of his sight and speech to his black art, ordered his servants to arrest him and cast him into prison. But a dense veil coming over their eyes

concealed S. Clement from them, and seizing a column
that was lying hard-by, they began to drag it along
thinking they were dragging their prisoner. The
holy man advised Theodora not to cease praying
until the Lord should enlighten her husband with
his heavenly light; and while she was praying, S. Peter appeared to her and said: « Your husband
» shall be saved in order that the words of Paul
» may be fulfilled : ' The unbelieving husband is
» sanctified by the believing wife. ' »[1] Sisinius
struck with remorse of conscience for his treatment
of Clement, desired Theodora to send for him. He
came and instructed him, together with 424 members of his family and slaves, in the mysteries of
the faith, and received them into the religion of
Christ. The words « *falite de reto colo palo Carvon-*
» *celle* » may be a corruption of the Latin « *fac ibi*
» *te retro cum palo Carvoncelle,* » « get behind the
» column with the lever (or stake) Carvoncelle. »
« *Albertel, Cosmâris,trai,* » «Albertel, Cosmaris, draw.»
« *Fili dele pute traite,* » « sons of—draw it up, » to
which a voice replies: « *Saxa traere meruistis: du-*
» *ritiam cordis vestris,* » « you have deserved to draw
» stones on account of the hardness of your hearts. »
Other interpretations might be given of these anti-

---

[1] Corinth., VII, 14.

quated sentences, but we shall leave them to those who are more profoundly versed in philology than we can have any claim to be.

The date of this painting has afforded a theme for discussion to some of the most eminent living archaeologists, philologists, and painters : some referring it to the twelfth century, others to the ninth, and others to the seventh. Without pretending to decide so difficult a question, we may observe that even the most modern pictures found here must be anterior to Robert Guiscard's devastation of the city in 1084, when very probably the basilica was abandoned, and it was found necessary to fill it with earth on account of the immense piles of ruins with which it was surrounded. But it may be objected that we cannot prove that the prefix (if it be a prefix) to Beno's cognomen [1] or even the cognomen itself, or any family of that name flourished in Rome before the twelfth century. We reply that this is a negative argument, and consequently proves nothing. Moreover there is a manuscript in the Lateran archives in which mention is made of a family of that name living in Rome in the eleventh

---

[1] Beno's cognomen has a very Dacian and Barbarian sound: but among the freedmen and their families descended from slaves from every part of the world it would not be difficult to find names equally barbarous. See Suetonius, *XII Caesarum* and *Taciti Annales* passim.

century, and that same family may have flourished
for centuries before. Finally it has been objected
that some of the inscriptions are in vulgar Italian,
which was not spoken before the twelfth century.
To this we oppose the authorities of the learned cardinal Bembo and Cesare Cantu. The former, in his work
« on the origin of the Italian language, » says: « It
» is asserted by some writers that the vulgar Italian
» language is coeval with the Latin, on the suppo-
» sition that the common people always had a lan-
» guage of their own; but it is certain that the
» vulgar Italian language was spoken shortly after
» the incursions of the barbarians, and as early as
» the sixth century. » The latter, in his complete
analysis of the formation of the Italian language [1]
furnishes us with phrases similar to those in our fresco, which were in use in the eighth and ninth centuries « *Da ipsa casa - ire ad marito - a scrivere tolli -
crotta, fenile - granario, orto, orticelle, corte.* » Therefore taking such examples into consideration perhaps
the ninth century may not be too early a period to
assign to these paintings. The style of the figures,
their execution and drapery, induced the renowned
painters Overbeck and Minardi to ascribe them to a
much earlier date.

---

[1] **Storia** universale, schiarimenti del libro **XI.**

S. ANTONINUS. — DANIEL IN THE LION'S DEN.

On the side of this pier, at the top, is the lowest half of a figure of a bishop in a richly ornamented dress, and jewelled buskins. His name, **Antoninus**, is painted under his feet. It may be Domitian's martyr of that name; or S. Antoninus, or Antoninus Cauleas, patriarch of Constantinople in 893, who laboured to extinguish the Greek schism begun by Photius,[1] and

---

[1] Photius was son of the patrician Sergius and of Irene, daughter of the pious empress Theodora. His parents committed his education to the celebrated Bardas, and so great was the proficiency he made in his studies that he became a prodigy of genius and learning. Poet, mathematician, orator, jurist, theologian, and statesman, Photius possessed the most refined intellect ; but his great qualifications were debased by a consummate depravity of soul; for he was the most cunning and deceitful of men, and always ready to sacrifice everything to his unbounded ambition. He held two distinguished offices at the court of Michael III, being Protospatharius and Protosecritis, that is, master of the horse, and chief secretary to the emperor. Religion, which he always looked upon with contempt, had everything to fear from an enemy of such a character. The eastern church, long since fallen from its primitive splendour by the neglect of holy teachings, now only wanted the impulse of an unfriendly hand to plunge it into the abyss of ruin. Photius became the instrument of this fearful catastrophe : he adhered to Gregory Abestas the schismatic bishop of Siracuse, in Sicily, who had raised a faction against S. Ignatius from the time of his promotion to the patriarcate of Constantinople. The saint had endeavoured to reclaim this prelate, but in vain ; so that at length he condemned and deposed him for his crimes, in a Council he held in 854. Photius continued to protect him, and being nominated patriarch by Bardas, in contempt of all canonical rule, and without even the form of an election, he was consecrated by the bishop of Siracuse, and on Christmas Day A. D. 858, the future author of the great eastern schism ascended the Patriarchal throne of Constantinople. Pope S. Nicholas I excommunicated

held a Council for that purpose, the Acts of which were purposely destroyed by the schismatics. In 846, S. Cyril told Photius: « Your passion against Ignatius » deprived you of your sight: » and in a series of pictures with which S. Cyril is intimately connected, the patriarch, who proceeded against that schismatic intruder (Photius), might be here appropriately introduced. Below, in the centre, is the prophet Daniel. He is dressed in Roman costume, and has

the sacrilegious intruder. The emperor Basil the Macedonian, two days after his accession to the throne removed him from the Patriarchal See, as a disturber of the public peace and S. Ignatius was reinstated. After the death of S. Ignatius, Basil recalled Photius who by his crafty machinations persuaded the Legates of Pope John VIII to restore him to his former rank. The eastern bishops terrified into submission by the proofs of the wonderful power so lately shown by Photius, dared not oppose his restoration. Basil wrote to urge the Pope's approval of Photius' nomination, which was granted on four conditions: 1st, that on the death of Photius, his place shall not be filled by a layman: 2d, that the Patriarch claim no jurisdiction whatever over the province of Bulgaria; 3d, that the bishops and clerics ordained by Ignatius shall hold their present rank and positions, and suffer no persecution; 4th, that Photius convene a council to receive the disavowal of his past conduct. The last clause was particularly displeasing to Photius. Its fulfilment would have cost his pride too dear, and he endeavoured to elude it. But the Pontiff having been informed of his faithlessness, in the presence of the clergy and faithful of Rome assembled in S. Peter's Church, renewed the anathemas pronounced against him by Nicolas I, Adrian II, and the eighth general Council. Marinus, who succeeded John VII in the potificate, and his successors Adrian III, and Stephen V, also condemned Photius. The letters of this last arrived in the east after the death of Basil the Macedonian in 886, and were delivered to his son and successor Leo the Wise, who immediately turned out Photius, and banished him into a monastery in Armenia, where he died after having lived thirty years in schism.

LIFE DEATH AND RECOGNITION OF S.ALEXIUS

the ephod on his breast; his hands are outstretched, and his eyes raised to heaven, while two lions gambol at his feet beneath which his name - Ss. Danihel - is written. The incorrect drawing of these animals, and of five others in the panel below, show that the painter never saw a lion in his life. In the earliest known painting of this subject, which is in Domitilla's cemetery, the prophet stands on a mount with his hands extended in prayer, but without the nimbus, and the two lions are very natural as well as lively. They seem to have been painted by one who heard the cry: « The Christians to the lions. » On Christian sarcophagi the saint appears in a state of gladiatorial nudity, and the beasts, on either side, squatted on their haunches, have not quite lost the ferocious character of their nature, though approaching the stiff quaint heraldic character we see here. An ornamental border separates the middle from the lower panel, and shows a good deal of fancy and taste.

LIFE, DEATH, AND RECOGNITION, OF S. ALEXIUS.

Called from a palace to a pilgrimage, from Roman espousals to a hermit's life, in a hut near our Lady's church at Edessa; in youth's bloom to the austerity of solitary old age; from wealth to privations; in privations to return home, not as the prodigal son, but, that hardest trial of merely human nature, to his birth-place, self-stript of its ties and associations, to parents no longer knowing him as their child, forgotten by all, a mendicant asking for charity, and with no place to lay his head ; this young nobleman, who lived in the beginning of the fifth century, Alexius, has bequeathed to the city of the Pontiffs an imperishable name. The artist, who painted the subject we are about to treat of, seems to have felt that the sweet odour of grace was wafted from that story of inspired devotion, and to have sought for appropriate ornament. The honey-suckle supplies the border below the picture of his death , the lower panel, of flowers, fruits, and gay birds of paradise, is resplendent in colour and in excellent taste. Above, the angels of our Lady and of the strength of the Church, Gabriel and Michael, censor in hand, stand beside the magnificent throne on which our Lord sits holding in his hands a scroll with the words « Fortis ut vincula mortis, » « strong » as the bonds of death. » Thus He presides over the life and death of the saint. Saints Clement and Nicholas are there also. Upon the Aventine Hill, the beautiful campanile of S. Alexius, on his father's house, looks down on one side upon the Tiber and the great hospice of San Michele, upon the Ripa

Grande, the port of ancient Rome, and upon S. Francesco a Ripa, built on the ancient church of S. Blaze where the saint of holy poverty, S. Francis, used to live. On the other side upon the ruins of the Forum and Coliseum, and the hills of Latium. The remains of the palace of Pope Honorius III, and of an antique Roman house are on the steep of the hill below towards the river. Honorius confirmed the rule of the order of S. Dominic in 1216, in which year the relics of S. Alexius were found in his church near the Dominican convent of S. Sabina. S. Adelbert of Prague, S. Boniface, the apostle of Germany, martyred at the age of seventy five, in 755, and S. Thomas of Canterbury martyred in 1170, lived in the convent of S. Alexius. There, once overlooking the busy grandeur of the world, the palace of the rich, and noble Roman Senator, Euphimianus, held a hidden treasure - the heart of his only child. Dear lover of the poor he gave incessant alms, and God rewarded him, calling him to a higher state, the greater sacrifice of voluntary poverty. « Yet one » thing is wanting to thee: sell all that thou hast, » and give to the poor, and thou shalt have trea- » sure in heaven; and come, and follow me. »[1] His chaste soul was vowed to God alone. His parents

---

[1] Luke, XVIII, 22.

urged him to marriage. His heart had already forsaken the world. If men have freedom, they should have freedom to live for religion. « Amen, I say » to you there is no man that hath left house, or » parents, or brethren, or wife, or children, for the » kingdom of God's sake, who shall not receive much » more in this present time, and, in the world to » come, life everlasting. » [1] He fled. In the eyes of the world he was eccentric or insane ; a son who rebelled against his parents, a husband who abandoned his bride. The Church, in him, vindicates the right, to make choice of a more perfect state, before the consummation of marriage; the pilgrim who hated father, and mother, and wife to come to Christ; the ascetic who hated his own soul that he might thereby save it, and shouldered his cross to be Christ's disciple; the saint obedient to grace and faithful to death. And the eye that gazes, from the cloister of S. Sabina, by the orange tree S. Dominic planted there, upon the palm tree waving its branches against the tower of S. Alexius, may turn itself within, and the soul ponder how sin is purged by suffering, and by what mysterious compensation young innocence seems to be called upon, in the hardship of a religious life, to do penance for hardened vice. At Edessa,

---

[1] Luke, XVIII, 29.

Alexius was miraculously recognized as a person of distinction, and saintly life. [1] He returned to Rome and as a pilgrim received hospitality in his father's house, where he spent many years bearing with joy the taunts of the servants. The staircase under which he was allowed to stay is still preserved over one of the altars in his church on the Aventine.

In the central compartment of the painting we see him on his return to Rome, in the garb of a pilgrim, with his wallet and staff, accosting Euphimianus who is on horseback followed by two attendants, and evidently asking hospitality of him. Euphimianus is pointing with his right hand to his palace (from the balcony of which a lady is looking,) and saying to Alexius: « That is my residence, in it you » shall find an asylum. » During his stay in his father's house he wrote an account of his life, but would not consign the manuscript to any one. At length, sickness came upon him, and he died holding the manuscript in his right hand with so stiff a grasp, that it could not be removed. At that moment the

---

[1] See Pinius the Bollandist, t. 4, Julii, pag. 239, who confutes the groundless and inconsistent surmises of Baillet regarding S. Alexius. Nerinio abbot of the Hieronymites at Rome who has fully vindicated the memory of S. Alexius in his Dissertation *De Templo et Coenobio SS. Bonifacii et Alexii,* in 4to, Rome, 1752. Also see Joseph Assemani ad 17 Martii in Calend. Univ. t. 6, pag. 187-189. And Bibl. Orient. t. 1, p. 401.

bells of the adjacent church began to ring a joyful
peal, of their own accord. The inhabitants of the
neighbourhood were seized with astonishment: the
phenomenon could not be explained. After a little
the news reached S. Boniface who then governed the
Church. Euphimianus requested him to come and
explain the marvel. The Pope consented, and he
went up to the Aventine accompanied by his clergy
and cross-bearer. On his arrival at Euphimianus' palace, he was conducted to the staircase where the
dead pilgrim lay. He recited a short prayer, and
leaning towards the pilgrim he took, without any
difficulty, the manuscript from his hand, and blessed
him. Euphimianus is standing by with an expression
of compassion, not knowing, of course, who the dead
man was. A little more to the right of the spectator
is depicted his recognition. He is laid on a bier covered with a pall, decorated with crosses, and birds
holding snow white lilies, symbols of purity in their
beaks. His aged parents tear their hair through grief
for not having known him, and the bride covers his
face with kisses, The inscription below says: « The
» father does not recognize who asks his pity. » The
Pope holds the scroll which tells his austere life. His
interment was celebrated with great pomp by the
whole city of Rome. How many parents have wept
when the spirit whispers to the young heart: « Hear,

« my daughter, and see, and incline thine ear; and
» forget thy people, and the house of thy father, and
» the king will desire thy beauty, for he is the Lord
» thy God and they shall adore him. » [1]   The final close of the devoted soul is well indicated by the
words upon the scroll in the Pontiff's hands: « Come
» to me, all you that labour. » [2]

S. AEGIDIUS, OR GILES. — S. BLAZE.

On the side of this pier, at the top, is part of a
figure with the name Egidius, that is Giles.   The
celebrated Athenian hermit of this name lived at the
end of the seventh century near Nismes, and was
greatly honoured in France where he built a monastery which became a great Benedictine Abbey, and
gave his name to the town of S. Giles.   But from the
position of S. Giles here in connection with S. Alexius
who lived in the fifth century, he may be the Abbot
who was sent in 514 by S. Caesarius of Arles to seek,
confirmation of the privileges of his metropolitan
church, from Pope Symmachus.   The election of Symmachus, at the end of that century, was contested by
an Eutychian antipope, and S. Caesarius condemned
the Semipelagians in the second Council of Orange

---

[1] Psalm. 44.
[2] Mathew, XI, v. 28.

in 529. S. Alexius lived in the same century with
Zosimus and Celestine, whom we have seen condemning the Pelagians, Eutychians, and Semipelagians,
and Leo the Great who by his presidency over the
Council of Chalcedon may be said to have torn up this
class of heresies by the root. In fact, S. Prosper,
whose portrait we shall find near this, and for whom
S. Leo sent from the South of France to become
his secretary, wrote vigorously against the Semipelagians. Their error consisted in admitting grace,
but stickling for man's own free will as moving to
virtuous actions before the call of grace. One might
suppose that the life of S. Alexius, so opposed to
natural free will, and so inexplicable without the
most powerful call of grace, was a practical refuta-
tion at the time; that that miracle of grace, the life
of a young saint choosing privations and abstinence
of every kind, in the very lap of fortune, and wooing
of the world, might consume the error in the flames
of divine love.

It is difficult to account for the selection of the
martyr bishop S. Blaze placed below S. Giles, except by
a reference again to S. Leo the Great, and the relics
under the high altar, among which are those of the
Forty martyrs of Sebaste in Armenia, of which city
Blaze was bishop. A year after S. Sylvester had
gazed from the walls of Rome in the direction of that

battle which gave her a Christian emperor, he was chosen Pope, and sent his Legates to the Council of Arles against the Donatists, a sect then seven years old, which pretended that the Catholic Church had failed elsewhere, and was to be found in its purity only in Carthage their own local metropolis.[1] But if S. Sylvester was condemning heresy, and Constantine supporting his decisions, Licinius was persecuting Christians, and, in 316, S. Blaze was put to death. Four years afterwards, the twelfth legion, quartered in Armenia, was ordered to sacrifice. Forty stepped out before the governor, Agricola, who had tortured the bishop, declaring themselves Christians; and, like S. Blaze, their sides were torn with iron hooks. Were we to take this image of their bishop, placed beside the sudden call of S. Alexius, as a sufficient reference to their history, no more instantaneous and effective call of grace could be found; for when they were stripped upon the ice to perish by lingering cold, one only apostatized, and his place was instantly occupied. « Lord, we are forty who are engaged in » this combat; grant that we may be forty crowned,

---

[1] The Donatists, in an assembly they held at Carthage, had the insolence to unchurch the whole Christian world except themselves, and commanded all, who had been baptized by Catholics, to be again baptized. To prevent so great a sacrilege, Constantine made it a capital offence for any one to rebaptize another - see Codex Just. tit. Haeret. lib. 2.

» and that not one be wanting to this sacred num-
» ber. » Such their prayer. A sentinel, moved by
a vision of spirits descending and distributing gifts
to all except the apostate, threw down his arms, stript
himself, and took the deserter's place. S. Blaze appears extracting a thorn from a boy's throat, who is
supported by his mother. He was patron of the wool-
combers at Norwich, who kept his festival in the
last century. In Rome, upon his feast (February 3),
which is celebrated in the church of S. Maria in Via
Lata, where S. Paul was lodged, a relic of his throat
is venerated; and also in a church dedicated to him
in Via Giulia, persons with diseased throats are
touched with another of his relics. The wolf carrying off a pig, which he is said to have saved by his
prayers, refers to a story recorded in his life.

S. PROSPER OF AQUITAINE.

Passing down the aisle by two beautiful columns
of *bigio* marble, one spiral, the other plain, we must
take the picture of S. Prosper of Aquitaine as the
only memorial left here of the condemnation of Pelagianism. A Welshman and Scotchman together were
its patrons: Morgan a monk of Bangor who took the
name of Pelagius, « by the sea, » and his pupil a
noble Scot, and *quondam* lawyer, known as the monk

Celestius « from the skies. » But neither was the original inventor of this heresy which denied the necessity of grace. Morgan picked it up at Rome, about the year 400, from Rufinus the Syrian, and then went off to Palestine to perfect it. The root of it was disbelief in the divinity of Christ, a heresy vigorously maintained by the Nazarenes and Ebionites at Pella whither the Christians had retired before Vespasian attacked Jerusalem. « Is not this the car-
» penter's son ? is not his mother called Mary, and
» his brethren James, and Joseph, and Simon, and
» Jude: and his sisters are they not all with us?
» whence therefore hath he all these things? » [1]
Ebion and Cerinthus attributed other children to the ever Virgin Mary before the birth of Jesus, as their followers since have done after that event: the whole being nothing else than a denial of the supernatural power of God and the fall of Adam, for if Adam had no grace to fall from, and Jesus were simply such as he, mere man, His blessed Mother needed no fullness of grace, and there was nothing but natural talent to recommend the New Testament to the human race. To follow its precepts became mere matter of choice, and no authoritative worship of the Creator could exist. The crucifixion became

---

[1] Mathew, XII, 55-56.

only a natural consequence of opposition to the world, and its victim a virtuous enthusiast. The presence of God in the pillar and cloud had passed away, and was expunged from the tabernacle, by the destruction of the only authorized Temple. The renewal of it by the Catholic Church could only be an illusion, or a trick. Sacraments were superfluous where grace, if they could confer it, was not needed. Preaching could only be, at best, of the natural law: Christ a capital philosopher, the best exponent of God the Creator, and of the moral duties of His creatures : heaven the birthright of man, if this world was not to last for ever : eternal hell an unnecessary invention repugnant alike to the affections of man, and his Maker who loved him. In short, as the rites, and ceremonies of the synagogue, were come to an end, and man ought not to go back to all that preceded it, the perfectibility of his reason, and natural appetite for good, would lead him on in an indefinite progress of intelligence, and moral virtues to be happy for ever. This desolating system was a renewal of Satan's old trick: « No, you shall not die the death. For » God doth know that in what day soever you shall » eat thereof, your eyes shall be opened: and you shall « be as gods, knowing good and evil. »[1] A voice from heaven: « This is my beloved Son » died away in idle

---

[1] Genesis, Chap. III, Ver. 4-5.

echoes when men said it thundered, or an angel had spoken. The only answer was the conduct of the Church, which, as each phase of heresy appeared, condemned it in its turn. It is not worth while to pursue the subterfuges of Pelagius and his disciples. At Carthage in 412, and at Diospolis in 415, accused by the exiled bishops of Arles and Aix, and in both cities condemned, he adopted that policy, which we have seen in our own day, of private conversations, and letters to friends; and such a system received its check, when the Bishop of Rome was written to for information with a will to abide by his answer. In 415 the bishops of Jerusalem took this course. In 416 again at Carthage and Milevis; and in 417 Innocent excommunicated the two, Pelagius and Celestius. Celestius came to Rome. Pope Zosimus, in March 417, without removing the excommunication, deferred sentence for two months. In 418 a great Council at Carthage renewed the excommunication; Zosimus confirmed it, and sent the sentence to Africa and all the chief churches of the East.

It often happens in the history of the Church, that error is answered not merely by the pen, but by a living saint. Augustine the Manichaean,[1] who

---

[1] The fallen Chaldaean priest Manes had got his notion of two necessarily existing principles, good and evil, creating their like, from Scythianus, the lapsed Arab Christian merchant.

at twenty two tested everything by reason, and
turned his wit against the Catholics, was yet to be
the converted child of his mother's tears, S. Monica;
yet to hear of S. Antony of the desert; yet to hear
the child singing « take up and read; » to snatch
up S. Paul's epistles from the garden bench, and
read with smitten heart: « Not in rioting and drunk-
» ness ; not in chambering and impurities, not in
» contention and envy: but put ye on the Lord
» Jesus Christ, and make not provision for the flesh
» in its concupiscences ».[1] As yet this African, im-
mersed in the pride of life, and the lust of the eyes,
was to become a convert, priest, bishop, founder of
a religious Order, doctor of the Church, saint. On
the grace of Jesus Christ, on original sin, on marriage
and concupiscence, on the soul and its origin, are
some of the works which, then thirty years a priest,
he wrote against Pelagianism. Pelagius was scotched,
not killed. In 429, Pope Celestine had sent his two
vicars against him to Britain. Both were French.
S. Lupus bishop of Troyes, who abandoned the married state to become a priest, and at the head of
his clergy boldly met Attila « the scourge of God, »
and saved his city. S. Germanus bishop of Auxerre,
called by compulsion to the ecclesiastical state, for

---

[1] Rom, Chap. XIII, ver. 13-14.

he was a military man, when the then bishop shut the church doors upon him and tonsured him. On his journey he received the virginal vow of S. Genevieve the future patroness of Paris, and foretold her sanctity. Confounded by their successful preaching, the heretics came to a conference at S. Alban's. It ended by Germanus taking his reliquary from his bosom, and laying it on the eyes of a blind girl who was restored to sight. He ordered the protomartyr's tomb to be opened, placed the reliquary within it, and took a little of the martyr's dust which he used in the consecration of a church at Auxerre. The devil, finding himself checkmated at S. Alban's, carried his warfare to the South of France. Some priests thought that by grace Augustine destroyed free will; and they compromised by granting that supernatural grace was necessary for actions conducive to eternal life but that free will must start the first desire. Like most compromises it was a bad one. Thus, Semipelagianism, ascribing to the creature alone the beginning of virtue, gave the whole to him and not to God. S. Prosper of Aquitaine applied to Augustine who replied, two or three years before his death, by Books on the predestination of the saints, and the gift of perseverance. Prosper went to Rome about it, and Celestine commended Augustine's doctrine to the bishop of Marseilles and others. When Leo the Great

18

became Pope in 440, he called Prosper to Rome and
made him his secretary. The final overthrow of the
heresy was due to S. Prosper; or as he himself describes it in his poem upon the Semipelagians ungrateful to divine grace. [1]

> « *Pestem subeuntem prima recidit*
> *Sedes Roma Petri, quae pastoralis honoris*
> *Facta caput mundo quicquid non possidet armis*
> *Religione tenet.* »

> « The stealing pestilence, the first cut off
> Rome Peter's Seat of pastoral honour made
> Head to the world ; what'er not owned by arms
> By true religion held. »

CRUCIFIXION.

On the pilaster, forming a right angle at the
end of the nave, is a group of subjects, if not arranged in connection with S. Prosper to vindicate the
doctrine of original sin and sacramental grace, yet
happily illustrating them. We turn with pleasure
from the discomfited heresies to the Author of grace
upon the cross. The painting is old and rude, but true
human hearts stand beside it. « You are they who
have continued with me in my temptations. » [2] Our
Lady is appealing to her Divine Son. S. John with
his Gospel roll stretches a supplicating hand to Him.
Could the painter better indicate the words : « Wo-

---

[1] Carmen de ingratis. — [2] Luke, XXII, 28.

CRUCIFIXION.THE MARYS AT THE SEPULCHRE

DESCENT INTO LIMBO.MARIAGE AT CANA

» man, behold thy Son; after that he saith to the
» disciple: ' Behold thy Mother ; ' and from that
» hour the disciple took her to his own ? » [1]
Mistress of the little house of Nazareth ; Mistress of
every Christian home, in the house and in the temple
wherever the Cross of Christ is venerated that Mother is found beside it. Our Lord is not represented as dead : there is suffering compassion in His
face. This is probably the earliest church picture
we have of the Crucifixion, and, if poor in art,
there is Christian feeling in the simplicity which
gives us the union of those three hearts in the hour
of agony and death. Red streams of grace flowed
down upon the guilty earth : the appointed Mother
stood. That loud cry rent the veil of the useless
temple, and so shook nature that the dead came
forth from their graves; still she stood. For in that
temple she had presented the Child, and for her a
prophecy was yet to be fulfilled. His heart was
pierced and her's; and as the blood and water flowed
that marriage type of Cana lived again before her
eyes. The mystery of the Cross was consummated.

THE MARYS AT THE SEPULCHRE.
DESCENT INTO LIMBO. — MARRIAGE FEAST AT CANA.

High up on the pilaster, at right angles with the
one we have just noticed, is depicted the open arch

___
[1] John, XIX, 27.

of our Lord's sepulchre with the lamp suspended
from it. The angel seems saying to the two women bringing the spices they had prepared : « He
» is risen, he is not here, behold the place where
» they laid him. »[1] The roll in the hand of her
with the alabaster box may refer to the pre-
diction « Wheresoever this Gospel shall be preached
» in the whole world, that also which she hath
» done, shall be told for a memory of her. »[2]
The last unction of His feet for burial was no common act. It was done with a pound of ointment
of rich spikenard of great value, and the house was
filled with the odour of the ointment. « If, » says
Augustine, « you will be a faithful soul, anoint
» the Lord's feet with the precious ointment. But
» that ointment was that of faith. By faith the
» just man lives; anoint the feet of Jesus by living
» well. Hearken to the Apostle when he says: ' We
» are the good odour of Christ unto God, in them
» that are saved, and in them that perish. To the
» one indeed the odour of death unto death : but
» to the others the odour of life unto life.' »[3]

---

[1] Mark. XVI, v. 6.

[2] Mathew XXVI, v. 13.

[3] Corinth. Chap. II, v. 15-16. — *The odour of death etc.* The preaching of the Apostle, which, by its fragrant odour, brought many to life,
was to others, through their own fault, the occasion of death; by their
wilfully opposing and resisting that divine call.

The subject below the sepulchre is the descent into Limbo, to release the souls which could not be admitted to the presence of God until the merits of Christ's passion had been applied to them. When the women returned from the sepulchre, their words seemed to the Apostles as an idle dream. But to Adam it was no dream when our Lord entered and raised him by the hand. In his state of glory, indicated by the azure cloud in which He is enveloped, our Saviour, with a grave and affectionate action, is releasing the parents of the human race. Adam presses one hand upon his breast, whilst Eve, behind, extends both in energetic supplication. Adam by his fall had not lost the inherent qualities of human nature, but forfeited the grace with which that nature had been endowed. To recover grace was the whole aim of a virtuous life, and purgatory the means to clear away the faults which marred the aim. So S. Gregory of Nyssa expresses it : « Some » there are who throughout their life in the flesh » regulate their lives in a spiritual manner and free » from passion : such we are told were the patriarchs » and prophets, and they who lived with them and » after them, men who hastened back to the per- » fect by means of virtue and the persuit of wisdom. » While others, through their entry into the future » state, have cast aside in the purgatorial fire their

» propensity to the material, and have returned
» gladly from an eager desire of good things to
» that grace which was at first the inheritance of our
» nature. » [1] The most efficacious means to obtain
this grace is the sacramental action of the Eucharist; and the Catholic painter ends his group of
mysteries with its type in the miracle of Cana. The
master of the feast who is addressing Christ, is
indicated by ARCHITRICLINVS written vertically over
his head. Our Lady with the nimbus stands next
to him. In the grave look of our Lord, with his
eyes cast down, there is an expression becoming
the importance of the Sacrament. All flows from
the life-blood of Christ. « A cluster of Cyprus my
» love is to me in the vineyards of Engaddi. » [2]
« We preach, » says S. Ephrem, « the cluster which
» when squeezed has filled the chalice of salvation
» with its own liquor. » And he represents our
Lady saying to the Magi: « I do fear Herod the
» polluted wolf, lest he disturb me and grasp the
» sword to cut off the sweet cluster yet unripe. »
For the Daughter of Sion knew what David had
sung: « Thou hast prepared a table before me,
» against them that afflict me. Thou hast anoint-

---

[1] De anim. et resurr. , p. 676.
[2] Canticle, 1, 13.

» ed my head with oil; and my chalice which inebria-
» teth me, how goodly is it! » [1] We easily connect,
the vintage scenes of the catacombs and the dove
with the full cluster of grapes, with the juice poured
into the chalice. Christ described in various figures
pours himself through the Church: Himself with
His grace under the veils of the bread and the wine,
but His grace alone in the other Sacraments. Grace
is the sap of the Church, the life blood of the
mystic vine. Those who reject it, cry with the Jews:
« His blood be upon us and upon our children. »[2]
Reject any fact of the divine testimonies, and
the connexion of the fact is lost; but deny the
necessity of grace, and the whole of the testimonies are whithered, for the Church exists only to
distribute it. When treason was at the table upon
the very issuing of the great Sacrament of Grace,
the words of warning were added. « Abide in me,
» and I in you. As the branch cannot bear fruit
» of itself, unless it abide in the vine, so neither
» can you, unless you abide in me. I am the vine ;
» you the branches: he that abideth in me, and
» I in him, the same beareth much fruit: for without
» me you can do nothing. If any one abide not in

---

[1] Psalm. XXII , v. 5.
[2] Math., XXVII, v. 25.

» me he shall be cast forth as a branch, and shall
» wither, and they shall gather him up, and cast
» him into the fire, and he burneth. » [1]

ASSUMPTION OF THE BLESSED VIRGIN.

As we approached with reverence that old niche
where, in the northern aisle, we found the Mother
in glory with the Son, here again we greet the sequel
and consummation of the triumph of the Cross in
her Assumption. Come, cried the Jews blaspheming
in the ears of that faithful Mother, « let Christ the
» King of Israel now come down from the Cross that
» we may see and believe.» [2] Come, « let us put the
» wood on his bread, and blot him out from the land
» of the living, and his name shall be remembered
» no more. » [3] The Church replies :

> « Impleta sunt, quae concinit
> David fideli carmine,
> Dicendo nationibus :
> Reynavit a ligno Deus. » [4]

> « O sacred Wood ! in thee fulfill'd
> Was holy David's truthful lay ;
> Wich told the world, that from a tree,
> The Lord should all the nations sway. »

[1] John, XV, v. 4-5-6.
[2] Mark, c. XV. v. 32.
[3] Jerem, II. v. 10.
[4] Hymn « Vexilla regis. »

ASSUMPTION OF THE BLESSED VIRGIN

That triumph would not, in a certain sense, be complete if she who had borne the heat and burden of the day where not beside the throne to share it. S. Alphonsus Liguori, considering why Mary, altogether sinless in soul and body, was yet permitted to undergo the common penalty of death, says that God wished to give the just the model of a sweet and happy death. It is a sweet thought that the Son who gave himself to the human race in the form dearest to their affections, that of the first born child, and had no dearer gift upon the Cross than her he loved so well, was showing S. John, in her, how to die. That living death of her's - the constant anticipation of Simon's prophecy in the passion of her Son, all those toils and travails she had borne for Him, all those pangs and insults, that patient woman was meekly sharing at the foot of the Cross, so naturally prepared her to minister at the bed of death, and disposed her so well to die, that were there nothing supernatural in the invocation of her name, it would rise of itself on dying lips with that of Jesus. As Irenaeus says : « As the human race was bound to death » by a virgin Eve, it is saved through a Virgin ; the » scales being equally balanced, virginal disobedience » by virginal obedience. » If Henoch and Elias were translated, that perfect will of Mary was not to lose the merit of « obedient even unto death. » And if

the Collyridian heretics strove to worship Mary, as
Gentiles did Astarte queen of heaven, death proving
her mortality gave her a triumph in the act. For
that pure body (such is the tradition of the Church)
was not to know the corruption of the grave, but,
reunited with her soul, anticipated the general resurrection, and abides with God in glory for ever.
Before this picture, of nigh a thousand years ago,
the theologian must bow his head. It is the earliest
known picture of the Assumption; [1] and in the fact
of her Assumption is contained the reprobation of
that heresy which Pius IX has had occasion to condemn, that life is distinct from the soul. For if the
most perfect and privileged creature of divine love,
after the sacred humanity of Christ, thus lost life and
recovered it by the reunion of the soul, the triumph
which the Church celebrates in this circumstance is
an evidence of the true faith on this point. « Arise, o
» Lord, into thy resting place ; Thou, and the ark
» which Thou hast sanctified. » [2]   The angels and

---

[1] The feast of the Assumption of the blessed Virgin is mentioned, as
having been celebrated with great pomp before the sixth century, both in
the Greek and Latin Churches, as appears from the most ancient sacramen-
taries extant, with complete calendars, before the time of Pope Sergius, as
is clear from the Pontifical ; and before the reign of the emperor Mauritius,
as is gathered from Nicephorus, lib. 17, 28. See also Baronius Annot. in
Martyr. Mabillon in liturg. Gallic. lib. 2, p. 118. Pagi in Brev. Gest. Rom.
Pont. in Sergio n. 26. Martene de Eccl. discipl. in diviu. Offic. c. 33, n. 25.
Thomassin etc.

[2] Psalm. 131.

saints, accustomed though they were to the wonders of heaven in which God displays the magnificence of His power, at the sight of the dazzling beauty with which Mary was adorned as she ascended on high full of grace, cried to their Lord: « Who is she that » cometh up from the desert flowing with delights, » leaning upon her beloved. » [1] And if human will would seek to persuade itself that this refers to the beauty of the soul of the just, to what soul so much as to hers? If it were expedient that their Master should depart, and prepare a place for the Apostles, His mother, surely, would not be left behind, and her place is at His right hand. « At thy right hand the » queen hath stood in a vesture all of gold, girt » about with variety. » [2]

Our Saviour is above, seated on His starry throne, in a nimbus supported by four angels. In His left hand He holds a closed book, while the right is extended. The design is not unworthy of Beato Angelico. Below, the Apostles, finding the tomb empty, are in various attitudes of emotion and surprise, and all have their eyes fixed on Her who is mounting aloft, and disappearing from their sight. They are in two groups, six on each side of the

---

[1] Canticles, 8, 5.
[2] Psalm. 44.

tomb, and two have their hands elevated, probably to indicate the desire they had to follow Her. The beloved disciple, who took his Mother to his own house, holds the Gospel roll with one hand, and places the other before his mouth in a manner reverential and full of astonishment. S. Vitus, holding a small cross in his right hand, stands at the extreme end to the right. He has his name - Sanctvs Vitvs - written vertically near his head, which is tonsured and surrounded with the halo. We cannot positively affirm which of the saints of that name he represents ; but very probably he was a member of the Order of the *Crociferi* -- Cross-bearers, -- founded by Pope S. Cletus. Or it may be that he was the celebrated S. Avitus archbishop of Vienne in France, who died in 525, and that he is placed near S. John on account of his opposition to the Arians who by denying our Lord's divinity deprived the incarnation of its supernatural value as a remedy for sin, and by thus degrading the Son to their own level reduced the Mother whom all generations shall call « Blessed, » and the Angel saluted « full of grace, » to the condition of any ordinary woman. S. Avitus was held in great esteem by Clovis, king of France, while, yet a Pagan, and by Gundebald the Arian king of Burgundy, whose son, and successor, Sigismund, he converted to the

Catholic faith. Ennodius, in his life of S. Epiphanius, says of him « that he was a treasure of learn-
» ing and piety. » Perhaps if we may conjecture
why a prelate of Vienne is found in the same composition with Pope Leo IV, A D. 847, 855, the reason
is that S. Ado, who was consecrated bishop of that
See in September 860, and next year received the
pallium from Nicholas I, with the decrees of a
Roman Council to check disorders which hadcrept
into several churches in France, had lived five years
previously in Rome, and from his distinguished character, and connexions with that See, may have had
an influence in the selection of the saint. On the
corresponding extremity to the left is Pope S. Leo
with the square green nimbus, or glory, to indicate that he was living at the time this picture was
painted, either by himself while yet a simple priest,
(for the halo and pallium might have been added
after he had been made Pope), or by a priest of
the same name, for the inscription underneath records « Quod haec prae cunctis splendet pictura de-
» core, componere hanc studuit presbyter ecce Leo. »
« That this picture may outshine the rest in beauty,
» behold the priest Leo studied to compose it. »
From the inscription « Sanctissimus Dom. Leo . . rt.
» PP. Romanus, » « Most holy Lord Leo. . . Pope of
» Rome, » it is not easy to determine whether he

is Leo III, or Leo IV, for the letters preceding it
are almost effaced, and cannot be read. If it be
Leo III, it must have been painted before 795; if
Leo IV, before 847. The latter had been priest
of the church of the Four crowned martyrs opposite S. Clement's. His feast is on the same day as
that of S. Alexius, July 17. The following names
are scratched on two narrow fillets running parallel
to the inscription under the feet of the Apostles:
« Hier. Ego Mercurius. Mercurius Presb. Petrus Lu-
» rissa. Ursus Presb. XXX Novembris obiit Kalaleo.
» † Salbius Presb. Flori. Florus Presb. S. Theodori.
» Joannes Presb. de Titu. Ego Rufinus Presb. Ven.
» Dom. Clemens Presb. Georgius. Ego Mercurius
» Presb. » Probably they are the names of the priests
who were attached to this basilica, except that of
Florus of S. Theodore's: but at what period they
lived we have not been able to ascertain. The priests
John and Salbius may be the same who scratched
their names in the niche of the Madonna in the
north aisle.

NARTHEX.

Two of the paintings in the narthex, as well
as the one we have noticed, at pages 248-9-50, of

the miracle of Sisinius, refer to the history of S.Clement. It is not easy to describe them without repetition. They have this peculiar interest that they are the earliest votive pictures we possess; or at least that we are acquainted with. No doubt the Catholic custom of giving expression in this way to feelings of religious gratitude for the benefits of Providence, for hair-breath escapes, graces of healing, and answers to prayer, always existed; and just as Pius IX invoked the help of our Lady when the floor was giving way beneath his feet at S. Agnese, and that most remarkable escape was followed up by the restoration of the church, and by commemorative pictures; so the authors of these pictures in our church seem to record their great devotion to S. Clement. « Who then, » says S. Basil of Seleucia, « will not be in admiration of the great power » of the Mother of God, and how far she goes beyond » whatever other saints we honour? For if Christ » bestowed so much power upon his servants as » not only to cure the afflicted by their touch, but » to do this even by their shadow, what must we » think of the power given to the Mother? » He describes many miracles in answer to prayers addressed to the virgin martyr S. Thecla (who suffered martyrdom in the first century, and he wrote in the middle of the fifth), so that her church was, in some way, a public hospital, celebrated throughout the east for curing diseases, alleviating sufferings, and casting out demons; and men went their way from it singing hymns, giving thanks, and blessing. In the preceding century S. Basil of Cappadocia says of the Forty martyrs of Sebaste: « The » afflicted flies to the Forty, the gladdened runs to » the same : the former to find deliverance from his » troubles, the latter that his more fortunate lot » may be continued to him. There the pious mo- » ther is found praying for her children, supplicating » for her husband on his journey, and begging health » for him when afflicted with sickness.» S. Augustine says : « This question surpasses the power of my » understanding, in what manner the martyrs suc- » cour those who are certainly helped by them. » He says he was himself a witness of the great glory of the martyrs, SS. Protasius and Gervasius, disco- vered in Milan by S. Ambrose. Nor was the belief in miraculous cures in the fourth century confined to Milan; for S. Asterius of Amacea says: « Thus » does a father, or a mother taking her sick child » and folding it in her arms, hurry by hospitals » and physicians, and fly unto help that knows no- » thing of their art; and having come to any of the » martyrs, through him she offers up a prayer to » the Lord. » And he adds, what travellers to Italy

will recognize as an evidence of the continuity of
Catholic habits in the West: « The crowds of beg-
» gars and the swarms of poor regard the resting
» place of the martyrs as their common asylum. »
And if any of them have shared in the sprinkling
of the holy water at S. Antony's at Rome, they may
witness an exemplification of what S. Paulinus says:
« You may see not only parents from the country
» bearing in their arms the pledges of their affection,
» but even oftentimes bringing in with them their
» sick cattle.» Or they may have been scandalized
by the practice mentioned by Theodoret, « that
» those, who faithfully petition, obtain their requests,
» the votive offerings, significative of their cures,
» plainly testify. For some bring representations of
» eyes, others of feet, others of hands, some of which
» are of gold, others of silver. For the God of
» those martyrs receives the gifts though small, and
» of little cost, computing the gift by the means of
» the giver. » It is evident that the donors of these
three pictures in our church were of the same way
of thinking, and wished to record their great devotion to S. Clement. One is given by Beno Derapiza,
another by Beno with Mary his wife, and another
by Maria Macellaria. As they all pointedly refer
to S. Clement, all are in the same style and give the
same formula « P. G. R. F. C. - pingere fecit, » « had

it painted: » and has to joint gift of the husband
and wife shows the motive for their grateful devotion to the saint, we suppose them to be the same
people. An eminent authority ungallantly suggests
that Maria Macellaria was the wife or daughter of
a butcher. We feel bound to shed every drop of
our ink in her defence; and if we cannot trace her
origin to the Sicilian town of Macella, and cannot
prove that she was not Maria of the provision
market, and no dealer in meat, fish, or vegetables,
we appeal to our fair readers whether Lady Mary
and Beno, on the other side of the medallion of
S. Clement, have the least look of the slaughter
house about them. S. Ambrose says of S. Helen,
whom the Jews and Pagans nicknamed *Stabularia*,
« a good Stabularia who sought so diligently the
» will of the Lord, and chose to be reputed as
» dung that she might gain Christ. » A good Macellaria, we think, who did not scruple to paint
the penitential spirit of her fear of God upon the
walls of our basilica. [1]

---

[1] Among the ancients *macellum* was a provision market, and got
its name from Macellus, a thief whose house was pulled down by the
censors and the ground used for the sale of victuals. Plautius says:
« I come to the market (*macellum*) ask for fish, they show them dear:
» lamb dear, beef, veal, dogfish, pork, all dear. » There was a very large
macellum on the Coelian, probably near to where S. Stefano Rotondo
now stands, and whoever knows how local names are kept up for cen-

Maria Macellaria's votive picture **is** a funeral procession, and there is a difference of opinion whether it is intended for the translation of the relics of S. Cyril or S. Clement. Our own opinion is that it represents the latter. We have spoken of S. Cyril and his missions before. Now we will step a few paces further on and consider first the upright picture referring to the place whence S. Cyril brought the relics of S. Clement. Those who in thought, or in printed articles, have accused Christ's Church of eight hundred years idolatry, have made a mistake in the date. Men are certainly prone to idolatry; and, long after Simon Magus and his Helena, one of

---

turies in Rome, and how nicknames are given, may see that Lady Maria lived thereabouts long after the *macellum* had disappeared. The Livia *macellum* was on the adjoining hill of the Esquiline. The Suburra, which the Roman antiquaries have shifted so often, seems to have **been** connected with those two hills. There, in the evening, stolen things were sold and **ladies walked: the** barber clipt and eatables were bought.

> Birds **of the hoarse** crowd, their mother's eggs,
> And **yellow Chiau figs** the steam **among,**
> The plaintive goat's rough progeny,
> Olives **as yet unequal** to the cold,
> Hoary **the greens** with chilling rime,
> Think'st thou our country sent to thee?
> How **diligently dost thou wander** boy!
> Nought ours, **myself** except, the fields do bear.
> What'er the Umbrian bailiff sends to thee,
> Rustic of Tuscia, **or of Tusculum,**
> Or country **by third milestone pointed out,**
> The whole for me is in **Suburra born.**

Martial.

the most pretentious capitals of Europe saw the
goddess of reason, and the streets she presided over
reeking with the blood of Christian priests. Eight
hundred years after their Master had died for man,
Cyril was striving to extirpate that Paganism among
the Sclavonians against which in Holland and Germany, a century before, so many English and Irish
missionaries were spending their toil and blood:
for that Apostolic seed which Celestine and Gregory had sent to Ireland and England, was to bear
rich fruit in the northern regions of Europe. The
Vandals of Prussia, the people about the Baltic,
the Hungarians and Poles, parts of Germany and
Sweden, were to welcome the harbingers of the
good tidings a century after S. Cyril. The Norwe-
gians, the Swedes, and the Russians, of the eleventh century, have left us the names of many
of their missionary saints, and in the twelfth century Pomerania, Finland, and Sweden bore witness
to the zeal of Rome for conversion. Pagan habits
were more inveterate than faith, and relapses frequent, though priests and kings watered the ungrateful soil with their own blood: and the thirteenth
age, which saw the reconciliation of the Greeks
at Lyons, also saw that Hyacinth who, in March
1218, received his habit from S. Dominic at S. Sabina,
and died at the age of 72, on the feast of the Assump-

tion of our Lady in 1257, a saint and apostle of the barbarous idolaters of the North. Scarce three hundred years after, was the charge of idolatry made against the Church; and it is evident, were we to accept it, that the unhappy infidels of Europe had been converted from one form of idolatry to another. If we get a little out of this chained cycle of years, we shall find the Jews of Smyrna suggesting that the mangled limbs of Polycarp might be worshipped instead of Christ, and the Centurian, to get rid of their contention, putting the body into the fire. We shall find the Pagan persecutors threatening others to have their remains utterly destroyed that silly women may not wrap them in linen cloths, and venerate, and anoint, and worship them. We are brought back to the first century; to that priceless treasure of the church of Antioch, to what the lions had left of S. Ignatius in the amphitheatre at Rome, and to the relics of Trajan's other victim S. Clement. We see again the Christians weeping on the shore when their venerable benefactor was carried out three miles at sea, and his body anchored there, as his executioners thought, for ever. Incorrigible idolaters they weep that they cannot prostrate themselves before a dead man's bones. At least they did not need the warning given by S. John Chrysostom in the fourth century: « Do not fix thy

» contemplation on this, that the martyr's body lies
» there deprived of the energizing power of the soul,
» but reflect on this that there reposes in that body
» a power greater than that of the soul itself, the
» grace, to wit, of the Holy Spirit, which, by the
» miracles that it performs, gives proof to all of the
» resurrection. » Eusebius is not ashamed to say
of another martyr : « The body of the divine martyr
» was cast up at the gate of the city by the waves
» of the sea, as though unable to hold it. » In the
case of S. Clement, the sea simply receded, and repeated the miracle every year.

MIRACLE AT THE TOMB OF S. CLEMENT.

In this beautiful composition we have lost the
first finding of the relics of our Saint. High up on
the wall, the inscription, now nearly obliterated,
only remains - « in mare submerso tumulum parat
» angelus istud » « the angel is preparing that
» tomb » (to S. Clement) « submerged in the sea, »
refers to the tradition that when Trajan had S. Clement thrown into the deep with an anchor about
his neck, and the Christians on the shore wept that
they could not recover his body, the sea retired
three miles, and it was found with the anchor in
a little marble temple prepared by angelic hands.

MIRACLE AT THE TOMB OF S CLEMENT

The miracle of the receding waters was repeated, for two centuries, on the anniversary of his martyrdom, and during the octave of his festival, thus leaving a dry path for the Christians to go and venerate his relics. The temple surrounded by the sea full of fishes is seen in the central compartment, and within it a marble urn containing the sacred treasure. The urn serves for an altar which is covered with a white cloth, and upon it are two candlesticks with lighted candles. Three lamps are suspended from the vaults, and from the canopy over the altar hang two looped curtains very gracefully arranged. On the left is a city, from one of the gates of which a procession issues headed by the bishop going to say mass, and carrying a crosier in his left hand, while his right is raised towards his breast. His assistants clothed in the vestments of their order accompany him, and an immense crowd of people follow behind. The name of the city is designated by the word *Cersona*, or Cherson, which is written under the arch of the gate. This ancient city has been, long since, destroyed, and modern Kertch built on its ruins. Between the bishop and the temple is a woman of comely aspect, and in a graceful dress, carrying in her arms her child who is lovingly embracing her. Again at the altar we see the same woman

and child : she is stooping to raise him up, while
he extends his little arms towards her. The words,
mulier vidua, widow woman, are written in the form
of a cross over her head, and *puer*, or little boy,
over the head of the child. Underneath, in one
line, is the inscription « *integer ecce jacet, repetit
» quem praevia mater* » « behold unhurt he lies whom
» his returning mother seeks again. » The scene
here represented and expressed by this epigraph
is recorded by S. Ephrem martyr bishop of Cherson,
by S. Gregory of Tours, the blessed James of Voragine, S. Antoninus, and many other early writers.
They tell us that when S. Clement was thrown
into the sea, about three miles from the shore, the
Christians who were spectators of his martyrdom
were grieved that they could not recover his body,
and begged of God to let them know how it could
be found. The Lord hearkened to their prayers,
and consoled them by causing the sea to retire to
the very spot where the holy Pontiff was drowned.
Following the receding waters they found his body
enshrined in a marble temple, with the anchor that
was attached to his neck. For two centuries, on
the anniversary of S. Clement's martyrdom, a similar reflux of the sea took place, and continued
throughout the octave of his festival, during which
the martyr's shrine was visited not alone by the

pious inhabitants of Cherson, but by pilgrims from
remote regions. On one occasion, a woman brought
her little boy with her to visit the tomb of our
Saint, and after having satisfied her devotion she
went away thinking that he was following her.
Having missed him, she determined to go back to
the temple, but after travelling a short distance,
she saw the sea flowing in and could not proceed
any farther. She then retired slowly before the
advancing waters, bewailing her only child whom
she thought she had lost for ever. On the following anniversary she returned hoping to find even
the bones of her dear little one, but, to her great
consolation and joy, she found him alive at the
tomb of the Martyr, and opening his eyes, as if
awaking from sleep, he stretches out his little arms
to his mother who takes him up and embraces him.
This touching fact should teach us that we should
never despair of God's protecting providence, and
that we should not measure His ways by those of
man. Lower down is a medallion of S.Clement, of
the finest style of art. He is tonsured and has the
nimbus. In his left hand he holds a closed book,
and is blessing with his right. On a beautiful border, which is intersected by the medallion, are four
doves turned towards the Saint. Beno, the donor
of the picture, holds a candle on one side of the

medallion; the Lady Mary is on the other side with her little boy Clement, both holding candles in their hands. Little Attilia, the sister of little Clement, has also her candle, and stands with her governess behind her father. Under the medallion-head of S. Clement is painted the very expressive and suggestive motto « *me prece querentes estole nociva ca-* » *ventes* » « seeking me in prayer beware of hurtful » things. » At the extreme left is the following inscription showing that this picture was a votive offering made by Beno to S. Clement, the patron of his boy.

† IN NOMI
  NE D̄N̄I
  EGO BENO
  DERAPIZA
  F̄ AMORE
  BEATI CLE
  MENTIS
  ET REDEMP
  TIONE ANI
  MEE PIN
  GERE FE
    CIT (sic)

« In the name of the Lord,
» I Beno Derapiza,
» for the love of blessèd Clement
» and the salvation of my soul,
» had it painted. »

TRANSLATION OF S.CLEMENT'S RELICS

TRANSLATION OF THE RELICS OF S. CLEMENT
FROM THE VATICAN TO HIS OWN CHURCH.

The devotion of the Derapiza family being accounted for, we have had at their hands the miracle of Sisinius' conversion; and that of the original
locality of S. Clement's relics, of a miracle wrought
there, and of their own connection with his name.
But is there none of an event so important to his
church, and so consonant with their devotion, as
the deposition of his relics here? The funeral procession may perhaps be the answer. S. Nicholas I
invited S. Cyril to Rome. S. Cyril, from the time
he had stirred up the bishop of Cherson to recover
the relics, took boat and found them, had borne them
back to the metropolis and ultimately begged them,
always carried them about with him. He brought
them to Rome, died and was buried in the Vatican, and
was translated to S. Clement's. Certainly there was
nothing to warrant the licence which the painter took
in representing him carried bodily on the bier wearing the pallium, borne by four youths, and two
others swinging their censers in the air; because
they were only the bones of S. Clement, which were
in a marble ark; and even if S. Cyril's body were
embalmed, it was similarly shut up in another ark
sealed by the Pope. The painter for pictorial effect

has not chosen to paint a mere ark. The body is followed by a youth with uplifted hands, incongruous if a mourner, but appropriate if hymning the glory of his relics. Nicholas was dead or dying when Cyril arrived, and Adrian did the rest. The anachronism of the painter, in representing Nicholas with his nimbus accompanying the funeral procession, is deliberate. The cross is borne behind the Pope who is between two eastern ecclesiastics, and two crosiers near them seem to denote two bishops. The one on his right has the nimbus. This might well be Cyril, and the other Methodius ; for, like Nicholas, Cyril was reputed a saint at his death, which followed soon after the deposition of S. Clement's relics ; but Methodius survived him many years, and could not be considered a saint at the time of either translation. The painter has also lowered the pall which covers the body to show the crosses of the pallium on the shoulder , precisely as he gives them on that of the Pope. If the venerable head with the nimbus on the bier is that of Cyril, we have no picture of the recovery of S. Clement's relics ; and the saint on the Pope's right, thus supposed to be Methodius, occasions a double anachronism by being sainted with Nicholas, though he certainly was not till probably fifty years after him: and the eastern bishop on the Pope's

left is altogether unaccounted for. The three span-
gled banners surmounted by Greek crosses, at the
back of the crowd, were most probably intended
to carry the imagination to the first mission from
Constantinople, and the triple conversion of the
Cham of the Chazari, the king of the Bulgarians,
and the duke of Bohemia. The artist has shown
ingenuity in breaking the line of the procession so
as to bring the Pope prominently forward. As the
head of the procession arrives, the Pope is celebrating at the altar, upon which is the missal, the paten, and the host. The deacon has the chalice upon
a cloth, as we see it in the picture opposite to the
temple in the sea. Upon the missal, which is open,
are the words « *per omnia saecula saeculorum -- pax*
» *Domini sit semper* » « for all ages: may the peace
» of the Lord be ever with you. » Over the altar
is a large circular lamp, and two smaller ones. The
inscription underneath repeats the anachronism
« † *Huc a Vaticano fertur pp. Nicolao hymnis divinis*
» *quod aromatibus sepelivit.* » « Hither from the Va-
» tican is borne (Nicholas being Pope) with divine
» hymns what with aromatics he buried. » The
notices we have of the circumstances attending the
arrival of S. Clement's relics and the burial of S. Cyril are too brief and obscure to supply any accurate details. That S. Cyril was first buried at the

Vatican, and afterwards removed to S. Clement's, they do say. It is most probable that S. Clement's relics were also presented to the Pope at the Vatican; but there is no mention of it. The artist clearly chose to represent the subject in his own way, and without strict historical accuracy either in the event or the accessories. The time at which these pictures were painted might be supposed rather soon after Rome was moved by the arrival of the relics than a couple of hundred years after. Besides the devotion of the Derapizas to S. Clement, and not necessarily to S. Cyril, there is in the picture opposite the temple in the sea a sufficient exhibition of the devotion of the Romans to the stranger saint.

OUR SAVIOUR BLESSING
ACCORDING TO THE GREEK RITE.

This large votive picture opposite the temple of S. Clement in the sea presents some difficulties: and unfortunately the funeral or liturgical inscription beneath it is illegible. Whether this was the very ancient chapel mentioned by Baronius, in which S. Cyril's relics were said to be discovered in his time, or why this composition should be found here and the miserably painted actions of his life (the au-

THE SAVIOUR. S.S. CYRIL AND METHODIUS

dience of Michael and the baptism) be in the sanctuary, who can say? The style is bolder and somewhat
more Byzantine than that of the other two pictures
in the narthex ; but looking to the larger scale and
votive nature of the subject it is not of a different
age. It was evidently meant for a grand commemorative picture of S. Cyril; and was probably an
altar-piece, framed as it is between two pillars,
and immediately opposite the temple from the ruins
of which he removed S. Clement's relics to Rome.
And, whether to a person entering by the great
door of the basilica, or passing from the church
into the narthex and turning to look at the patron
saint of the basilica, it is on the right hand, as
the place of Cyril's deposition is described by Baronius, Panvinius, and Panciroli, and where the devotion of the Romans would naturally place his
honourable memorial. In the centre our Lord, represented as a young man with parted hair and
very little beard, stands upon a footstool. In one
hand he holds the book of the Gospels, and with
the other gives his blessing according to the Greek
rite, a peculiarity appropriate to the saint from the
Bosphorus. Two ecclesiastics kneel one on each
side : the elder tonsured and bearded, not unlike one
of the bishops beside Pope S. Nicholas in the procession, does not aspire to the honours of a saint, for

has no nimbus. His dress is rather that of a philosopher, or monk, and in his left hand he holds
the Gospel while his right seems to appeal mo-
destly to the Saviour. The younger, close-shaved
after the manner of the Latins, and wearing a
rich chasuble, kneels reverently holding a jewelled
chalice upon the cloth which covers both his hands.
It is natural to suppose that the elder represents
S. Cyril. S. Clement, whose name is written vertically behind him, wearing the pallium, precisely
as S. Nicholas, and as it is represented on the body on the funeral bier before described, is very
conspicuously presenting him to our Divine Lord;
a natural action for one to whom he was in-
debted for the finding of his relics and bringing
them to Rome. The angel Gabriel stands behind
the aged ecclesiastic, whom we suppose to be Cyril,
with one hand in the action of prayer, and with
the other affectionately shielding the bosom of his
client, his hand reaching down almost to touch the
Gospel which that client holds in his left hand.
This appears a natural action in the angel inter-
ceding for a missionary of the Gospel in the circumstance of his death, pleading for that blessing
which our Lord, if he is blessing either of the
persons in this picture, is directing to the elder.
Were we to suppose that the younger, notwithstand-

ing the incongruity of his Latin appearance, is
meant to represent Methodius, he is not so presented nor so shielded, and might be simply offering
the chalice of his affliction. Behind him is the
angel Michael appealing to the Saviour, with his
left hand, in behalf of his client, and holding his
rod in his right. « And he that spoke with me
» had a measure, a golden reed to measure the
» city, and the gates thereof, and the wall. » [1]
In the mosaics of S. Agatha in Ravenna, supposed
by Ciampini to have been executed about 400, our
Lord is seated giving his blessing, and on either
side of him an angel with a rod. If this client is
Methodius, we remember his conversion of Boigo-
ris-Michael. If we had any doubt that this picture
referred to the missionary enterprise of S. Cyril, the
figure of S. Andrew on this side, which corresponds
to that of S. Clement on the other, would remove it.
The Apostle takes no part apparently in the subject
of the picture, but with his right hand refers to
the Gospel roll in his left. He was the earlier
Apostle of the countries traversed by Cyril and
Methodius, and the Russians have long gloried that
he carried the Gospel as far as the mouth of the
Borysthenes, to the mountains where Kiow stands,

---

[1] Apoc., 21, 15.

and the frontiers of Poland. Immediately under this picture a tomb of brick was discovered, on 10th of February 1868, containing the skeletons of two men of more than ordinary size. Could they be those of the brother missionary saints?

S. FLAVIA DOMITILLA V. M.

On the wall under the *luminaire*, or skylight, at the south end of north aisle is the head of a female with the halo. It is of a high style of art, and is supposed to have been painted towards the end of the fourth or the beginning of the fifth century. According to the learned Father Garrucci, it represents S. Flavia Domitilla.

S. FLAVIUS CLEMENT M.

Nearly opposite the fresco of our Saviour blessing according to the Greek rite, is another head painted on a brick wall of early Roman construction. The abovenamed eminent archaeologist thinks that it represents S. Flavius Clement. It belongs to the old Roman school of painting, and is supposed to have been executed about the year 300. Beneath it is an inscription, scratched on the plaster between the bricks, which has puzzled the ingenuity of paleographers to decipher.

OUR SAVIOUR DELIVERING ADAM FROM LIMBO.

The Saviour of the world having expired on the
Cross, and by His death paid the ransom due to the
Divine Justice for the sins of men, descended into
the infernal prisons to deliver thence the souls of the
just, who were so long debarred from Paradise, their
heavenly home. The fresco before us, which is on
the right of the hight altar, represents that scene.
Our Divine Lord wears a flowing mantle, and is surrounded with a cerulean halo. He takes Adam by the
right hand and tramples on the demon who is vomit-
ing balls of fire at Him. The enemy of the human
race, unwilling to let Adam go, holds him by the
foot and knee. Hovering in the dark back-ground,
are heads and hands, symbolizing, according to archaeologists, the *shades*, or souls of the disconsolate
prisoners. Our Redeemer holds the Cross in His
left hand, and behind Him is the monogram C-S-
Christus Salvator-Christ the Saviour. Behind Adam,
only three fingers remain of a figure which is supposed to have represented Eve. The father of the
human race is in a standing posture, and there is
an expression in his face which says, he has been
long enough here. A small spiral pillar separates this from another compartment to the left.
It contains a half figure of a venerable ecclesia-

stic of oriental type, holding in his left hand a
gemmed closed book, while the right is raised in
the attitude of supplication. He wears a gemmed
chasuble, and an embroidered amice, or cowl, decorated with five Greek crosses. If we do not very
much mistake, this figure represents Methodius, the
brother of S. Cyril, who, as Dubravius writes, was
interred in the church of S. Clement.

It is somewhat singular that Limbo should be
found twice in this church, and if the picture raises
fresh antiquarian guesses at dates and styles, the
middle state of souls is too old and Catholic a doctrine to be disturbed by its incredulous opponents.
S. Cyril of Jerusalem says : « Then we also commem-
» orate those who have fallen asleep before us, first
» patriarchs, prophets, apostles, that God, by their
» prayers and intercessions, would receive our peti-
» tion: then also on behalf of the holy Fathers, and
» bishops, who have fallen asleep before us, and of
» all, in short, who have already fallen asleep from
» amongst us, believing that it will be a very great
» assistance to the soul, for which the supplication is
» put up, while the holy and most awful Sacrifice lies
» to open view. And I wish to persuade you by an
» illustration: for I know many that say this : 'What
» is a soul profited, which departs from this world,
» either with sins, or without sins, if it be commem-

» orated in prayer ?...' Now surely, if a king had
» banished certain persons who had offended him,
» and their connexions, having woven a crown, should
» offer it to him on behalf of those under his venge-
» ance, would not he grant a respite to their punish-
» ments ? In the same way, we also, offering up to
» him supplications on behalf of those who have
» fallen asleep before us, even though they be sinners,
» weave no crown, but offer up, for our sins, Christ
» crucified, propitiating, both on their behalf and our
» own, the God that loves man. » [1]

SARCOPHAGI
MONUMENTAL AND LAPIDARY INSCRIPTIONS.

The sarcophagi arranged along the walls of the
narthex were found during the progress of the excavations. That on the right, near the bell-tower, contains the remains of a man and woman, probably
Beno and Maria already noticed; and the one opposite it those of a man. The small sarcophagus, vis-à-
vis the miracle at the tomb of S. Clement, contains the
bones of a little boy, or little girl, each in its natural
place. The inscription on it is Pagan, but we know

---

[1] Catech. Mystag. V. (Alit. Catech. 23). n. 9-10, p. 328.

that the Christians sometimes appropriated, for the purpose of interment, pagan sarcophagi. It is:

D.   M.
JVLIAE C. FIL.
FELICITATI
SPIRITO DVLCISSIMO
DEFVNCTO ACERVO
QVAE VIXIT ANNO VNO
MENSIBVS XI. DIEB. TRIBVS
FECERVNT JVLII VERNA
ET FELICITAS PARENTES
SIMILITER ACERVI ET
INFELICISSIMI

Near the stairs is a large *terra-cotta* coffin which contained the body of a bishop, or mitred abbot: but the moment it was exposed to the air, the human form disappeared; for it was not thicker than a cobweb. There are three other sarcophagi containing human bones, but they have no inscriptions.

Opposite the door leading to the nave is a large marble slab with the following inscription:

MIRE INNOCENTIAE IENNARIO V. P. QVI
VIXIT AN: LI. MENS V. D XXV. NAM MECVM
VIXIT AN: XXV. MEN. V. D. XXV. SINE ALIQVA
DISCORDIA AVT CONTROVERSIA . FLO-
RENTIA VXOR BENEMERENTI IN PACE
FECIT ET SIBI DEPOSITVS PRID:
IDVS IVNII VRSO ET POLEMIO
DP. FLORENTIES NONIS AVG. VIXIT ANNIS V
.M X. VIXIT SVPER MARITVM SVVM ANNVS III. M. II.IN PACE

De Rossi in his « Inscriptiones Cristianae » [1] gives a part of the above ; for the slab was broken, and only about one half of it was found at the time this eminent archaeologist published that work. Ursus and Polemius were consuls in 338.

Over a grave, nearly opposite the door that leads to the nave was found the following epitaph. It is now in the wall near the entrance to the narthex.

SVBTVS HAC TERRA NRA . SEPVLTA SVNT MEMBRA
NEPTIS CVM AVA, DVLCISSA NEPE . VOCATA
PETRVS ET DARIA . BIOLA SIMVLQ. MARIVLA
CVM HIS QVIB: ADJVNCTIS ALIIS TRIBVS
CAL . MAD . OB DVLCISSA . TEP . GREG . VI.
PP, IND: IIIIX.
ANN . I . NICL . PP . OB . MARIA IND :
M . SEPT . D . XVIII.   IIIX.

Gregory VI governed the Church in 1045.

Another slab has an inscription on both sides, one pagan, the other christian.

D.   M.

M. AVR. SABINVS CVI FVIT ET SIGNVM VAGVLVS
INTER INCREMENTA COAEQVALIVM SVI TEMPORIS
VITAE INCOMPARABILIS DVLCISSIMVS FILIVS

---

[1] Vol. I.

 SVRO IN PACE QVESQENTI
EVTICIANVS FRATER FECIT

IOVINIAN . . .
NEOFITO

On the floor opposite the picture of S. Alexius:

DEPOSITVS LEONAS VI . KAL . FEB .
IN PACE

† PRAESBYTER

and various other fragments of inscriptions in Damasine characters.

INNOCENQVAE VIXIT ANN V
M. V.

This epitaph is of the second century.

CLEMES VIXIT
ANNIS X̄X̄V

DIS . MAN
CLAVDIAE VITALI . TI
CLAVDIANVS
SABINIANVS
NVTRICI PIEN
TISSIMAE

M. LVCCIVS . CRESCES
VIXIT . ANNIS XXVIII

SCIATHIS . MAGIAE . LIBRAR
VIXIT . ANNOS . XVIII
PROS . POCTAVI . CVBICVL . FECIT
FECIT . CONIVGI . 8VAE . ET . SIBI

Inserted in the wall of the narthex are several other inscriptions and fragments of inscriptions,
some of which are pagan, and others Christian :
also exquisitely sculptured capitals, divers pieces
of broken columns, fragments of marble candlesticks
ornamental sculpture, pieces of mosaic pavement,
and tiles with the names of the makers, and of the
Consuls who lived at the time. The following
are a few specimens of them.

I
... VLIAE
. RYPHOSAE

II

LTARQV . T . ERO...

III

APRILIS CN. DOMITI ...
AGATHOBVLI
DOL

IV

RATIONIS PATRIMONI

V

APRO ET PAE COS   Ann.
MFAB LIGYMNI   123

VI

APRON ET PA
POMPVLI EX
ANNVERI   id.

VII

... XPRARMCEST   id.
... IAPRONI COS

VIII

EXPRS. . . . .   id.

IX

EARINI DOMITIAE LVCILLAE   120-125
DOL
.

X

... TSOSSI . IANVAR ...... F MACED   id.
EXPRSTA................. MAXIM

XI

O · D · EX . PR · D . L . OF . Q . F . A
LSTQVADRETCCRVF   Ann.
                    COS   142

XII

EX FIGLINIS TONNEIANIS FLAVLAVRI
        OP DOL ALLI RVFI   165

XIII   XIV

RDPRIIIOS   ЯЗЯTJA . . .

XV

CCVLDIAS. . . .

XVI

† OFICI . BENIGNI †   100

MODERN BASILICA OF S. CLEMENT.

PRELIMINARY REMARKS.

The Church of God is a society existing everywhere throughout the world, bound by its own laws,
acknowledging its own head, comprised, as to some
portion or other of its members, within the limits
of temporal kingdoms, but bound in conscience by
the secular laws of those kingdoms only so far as they
agree with her laws, and are accepted by her. It is
evident, therefore, that in every case of conflict
between the liberties of the Church and the law
or · practice of any temporal kingdom, the subjects
of the Church must appeal to the decision of their
own tribunal; that is for the direction of their
consciences on the point, to the judgment of the
Pope who is their supreme judge in morals. In
point of practice, whatever intermediate judgments
may be given by theologians, doctors, or bishops,

the last resort is the conscience of the Vicar of Christ. The Church does not judge those who are without ; and whether the Sultan is right or wrong in practising polygamy, whether the government of England is right or wrong in setting up divorce-courts, the Church merely prescribes to her own subjects, that is to the faithful of Christ, that they cannot avail themselves of such relaxations or inducements held out by sovereigns and governments to those who obey them. Hence, without going into theories or details, it is easy to understand the principle of sentences of deposition which the Pope has pronounced, from time to time, against Catholic sovereigns. He released their subjects from their oath of allegiance, because he is the sole judge of all oaths. He is the final judge of the morals of Catholics, and a sovereign is no more exempt from his excommunication than a slave ; and were the subjects of the sovereign truly Catholic, he would find himself, as isolated and helpless as the merest beggar in his dominions, when once named as a person excommunicated, and to be avoided. Under what circumstances, or for what crime, a thief or a king is to be so sentenced, rests entirely with the judgement of the Pope. This, indeed, is a tremendous power; but it is tremendous only because the Church has a real existence, and not one of mere opinion. The atheist is free from it: the infidel is free from it: all who despise it, in a certain sense, are free from it; for, to enforce the sentence, the Pope has only the word of Him who said: « Vengeance is mine; I will repay, » saith the Lord. » When the society of Europe was more Catholic, and more free, the sentence of the judicial power of the Pope reached sovereigns in spite of their array of physical force; because men of good will did not choose for their sake to encounter the vengeance of God. Rebellion, hateful to the Church, was equally denounced with the crimes of the sovereign, which might seem to justify it. The extreme sentence of deposition from the throne was a proof that Christian men were not chattels to be squandered by the caprice of a man mad, or wicked enough, to set at defiance, with impunity, the laws of man and God.

We have often heard it asked: « What right » have Popes to dethrone kings? » but few take the trouble to inquire what right have emperors, or kings, to rob, and dethrone Popes. We have heard the cry of « vox populi, vox Dei, » and have generally seen the omnipotent voice ending in mock elections under loaded cannon. We have heard the wail of suffering populations, and it has risen louder when they found themselves stript the more, the more they were supposed to be enjoying the sun-

shine of new liberty, a precious possession of which
Brutus seems to have bequeathed nothing to his
admirers but the dagger. We have seen nations
all professing peace, all anxious for unity, inimitably
national, marching hither and thither, strewing
the earth with the thousands of their dead, boast-
ing of their virtues in the list of which they
left out self denial. It is an old story. Let us look
at the Germans playing their part under Henry IV.
In 1054 Hildebrand had been sent legate to France
against simony in the collation of ecclesiastical be-
nefices. In 1073, upon the point of being elected
Pope, he begged Henry to use his influence against
it, telling him that he could never tolerate his scandalous crimes. We will take the new Pope's character from his adversary Du Pin. « It must be
» acknowledged that Gregory VII was an extraordi-
» nary genius capable of great things, constant and
» undaunted in their execution, well versed in the
» Constitutions of his predecessors, zealous for the
» interests of the Holy See; an enemy of simony and
» libertinism (vices he vigorously opposed), full of
» Christian thoughts, and of zeal for the reformation
» of the manners of the clergy; and there is not
» the least colour to think that he was not un-
» blemished in his own morals. This is the judgment
» which we suppose every one will pass on him

» who shall read over his letters with a disinter-
» ested and unprejudiced mind. They are penned
» with a great deal of eloquence, full of 'good
» matter, and embellished with noble and pious
» thoughts; and we say boldly that no Pope, since
» Gregory I, wrote such strong and fine letters as
» this Gregory did. »   To what emperor shall we
compare Henry IV? The bastard of Normandy who
swept away the village churches of England to make
room for his deer, was a bold soldier; bold in his
vices, and not a mere plotting debauchee.   To
what king? Henry was more like the passionate
church-robbing murderer of Thomas a Becket. He
caused the seals and crosses of every deceased bishop and great abbot to be delivered to him, and
sold them to whom he pleased; but we do not know
that he stooped so low as the cabbage gardens, and
poor convents of Capuchin Friars, and Franciscan
Nuns. Brutish in his life, affecting penitence for
his usurpations of the temporalities of the Church,
as if he were urged on to draw the sword by his
unhappy fate, receiving the letters of the Pope with
tears, not ashamed in his insatiable lust even to
offer violence to women who had the misfortune
to be his subjects; ever bold to do wrong and, like
the drunken sot, never able to do right, personally
endowed with the animal courage of the chamois-

hunter, or the *condottiere:* to what king shall we liken Henry IV? In an age when Romans wore swords and knew how to use them, when, under the sanction of religion, there was some show of justice in Italy to punish the violation of morality, and a condemnation by the Pope, even though frustrated by violence, was not yet become mirth for the printers of pamphlets at Paris, or the street preachers of London or Turin, we may imagine a scene that followed in the capital of the Christian world. The Sovereign Pontiff upon his throne was presiding over a Council in the Vatican when a priest from Parma, Roland by name, entered and presented his credential letters. His errand was to deliver two letters from the emperor of Germany and the sentence of a mock Council held by him at Worms. In the name of his sovereign, Roland commanded the Pope to resign the Chair of Peter; and turning to the bishops and clergy bade them present themselves on the festival of Pentecost to Henry IV, who would appoint for them a lawful Pope in the place of the ravening wolf and tyrant Hildebrand. The soldiers and nobles on duty at the Council rushed towards the debased priest, who was scarcely saved by taking refuge at the feet of his Holiness. When this imperial messenger had been removed, and order restored, Gregory opened Henry's letter and read it in a loud voice to the bishops. « Henry, not by usurpation but by the will » of God, king of Germany, to Hildebrand not a Pope » but a hypocritical monk. » The reading of these words caused such indignation that the Council had to be prorogued to the following day.

The question in dispute was simple. In 1075, the Pope directed his legates to summon Henry king of Germany and emperor elect, to Rome, under pain of excommunication for having simoniacally usurped the investiture of bishoprics, and promoted unworthy persons to ecclesiastical dignities. The enraged king ordered the legates out of the country, and he himself presided over a number of excommunicated simoniacal bishops at Worms, where cardinal Hugo distinguished himself by his invectives against the head of the Church. Ambassadors were at once dispatched to Italy to persuade the Italian bishops to accept their mock sentence of deposition; those of Lombardy, and the Marches of Ancona, were easily gained over, and in their assembly at Parma ratified the work of Worms. Henry sent the Romans a copy of the sentence: « I Henry, king » of Germany, finding that you have forfeited all » your rights, and usurped the Papacy, command » you to descend from the Chair of that city of » which I have been elected patrician and sovereign

« by the free suffrages of the people. » And in
another letter he urged them to rebel, and condemn
and dethrone Hildebrand the tyrant, the usurper of
the Holy See, the betrayer of the Roman empire,
and the enemy of the common weal. These were
the two letters Roland undertook to present to the
Pope. History repeats itself. The only difference
appears to be that, the blustering violence of the
lansquenet is replaced by the impudence of the « pe-
» tit-maître » of the salon ; the cajoling of the
multitude, and the actual use of military oppression,
remaining constant quantities in diplomatic permu-
tations. In countries that boast of more conspicuous
plain-dealing, the statesman writes the pamphlet
of the prison-spy; the conspirator is supplied with
the passport, the fleet protects the landing of the
brigand. In others more jealous of military empire
than of liberty or peace, the pamphlet, the plot,
and the purse, the advice of the envoy, and the
judicious presence of a few troops to preserve order,
and countenance fair play, pave the road to the
modern ovation, and the ballot-box brings to perfection what some discharges of artillery, rendered
necessary by the inconceivable stupidity of the human race, had begun.

The Council which had been so rashly interrupted, met again the next day, and Gregory ad-

dressed the one hundred and ten bishops and prelates present at it, palliating as far as he could the conduct of the German king and exhorting him to liberate the bishops and abbots he had cast into prison. The fathers all rose and besought the Pope to unsheathe the sword of Peter, and cut the rebellious, blasphemous, and tyrannical monarch off from the Church. Standing on his throne, his Holiness pronounced this sentence amidst the acclamations of the Council: « Strong in the faith that
» the Vicar of Christ can loose and bind on this
» earth whatever should be loosed or bound in
» heaven, not through any worldly intention but
» for the safety and honour of the Church, I, the
» legitimate Pope and Vicar of Christ, excommu-
» nicate, in the name of the Father and of the Son
» and of the Holy Ghost, Henry king of Ger-
» many, son of Henry emperor of the Romans, who
» with unexampled pride persecutes and oppresses
» the Church : I interdict him the government of
» the kingdoms of Germany and Italy: I absolve
» all Christians from their oath of allegiance to
» him, and prohibit obedience to be rendered to
» him as king, because whosoever renounced the
» authority of the Church forfeits the authority
» he has received from her. » It was not the fashion of that age for imperial librarians to vilify

the life of Jesus Christ: nor could an emperor out-
rage the moral sense of his countrymen, with impunity. When the Frenchman Berengarius broach-
ed errors against marriage and infant baptism,
and his impiety denied transubstantiation and the
real presence, a Council at Paris unanimously condemned him; and the Catholic king deprived him
of the revenue of his benefice, and an archbishop
of Canterbury, Lanfranc, wrote an excellent con-
futation of the heresy. In his letters to the Germans the Pope stated « that Henry was guilty
» of crimes so heinous and enormous as to deserve
» not only to be excommunicated, but, according
» to all divine and human laws, to be deprived
» of royal dignity. » The imperial appetite was
not satisfied to pick up vile mistresses in public
places. The head of the state was charged with
dishonouring the wives and daughters of the princes, with cruel oppression of his subjects, with
disregard of public interests, and the murder of
many innocent persons. The German princes declared in the national Council they held in 1076,
that he had wantonly shed the blood of his subjects and laid an intolerable yoke on the necks
of a free people. In modern days, it would be
that he had broken his promise to protect the
Church. But then the Germans had not adopted

that heresy which lines the royal mantles of the nineteenth century. « For many there are who, » set over the handling of public affairs, call them- » selves patrons and champions of religion, extol it » with their praises, cry it up as most especially » suited and useful to human society; neverthless » wish to moderate its discipline, to rule the sacred » ministers, to put hands upon holy things: in a » word, strive to encompass the Church within the » limits of the civil state, and lord it over her, who, » however is *sui juris,* and by divine counsel ought » to be pent up within the boundaries of no empire, » but to be propagated to the utmost bounds of » the earth, and embrace every race and nation, to » point out to them, and set free, the way of eternal » blessedness. »

In the language of the modern historian « Free- » men put over themselves Henry as king, on condi- » tion that he should judge his constituents with » justice, and govern them with royal care, which » compact he had constantly broken and disregarded. » Therefore, even without the judgment of the Apos- » tolic See, the princes could justly refuse to acknow- » ledge him any longer as king, since he had not » fulfilled the pledge which he gave at his election, » the violation of which brought with it the vio-

» lation of kingly power. « [1] But the Germans,
holding yet to the unity of faith, and unwilling
to become mere tools of a military theology, did
not think the common Father of the faithful an
alien to their welfare; nor did they need to exclude
the judgment of the Apostolic See from what affected its own supremacy. They had not learned
that Cisalpine hypocrisy with which the satellites
of rebellion rejoice in the liberty of the Church,
whilst they trample its laws and rights under foot,
drive religious women from their homes, strip them
of all that could be sold, and thrust the clergy
and prelates into prison. When such things were
done in the eleventh century they were not supposed to savour of liberty, but to be acts of violence
against the common conscience; acts of shame which
no pretext or excuse could palliate; nor were kings
held to be religious who violated, more conspicuously than other men, the common obligations
of humanity. If great crimes too often disgraced
the throne, men who had not laid aside the traditional respect of the German tribes for chastity,
and reverenced the Church which taught and practised it, were not easily to be persuaded that the
sceptre in the loathsome grasp of the vulgar de-

[1] Muratori, An. d'Italia, tom. IV, pag. 245, 246.

bauchee gave him a right to proclaim himself to
the civilized world as the man of destiny, the saviour of the nations, the Caesar harbinger of universal peace. The tradition was not lost, that when
the Pope of Rome confronted Attila, the Hun had
seen S. Peter and S. Paul standing by him. And
if common sense could not teach men that royal
power was a great responsibility before God, the
words of S. Leo to another prince were not yet
expunged from Europe, that the royal power had
been conferred upon him not alone to rule the
world, but chiefly to protect the Church. [1] It
was the law of the empire that a king or emperor who remained a whole year under excommunication was virtually dethroned; yet if the Germans
had acted on their own opinion, as Muratori suggests, they would simply have been violating fun-
damental law and rejecting the ultimate court of
appeal. They sought the sanction of the Pope.
Whether the ideas of the men of that age were lo-
gical or not, whether the pretensions of the Holy
See were rightful or not, there was at least this
advantage that there was somebody to appeal to,
and that somebody must of necessity have some
fixed principles, or he would not be appealed to. It

[1] S. Leo III to Charlemagne.

was not a common hodge-podge of interests pitched into a congress to be got out of it in what condition they might be, and with no power but the fortuitous concurrence of interests to enforce a decision, if it were worth while to enforce it. The Pope had interests to maintain which he believed to be sacred: which Popes have maintained at Fontainebleau, at Gaeta, or when reduced by a robber king almost to the gates of Rome. It is an advantage to have something tangible to defend, and that something is the Cross of Christ which Judas and the Caesars have made more glorious by their treason and their hate.

Anxious to get absolution before the years's end, Henry crossed the Alps in the depth of winter, and prostrated himself, in the garb of a pilgrim, at the gates of the fortress of Canosa, where Gregory was stopping on his road to Augsburg to preside over the Council in which the question about the throne was to be decided. For three days he was not admitted; judging, by his former duplicity, that the sincerity of his professions was not to be relied on. He received absolution on condition that, if his trial before the German nobles at Augsburg were against him, he should renounce all pretensions to the crown. Promising this, the Pope embraced him, and gave him the kiss of peace, after which he prepared to

celebrate mass. At the time of communion, holding
the Blessed Sacrament in his hand, Gregory appealed to his Lord as witness of his innocence, and invited the king to do the like. Conscious of his guilt
he dared not, but promised to do it at Augsburg.
Six days after he made a league, with the excommunicated bishops of Lombardy and Tuscany, to
make the Pope a prisoner; and not succeeding declared war against him. The archishop of Mayence
with the bishops of Wurtzburg and Metz, and other
prelates, dukes Rodolph, Guelph, Berthold, with the
Margraves, counts and barons, assembled at For-
cheim, were informed by the papal legates of Henry's perfidy. Rodolph proposed to elect a new king,
but the legates suggested that the Pope ought to
preside at the election. The nobles maintained that
procrastination was detrimental to the vital interests
of their country. The legates persisted that the
Pope as head of the Christian world should first
be consulted. At last the right of election was ceded
to the prelates, and Rodolph duke of Swabia was
chosen. Otho of Nordheim, Guelph and Berthold
approved of the election, the legates sanctioned it,
the people acclaimed it; and messengers were dispatched to beg the Pope to anathematize the dethroned king. Still Gregory hesitated, hoping for
Henry's amendment. At length, in 1080, seeing

that he went on adding crime to crime, he excommunicated him anew in a Council at Rome, and acknowledged Rodolph. War ensued between the competitors, and Rodolph was slain. In 1081, Henry descended into Italy with a powerful army and besieged Rome, but was repulsed by the people who adhered unflinchingly to the Sovereign Pontiff. In 1082 and 1083 he renewed the siege, but without success. In 1084 he returned a fourth time bribed the nobles, whose castles and estates had been ruined in the three preceding sieges, and the gates of the city and fifty hostages were delivered into his hands. The antipope Clement III, Guibert archbishop of Ravenna, titular of S. Clement's, who had been chosen, by Henry's party at Brixen, upon the election of Rodolph, was consecrated at the Lateran, and in turn he, in the Vatican, crowned his protector who took up his residence on the Capitol as the lawful successor of Augustus and Charlemagne. Gregory took refuge in the Castel S. Angelo; whilst Rusticus, his nephew, defended the Septizonium, an insulated mausoleum built by the Antonines where the church of S. Lucia in Selce now stands, near the basilica of S. Maria Maggiore. Twenty five years before, at the end of Easter, Rome had seen the bishop of Toul, in the habit of a pilgrim, alighting from his horse some miles from the city and walk-

ing barefoot to be crowned as **Leo IX**. To repress
the Normans who, after having expelled the Saracens and Greeks out of the kingdom of Naples,
became very troublesome neighbours to the Holy
See, he made over his German lands of Fuld and
Bamberg to Henry III, receiving in exchange Bene-
vento and its territory. By means of this exchange
he hoped to check the Normans, but his army was
defeated by them and himself made prisoner. After
about a year he was honourably sent back to Rome.
In his last illness, he had himself carried before the
altar of S. Peter, where he remained prostrate for
an hour, then heard mass, received the viaticum and
expired. Now, the Norman duke of Calabria, Robert
Guiscard, Henry's implacable enemy, advanced from
Salerno with an army of six thousand horse and
thirty thousand foot. Three days before he reached the gates of Rome, Henry retreated into Lombardy, exhorting the Romans to drive back the
Normans and persevere in their rebellion on his behalf. In Lombardy the Tuscans gave his army a
great overthrow. Within twelve years his eldest
son Conrad and his second son Henry rebelled against
him. The latter, crowned emperor of Germany, stript
him of the imperial insignia and forced him to renounce the throne. He took refuge at Cologne,
and then at Liege, where he mustered an army against

his son Henry V, who defeated him. Reduced to
.extreme misery, he supplicated the bishop of Spire
to nominate him to the prebend of a lector or
precenter in his cathedral church, but was refused.
At length abandoned by every one, he implored
the bishop of .Liege to afford him an asylum, and
there he died in 1106. The antipope Guibert, after
wandering through various parts of Italy and Germany, died suddenly at Ravenna in 1100 or 1101.
Meantime schism and rebellion had wrought their
usual calamities. Guiscard fought his way into Rome
by the Porta Asinaria on the Naples road, and
took up his quarters at the fortified monastery of
the four crowned Martyrs opposite S. Clement's.
The imperial faction, still strong in the city, rose
against the Normans, and a hasty word from the
conqueror was the signal for fire and pillage. As
Italy has seen the Arab infidels of Algiers imported
by the occupant of the throne of Catholic France
against the Christian forces of Austria, so the Saracens of Sicily formed a large contingent of Guiscard's army, and seized the opportunity of plunder.
From the Lateran to Castel S. Angelo, and from
the Flaminian gate to the church of S. Lorenzo in
Lucina, was a scene of wreck and ruin. A great
part of the buildings of ancient Rome were then
destroyed, and the fragments that remained sup-

plied materials for ordinary buildings. Whatever
was habitable from the Lateran to the Capitol was
swept away. We might surmise that the basilica
of S. Clement perished in the general wreck at that
time; and that the clear waters which fill the subterranean chambers of Clement's palace had filtered
through the soil after the destruction of the baths
of Titus on the hill hard by. But in the absence
of information lost, or possibly existing still in manuscripts of the Vatican and other libraries, though
we have searched for it in vain, we have no proof
that the churches were then destroyed. The suc-
ceding century was one of church restorations.
Paschal II, in 1118, re-dedicated S. Adrian's in the
Forum, and it is said that he rebuilt that of the
four crowned Martyrs. In 1145, Lucius II, placed
the Lateran basilica of the Salvatore under the invocation of the Baptist and Evangelist S. John, and
repaired and consolidated the foundations of S. Croce
in Gerusalemme. In 1491 Celestine III made the
ceiling of S. Maria Maggiore. But these are all
negative indications. On the 13th of August 1199,
a conclave was held in S. Clement's, and its titular
cardinal Raynerius elected Pope. This was only
fifteen years after the devastation by Guiscard's
troopers, and it is difficult to understand how in
so short a period of time the subterranean basilica

could be filled up, and a new one built upon its site. But this difficulty disappears when we view the carelessness and evident haste with which the walls of the modern basilica were constructed; and moreover S. Clement's being obnoxious as the title of the antipope, and standing in the valley at the foot of Guiscard's position, it is probable that it was not spared in the fight. But in that case how can we account for the preservation of the pictures whose colours were so wonderfully bright when first cleared of the soil? By assuming that the church was only partially destroyed and immediately filled up after the devastation. Those who refer these paintings to the years intervening between 1085 and 1099, do so without a shade of probability; for, as we have already stated, they must have been executed when the circumstances they represent, and the devotion of those saints were fresh and fervent in the minds of the Romans. We confess, however, that in the midst of this obscurity of data, and dearth of positive proof, we can find only two facts of which we are certain - 1st that the original basilica existed in 1058, as we learn from a monumental inscription lately found in the pavement of the narthex with the names of Gregory VI and Nicholas II; 2^{d} that the modern church was built before 1299, because the

VIEW OF THE INTERIOR OF THE MODERN BASILICA

tabernacle of the holy oils bears that date, and is an insertion later in style than the rest of the church.

MODERN CHURCH.

The modern church of S. Clement was restored, by Clement XI, in 1715, as is recorded by this inscription over the door:

ANTIQVISSIMAM HANC ECCLESIAM
QVAE PENE SOLA AEVI DAMNIS INVICTA
PRISCARVM VRBIS BASILICARVM
FORMAM ADHVC SERVAT
EO IPSO IN LOCO AEDIFICATAM
AC IN TITVLVM S. R. E. PRESBYTERI CARDINALIS ERECTAM
VBI S. CLEMENTIS PAPAE ET MARTYRIS PATERNA DOMVS
FVISSE CREDITVR
A SANCTO GREGORIO MAGNO
GEMINIS HIC HABITIS HOMILIIS
ET SACRA QVADRAGESIMALI STATIONE
CONDECORATAM
CLEMENS XI. PONT. MAX.
IPSO ANNIVERSARIAE CELEBRITATIS EJVSDEM S. CLEMENTIS DIE
AD CATHOLICAE ECCLESIAE REGIMEN ASSVMPTVS
IN ARGVMENTVM PRAECIPVI IN EVM CVLTVS
INSTAVRAVIT ORNAVITQVE
ANNO SALVTIS MDCCXV. PONTIF. XV.

22

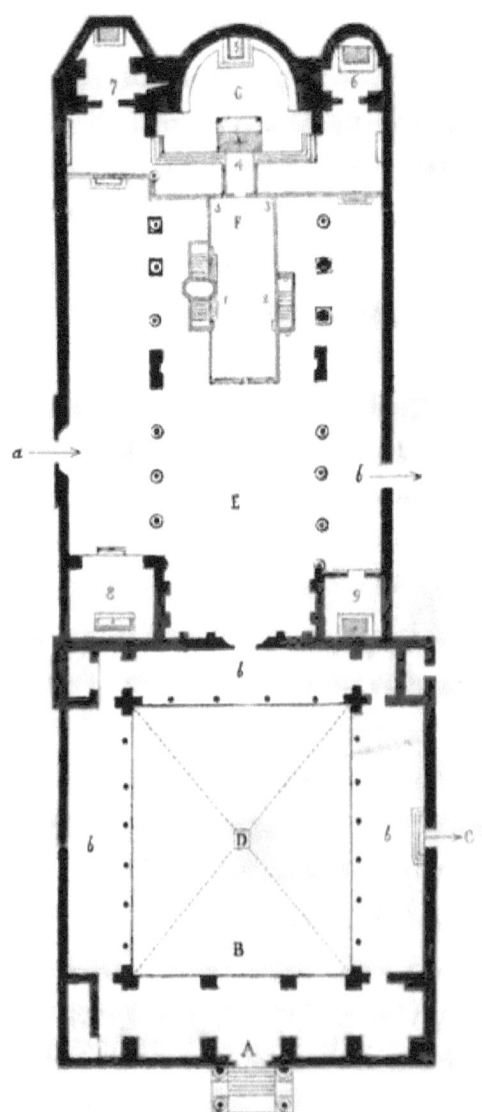

Ground-Plan of external portico, quadriportico, and modern Basilica.

A. Entrance to. B. Atrium. bbb. Quadriporticus. C. Entrance to convent. D. Fountain in which the Faithful used to wash their hands before
entering the church. E. Nave. F. Choir. 1. 2. Ambones. 3. Ancient
marble screens. 4. High altar. G. Presbyterium and tribune. 5. Episcopal
chair. 6. 7. 8. 9. Chapels of S. John, of the Rosary, of the Crucifixion,
and of S. Dominic. a. Side entrance to the church from the street. b. Entrance to the sacristy and subterranean basilica.

« This very ancient church which almost alone,
» unconquered by the damages of time, yet pre-
» serves the form of the old basilicas of the city,
» built upon the very spot, and erected to a Title
» of Cardinal priest of the Holy Roman Church,
» where the paternal house of S. Clement Pope and
» Martyr is believed to have been : graced by
» S. Gregory the Great with two homilies delivered
» here and the holy station of Lent. The Supreme
» Pontiff Clement XI elected to the government of
» the Catholic Church on the very day of the an-
» niversary celebration of the same S. Clement, in
» token of his particular devotion to him restored
» and ornamented it, in the year of salvation 1715,
» of his Pontificate the fifteenth. »

We must regret that the restorations are not
in keeping with the style of the church; and particularly that the heavy carved and gilt flat ceiling
substituted for the open timber roof, existing in 1690,
presses upon and conceals some parts of the mosaic
apse. The stucco ornaments and pictures above the
arches of the nave are also of the last century.
A series of frescoes is painted over the colonnades
that divide the nave and aisles. We give them in
the following order.

Death of S. Servulus. — On the right next the door, is depicted the death of S. Servulus by Chiari, a Roman artist, 1654-1727, and pupil of Carlo Maratta. The saint is sitting on a pallet listening to a man who is reading the scriptures: a pilgrim kneels before him, and two other men are earnestly looking at him: his aged mother leans on her staff behind, and an angel is distributing bread to the poor. S. Gregory the Great, in his first Book of morals, [1] thus speaks of Servulus : « In the porch » of S. Clement's church, Servulus, whom many of » you knew as well as I, passed his days. He was » poor in this world's wealth, but rich in heavenly » treasures. He was paralyzed from his infancy. » His mother and brother attended him, and the » alms he received he caused them to distribute » among the poor. He was utterly ignorant of let- » ters, but he bought the books of the sacred scrip- » tures, and had them continually read to him by » the pilgrims and other pious persons to whom he » gave hospitality, so that he committed them all to » memory. In his sufferings he never ceased, either » day or night, to give thanks to God, and sing His » praises. But when the time arrived for him to » receive the reward of his sufferings, the pain

---

[1] Homily 15, n. 4.

» attacked the vital parts, and knowing that he
» was near death, he asked the pilgrims, and those
» persons whom he had lodging with him, to arise
» and sing with him the psalms for his death. And
» while they were singing, he suddenly interrupted
» them, saying with a loud voice: ' Hush! do you
» not hear the melodies of the heavenly choir?'
» And while listening to the angelic chant, he
» expired. »

S. Ignatius condemned to death by Trajan. —
This fresco, by Piastrini, represents the emperor
Trajan sentencing S. Ignatius to be sent to Rome
to be devoured by wild beasts, in the Colosseum, for
the entertainment of the people. Two soldiers are
shackling his left hand, whilst he points with his
right to heaven , joyfully exclaiming: « I thank
» thee, o Lord, for vouchsafing to honour me with
» this token of perfect love for thee, and to be
» bound with iron chains in imitation of the apostle
» Paul for thy sake. »

Shipped at Seleucia, sixteen miles from Antioch,
bound to ten leopards, (so he calls the soldiers who
guarded him night and day,) at Smyrna he met the
bishop S. Polycarp his fellow-disciple under the
Evangelist S. John. To reach Rome before the shows
were over, they hurried him again aboard. From

22 *

Troas he wrote to the church at Smyrna, styling
the heretics who denied that Christ had taken true
flesh, and that the Eucharist is that flesh, wild
beasts in human shape, and prohibiting all communion with them.

S. Ignatius parting from S. Polycarp. — The two
martyr bishops are embracing each other, and the
soldiers hurry S. Ignatius, who is in chains, to the
ship in the back-ground. In front of a building
behind the saints, is a group of men and women;
some of them earnestly conversing with each other.
The composition is very good, and tastefully executed. It is by Triga.

**S. Ignatius devoured by lions in the Flavian am-
phitheatre.** — Ghezzi of Ascoli, 1634-1721, an imitator of Pietro da Cortona, gives the last scene of
the holy martyr's life. Ignatius longed to land on
the track of S. Paul at Pozzuoli, but a strong gale
drove the ship to Ostia. He reached Rome on the
last day of the shows, December 20 ; was presented
with the emperor's letter to the prefect, and immediately taken to the amphitheatre. He had begged
Polycarp and others, and wrote the same to the
Romans, to pray that he might be devoured at
once, lest, as happened to some Christians, the beasts

refusing to touch them, he should lose the crown of martyrdom. A letter of the church of Antioch reveals that the prayer was heard. « Thus was » he delivered to the wild beasts near the temple, » that so the desire of the holy martyr might be » accomplished, as it is written ' to the just their » desire shall be given, ' [1] that he might not be » burdensome to any of his brethren by the gather- » ing of his relics according as in his epistle he » had before wished that so his end might be. » For only the more solid parts of his holy relics » were left, which were carried to Antioch and » wrapt in linen, a priceless treasure bequeathed » to the holy church through the grace which was » in the martyr. » Four fierce lions were let loose and instantly devoured him, leaving only the larger bones. We see him kneeling with his arms extend-ed, his eyes raised to heaven: two lions upon him, a third rushing forward, and another looking gently at him. Angels are in the air, one of whom flies towards him with the palm. « After being present » at this sad spectacle, » say the authors of the letter, « which made us shed many tears, we spent » the following night in our house in watching and » prayer, begging God to afford us some comfort

---

[1] Prov. X, 24.

» by certifying us of his glory. » They add that several saw him in great bliss.

S. Clement giving the veil to Flavia Domitilla. — The pictures on the left of the nave are all of the life of S. Clement. Sebastian Conca of Gaeta, 1676-1764, a pupil of Solimene of Naples, and an imitator of Pietro da Cortona, painted, near the door, S. Clement giving the veil to Flavia Domitilla, who is kneeling before him.

S. Clement causing water to gush from a rock. — This is by Grechino. It represents the miracle at the marble quarries in the Crimea, recorded in the first responsory of S. Clement's festival. « At the » prayer of S. Clement there appeared to him the » Lamb of God: from under whose foot a living » fountain flows: the gushing of the stream makes » glad the city of God. I saw upon the mountain » the Lamb standing. » The Christians parched with thirst from their toil in quarrying and cutting the marbles, are gladly drinking.

S. Clement cast into the sea with an anchor tied to his neck. — Odasi of Rome, one of the chief fresco-painters of the day, 1663 - 1734, under the patronage of Benedict XIII, depicted the martyrdom of S. Clement. The Pope is seen on a precipice over the sea, with the anchor fastened to his neck. Two men are holding it, and an officer commands the soldiers to hurl him into the waves. An angel bears the palm above. « When he had taken his way to » the sea, the people cried aloud: ' Lord Jesus Christ » save him. ' Clement was saying with tears: ' Fa- » ther, receive my spirit. ' »[1]

Translation of the relics of S. Clement. His entrance into glory. — We might expect the last subject to be that of the third responsory. « Thou » hast given, o Lord, a dwelling to Thy martyr Cle- » ment in the sea, in the form of a marble temple » prepared by angelic hands: affording a way to the » people of the earth to tell forth Thy wonders. » But Chiari has chosen the more ordinary translation of the relics. At the head of the saint, laid on the bier in his pontifical robes, there are two torch-bearers, and the Pope and his attendants stand at his feet: angels hover in the air. The same painter has represented the glory of the saint in the large painting on the ceiling over the centre of the nave.

SS. Cyril and Methodius. — On the wall over the door opposite the apse are the figures of SS. Cyril

---

[1] Benedictus Antiphon at Lauds.

and Methodius, clothed in their episcopal robes. They wear the Greek pallium, and hold in their hands the Greek crosier. All these frescoes are very fair specimens of that feeble, mechanical, and conventional school, of which Carlo Maratta was the chief.

CHAPEL OF THE CRUCIFIXION.

Injured as they are, it is a relief to turn to the frescoes in the chapel of the Crucifixion at the east end of the south aisle. There is, at least, a unity in its Gothic conception; and if the costumes are quaint medieval, poetry and good drawing, and sweet expression, yet remain. They are the very opposite of the Academic style; and their Tuscan author, 1402 - 1443, Masaccio, as Tommaso Guidi was nicknamed, was a man who gave a great impulse to the art by studying individual forms. Masolino and Fra Filippo Lippi were of his age and school. Unfortunately for himself, the young Carmelite Lippi left his convent, and, after having been captured by a pirate and sold to slavery in Africa, became a painter of great repute, and carried off a young lady, Lucrezia Buti, from the convent of S. Margaret, at Prato, in which she was being educated. Their son Filippino became a great artist, and finished the frescoes of the Brancacci chapel, in the Carmine at Florence, interrupted by Masaccio's death. Vasari mentions twenty four eminent artists who studied Masaccio's style. His forms were similar to those of his contemporaries, the sculptors Donatello and Ghiberti. This is the only chapel he painted in Rome. On the isolated pier to the left, is S. Christopher who suffered martyrdom in Lycia under the emperor Decius. He seems to have taken the name of Christopher, that is, carrier of Christ, from the same motive as Ignatius did Theophorus, that is, carrier of God, to express his ardent love and intimate union with Christ whom he always carried in his breast. Vida, the poetical bishop of Alba, 1470 - 1556, quaintly says of him:

« *Christophore, infixum quod eum usque in corde gerebas,*
Pictores Christum dant tibi ferre humeris. » [1]

« O Christopher, whom thou in inmost heart didst bear
Thy Christ, the painters on thy brawny shoulders bare. »

And it is said that his great stature and wading through the stream represent his courage in his tribulations. But, seeing how very often our Lord appeared to saints in the form of a little child, it is very possible that a lost tradition of some such

[1] Hymn. 26, tom. 2, pag. 150.

vision applies to S. Christopher. The entrance to
the chapel is an introduction to the consideration
of the humanity of Christ. Our Lady at prayer,
in an arcade, receives the Angelic Salutation: « Hail
» full of grace. » We pass under an arch on which
are painted the twelve apostles, and stand before
the Crucifixion of our Divine Lord. The eyes raised
to heaven are met, upon the vault, by the only
sources whence the Christian can learn of the God
made man, to wit, the four evangelists with their
emblems, and the four doctors of the Church.
The still landscape behind the cross represents the
repose of that world which its Creator meant for
peace. Human passions, and the dereliction of the
chosen people, fill the foreground. « What more
», ought I to have done for thee, and did it not? I
» planted thee my vineyard most goodly to behold;
» and thou art made to me very bitter, for in my
» thirst thou hast given me vinegar to drink, and with
» the lance pierced through thy Saviours's side. »[1]
Nor is the author of evil absent, nor the quick help
given to repentance. The demon violently drags
the soul of the reviling thief; whilst an angel receives
the soul of the forgiven penitent. The centurion on
horseback, clasping his hands, gazes up at the world's

---

[1] Adoration of the Cross on Good-Friday.

victim. She to whom much had been forgiven, because she had loved much, embraces the Cross, at the foot of which the beloved disciple stands weeping; and the will of the Virgin Mother fails not, but her human nature, worn out by suffering, faints in the arms of the women supporting her. The individuality of the painter's conception is strongly marked in the boy with a basket, and in the group of four men, one of whom is pointing to the Cross, while the others seem to listen to him.

On the wall to the left is depicted the martyrdom of S. Catharine. The first act of the saint shows her discoursing of the Trinity to the pagan Philosophers of Alexandria. She converted them, and the consequence of their conversion is seen in the fiery death they are doomed to suffer, under which the virgin encourages them to perseverance. Higher up, the idol she despised stands upon the pillar before which she is reproving the idolaters. Then from the window of her prison-cell she converses with the empress Maximin, and converts her. The convert is decapited by orders of the emperor, and an angel receives her soul. Ordinary tortures were not sufficient to punish, what seemed to the Pagans, crimes so enormous. The wheel, which bears her name, is contrived to tear her in pieces, but an angel descends and the broken engine wounds the executioners. In the presence of the soldiers leaning on their shields, the martyr kneels to receive the last stroke of the executioner, and an angel carries her soul to its reward. A small, but very delicate and graceful design shows three angels laying her body in the tomb on the summit of Sinai. When we praised Masaccio for turning to nature, it was not as if he were a mere copyist of living forms: the difficulties he had to contend against in painting eastern costumes, certainly not familiar to him, and of using medieval soldiers for Roman legionaries, or spectators in the dress of Florentines, would have overcome the mannered artist who had not his talent for giving expression to the face. The subjects on the opposite side, next the street, have recently been detached from the wall, put on canvas, and replaced, in order to prevent their perishing altogether from damp. The one near the altar represents a flood which inundated the city of Alexandria as a punishment for the death of the martyrs. Several persons are seen drowning in the waters, while S. Catharine is praying at the window of a palace. We do not know what the others represent, and therefore must leave them unnoticed.

We are enabled to fix the date of an inscription on the outer wall of this chapel, near the great door of the church, by the introduction into it, of the

name of Pope S. Zachary. He succeeded Gregory III,
in 741, and died in 752. The inscription records
a gift, by Gregory the titular of our church, of the
deutero-canonical and other books of the Old and
New Testament. It is as follows:

« Hisraheliticus dona offerebat populus ruri
Alius quidem aurum, alius namque argentum,
Quidam quoque aes, quidam vero pilos caprarum,
Infelix autem ego, Gregorius primus presbyter almae
Sedis Apostolicae, hujusque tituli gerens,
Curam beati, supremus cliens Clementis,
Offero de tuis, haec tibi Christe thesauris
Temporibus SSmi Zacchariae Praesulis summi
Per martyrem et sanctum, parva munuscula tuum,
Clementem cujus meritis merear delictis carere,
Atque ad beatam aeternam ingredi vitam.
Aisti quantum habes, regnum valet coelorum.
Suscipe hos Domine, velut minuta viduae quaeso,
Veteris novique Testamentorum denique libros
Octateuchum, Regum, Psalterium, ac Prophetarum
Salomonem, Esdram, historiarum illico plenos.

. . . .
Require syllabarum, lector, sequentiam harum. »

The last line is engraved on a different quality
of marble which shows that the iscription is in-
complete.

CHAPEL OF S. DOMINIC.

The little chapel of S. Dominic, on the other
side of the great door, is incrusted with rich and
various marbles. The altar-piece which represents

the saint dying in the arms of angels is said to be
by Roncalli, a follower of Barocci of Urbino; and the
two paintings on the side walls are attributed to Sebastiano Conca. But, judging from their style, it is
much more probable that all three are by Ignatius
Hugford who was born in Florence of Scotch parents
in 1695, and afterwards became president of the Aca-
demy of the « Fine Arts » in that city. The two last
subjects have been repeated by the late Father Bes-
son O.P. on the walls of the chapter-room in S. Sisto
where they actually occurred. The painting on the
right represents S. Dominic restoring to life a mason
who had been crushed to death by the fall of a vault,
during the building of the convent of S. Sisto. That
on the opposite wall represents the same saint restoring to life the young prince Napoleon Orsini, the
only surviving stock of the Orsini family. Theo-
doric Apolda,[1] Fr. Humbert,[2] a third historian
quoted by Echard,[3] Fleury,[4] John Longinus,[5] and
many others record this miraculous fact to have
occurred in the following way. Honorius III, com-
mited to S. Dominic the reformation of the nuns in
Rome, many of whom then lived without keeping
enclosure, some dispersed in small convents, and

[1] C. 7, n. 80.   [2] C. 33.   [3] T. 1, p. 30.
[4] 1, 73, n. 32.   [5] C. 6, Hist. Poloniae, ad an. 1218.

others in the houses of their parents and friends. In order to facilitate the success of this commission, the saint requested that three Cardinals should be appointed to assist him, to which the Pope assented, and named for that purpose Hugolini, dean of the Sacred College, Nicholas bishop of Tusculum, and Stephen, of Fossa Nuova, cardinal priest of the twelve Apostles. S. Dominic, having obtained the consent of the Pope, offered to give his own convent of S. Sisto to the nuns, and to build a new one for his friars on the Aventine. The nuns who lived in the small convents were easily induced to embrace the reform, but those of the great convent of S. Mary's beyond the Tiber obstinately refused. The saint repaired thither with the three Cardinals already mentioned and addressed the nuns with such force of reasoning, and so much charity, that they all, except one, promised to obey. But the devil was not to be discomfited so easily. Immediately after the Cardinals and S. Dominic had gone away, the parents and friends of the nuns went to S. Mary's to implore them not to take a step which could never be recalled; that, if they did, they would repent it; and that they ought never to abandon their convent which was enriched by so many privileges. Such discourses were too flattering not to please women, who, although vowed to religion, held a certain

23

amount of uncontrolled freedom too dear; so they all changed their minds and resolved to remain where they were. On hearing this, S. Dominic returned to S. Mary's to say mass, and after he had offered the holy sacrifice he addressed them with tears in his eyes, saying: « Can you then repent of a pro-
» mise you have made to God ? Can you refuse to
» give yourselves up to Him without reserve,
» and to serve Him with your whole hearts? »
He went on in a strain of such affecting exhortation that after his discourse, the abbess and all the nuns confirmed by vow their readiness to comply with his directions. On Ash-Wednesday (1218) they took possession of their new convent, and while they were assembled in the chapter-room with the three Cardinals treating of the rights and administration of the community, a messenger came to inform them that the young prince Napoleon, cardinal Stephen's nephew, had fallen from his horse, near the Porta S. Sebastiano, and was killed. The news so stunned cardinal Stephen that he fell speechless on the breast of S. Dominic who was sitting by his side. The saint, after in vain endeavouring to alleviate his grief, ordered the lifeless body to be brought to the chapter-room, and told brother Tancred to prepare the altar that he might say mass. The holy sa-

crifice being ended, the man of God put the broken limbs in their proper places, and, after spending some time in prayer, made the sign of the Cross over the body, and lifting up his hands to heaven, cried out with a loud voice: « Napoleon, I say to » thee, in the name of our Lord Jesus Christ, arise. » That instant the young man arose safe and sound, in the presence of the three Cardinals, the friars, and nuns, and an immense concourse of people.

CHAPEL OF THE BLESSED SACRAMENT.

This chapel, at the end of the aisle opposite S. Dominic's chapel, is dedicated to S. John the Baptist, whose statue, by Simon the brother of Donatello, is over the altar. On one side is painted the Baptist reproving Herod for having married his brother's wife; and on the other side his decapitation, and his head given to the dancing girl on a dish. The chapel is vaulted, in a manner rare in Rome, with white glazed terra-cotta sunk panels, in the centre of each of which is a rose in alto-rilievo.

The two monuments immediately outside the chapel are very good specimens of cinque-cento work, especially that of cardinal Roverella, which bears the date of 1476. The cardinal is in a recumbent posture with two angels keeping watch over him, one at his head and the other at his feet. In the arched top of the monument is the Almighty surrounded by angels, and below them the Blessed Virgin with the Divine Infant sitting on her knees. Two angels stand by their side. On the right, S. Peter is presenting the cardinal to our Lord and His Blessed Mother. S. Paul is on the opposite side. Two exquisitely carved candelabra, in bas-relief, form a border for the sides of the monu-ment; and the sarcophagus is highly decorated with very graceful arabesques, and the symbols of the fine arts of which it would appear the Cardinal was a generous protector. At the base of the tomb there are angels, one on each side, admirably designed and executed. A little to the right, towards the sacristy, is the tomb of John Francis Brusati, nephew of cardinal Roverella, and arch-bishop of Nicosia in Cyprus.

CHAPEL OF THE ROSARY.

The altar-piece of the Rosary chapel, on the left of the apse, representing the Madonna and Child giving Rosaries to S. Dominic and S. Catharine, is by Conca. It is well designed and admirably exe-cuted. On the wall to the left, S. Francis of As-sisi is depicted receiving the Stigmata on Mount

Alverno, and on the right S. Charles Borromeo distributing alms to the poor. Outside the chapel to the left, is the monument of cardinal Venerio of Recanati who died in 1479. The columns sculptured with vine-tendrils, and birds pecking at the grapes, are very beautiful. The capitals are admirable specimens of fine pierced work. On the rim of one of them is engraved the name « Mer- » curius Presb. S. Clementis: » very probably the same John Mercurius, titular of the basilica, who erected an altar in it under the Popedom of S. Hormisdas, 514-523, and therefore they must have been removed from the underground basilica. On a pilaster, opposite this monument, is a pleasing picture, by an unknown artist, of the Virgin and Child, and S. John. The children are playing together, and our Lady, kneeling with her hands joined, earnestly looks at them. Angels are scattering roses over their heads. On the floor, to the right, is the tomb of cardinal Henry of S. Allosio who died in 1450.

PORCH, QUADRIPORTICO, AND VESTIBULE.

Having described the modern portions of the church, we will proceed to examine it as carrying out the primitive arrangements of a Christian basilica reproduced from the original beneath. First the porch, once painted, is roughly built with four antique columns sustaining a Gothic canopy, three of the columns being of granite and one of cipollino, differing in order and diameter, two having Corinthian and two Ionic capitals; the door-jambs are rudely sculptured with tracings of dissimilar designs; there are also remains of other buildings, and the whole is carelessly constructed.

The hangings and tapestry at the door of Roman churches on feast-days keep up a custom Pagan as well as Christian. Pliny says Zeuxis was so rich that he displayed his name woven in gold in the curtains shown at Olympia. And Aristotle gives a minute description of one of purple bought from the Carthaginians, embroidered with animals and gods, which when it was exhibited by Alcisthanes at the great festival of Juno Lacinia, to which all Italy used to flock, drew all eyes from the others. The iron rod is still in its place for those curtains of which the poet, of the fourth century, Aurelius Prudentius Clemens says: « Quae festis suspendam » pallia portis? » The bishop of Uzales in Africa, who lived in the fifth century, mentions that before the oratory, in which were preserved the relics of the protomartyr S. Stephen, a veil was placed on which the saint was painted carrying a cross upon his shoulders. From this outer porch we enter the quadriportico which is oblong, being 62 feet by 50, and surrounded on three sides by 16 pillars, twelve of grey Bigio marble, three of Numidian marble, and one of Oriental granite. The pavement of the atrium contains many fragments of green and white serpentine, and in the centre of the court is the *impluvium* to receive the rain. So far we have the usual arrangement of the Roman palace. The fountain at which the Christians purified themselves before entering the house of God, was restored in 1868. In the porticoes of the ancient palaces family busts and other ornaments were found. In those of the church were placed pictures. In the fourth century, S. Asterius, after having prayed at leisure in the church, was passing hurriedly through one of the porticoes when he was arrested by a painting representing the martyrdom of S. Euphemia. [1] It was in the fifth century, when the holy Cross was exposed for public veneration at Jerusalem, that Mary of Egypt was withheld, from entering a church, by an invisible hand, thrice and four times. Smitten by her bad life she retired into a corner of the court. There she perceived a picture of the Mother of God; and, fixing her eyes upon it, begged her by her incomparable purity to help

---

[1] Combefis, t. I. Enar. in Martyr. S. Euphem., p. 207-210.

a lost woman to consecrate her life in penance, and allow her to venerate the sacred wood of her redemption. Then with ease she went up to the very middle of the church, kissed the pavement in tears; knelt again before the picture, and asked the witness of her promise to guide her. She seemed to hear a voice « if thou goest beyond the Jordan, thou » shalt there find rest and comfort. » Weeping and looking at the image, she begged the Blessed Virgin never to abandon her; and followed up her conversion by that forty years' solitary penance in the desert, which has made her one of the most marvellous penitents in the history of the Church. We might accuse Jerome the austere, beating his emaciated breast in the wilderness, of harshness when he writes: « Gird yourselves and lament. » [1] « He that is a sin- » ner, whom his own conscience reproves, let him » gird himself with sackcloth, and lament both his » own sins and those of the people; and enter into » the church which he had left on account of his sins, » and let him sleep in sackcloth, that by austerity » of life he may compensate for his past delights. » The bishop of Barcelona, S. Pacian, writes about 374: « What shall I do now, the priest that am required » to effect a cure? It is late for such a case: still, if

---

[1] Joel, 1. 16.

» you can bear the knife and the caustic, I can yet
» cure. Here is the prophetic knife: 'Be converted to
» the Lord your God, in fasting, and in weeping, and
» in mourning, and rend your hearts.'[1] Be not afraid,
» dearly beloved, of the cutting. David bore it; he
» lay in filthy ashes, and was disfigured by a robe
» of a mean sackcloth ... I beseech you, therefore,
» brethren, by the faith of the Church, by my soli-
» citude for you ... let not shame overcome you
» in this work: let it not be irksome to you to
» make your own, the seasonable remedies of sal-
» vation; to humble your minds with sorrow; to
» put on sackcloth; to strew yourselves with ashes;
» to wear yourselves with fasting and grief; and
» to obtain the help of others' prayers. In pro-
» portion as you have not been sparing in punishing
» yourselves, in that same measure will God spare
» you ... Here is my promise and pledge, that if you
» return to your Father by a true satisfaction, by
» going astray no more, by not adding to your for-
» mer sins, by uttering also words of humility and
» of plaintiveness: -- *Father, we have sinned be-*
» *fore Thee, we are not now worthy to be called Thy*
» *sons;*[2] -- at once the unclean herd will leave you,
» and the foul husks their food. He will at once

---

[1] Joel, 2, 12.   [2] Luke, XV.

» *clothe* the returning sinner with his *robe*, honour
» him with *a ring*, and receive him again to a father's
» embrace. »[1] Let us now turn to a bishop, who
when told that the emperor, who had already
done eight months' penance after he had met and
repelled him from the church-porch, was again approaching, answered : « If so, I tell you plainly
» I shall forbid him to enter the church porch;
» and if he think good to turn his power into
» force and tyranny, I am most ready to under-
» go any death, and to present 'my throat to
» the sword. »   S. Ambrose again says: « I have
» known some who in penitence have furrowed their
» cheeks with tears, have worn them away with con-
» tinual weeping, have cast themselves down to be
» trodden on by all, and with a countenance pallid
» with fasting have had the appearance of the dead
» in a breathing body. «   In another place he says:
« I have more easily found those who have pre-
» served their innocence, than those who have done
» penance in a befitting manner.   The world is to
» be renounced, sleep less indulged in than nature
» demands: disturb it with groans, interrupt it with
» sighs, set it aside for prayers: a man must so
» live as to die to the uses of this life , he must

---

1 Paraen. ad Poenit., n. 9, 12. Galland., T. VII, p. 272-3.

» deny himself and be entirely changed. » [1] If we would turn to S. Augustine the convert of S. Ambrose, we are encouraged by the communion of saints: « As regards, daily, momentary, light sins, » without which this life is not passed, the daily » prayer of the faithful satisfies. » [2] But he advises a man who is conscious of deadly sins to come to the prelate through whom the keys are ministered to him in the Church. « So that if his » sin is not merely to his own injury, but also to » the great scandal of others, and it seems to the » prelate a thing expedient for the utility of the » Church, let him not refuse to do penance in the » presence of many, or even of the whole people: » let him offer no resistance, nor, through shame, » add the tumour of pride to his deadly mortal » wound. » Two hundred years before, Tertullian enforced the same practice: « Confession is a di- » scipline for the abasement and humiliation of man, » enjoining such a manner of life as invites mercy. » It directs also even in the matter of dress and » food, to lie in sackcloth and ashes, to hide the » body in filthy garments, to cast down the spirit » with mourning, to exchange the sins which he

---

[1] T. II, Lib. II, de Poenit., c. X, n. 96, 436-7.
[2] T. II, Enchirid. de Fide. n. 17.

— 364 —

» has committed for severe treatment; for the rest,
» to use simple things for meat and drink; to wit,
» not for the belly's, but for the soul's, sake; for
» the most **part** also to cherish prayer by fasts, to
» **groan, to** weep, and to moan, day and night, unto
» **the** Lord his God; to throw himself upon the
» ground before the priests, **and to fall on** his knees
» before the Altar of **God**; to enjoin all the brethren
» to bear the message of his prayer for mercy. » [1]
Besides **hearty** repentance and private penance, the
sinner had in some cases to humble himself, **as**
S. Augustine notices, in the sight of all the people,
and beg to be restored to their communion. For
in the unity of the Church it never entered men's
minds to haggle, and make terms as to the conditions on which they would condescend to be received, but they deplored their separation as an evil
intolerable to their own consciences, worth any humiliation in exchange for that kiss of peace which
they could only deserve by submission to authority.
« Should any one, having secret sins, yet, for Christ's
» sake, heartily do penance, how shall he receive
» the reward, if he be not restored to communion?
» I would have the guilty hope for pardon: let him
» beg it with tears, let him beg it with sighs, beg

---

[1] De Poenitentia, n. 8-12, p. 126.

« it with the tears of all the people: that he may
» be pardoned, let him implore. And, in case com-
» munion has been deferred a second and a third
» time, let him believe that he has been too remiss
» in his supplication : let him increase his tears, then
» let him return in deeper distress, embrace their
» feet, cover them with kisses, wash them with his
» tears, nor let them go that the Lord Jesus may
» say of him : ' Many sins are forgiven him, because
» he hath loved much. ' » [1]

When such was the spirit of the Church we know
with what vigour the archbishop repulsed the guilty
Theodosius; yet S. Paulinus of Milan relates, in his
life of S. Ambrose, that whenever any one confessed
his sins to him, he wept so as to compel the penitent
also to weep. Sozomen of the Greek Church, A. D. 450,
who remarks that « it is a sacerdotal law that the
» things done contrary to the sentiment of the Bishop
» of the Romans be looked upon as null, » has preserved for us a graphic picture of the public penitents. Of auricular confession he says: « As not to
» sin at all, seems to belong to a nature more divine
» than that of man's, and God has commanded pardon
» to be granted to the penitent even though he may
» often sin, and as in begging pardon, it is necessary

---

[1] S. Ambrose, T. II, L. I, de Pœnit., c. XVI, p. 414.

» to confess also the sin, it, from the beginning, deser-
» vedly seemed to the priests a burthensome thing
» to proclaim the sins, as in a theatre, in the cogni-
» zance of the whole multitude of the church, they
» appointed to this office a priest from among those
» whose lives were best regulated, one both silent
» and prudent, to whom they who had sinned went
» and acknowledged their deeds. » And, in 460,
S. Leo the Great prohibited public Confession. « I
» ordain that that presumptuous conduct, which,
» I have lately learned, is by an unlawful usurpa-
» tion pursued by certain persons, in opposition to
» an apostolic regulation, be by every means set
» aside. That is, as regards the penitence which is
» applied for by the faithful, let not a written de-
» claration of the nature of their individual sins
» be publicly recited; since it is sufficient that the
» guilt of their consciences be made known to
» priests alone by secret confession. » [1] The priest,
in fact, gave his absolution upon condition of the
penitent performing his penance. « But, » says Sozomen, « nothing of this was required by the No-
» vatians, who make no account of repentance; though
» among the other sects (heresies,) this custom pre-

---

[1] Ep. CLXVIII, ad universos Episcopos per Campaniam, Samnium et Piscenum constitutos, c. 2, p. 1430-1.

» vails even unto this day. And in the church of
» the Romans, it is carefully preserved. For there
» the place of those who are doing penance, where
» they stand in sadness, and with signs of grief,
» is visible (to all.) And when the liturgy of God
» is at length completed, without partaking of the
» things which are the privilege of the initiated;
» with groans and lamentations they cast themselves
» prone upon the ground, and the bishop meeting
» them face to face, in tears, falls in like manner
» upon the pavement, and with loud lament, the
» whole assembly of the church is drowned in tears.
» And after this, the bishop raises the prostrate:
» and having offered up a suitable prayer for the
» sinners who are penitent, he dismisses them. But
» privately each one being voluntarily afflicted, either
» by fasts, or abstinence from food, or in other
» ways appointed him, he awaits the time which
» the bishop has assigned to him. But, at the ap-
» pointed time, having discharged the punishment,
» as it were a debt, he is freed from sin, and as-
» sociates with the people in the church. The priests
» of the Romans observe these things, from the be-
» ginning, even unto our days. » [1] And we have
from an African Synod of the fourth century the

---

[1] H. E., Lib. VII, c. 16, p. 290, 301.

rationale of this conduct of the bishop, and the place appointed for the penitent. « Let the periods » of penance be adjudged to penitents, by the de- » termination of the bishop according to the dif- » ference of their sins: and a priest shall not re- » concile a penitent without consulting the bishop » except necessity, arising from the absence of the » bishop, compel him: but as to the penitent whose » crime is public ànd most notorious, disturbing the » whole church, he shall impose bonds on him before » **the** apsis. » [1] S. Basil mentions all the classes of these penitents when he says in his 44th Canon that the adulterer should be excluded from parti- cipation in the holy mysteries for fifteen years: to spend the first four among the mourners, then five among the listeners, then four among the prostrate, **and** the remaining two among the standers. The Council of Nicaea directs that persons who fell away without compulsion, as happened under the tyranny of Licinius, if truly repentant, should pass three years among the hearers as believers, and during seven years shall be among the prostrate, and du- ring two years shall communicate without the obla- tion. The Council of Ancyra directs that persons who fell before the idols, but had not eaten the

---

[1] Codex Can. Eccl. Afr. Can. XLII, **Col.** 1069, Labb. T. II.

meats that had been offered to them, should prostrate for two years, and communicate in the third, without the oblation, in order that they might receive full communion in the fourth year. « But the bishops have the power, having considered the manner of their conversion, to deal indulgently with them, or to add a longer period. But above all things, let their previous, as well as their subsequent life, be enquired into, and so let the indulgence be measured out. »[1] S. Gregory of Nyssa says: « The Canon law for fornicators is that they shall be utterly cast forth from prayer during three years, and be allowed to be *hearers* only for three further years. But, in favour of those who with special zeal avail themselves of the time of conversion, and in their lives exhibit a return to what is good, it is in his power, who has the regulation of the dispensation of the church for a beneficial end, to shorten the period of *hearing,* and to introduce such men earlier to the state of *conversion,* and, further to lessen this period also, and to bestow *communion* earlier, according as, from his own judgment, he comes to a decision respecting the state of the person under

---

[1] Can. V, Col. 1456-7. Labb., t. I.

» cure. » [1] Evidently under such discipline persons could not travesty the religious dress and sneak into Catholic churches to commit sacrilege against the Eucharist by receiving it. S. Gregory notices that penitents were not to be deprived of the Viaticum, but, if they recovered, were to complete their period of penance. Of the practice of the West, S. Innocent I, a. d. 417, writes: « As regards pe-
» nitents, who do penance, whether for more grie-
» vous or for lesser offences, if sickness do not in-
» tervene, the usage of the Roman Church demon-
» strates that they are to have remission granted
» them on the Thursday before Easter. For the
» rest, as to estimating the grievousness of the
» transgressions, it is for the priest to judge, by
» attending to the confession of the penitent, and
» to the grief and tears of the amending sinner,
» and then to order him to be set free when he
» sees his satisfaction such as is suitable: or, if any
» such fall ill, so as to be despaired of, he must be
» pardoned before Easter, lest he depart this world
» without communion. » [2]

As we passed through the quadriportico to the great door of the church, persons excommunicated

---

[1] T. II, Ep. Can. ad Letoium, p. 119.
[2] Ep. XXV, Decentio, n. 10, Galland, T. VIII, p. 589.

and utterly cast forth from prayer for a time, weepers, and mourners in sackcloth and ashes, winterers as abiding the elements, would lament their exclusion, and beg for prayers. The vestibule of the modern church being precisely over the ancient one, the first step into it would bring us among the catechumens and penitential hearers, both of whom were obliged to withdraw before the offertory. They were under the rod of the ostiarius, and hence this place probably got its name *Narthex*, which signifies a rod.

INTERIOR OF THE CHURCH.

The interior of the church before us is 170 feet 6 inches long, by 70 feet 9 inches in width. On either hand the sixteen antique columns separating the nave from the aisles form a perspective to the apse: five of them are Parian marble, and of these four are fluted and one plain; five others of Numidian marble, three of granitello, two of Oriental granite, and one of *bigio*. The pavement is of beautiful « *Opus Alexandrinum*, » in varied patterns. More than one third of the nave is occupied by the choir with its paschal candlestick and elevated ambones on either side. At its further end is the shrine of the Martyr to whom the church is dedi-

cated, with the altar over it, raised in front of
the bishops throne and the sedilia for the priests.
The sight is arrested, at this most important point
of a Christian basilica, by the ciborium over the
altar and the rich mosaics of the apse. The floor
of the church was given up to the laity. We will
not attempt to assign the precise places occupied
by the other penitents after passing the catechumens and *hearers* in the narthex. Butler says that
the *prostrate* were at the bottom of the nave,
and the *standers* above the ambones. S. Charles
Borromeo revived the separation of men and women;
and Ciampini says, the men were in the south aisle,
and the women in the north. The Pontifical book
says, Pope Symmachus made the Oratory of the holy
Cross on the men's side, Sergius I made a golden
image of S. Peter on the women's side: Gregory III
an oratory next the triumphal arch on the men's
side. In the East the separation was made effectual
by enclosures with doors. The empress S. Helen
would be in her proper place in the women's depart-
ment. Theodosius prayed in the chancel till S. Ambrose reproved him for it; and the emperor's throne
was placed in the upper end of the men's apartment
next the sanctuary. In the plan which Ciampini
gives of S. Clement's he assigns the chapel of the
Blessed Sacrament as the *Matronaeum*, or the place

appointed for matrons: and the chapel of our Lady of the Rosary, as the *Senatorium,* or place for the Senator and other persons of distinction.

The object of the separation was not merely to prevent remarks upon bonnets and dress, and glances directed anywhere but to the altar. It was most important for the **sacrifice** and the communion. **The** Apostolical Constitutions of the **third century direct some of the** deacons to attend upon the oblation ministering the body of our Lord with fear, and others to watch the multitude, and keep them silent. During the sacrifice the people were to stand and pray in silence: then to communicate each rank by itself, women with their heads veiled: the doors guarded lest an unbeliever, or one **not** initiated should enter. S. Hilary says: « **We must** » not treat indiscriminately, nor unwisely, and with- » out caution, of the Incarnation of the Word of » God, and the mystery of the Passion and the power » of the Incarnation. » [1] In the nineteenth century when grace is made a jest for flippant lawyers, baptism an open question, ordination a ceremony signifying nothing, theology the staple of lay reviews, and the filth of the divorce court the entertainment of the people, the reticence of the fourth century about the

---

[1] Comm. in Matth., c. **VI, n. 1,** p. 696, t. **I.**

mysteries will, doubtless, appear, to the scoffers of religion, antiquated and over nice. S. Ambrose remarks that he was on the Lord's day, after having dismissed the catechumens, expounding the creed in the baptisteries of the basilica. « These » mysteries which the Church now makes known » to thee who art transferred from among the ca- » techumens, it is not the custom to make known » to the Gentiles; for to a Gentile we do not » make known the mysteries concerning the Father, » Son, and Holy Ghost: neither do we speak plainy » of the mysteries before catechumens. » And precisely because the doctrine of the Trinity was not communicated to them, the Lord's prayer was not to be published, nor the Apostles' creed written. « A fortiori » the real presence was not to be exposed, as S. John Chrysostom says, before Gentiles who might scoff at it, or before catechumens whose curiosity might be roused and ignorance scandalized. In the present day the depths of ignorance cast a dark cloud, indeed, about the consecrated host, but do not prevent the scandal. The ancient practice was effectual. « When the catechumen has » joined his praise to that of the initiated, he » withdraws from the more secret mysteries, and » is excluded from Christ's sacrifice. » [1] In the

---

[1] S. Cyril of Alexandria de Ador. in Sp. et Ver., p. 445.

same fifth century, Theodoret says of the divine
food, and the spiritual doctrine, and the mystic
and immortal banquet which the initiated recognize:
« These things are plain to the initiated and do
» not need explanation; for they are acquainted
» both with the spiritual oil wherewith they had
» their heads anointed, and with that inebriation
» which weakens not, but strengthens, and that
» mystic food which He, who has become bride-
» groom, as well as a shepherd, sets before us. » [1]
We are thus prepared to listen to the ancient discipline of the Church, to see the propriety of not
tempting ignorant persons by their own ignorance
to accept the teaching of the Church without which
ignorance is an inheritance; and even, in the rite,
to see the utility of these eastern flabella which
excite the derision of the uninstructed, when the
chant rises in S. Peter's, and the tiare'd Pontiff is
dimly seen in the distance borne onwards upon
the shoulders of the faithful to the altar of sacrifice.
« Let other deacons walk about, and watch the
» men and women that no noise be made, that no
» one nod, or whisper, or slumber; and let the
» deacons stand at the doors of the men, and the
» subdeacons at those of the women, that no one

_____

[1] T. I, in Ps. XXII, p. 746-50.

» go out, nor a door be opened, although it be
» for one of the faithful, at the time of the obla-
» tion.   Let one of the subdeacons bring water to
» wash the hands of the priests, a symbol of the
» purity of souls devoted to God.   Then shall the
» deacon immediately say : ' Let none of the ca-
» techumens, none of the hearers, none of the un-
» believers, none of the heterodox stay; you who
» have prayed the foregoing prayer depart, let the
» women take their children. Let no one have aught
» against any one: let no one come in hypocrisy:
» let us stand upright before the Lord with fear
» and trembling to offer.'   When this is done, let
» the deacons bring the gifts to the bishop at the
» altar; and let the priests stand at his right hand
» and at his left, as disciples standing by their
» master.   But let two of the deacons, on each side
» of the altar, hold a fan made of thin membranes,
» or of peacock's feathers, or of linen, and let
» them silently drive away the flies, and the gnats,
» that they may not come near the chalices. » [1]
Before we consider the part of the church especially
devoted to the clergy, we will ask any of our
readers who have been at the ceremonies by the
tomb of the Apostle whether if religion is venerable

---

[1] Apostolical Constitutions.

by antiquity as well as by precept, the things they
have seen there, and not understood, deserve to be
laughed at?

The high altar is separated by marble panels
from the laity, the penitents, and catechumens.
We have the authority of S. Clement himself, for this
separation of the clergy from the lay congregation.
He says: « There are proper liturgies delivered
» to the chief priest, and a proper place assigned
» to the priests: and there are proper ministrations
» incumbent on Levites, and the layman is adjudged
» to the appointments of laymen. » And we suppose S. Jerome speaks of what was the custom in his
day, when the church of S. Clement kept his *memory*
still. « It is not the same thing to shed tears for
» sin, and to handle the body of the Lord: it is not
» the same thing to lie prostrate at the feet of the
» brethren and to minister, from an elevated spot,
» the Eucharist to the people. » Before we approach
that elevated spot, which, in all the ancient basilicas is nearly the same, a platform, from wall to
wall, mounted by steps on either side of the altar,
let us examine the choir on a lower level, but raised
also, by one step, above the floor of the church. It
is paved with Alexandrine work; the entrance gates
are enriched with mosaics: the great marble panels
are carved with wreaths, and crosses, and one conspi-

cuous monogram frequently repeated: and on the jambs supporting them are engraved the fish, the dove, and branches of the vine. The monogram is one of those puzzles of which Symmacus says to his friend: « I should like to know whether you got all » my letters sealed with the ring in which my name » is more readily understood than read. » S. Avitus of Vienne, like a sensible man, had his name in full round his monogram, that people might readily make it out. When Roman antiquaries confounded this choir, or *schola cantorum*, with that of the basilica whence the beautiful marble panels containing the monogram had been brought up, they used to say that it (the monogram) meant *Nicholaus*. Ugonius, Alemannius, and Du Cange said so; but Ciampini thought it was *Johannes*, though what John he did not know. The distinguished author of Murray's Guide-Book said « John VIII. » But the following inscription, recently discovered, upon one of the marble beams under the panels to the west of the Gospel *Ambo*, enables us to solve this question : « *Altare tibi d̄s salvo Hormisda papa. Mercurius Presbyter cum sociis offert.* » « In the Pontificate of Pope Hormisdas, Mercurius the Priest, with his companions, offers an altar to Thee, O God. » On the capital of one of the exquisitely sculptured pillars that decorates the monument of Cardinal Venerio, near the chapel of the Rosary, at the west end of the south aisle, is another inscription, which runs thus:

† Serbus † Dn̄i Mercurius P̄B̄. † Sc̄e Ecclesiae Catholicae off.

It is but natural to infer from this inscription that the pillar, at one time, supported the *ciborium* or *baldacchino*, which the Priest Mercurius with his colleagues had erected, and that both *ciborium* and altar stood in the lower church. S. Hormisdas governed the Church from 514 to 523. Mercurius, Cardinal Priest of S. Clement, was elected Pope in 532, and died in 534, as we are informed by the well known inscription in S. Peter's *ad Vincula*: « Joannes cogno- » mento Mercurius ex Sanctae Ecclesiae Romanae » presbyteris ordinatus ex titulo S. Clementis ad glo- » riam Pontificatus promotus etc. » Thus, in Mercurius, Pope John II, we have the person whose monogram is frequently repeated in the marble panels of the screen, the classical style of which agrees far better with the sixth than with the middle or close of the ninth century. Moreover the fact of John II, having erected an altar, while he was Cardinal Titular of S. Clement's, makes it almost evident that he would, during his Pontificate, take a special interest in this Basilica, and complete the work he had commenced while he was its Titular.

As to the guesses about the period of the
destruction of the old basilica and the building of
the modern one, it is not improbable that the great
earthquake of 896, twenty nine years after the
death of Nicholas I, may have shaken the basilica,
and perhaps thrown down the roof, when the fres-
scoes of S. Clement, S. Alexius and S. Cyril, were
fresh upon its walls. In which case the basilica,
which was not filled up with casual ruin, but with
soil and débris purposely compacted, may have
given place to the new church two hundred years
before Gregory VII, and Paschal II, and thus it
(the new church) was not destroyed by Guiscard at
all. Paschal II may have repaired it, and executed the mosaics of the apse, in memory of his
election in it, when he was repairing or rebuilding
the four crowned Martyrs. And two hundred years
after him, the nephew of Boniface VIII restored
the mosaics in the concavity of the apse and inserted the tabernacle for the holy oils. The erudite
author of Murray observes that the blocks of the
choir are adjusted in a careless manner; and that
the gospel-ambo being on the left instead of the
right hand, as in the basilica of S. Lorenzo, and in
some other churches, is another reason for supposing
that the choir, was carelessly set up, when removed
from the church beneath. But the panels and pave-

ment appear to have been carefully removed, and
the different parts of the ancient choir accurately
copied; and it is not likely that the builders did not
know on which side the *ambo* ought to stand, although, without any haste or want of accuracy in
placing the blocks, the settlement of the soil dislo-
cated the joints and threw the panels out of the horizontal line. That very careful antiquary, Ciampini,
engraves the gospel-ambo of S. Lorenzo without a
hint that its position is more correct than that of
S. Clement's. « We have thought, » says he, « to
» note these things first, that as this kind of join-
» ings of dissimilar parts is everywhere occurring
» as well in S. Clement's as in the other very old
» basilicas, persons entering the vestibules of these
» churches may not stick in over nice animadver-
» sions, but rather go on with us to the more useful
» observation of the chief internal parts. » An ancient heretic used to ask: « What is the Easter that
» you celebrate? You are again made to take up
» with Jewish fables. There is not to be any cele-
» bration of the Passover; for Christ our Passover is
» sacrificed. » To such a one the lofty spiral mosaic of our paschal candlestick is an eyesore, and,
instead of being lighted at the Gospel, the blest
candle ought to be extinguished for ever. That
striking of the flint on Holy Saturday, and blessing

of the new light in the church; that prayer « Lord
» God, Father Omnipotent, light never failing, who
» art the Maker of all lights, bless this light which
» is blest and made holy by Thee who hast en-
» lightened the whole world, that with that light
» we may be enkindled and illuminated with the
» fire of Thy brightness; and as Thou wert a light
» to Moses going out of Egypt, so do Thou give light
» to our heart, and sense that we may deserve to
» come to light through Christ our Lord: » and
the successive lighting of the church-lights when
the sun is shining in the heavens, is surely superfluous and ridiculous excess. That chant of
the deacon has no meaning when he goes up to
the gospel-ambo and sings: « Now let the angelic
» host exult: the mysteries divine exult: and for
» the victory of so great a King the trumpet of
» salvation sound! Let the earth also rejoice illu-
» minated with such splendour, and enlightened
» with the brightness of the eternal King: let it
» feel that the darkness of the whole world is dis-
» persed. Let mother Church rejoice, adorned
» with the brightness of so great a light; and may
» this temple resound with the loud voices of the
» people. Wherefore I beseech you, most dear
» brethren, who are here present in the wonderful
» brightness of this holy light, to invoke with me

» the mercy of Almighty God. That He who has
» vouchsafed to number me among the Levites,
» without any merits of mine, would pour forth His
» brightness upon me, and enable me to perfect
» the praise of this light. »

And then follows : « Oh surely necessary Adam's
» sin which by the death of Christ is blotted out!
» Oh happy fault which deserved to have such and
» so great a Redeemer ! Oh truly blessed night,
» which alone deserved to know the time and the
» hour in which Christ rose again from worlds be-
» low. This is the night of which it is written :
» ' And the night shall be illumined as the day,
» and the night is my light in my delights. ' »
And when the ceremony goes on and the consecrated hand waves the water to the four quarters
of the world, and the mystic candle thrice plunged in the plenitude of the Holy Ghost within the
baptismal font, we cannot think without pain of
the thousands of children, who, in some countries
where Christianity is said to be part and parcel of
the law of the land, are never purified by that water, and whether baptism is a sacrament at all is
a question free to dispute. Ennodius of Pavia, who
died in 521, and was styled a glorious Confessor
by Nicholas I, wrote two forms of blessing the paschal candle in which the divine protection is im-

plored against storms and all danger from the malice
of invisible enemies. Some attribute the rite to Pope
Zosimus A. D. 418: and the *Agnus Dei*, found with
the relics under the altar of our church, may be
of that date, for the archdeacon used to bless, on
Holy Saturday, wax mingled with oil and impressed
with the figure of a lamb, such as was found in
the tomb of Mary Stilicho. S. Zeno, A. D. 362-383,
says of the font : « Haste ye, brethren, who are about
» to be washed. The living water tempered by
» the Holy Spirit, and with the pleasantest fire,
» with soothing murmur now invites you. » [1]   And
S. Pacian, A. D. 371, says « that the justice of Christ
» must need pass into the human race, Christ be-
» getting in the Church by means of the priests.
» These things cannot be otherwise fulfilled than
» by the sacrament of the laver, and of the chrism
» of the bishop. » [2]   And any one who considers
that lights were borne before the emperors, and the
fondness of the Christians for lights, incense, and
balsams, in the catacombs, will hardly suppose that
so obvious a figure as the descent of light into the
illuminative waters was neglected.

On either side of the choir are the *ambones*. The

---

[1] Lib. II, Tract. 35. Invit. 6, ad Font. Galland., T. I, p. 140.
[2] Sermo de Baptism., n. 3. Galland., T. VII, p. 308.

word *ambo* is said to be derived from the Greek word
ἀναβαίνειν, to go up, which might apply to any other
staircase, so that it is possible that *ambones* may be
a colloquial corruption of *umbones*, that is convex
projections, or elevated promontories. They are of
remote antiquity. S. Augustine recounts [1] that Vic-
torinus, the Rhetorician, read his profession of faith
from the *ambo*. On the east side of the gospel-*ambo*
is a beautiful spiral candlestick, in mosaic, for the
paschal candle. The connection between the light to
enlighten the Gentiles represented by the paschal
candle, and the higher step in the *ambo* from which
the deacon reads the gospel is evident. Ciampini says
that S. Cyprian calls *ambo* the tribunal. The gospel-
ambo in our church has a double staircase, on one side
towards the altar, on the other towards the narthex.
According to an old Roman *ordo*, the two accolytes
with their candles separated when they reached the
ambo, two subdeacons with thuribles, and the deacon
with the gospel passing between them; and going up
into the *ambo* by one staircase, the subdeacons immediately descended by the other and there stood.
A third subdeacon, preceding the deacon, held in his
left hand the gospel to be opened at the mark, and

[1] Confessions of S. Augustine, book VIII, c. 11.

the deacon read on that higher step in the *ambo* which
a subdeacon was not to mount, it being especially
reserved for the gospel. The deacon read the gospel
with his face turned to the North. The gospel ambones in S. Lorenzo and S. Pancras are similar to
these in S. Clement's, all three having that central
projection from which the modern pulpit is taken.
In S. Pancras, put up, in 1249, by Innocent IV, it is
ornamented by twisted columns, and supported by a
pillar below, as some pulpits are. But Ciampini remarks that S. Clement's has a double *ambo*, and that
it is an indication of the greater antiquity of the
church to suit that very ancient rite of the Roman
Ordo, by which the deacon stood turned to the south
aisle in which the men were wont to be, but otherwise to the north, a rite not everywhere observed in
the eighth and following centuries. The explanation,
he supposed to be, is, that if the southern aisle was
quite full of men and the middle of the nave also,
the deacon turned to the women's side on the north,
thus comprising the centre nave as well: but if the
men were fewer and the southern aisle held all, then
he turned to that side. On the women's side to the
north we have another *ambo*, but lower, with its two
marble desks, of which the highest, next the altar,
was for the subdeacon who turned towards the altar
to read the Epistle without regarding East or West.

The altar in S. Clement's is at the west end, but the celebrant, standing in front of it, always faces the East. The lower desk turned to the East was for the cantor to sing the gradual, responsories, and allelujas; and is only found where the subdeacon by turning to the altar had his back to the East, whereas, if he faced the East, a second desk for the cantor would be superfluous. Anastasius the librarian says it was Celestine I who, before the year 432, had the gradual sung at Mass.

Leaving the *ambones* behind, and returning with the deacon up the choir, the following arrangement is before us ; a porphyry slab with the inscription :

FLAVIVS CLEMENS
MARTYR
HIC
FELICITER
EST TVMVLATVS

« Flavius Clement martyr is here happily buried. »

Lower down, on the cornice over the *transenna*, behind which are preserved the relics of SS. Clement and Ignatius, is the following inscription :

HIC
REQVIESCVNT
CORPORA SANCTORVM
CLEMENTIS PAPAE
ET
IGNATII EPISCOPI
ET MARTYRVM

In the basilicas, with some rare exceptions, the body of the saint was placed beneath the altar protected by *transennae ;* and at S. Alexander's, on the Nomentan way, were discovered, in 1854, the remains of such an altar, and the *transennae*, with the names of the saints and of the bishop who dedicated it. As we stand below the altar before the slab of the martyr consul Clement, on either hand are two white marble *transennae* admirably worked, and they were once, probably, in their proper place in the lower basilica. These net-work panels sufficed to admit air to the lamps within, and did not hide the martyr's body from the sight of the worshipper. In the more ancient *transennae* the interstices were larger that cloths might be passed through them to touch the body ; for the corporeal relics were not then generally distributed. On either side of the shrine, steps lead to the platform upon which the altar stands : and to know the use of the altar, we must turn to the episcopal chair behind it, raised by three steps above the sedilia, for the priests, diverging from it on both sides. The back of this chair is of white Grecian marble on which the word « *Martyr* » in large letters is not inappropriately read. The bishop presiding there has passed step by step through the four minor Orders, beginning with the door-keeper; then through the holy orders of subdeacon and deacon, before the sacramental seal of the priesthood imprinted an indelible character for weal or woe upon his soul; and if in rank and order he now possesses the fulness of the priestood, and the Orders necessary for the altar can be conferred by him alone, there is one greater still to whom *ad limina apostolorum* he must render an account. Although he has not borne the successive duties of each rank for so long a time as in the ancient discipline of the Church, he began by the denial of himself, and the dedication of his whole will to God. His power and his strength are derived from that altar before him, from that Θυσιαστήριον of sacrifice from which they cannot eat who do service in the tabernacle. [1] Once he need only have raised his eyes to the silver dove suspended by a chain, which is still preserved, from the ciborium over the altar, to know that *there* was light, and life, and love : that unspeakable Presence, life of the soul, perpetual health of the mind, the bread of angels, eaten by the priest at that table under the sacred veils, carefully reserved that the triumph of Christ might be consummated in that most glorious act when still upon earth He is carried to heal the sick, and give courage to the dying. The ciborium is sustained by four pillars, two of *pao-*

---

[1] Hebr., XIII, v. 10.

nazzetto and two of *marmo scritto*, precisely such as were found at S. Alexander's and might be seen in the last century in the church of SS. Peter and Marcellinus. Ciampini considered this part known as the Confession so important that he engraved the ciborium of SS. Peter and Marcellinus as well as that of S. Clement. The bishop then was most appropriately placed in that seat where the praetor had decided so many vulgar causes, for between him and the people is no longer the table upon which the death warrant of Christians had been signed, but the altar upon which the Lamb of God who taketh away the sins of the world is immolated. S. John Chrysostom says: « When thou art going » to approach the sacred table, consider too that » the King of all is present there: for, indeed, he » is present really, thoroughly acquainted with each » one's disposition, and seeing who comes with be- » coming holiness, who with a wicked conscience, » with impure and foul thoughts, with evil deeds. » [1] And it is precisely because, in the presence of that King, His human court must keep their proper pla- ces so as to discharge their limited service, the whole arrangements of His sacred palace have been made; not at random, but for his intelligent crea- tures to pay Him suitable honour.

---

[1] T. VI. In Illud. Vidi Dom., n. 4, p. 165.

The personality of Christ upon the altar is reflected in the magnificence of that highest place where the clergy are found; and the beautiful and elaborate mosaic with the inscription:

« *Ecclesiam Christi viti similabimus isti*
Quam lex arentem, sed Crux facit esse virentem, »

« The Church of Christ we liken to that vine
The law made dry, the cross all green to shine, »

was meant to teach what, long years after, the Council of Trent commanded bishops to teach « that by » means of the history of the mysteries of our re- » demption, portrayed by paintings and other re- » presentations, the people is instructed and con- » firmed in remembering and continually revolving » in their mind the articles of faith. » Over the heads of the clergy, and out of their sight, whose minds ought not to be distracted from the altar, and whose eyes, looking beyond the altar, fall upon the people for whose souls they are responsible, that symbolical profusion of coloured shapes was to the people a certain image of heaven, and of the connection between the Church on earth and the Church in heaven. In the highest centre is a small cross; and in the circle below it the head of our Saviour with the Gospel, a hint expressed also in the inscription (« *Gloria in excelsis Deo sedenti super thronum, et in*

» *terra pax hominibus bonae voluntatis*, » « Glory be
» to God on high sitting upon his throne, and on
» earth peace to men of good will,» into which the
circle falls) that the good tidings were to men of
good will, and his eyes vigilant to behold and bless
them. The emblems of the four Evangelists express
the connection between the prophetic vision of Ezechiel in the old law and that of S. John in the new.
« The face of a man signifies Matthew who began to
write, as it were of a man, the book of the generation
of Jesus·Christ: then Mark in whom is heard the
voice of the lion roaring in the desert, the voice
of one crying in the wilderness: the face of the calf
which sets forth that Luke began from Zachary
the priest: the eagle, John who, hasting to higher
things, treats of the Word of God. » And in the
Apocalypse [1] there is the same meaning where it
is said, « the first living creature like to a lion,
and the second like to a calf, the third having the
face as it were of a man, the fourth like an eagle
in flight. And the four living creatures had each
of them six wings, and round about and within they
are full of eyes, and they rested not day or night
saying: Holy, Holy, Holy, Lord God Almighty who
was and who is and who is to come. » The imme-

---

[1] C. 4.

diate connection between the church in heaven and
the things of earth, between our Lord in glory and
the diffusion of his Gospel here, is shown in the
apostles, and martyr saints who succeed them. On
the right is Peter instructing Clement with the inscription: « *Respice promissum, Clemens, a me tibi*
» *Christum,* » « Clement, behold Christ promised by
» me to you. » On the left Paul arguing with the
deacon S. Laurence, and the inscription : « *De cruce,*
» *Laurenti, Paulo familiare docenti,* » « Paul familiarly
» teaching Laurence about the Cross. » The latter
is probably an allusion to some tradition connected
with the Oratory of S. Laurence *super Clementem*
at the Scala Santa; we regret that we do not know
what it is. S. Laurence , broiled alive in 258 by
the enraged Praefect to whom he showed the poor
as the treasures of the Church, was taught the
scriptures and spiritual life by Xyxtus II. His last
prayer was for the conversion of the city ; and he
asked it for the sake of the two apostles Peter and
Paul who had there began to plant the Cross of
Christ, and had watered that city with their blood.
It is a pleasing thought that the most beautiful
lettered pectoral Cross yet discovered, a gold reliquary of the sixth century, with the inscription
« The Cross is life to me, death, o enemy ! to thee, »
was found in his basilica. The mind of the Chris-

tian artist was not satisfied without bringing down
the glory of God on high to the predestined places
of the earth. And he does it by placing, below
S. Peter, Jeremias who mourned over the city that
was to be forsaken. The prophet holds in his hand
the scroll of Baruch : « *Hic est Dominus noster, et*
» *non aestimabitur alius absque illo,* » « This is our
» Lord and there shall no other be accounted of
» in comparison of him. » The city of Jerusalem
is below him. Under S. Paul, he gives the prophet of the virginal birth of Christ, Isaias, with
the inscription « *Vidi Dominum sedentem super so-*
» *lium,* » « I saw the Lord sitting upon the throne; »
and below him Bethlehem with the child in the
arch over its gate. This part of the mosaic has
been very little restored, and was probably executed by cardinal Anastasius, about the year 1108,
whose name is on the episcopal chair in front of
the high altar: « † Anastasius presbiter Cardinalis hu-
» jus tituli hoc opus cepit et perfecit. » [1] That por-

---

[1] Anastasius died in 1126 and was buried in his titular Church.
In the 16th century the following epitaph engraved on a marble slab
was preserved in the portico of the modern basilica:

dudum IS SANCTE PATER CLEMENS TVA TEMPLA NOVAVIT
CVIVS IN HOC TVMVLO PVLVIS ET VMBRA JACENT
MORIBVS EGREGIIS ET VITA PRESBYTER VRBIS
FVLSIT ANASTASIVS NOMINE DICTVS ERAT
VITA DECENS STVDIVMQ. PIVM VIS RELIGIONIS
CONSPICVVM MERITIS EFFICIEBAT EVM
HVNC QVICVMQ. LEGIS TVMVLVM MEMOR ISTO LEGENDO
DICERE NATE DEI SVBSIDIERIS EI.

tion of the mosaic which fills the hemispherical vault
of the arch is the most elegant in Rome, and was
probably restored, if not made, by cardinal Cajetan, as is recorded by the following inscription over
the gothic tabernacle :

« Ex annis Domini prolapsis mille ducentis
Nonaginta novem Jacobus collega Minorum
Hujus basilicae tituli pars Cardinis alti
Haec jussit fieri quo plausit Roma nepote
Papa Bonifacius Octavus Anagnia proles. »

Therefore it is of the age of Giotto, who may have
designed it, as he did the *Navicella* over the door
of S. Peter's. Cavallini who executed the *Navicella*
was his contemporary, if not his pupil, and finished
the mosaics on the facade of S. Maria in Trastevere. Gaddo Gaddi, whose son was Giotto's godson
and pupil for many years, had a great reputation
for mosaics, and was invited to Rome by Clement V.
He finished Jacopo da Turitas' mosaics in S. Maria
Maggiore, and executed several others relating to our
Lady. The repairs in the mosaics of that basilica discovered the name of another artist Philippus Rusutus,
A. D. 1317. But, as far as we know, none of these
works show the elegant symbolism of the apse of
S. Clement's. Giotto painted several frescoes in the
Loggia of the Lateran, but the only one remain-

ing is the portrait of cardinal Cajetan's uncle, Boniface VIII, proclaiming the jubilee of 1300, still preserved in that basilica. The hemispherical vault of
the apse is the work of a great artistic mind in
its conception, and, as regards execution, we know
that Giotto improved the art of working in mosaics :
and there is a marked affinity of style in the mosaics
of the apse to that of the coloured marbles with
which he decorated the buildings 'in his pictures
and carried to perfection in his Campanile at Florence. Although the mosaics, of S. John in Fonte,
at Ravenna, show full-length figures inclosed in ara-
besque foliage, they have nothing in common with
the graceful curves we see here : and the whole
concavity, which is the crown of the work, is so
superior, in symbolical style, as well as in drawing,
to the rest, or any other mosaics in Rome, that it is
easier to refer the design to Giotto, than to imagine an unknown artist possessed of similar power.
Coming out of the gates of Bethlehem and Jerusalem, we have the usual subject of the twelve apostolic sheep with the mystic lamb, crowned with the
nimbus, in their midst. Above them is the following inscription which forms the lower border of the
florid arabesques of the concavity :

« *Ecclesiam Christi viti similabimus isti*
  Quam lex arentem, sed Crux facit esse virentem:
  De ligno Christi, Jacobi dens, Ignatüque
  Insupra scripti requiescunt corpore Christi. »

« The Church of Christ we liken to that vine,
  Which, the law parched, the cross makes green to shine:
  O' th' wood of Christ, of James a tooth, and of Ignace
  In body of that Christ have found a resting place. »

The representation of the Cross excited the devotion of the faithful the more from the knowledge that a particle of the true Cross was before them; and the union of our Lord with his saints, and of His passion with theirs, was more than shadowed by placing a relic of an Apostle, and of the martyr Bishop of Antioch, with the true Cross in the very figure of His body. A broad border, rich with flowers and fruit, goes all round the inner edge of the concavity; and we recognize in it the grapes, and ears of corn, symbolic of the Eucharistic species. In this border, just over the gate of Bethlehem, is a man with large bunches of grapes; in the crown of the arch is the Constantinian monogram of Christ, and below it, on the right, a hare among grapes. The meaning of the hare, which is often found in Christian monuments, is undecided. On a Siracusan lamp, round a jewelled cross, is a border of triangles and leaves, and hares running. In another is one hare, and in another the circular border terminates with a flying dove. It is suggested that the hare represents human nature prone to sin : and in the distinction of clean and unclean animals, given in Leviticus ch. XI, it is reckoned among the unclean animals, which the people were prohibited to eat, in order to restrain them from the vices of which these animals are the symbols. « And » the Lord spoke to Moses and Aaron, saying : Say » to the children of Israel : these are the animals » which you are to eat of all the living things of the » earth. Whatsoever hath the hoof divided, and » cheweth the cud among the beasts, you shall » eat. But whatsoever cheweth indeed the cud » and hath a hoof, but divideth it not, as the ca- » mel, and others, that you shall not eat, but shall » reckon it among the unclean. The cherogrillus » which cheweth the cud, but divideth not the hoof » is unclean. The hare also : for that too cheweth » the cud, but divideth not the hoof. » The vine itself, however , was called *leporaria*, as it were the hare-plant, perhaps from some idea that its leaves had a peculiar attraction for these animals. Here at least , placed in the midst of Eucharistic emblems, the little hare is, more probably, a figure of the soul leaping to its choice food. By this Eucharistic border (if we may so call it) the main subject is framed. At the top, the opening of the heavens is indicated by the waving prismatic circle, and the hand in the wreath in the sky is a common emblem of Almighty power. On either side of it are two lambs. In the centre of his composition, the artist no longer dwells upon apostles and martyrs, but goes straight to the Passion. The Cross let down from the hand of the Almighty roots itself upon the earth in wondrous foliage, spreading, as the mystic vine, in bold and graceful curved lines over the whole field. With that higher instinct, which did not suffer him to represent the naked crucifixion as we have seen it by the naturalist Masaccio, he places, upon the Cross the humanity of our Saviour, decently and devoutly draped. The Virgin Mother and her adopted Son stand beside it, and on its four extremities are twelve spotless white doves, symbols of the Apostles. For the rest, he fills every part among the graceful windings of the vine with an admirable variety of birds and flowers, thus evidently determined to surround the cross with beauty. Where, as he passes under it, he must give other human figures, he makes them mere accessories, distinct, indeed, but not disturbing the luxuriant harmony in which he sets them. A little hart is feeding at the foot of the Cross; perhaps symbolizing Adam in the garden of Paradise; or it might be that the artist had in his mind the ending of the Canticles: « Flee away, O my beloved, and » be like to the roe, and to the young hart upon » the mountains of aromatical spices. » The glad waters are gushing out below from four tongues, symbols of the four rivers which flowed through Paradise, and two thirsty harts, admirably drawn, are drinking from them. That mysterious 47th chapter of Ezechiel is before us. « And he brought » me again to the gate of the house, and behold » waters issued out from under the threshold of the » house towards the East: for the fore-front of the » house looked towards the East: but the waters » came down on the right side of the temple to » the south side of the altar. And he said to me: » Surely thou hast seen, O son of man. And he » said to me these waters that issue forth to- » wards the hillocks of sand to the East and » go down to the plains of the desert, shall go » into the sea, and shall go out, and the waters » shall be healed. And every living creature that » creepeth whithersoever the torrent shall come, » shall live: and there shall be fishes in abundance » after these waters shall come thither, and they » shall be healed, and all things shall live to which » the torrent shall come. » The Christian fishes of the catacombs could have no better origin than this torrent of healing waters from the house turned to the East. Whether the artist had intended to make this allusion, or not, he could not have expressed more ably, than he has done, his motto, that the Cross makes the vine dried up by the law vigorously to bloom: its sap gushes out in living streams, and the living creatures draw nigh to it to drink and live. There he has set the pelicans of the wilderness; and behind them the peacocks of the catacombs, symbols of immortality on account of their longevity; and on either hand where the streams are drunk up by the earth the good shepherd is feeding his sheep; and the Church, turned away from Jerusalem towards Bethlehem, is doing that office which the ungrateful city refused at His hands; not indeed gathering the little ones under her wings (for she is depicted as a woman,) but distributing to her chickens, symbols of her children, the corn of salvation. And, that the shameful circumstances of the passion may not be altogether forgotten in the exuberance of the cross growing lilies and the true vine, nigh Bethlehem the time of night is indicated by the owl, and, in that fatal night, the denial of Christ by Peter is represented by the cock below it. But to Jerusalem is turned the lance which, in the hand of a soldier of the Caesar, struck the last blow the faithless people could

inflict upon the sacerdotal King. « Before thee I
» opened the sea: and thou hast opened my side
» with a lance. » The subtle delicacy of the artist
is astonishing. Of the twelve white birds, symbols of the twelve Apostles, the lowest and last, probably symbolizes S. John the Apostle, **but**, as his
martyrdom, though attempted, was not actually effected, the upper half of the dove only appears,
and the rest is hid in the verdure of the cross.
There are two magpies and various other birds on
either side, **but** we do not know what they sym-
bolize. The serpent is indicated, but it is as a
beautiful curve, of crimson and gold, terminated by
a flower. In another line of subjects are the four
great Doctors of the Church with their names. On
the right S. Ambrose and Gregory, on the left S. Jerome and Augustine. S. Clement had been represented with S. Peter already, and there was **no occasion to** repeat him here: but the miracle of Sisinius is not forgotten. The object which the artist
had proposed to himself, to make the cross the
mystic vine, **and** to surround it with the gladness
of the vine, the fowls of the air resting in **its** branches, the living creatures of the earth partaking
of its abundance, did not leave space for an elaborate composition of the miracle. The figures are
separated, but the story is fully told. On the right

Sisinius is being led by the boy, and Theodora is behind. The Sacrifice is indicated further on by the detached ecclesiastical figure in a stole with a censer, or perhaps the ciborium inclosing the Host; for in the arabesques at Ravenna a similar object is seen with two deer stooping towards it. On the left Sisinius in full costume, no longer blind, stands turned away with two men behind him. Further on his conversion is finished, for he stands alone making a votive offering of the gospel roll.

On the wall beneath is painted our Saviour, and around Him the twelve Apostles separated by palm-branches. The Apostles are standing on the bank of a stream in which are seen various fishes swimming. The Saviour is in the attitude of blessing with his right hand, and in his left He holds a scroll on which are written the words « Pacem meam re-» linquo vobis, pacem meam do vobis, » « My peace » I leave you: my peace I give you. »

We have dwelt too long upon this magnificent mosaic. The brilliancy of the colours, and the minute delicacy of the objects, are set off by its ground of gold. It would be a mistake to suppose that it was only a newer and more excellent developement of mediaeval art; for the catacombic crypt of Praetextatus with its birds and its flowers, its roses and nests, its grapes, and ears of wheat, its harvest scenes and good shepherds, gives to its altar tomb as elegant and a more concentrated embellishment. There are some who with too fastidious philosophy, and too great a disregard of the mixed nature of man, would soar with the eagle, but not with the steadfast eye of S. John; would have no other vault for their devotions but the myriad constellations of the heavens. But the simple--minded faithful cannot attempt such lofty flights. They need the more domestic images of the Church. When they turn from the labours of their daily life to rest the wearied senses, and find some pleasure in the pictures with which men seek to do some honour to God's house, they have beyond it a gratification which is not confined to the philosopher and is enjoyed by the beggar.

APPENDIX.

TRANSLATION OF THE RELICS
OF SS. CLEMENT AND IGNATIUS.

IN the last century, Hannibal Albani, Cardinal
Titular of S. Clement's, and nephew of Pope Clement XI, wishing to take relics of S. Ignatius, threw
down the high altar, and destroyed the Confession [1]
which existed beneath it. He took the leaden reliquary out of the Confession, and had the contents carefully transferred to another; but he did not
restore the Confession. On the 22^d of June 1727, the
Dominican Pope Orsini, Benedict XIII, preached from
the gospel ambo in the choir; and after the sermon
he himself carried in the procession the reliquary on

---

[1] Confession, in *Church History*, is a place in churches, usually
under the high altar, wherein were deposited the relics of the martyrs.

his shoulders, assisted by cardinal Albani, and two archbishops, and placed it under the new high altar prepared, by the Cardinal Titular, the year before. Twelve cardinals, four primates, several archbishops, bishops, and prelates, and all the Dominican Friars in Rome with the most Rev. Father Thomas Ripoll, General of the Order, walked in the procession.

The excavations of the original basilica of S. Clement discovered, in 1857, by the writer of these pages, and cleared out and restored mostly by public subscription, made it necessary again to take down the high altar. The reliquary was removed on the 10th of June 1866, and, on Tuesday, the 20th of November 1867, was opened, and its contents examined by the proper ecclesiastical authorities. The reliquary contained :

1. Several bones of S. Clement and S. Ignatius.

2. A considerable quantity of earth, or ashes tinged with blood.

3. A glass vase, supposed to be as early as the first century, the inside of which is covered with a deposit of reddish hue.

4. A small phial, of very ancient date, also containing coagulated blood.

5. Two crosses, one of wood, the other of metal. The former, at one time, evidently contained some relics.

6. An Agnus Dei made of bees' wax, with the figure of the lamb impressed on either side.

7. A piece of stone, or slate, with the inscription REL . SCT . XL, relics of the Forty Martyrs.

8. A marble slab, on one side of which are engraved monograms, and on the other inscriptions. We give *fac similes* of both.

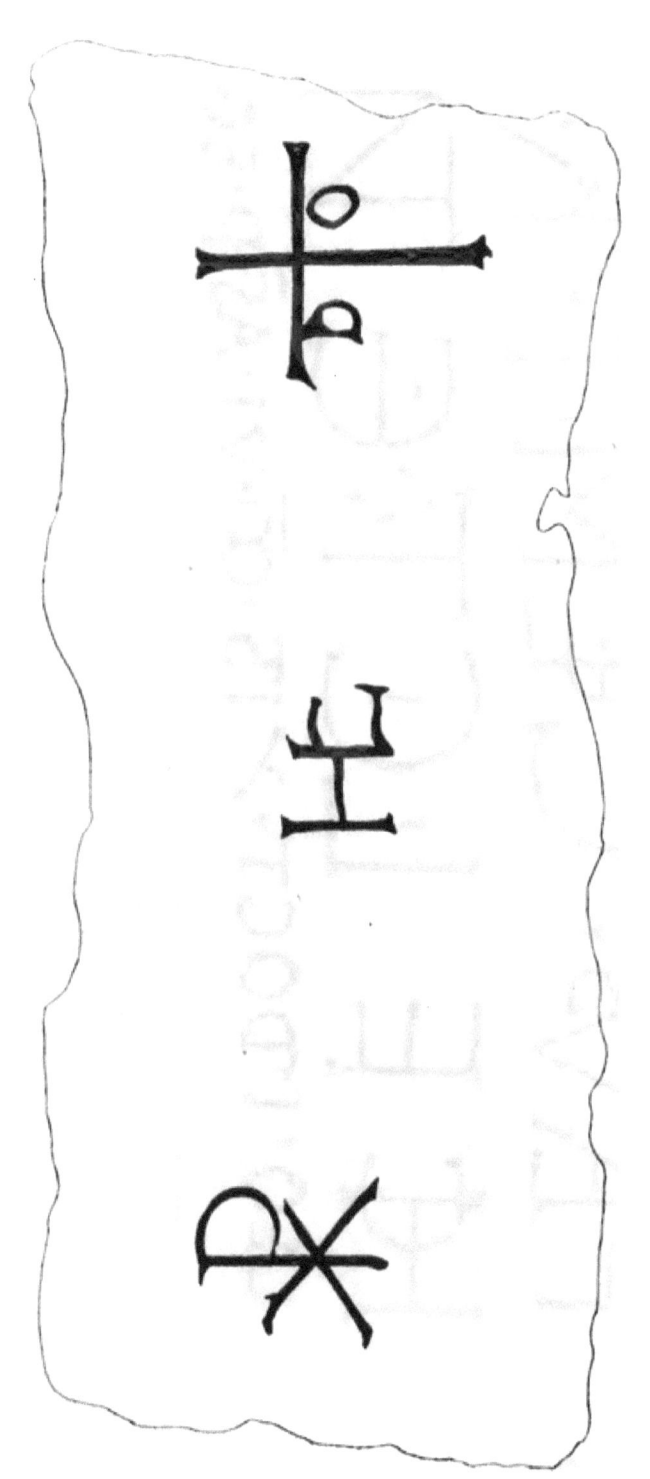

FAVS· C€MMR·

H€F LICT€Tↁ

LEO·IDOCT·XITS·Ꟈ·VI·AS·P·EG

The monograms may be read thus:

CHRISTVS . JESVS . DOMINVS

And the first two lines of the inscription, thus:

FLAVIVS CLEMENS MARTYR
HIC FELICITER EST TVMVLATVS

The third line is in small characters, and has puzzled the learned to decipher it. Vitry says of it: « It is easier to say how it should not be read, than » how it should be read. » [1] Some decipher it thus - **Leo I Doctor Christianitatis anno CDXL assumptus Pontifex Ecclesiae.**

Others explain it - **Leo I Doctor Xystus martyr VI a Sancto Petro Ecclesiae Rector.**

Others - **Leo I Doctor Christi 13 mensis VI ad S. Petrum eumdem gestavit.**

If we were allowed to venture a conjecture, we would say that it should be read - **Leo I Doctor Decembris mense VI anno sui Pontificatus egit.**

---

[1] « Tertia linea facilius est dicere quomodo non sit legenda, quam » quomodo legenda sit. »

The ceremony of examining the relics having been gone through, they were kept under seal in one of the ambries in the sacristy until the high altar was prepared to receive them. In 1868, when the altar was re-erected, Pius IX ordered them to be replaced. The Cardinal Vicar, who has the custody of relics in Rome, directed that they should be transferred to a new copper urn. We felt that, in so ancient a church ancient forms ought to be restored. To restore the Confession was impossible; but we obtained permission to put back the reliquary in its proper place, where the Confession once was, and where it was found; and as Cardinal Albani had taken away the lattice that was there, and closed all up with a pòrphyry slab, we had it removed and replaced by a *transenna* of the more appropriate ancient form. The reverence due to the relics of martyrs so early, and so renowned, in the history of the Church, as Clement first Pope of that name, and Ignatius, the Bishop of Antioch: and the recurrence of the feast of S. Ignatius, on the 1st of February, suggested a triduo of devotions to end on that day. His Holiness the Pope granted Indulgences for it.

The Cardinal Vicar came to the church on the 29th of January, and transferred the relics into the new reliquary, on which is the following inscription:

SALVO . BB . D . N . PIO . IX

ET . JVSSV . EJVS . C . CARD . PATRIZI

EPISC . PORT . ET . S . RVF .

RELIQVIAS . IN . THECA . ANTIQVA . DIE . X . JVNII . MDCCCLXVI

SVB . ALTARI . MAJORE . REPERTA

ITERVM . IN . HAC . THECA . REPOSVIT . DIE . XXIX . JANVARII

MDCCCLXVIII

Cardinal Guidi Archbishop of Bologna, the most
Rev. Father Jandel, General of the Dominican Order,
the Community, and a few others were present at
the ceremony of the translation.   During the whole
of that night the Community kept watch by the
relics, and Cardinal Guidi, representing Cardinal
De Bonnechose, Archbishop of Rouen, and Titular
of S. Clement's, consecrated the high altar the next
morning.   At 3 o'clock in the afternoon, the procession with the reliquary set out, in the following
order, from the altar of the subterranean basilica
which was brilliantly illuminated.

The cross and banner of the Order followed by
all the Dominican Fathers in Rome, the General
coming last next the bier, which was covered with
red velvet, and over it a pall of crimson silk and

gold, open on one side to show the inscription, and ornamented on the other side with the monogram of Christ, copied from the porphyry cover of Constantine's sarcophagus at Constantinople. The four bearers, in rich vestments, were:

The Most Rev. Father Leo Salua O. P.
The Very Rev. Father V. P. O'Doherty O. P.
The Very Rev. Father Paul Stapleton O. P.
The Very Rev. Father Joseph Mullooly O. P.

The following dignitaries of the Church, wearing gold mitres and copes, walked beside the bier:

His Grace, the Most Rev. R. L. E. Antici-Mattei, Patriarch of Constantinople.

His Grace, the Most Rev. P. R. Kenrick, Archbishop of S. Louis.

His Grace, the Most Rev. F. X. De Merode, Archbishop of Melitene.

His Grace, the Most Rev. P. De Villanova Castellacci, Archbishop of Petra.

After the bier came in cappa magna.

His Eminence Cardinal De Reisach.
His Eminence Cardinal Barnabò.
His Eminence Cardinal Pitra.
His Eminence Cardinal Bilio.
His Eminence Cardinal Mertel.
His Eminence Cardinal Guidi.

The Procession was closed by

His Grace, the Most Rev. P. Brunoni, Archbishop of Taron.

The Right Rev. J. A. Goold, Bishop of Melbourne.

The Right Rev. F. Marinelli, Bishop of Porphyrus; and several other Prelates, whose names we cannot recal to mind.

The Swiss Guard of the Pope walked beside the bier, and a Company of Zouaves kept the line of the Procession. It was followed by a great number of the Regular and Secular Clergy, who, accompanied by an extraordinary crowd of people, formed, as it were, a supplementary procession; and all seemed to profit by the following invitations addressed to them from the doors of the church of S. Clement:

1.

QVI . TRIDVANIS . SVPPLICATIONIBVS
SANCTORVM . CORPORA
IN . HAC   BASILICA . QVIESCENTIA
VENERATVRI . CONFLVITIS
FIDEM . AVGETE · PETITE . ACCIPIETIS

2.

HEIC . VBI
APOSTOLORVM . CHRISTI . ET . SVMMORVM . PONTIFICVM
ENIXAE   AD . DEVM   PRECES   OLIM . ASCENDEBANT
CONVENIENTES . EX . OMNIBVS . MVNDI . PLAGIS . FIDELES
SANCTORVM . IN . AEDE . D . CLEMENTIS . QVIESCENTIVM
SACRAS . EXVVIAS . VENERATVRI
SCINDANT . CORDA . SPEM . AVGEANT . EXAVDIENTVR

The quiet kneeling reverence with which the
reliquary was welcomed, as it moved above the cor-
tege of Prelates towards the Coliseum, was most
impressive. It was a picture of old Christian Rome
to see that simple chest, containing nothing but
the bones of men who had died for Christ, rising
over the flashing steel, and plumed helmets glistening
in the sun, and the crimson habits of the Princes
of the Church, seventeen hundred years and more
after the martyrs had passed through the waves of

the Euxine sea, and the jaws of the lions of the
Caesars, slowly nearing, with no sound but the Li-
tanies of the Saints, the lofty ruins of the Flavian
Amphitheatre, and descending into its midst. There
in the centre, by the plain wooden cross, but not
on the arena, where S. Ignatius, Trajan's victim,
was given to the lions; for time has heaped up moul-
dering decay, age after age, upon it, as if to hide,
from human eyes, the hellish rage and cruelty of
which men are capable who hold imperial power,
and has draped with moss, and grass-green shrubs,
and gay flowers, the tiers of seats up to which the
conquered gladiator cast an imploring look for life,
and where that ferocious race made the silent sign
that they might enjoy the sight of the blood gushing from his heart : there the Procession made a
pause. Doubtless angels looked down from the battle-
ments of heaven upon the scene, and *there* too the
hymns of martyrs ceased, when *here* the Magnificat
Antiphon rose upon the still air: « Hic est vere
» Martyr, qui pro Christi nomine sanguinem suum
» fudit, qui minas judicum non timuit, nec terre-
» nae dignitatis gloriam quaesivit, sed ad coelestia
» regna pervenit; » and the clear voice of the
Cardinal Archbishop of Bologna put up the prayer
for all. « Look down upon our weakness, Omni-
» potent God, and because the weight of our own

» actions is heavy on us, may the intercession of
» Thy blessed Martyr and Pontiff Ignatius protect
» us. » So it passed through the theatre of pagan
diversions, and, returning by the Lateran road,
entered, through the great door, the church of
S. Clement, amid the hearty « Te Deum laudamus :
» Te Dominum confitemur : » and proceeding at once
into the choir, the relics of the Martyrs were laid
in the Confession, and the marble *transenna* fixed
before them.

Every day of the triduo there was a high mass,
and vespers, in Gregorian chant, a sermon and benediction. The Most Rev. Father De Ferrari O. P.
preached, on the first day, the panegyric of S. Clement. He dwelt on the genealogy, conversion, learning, piety, exile, and martyrdom of the saint; and
on the discovery of his relics by S. Cyril who brought
them back to Rome and deposited them in the
church built on his paternal house, and dedicated
to his memory. On the second day, the Very Rev.
Father Caprì O. P. treated of the martyrdom of the
Consul Flavius Clement, of the holy life and saintly
death of the cripple Servulus, who used to beg alms
in the porch of our basilica, and of the missionary
labours, and zeal of SS. Cyril and Methodius, the
Apostles of Sclavonia. And on the third day Cardinal Guidi O. P. eulogized the virtues of S. Ignatius,

Bishop of Antioch, one of the most illustrious and
heroic martyrs of the early Church. His Eminence
pointed to the Roman empire in its luxurious and
cruel capitals of the West and East, Rome and Antioch, Rome filled with idols, Antioch pervaded by
Judaism, though with a large Christian population:
the Caesars vainly drowning S. Peter and S. Paul
in their own blood, vainly bandying from East to
West, and *vice versa*, their successors Clement and
Ignatius, proving the unity of the Church in their
very act: vainly sacrificing these and thousands of
other lives, for apostolic blood watered the tree of
faith, and on every side fresh heroes bore the Cross
and conquered. He spoke of the spirit of Judaism
never spent, and at work now in modern Europe.
He called upon the Romans especially, again to kindle
the fire of faith, again to rally by the shrines of
the martyr saint: and gravely warned them if they
failed. Then pointing at how faith, far from being
extinguished, was lighted anew by the violence of
the world; how the meek and suffering were the
chosen champions of Christ, he asked to whom, in
this our day, had God given these precious relics?
To the poor and humble Dominican Friars of Ireland, to the children of that long suffering race
whose faith no persecution of government could
crush, nor any repentance of rulers adequately re-

ward. There, **beneath the** altar, in that little chest, was their consolation, their hope, **and** their reward. And so as the evening drew in, and the lamps **and** candles in the old church grew brighter, again the *Te Deum* pealed, and a man, who has had no small part in the Pontificate of Pius IX, once a soldier, now **an archbishop**, Monsignor De Merode, slowly approached the altar, and lifted up in benediction the Body of our Lord before which every Catholic head and heart must **bow**.

THE END.

An anonymous friend has sent us the following lines which, presuming on the writer's permission, we insert in this place.

THE SCEPTIC'S DREAM.

It was the Festival of S. Clement. I was at Rome, and wandering with a friend among the stately ruins of the Colosseum. The gentle autumnal breeze brought to our ears the sound of distant church bells. ‹It is time to go to S. Clement's› said my friend, ‹ are you not coming with me? › ‹ No, thank › you, › I replied, ‹ the church itself is interesting, I grant › you, from its ancient architecture and frescoes, but as a › work of art alone, at least to me. The legendary meanings › of the paintings on its walls, are to me as mythical as the › history of Romulus and Remus. No, I leave such puerilities › to women and children. › ‹ I will not attempt to argue › with you, › was the answer, ‹ but, › opening his English Prayer-book, ‹ having seen you at the English Service last › Sunday, I fancied you might venerate a church in which the › remains repose of a Saint commemorated by our Communion, › and he pointed to the line in the Kalendar, marked Nov. 23, S. Clement Bp. and Martyr. ‹ My dear fellow, › I answered,

‹ all Communions are much the same to me. I went to church
› last Sunday because the rest of my party did so; but you
› must not take for granted in consequence that such is my
› habit. Christianity may have effected much, I do not say it
› has not, but civilization has done more, and we of the 19 th
› century, the age of free thought, cannot again put ourselves
› in leading-strings. **Look** at these piers, was this gigantic
› **pile erected by** Christians? After all, we are a set of pigmies
› **compared to those** whom you would term our less enlighten-
› **ed** progenitors. The very stones of Rome have a voice. ›
‹ Yes, › he answered, ‹ but like the writing on Balthassar's
› wall, there is only one true interpretation. › So saying, he
left me, and sitting down on a stone, half worn away by the
knees of pilgrims, I lazily watched the daws and listened to
their cawing, as they flew in and out of the upper arches, until
overcome **with drowsiness,** I fell asleep, and dreamt, and this
was my **dream:**

I dreamt that I was alone, pacing up and down one of
the aisles in the **church of** Clement, **when** suddenly, I *felt*,
without at **first** seeing anything, that some one was **near**
me. I turned my head, and saw that, close beside me, stood
a shadowy figure, whose features I could not distinctly discern,
the whole form being enveloped in a kind of mist; but a voice,
different from any I had ever known, fell on my ear: ‹ Even
› the stones of Rome speak, › it said, ‹ come with me, and I
› will tell you what they say. › An unseen power seemed to
constrain me to follow my conductor, and I hastened after the

shadowy form, down the flight of steps which led to the subterranean church. ‹ You reject as false all you cannot see with
› your bodily eyes, › it said, ‹ is it not so? All unwritten tra-
› dition is the same to you — a collection of idle tales; and
› much even that you see, you declare to be interpolated, if it
› does not exactly agree with your own ideas of what is rea-
› sonable. Am I not right? › I bowed my head in assent.
‹ You consider Romulus and Remus as mythical personages;
› you doubt whether such a patriot as Horatius Cocles ever
› existed, except in the poet's brain; but you believe, do you
› not, that there where such monarchs as Nero and Trajan? ›
I bowed again. ‹ Why do you believe in them? Perhaps
› they - perhaps none of the so called Caesars ever really
› lived. › I murmured something about the testimony which
not one, but several histories gave to their existence, recording
their deeds, entering into minute descriptions of their very
characters - also, that even the buildings in Rome added further
confirmation. ‹ Yet you have allowed the doubt to enter into
› your mind, whether Christianity itself is of divine origin,
› and you actually sneer at those who venerate with reverential
› affection, the martyrs who won their crown by embracing
› death in its most terrible shapes, rather than apostatize. ›
‹ I never sneered at a martyr himself, in whatever cause, › I
hastily answered, ‹ truth, self-devotion, self-denial, must al-
› ways command respect. › ‹ Look on this, then, › the figure
replied, ‹ but first cast from your mind scepticism and frivo-
› lity, which as poisonous exhalations interpose between you

> and the truth. Here you see the installation of S. Clement,
> the fellow labourer of S. Paul, as Bishop of Rome; here again,
> he is celebrating the Holy Eucharist: see the altar, paten,
> chalice, the very words in the open book, the same as those
> used daily in the Service of the Church. Will not what has
> been accepted *always* and *everywhere* have a little weight
> with you in helping to prove the truth of Christianity? You
> have seen these before, you have admired the depth of ex-
> pression in the faces, the freshness of coloring, the grace of
> the drapery, but those they represented were to you as
> myths. Yet not in one, but in many books, these Acts of
> the martyrs are recorded, and now these walls, decorated
> by the art of more than a thousand years ago, corroborate
> their testimony. You admire self-denial in the abstract;
> here you find it in reality. Here S. Alexis, leaving bride and
> parents and affluence, goes forth to lead a life of self-abne-
> gation, and putting his hand to the plough, until death, looks
> not back. Here again you have the apostolic words fulfilled
> and the unbelieving husband converted by the believing wife.
> Look down below into the chambers, turned by S. Clement
> into a retreat for prayer; he, the noble Roman, forsaking the
> gorgeousness of an imperial court, to labor with Paul the
> aged, one who wrought with his own hands for his living,
> and a prisoner. Is not that self-devotion? Walk round and
> round this ancient Basilica, you will find the same story on
> each fresco; all unite in silently but effectually preaching
> the same doctrine — death to the world, in order to attain

> to life in that which shall never pass away. Above us, but
> beneath the high altar, repose all that is mortal of S. Clement
> and S. Ignatius. Why were they martyrs? Because they
> loved the truth better than their lives. Because the ancient
> Romans, the conquerors of the world, delighted to see an
> aged man, against whom not a whisper of slander could
> be breathed, torn to pieces by wild beasts, or as he him-
> self expressed it: 'I am the wheat of Christ. I must there-
> fore be ground and broken by the teeth of wild beasts,
> that I may become His pure and spotless bread.' A few years
> ago, and those blessed relics were borne in triumph through
> the arena, once flowing with his blood, and the stones which
> echoed to 'Death to the Christians' resounded to the glorious
> *Te Deum.* What has effected this change, from bloodshed to
> peace, from the cry of the heathen persecutor to the trium-
> phant song of the Christian? Has civilitation? No, a thou-
> sand times no. A Fisherman of Galilee, a Jew of Tar-
> sus, a few disciples, some of them weak women and
> striplings have won a grander victory than ever did Alex-
> ander or Augustus. Rome conquered the world, but they
> conquered Rome. And your boasted reason, what does it
> say? Does it not bow to the Almighty Power which alone
> could effect this marvellous change? Is not Christianity
> divine? Do not the very stones of Rome attest it? Do
> not the walls of *San Clemente*, and of the Colosseum, suffice
> alone, without any other proofs, to bear requisite testimony
> to the truth, which the Church, watered by the blood of

› martyrs, teaches? Oh! wretched, miserable doubter, be
› sceptical no longer. You admire him who dies, for a prin-
› ciple, however faulty; venerate those who looked for no
› applause of man, but an unfading wreath in Heaven. You
› profess to love truth. Think of those who sealed their testi-
› mony to it with their blood, sooner than throw a few grains
› of incense before an imperial image. You feel your heart
› glow within you, while listening to the histories of Cle-
› ment, and Cyril, and Alexis, and their patient self-denial.
› Waver then no more, unstable mortal. Learn from these
› old walls and decaying paintings the eternal truths they
› eloquently, though silently proclaim , and years hence,
› may be, in your distant home, far away from this City
› of martyrs, you will remember with thankfulness as the
› Feast of S. Clement comes round in the Church's year, the
› lesson they taught you. Yes, these very walls, hidden for
› centuries, have now, as it were, been brought to light to
› add yet a testimony to the awful fact, in this age of in-
› consistency and incredulity, fast gliding from the mind of
› man, that this sphere is not to revolve for ever, that a
› pagan morality is not sufficient to cleanse its corruption,
› that the most virtuous heathen that ever lived lacked that
› consoling faith in a Communion of Saints, which sheds a
› soft, benignant light on the dreariest path trod by a Chris-
› tian, and so died, as he lived, without that peace, which
› the highest honors of earth fail to bestow. ›

The voice ceased, and I awoke. The sky was still a cloud-

— 427 —

less azure, the daws were still cawing above me, all around
appeared the same, I alone was different, and as I walked
from the great amphitheatre, I turned once more for a last
look at the central Cross, that holy symbol so dearly loved
by the early Christians, that even on their very tiles they
engraved it; and I felt that I too had been conquered by
its power, on the spot where the martyrs won their crown.

« Made co-heirs with Christ in glory,
  His celestial bliss they share;
May they now before Him bending
  Help us onward by their prayer;

That, this weary life completed,
  And its fleeting trials past,
We may win eternal glory
  In our Father's Home at last. »

Rome, Nov. 24th, 1872.

INDEX.

A

INDEX.

of Pagan Rome - 168 - Christian basilicas - *ib.* - some
of those of Pagan Rome converted into Christian churches - design of - 169 - modern of S.Clement - *ib.* - ancient
of - *see Clement's.*

C

with his brother, they translate the liturgy and mass into that language - 153 - comes to Rome on the invitation of Nicholas I - carries the relics of S. Clement with him - - *ib.* - dies in Rome - *ib.* - is interred in the Vatican - translated to the church of S. Clement - 164 - condemnation of Nestorian heresy by - 210 - painting of - 239 299 300 to 306.

D

E

Germanus Bp of Auxerre, legate of Pope Celestine to Britain - 205 272.

Gervasius and Protasius MM. - relics of discovered in Milan by S. Ambrose - 288.

Gnostics - 96.

Gracchus - 214 215.

Grafiti - 20¹ 286.

Grancolas - 108 note.

Gregory S. the Great, quoted - 9 note - his letter to the hermit of Ravenna, quoted by Adrian I when writing to Charlemagne on holy images - 30 186 340.

Gregory III - *see Cemeteries.*

Gregory S. of Nyssa - 33 - his description of a Christian shrine - *ib.* and following pages - 161 277.

Gregory of Tours - 144.

Gregory VII - 181 184 320.

Gueranger, Benedictine Abbot - *see Cemeteries.*

Guiscard, Robert - 333.

H

Hammond, Henry - 91.

Hefele - 62.

Henry IV of Germany - 320 and following pages.

Heinschenius - 66 89 166.

Hilaria - relict of Claudius M. - 176

Hilary S. quoted - 18 373.

Honoratus - 241.

Honorius emperor - 205.

Horace - 66 69.

Hyginus - 74 81 96 97.

I

Iconoclastic Mania - 51.

Ignatius S. Bp of Antioch - part of « letter to Philadelphians » attributed to - 70 130 - condemned to the wild beasts by Trajan - 131 - conducted to Rome - 132 - his interview with S. Polycarp at Smyrna - his letters to various churches - *ib.* - his letter to the faithful at Rome quoted - *ib.*

Permissu Superiorum.

D · M·
CL·MARTI
NAE·ANXI
ANENCLE
TVS
PROVINC·
CONIVGI
PIITISSIME
H · S · E

www.ingramcontent.com/pod-product-compliance
Lightning Source LLC
Chambersburg PA
CBHW052340110726
47901CB00005B/1306